Adam's
was frigh

It reminded Charmiane again that he was a stranger. But a stranger she had loved.

"Are you angry, Adam?" she ventured at last.

He opened his eyes. "Why should I be angry?"

"Because . . . because of what happened in the garden."

"God knows it was madness."

She bit her lip. "I'm not sorry."

"You're a little fool! Too young to know anything." His voice was a harsh bark.

"You *are* angry," she choked out, and covered her eyes with her hand.

He stared at her, at the soft trembling of her chin. "Charmiane, don't cry."

He kissed her gently, then pulled her into his strong embrace as though he would hold her forever. His kiss deepened—eager, hungry for the sweetness of her mouth.

Charmiane clung to him, lost once again in the passion of his demanding kiss.

Dear Reader,

Passion, the quest for glory, the struggle to surmount seemingly insurmountable odds, and romance—always romance—these are the hallmarks of Harlequin Historicals. In only three hundred pages we bring you all the excitement and action of a five-hundred-page historical, but compressed into a convenient length that many of you have said better suits your busy lives.

And our authors! Favorite names shine from our covers: Louisa Rawlings, Marianne Willman, Susan Johnson, Heather Graham Pozzessere, Lynda Trent—the list goes on and on. But we don't stop there, because we're also proud to present the stars of tomorrow: DeLoras Scott, Bronwyn Williams, Caryn Cameron and all the others who make your monthly reading such a pleasure.

From west to east, the United States to Europe, Mexico, Russia and around the world, explore the past through Harlequin Historicals and learn one undeniable truth: love is always the same. No matter where or when a man and a woman fall in love, the moment is always one to treasure forever. So share those moments with us now and every month to come, only in Harlequin Historicals.

Leslie Wainger
Senior Editor and Editorial Coordinator

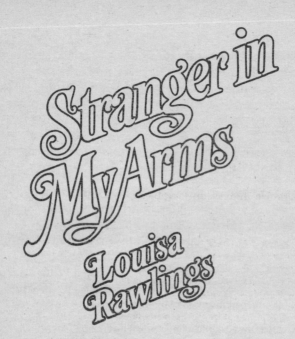

Stranger in My Arms

Louisa Rawlings

Harlequin Books

TORONTO • NEW YORK • LONDON
AMSTERDAM • PARIS • SYDNEY • HAMBURG
STOCKHOLM • ATHENS • TOKYO • MILAN

Harlequin Historical first edition December 1990

ISBN 0-373-28660-0

STRANGER IN MY ARMS

LOUISA RAWLINGS

has written eight historical romances, several under the pseudonym Ena Halliday. Interested in France since her school days, she has set most of her books in that country. She has received numerous awards for her work from the Romance Writers of America and *Romantic Times*. When her four children were younger, she enjoyed a suburban, domestic life: PTA, gardening, gourmet cooking and sewing her own clothes. With the children grown and gone, she and her husband now live happily in a Manhattan apartment and find more time for traveling and attending the opera.

The author would like to thank the following people
for their help, advice and expertise:
Professor Simon Schama of Harvard University,
David Kaplon and Dr. Richard Kaplon,
and my dear brother-in-law, in-house shrink
and psychiatric consultant,
Dr. Harvey Mazer.

Chapter One

If Charmiane de Viollet remembered the Reign of Terror at all, it was as a vision of Aunt Sophie running about and shrieking, her fleshy bosoms popping from her bodice as she snatched wildly at the canary that had escaped its cage. The rest of the story had been recited to Charmiane so often that it had assumed its own reality: the desperate flight from their town house in Paris—the carriage loaded with silver and luggage and oddments of furniture—the mad race for the Swiss border, the mobs and the looted carriage, Papa's final fatal stroke. Very dramatic, very graphic, especially as Uncle Eugène told it, but strangely unengaging. For Charmiane, the single emotion connected with that event would always be levity—the remembrance of those pink mounds bouncing absurdly against Sophie's stays in delicious counterpoint to her squeaks and wails.

It was different for Armand. As Charmiane watched her brother limp toward her across the vestibule of the Imperial Palace, she felt a twinge of guilt for being so unmoved, so untouched by their common past. She had been a child of four that terrible autumn of 1793; Armand had been eighteen, and charged with the care of the family's country estate near Blois. He'd been left behind in France during the Terror to claim and hold the château after Uncle Eugène and Aunt Sophie and Papa had been denounced by the Committee of Public Safety and had fled the shadow of the guillotine, taking Charmiane with them.

Armand had stayed—an ostracized aristocrat, deprived of his legal rights, scrutinized and harassed by the police, despised by the very peasants who had owed their lives and livelihood to the family for generations. And when at last Armand's name had been placed on the list of the proscribed and the country estate had been confiscated and sold to finance the Revolution, the

Armand who had joined them in their Swiss exile was no longer the Armand that Charmiane remembered.

She sighed. Such a long time ago—nineteen years, come September—and the pain was still etched on her brother's dear face.

She moved forward to join him at the foot of the grand staircase. The lights from the huge chandeliers picked up silvery threads in his dark curls. He managed a smile, but it was clear that he was unhappy about this evening.

"I recognized the old man who brushed my coat and took my hat," he muttered. "He was the Duc de Barthou's cousin. He didn't have a sou *before* the Revolution. His father disowned him. It probably saved his head. But to come to this . . ." He clenched his fist, his brown eyes flashing. "One of Napoleon's parvenus was berating the old man. A fop with a vulgar diamond on his cravat. Damned upstarts. Every one of them. Scarcely out of the gutter and parading about with their new titles. I'm glad Papa's not alive to see it. I pretended not to know Barthou, of course. We all live with shame."

She put her gloved hand on his sleeve in sympathy and tried not to hear the lively music coming from the rooms above. How could she enjoy herself when he was so miserable? "Oh, Armand, I'm sorry. I shouldn't have begged you to bring me. It's too painful. The memories."

He looked about the cavernous vestibule with its gilded marble columns and arches, its massive urns, its swagged draperies of deep green velvet strewn with golden bees—Bonaparte's symbol. The chandeliers were large and ornate, the patterned carpets harsh with strong colors. A gaudy imitation of Imperial Rome. Under the Monarchy, this had been the elegant Tuileries Palace; now, coarsened and redecorated in grandiose style, it served Napoleon and the Empire.

Armand's scowl deepened. "They drove the King and Queen from this very palace. Did you know that? And massacred scores of his loyal guards in this vestibule. And now Napoleon's minions dance here joyfully. As though they were dancing on their graves. And the graves of so many innocents who lost their lives." His bad leg began to tremble. He stilled it with an impatient slap. "You and Sophie should have stayed in Switzerland. I told you France would be a disappointment after all your hopes and dreams."

"Dear Armand, how often did your letters promise that all would be well? Have I learned my lessons for nothing? The arts, the graces, the ways of nobility? The old times will come again. The people will tire of being ruled by adventurers and plunderers. Isn't that what you've told me? And the old times will return. France will have a king again. You'll be the Duc de Chevrillon, as you were meant. And I'll reclaim Henri's estate and be the Marquise de Viollet, and..." She looked with longing toward the top of the stairs, where a laughing group of young people was waiting to be announced. "And we'll attend a party every night! Oh, please don't be sad, Armand. Not at my very first grand ball!"

"And you think those times will come again?" His mouth twisted with bitterness. "I'm no longer so certain. It's Napoleon's France now. Who remembers the old days? Who cares?"

She tried again to cheer him. She smiled and tapped her nose, affecting the expression of a clever schemer. "I have a plan. I intend to be bright and gay and capture the heart of a rich politician or a marshal of the army. For just one of my smiles, he'll buy back the Chevrillon lands for me. And then I'll give them to you!"

He grunted but said nothing.

"Oh, Armand!" Try as Charmiane might, she couldn't suppress the excitement in her voice, the glow of anticipation that warmed her cheeks. "I heard the ladies talking in the dressing room as I straightened my gown. Bonaparte is expected. Can you imagine? The Emperor himself! Surely that makes this a special evening. And what do you think I'll do?" She giggled. "I'll flirt with him and make him restore your title. Would that please you, dear heart?"

Armand's lip curled in scorn. "He may be the Emperor to those toadeaters who gather around, but I'll forever smell the garlic on his peasant breath!" He scowled at the toe of his black pump as a young woman passed them on her way to the ladies' dressing room. She wore a bright scarlet gown lavishly encrusted with silk flowers, fringes and scallops of Mechlin lace; the high waistband was further accented by a girdle of sparkling brilliants. A necklace of alternating pearls and rubies glittered at her throat, with earrings and bracelets to match, and every finger on her silk-gloved hands bore a twinkling diamond ring.

"Bon Dieu," muttered Armand. "Do you see what I mean? Not a thought for simplicity. All that money. And not the sense, nor wit, to spend it with any taste. Tricked out like a whore! While you...who should be wearing the tiara of a *marquise...*"

Unable to compose her face, Charmiane turned aside to hide the trembling of her lip. She was painfully aware of the inadequacies of her own toilette, for all her efforts this evening. Her yellow satin gown was sadly out-of-date, and she'd had to put an extra seam in one of her long white taffeta gloves to hide a stain. In place of the old evening redingote she'd outgrown was a cashmere shawl they'd borrowed from a kindly neighbor; it was beautiful, though slightly threadbare. But Aunt Sophie had carefully unwrapped the last fan she'd saved from the old days. It was of ivory and silk, painted with lords and ladies in a garden, and Aunt Sophie had carried it for the marriage of the Dauphin to Marie Antoinette. The few Chevrillon jewels they'd managed to escape with were long gone, of course—removed little by little from their hiding places in the hems of Aunt Sophie's gowns and sold to keep them in food and lodgings all these years. But Charmiane had scraped together a few francs to purchase a modest pair of earrings—cut-steel brilliants set into mother-of-pearl. And her glossy black hair had been smoothed into a coil on the top of her head and pinned up with a pair of rather handsome bone combs. She'd spent hours in the planning and assembling of her wardrobe so that Armand—so sensitive, so aware of their humble station in this new society—wouldn't be humiliated.

She sighed. The evening had scarcely begun, and she was already a disappointment to him. She made another attempt to salvage his mood. She turned back with a bright smile. "Well, I *might* have had a tiara, or at least a few jewels, if Uncle Eugène's judgment had been as solid as his paunch! When Henri swore he had money in France, who would have guessed that his claim was under dispute?" She laughed. "I remember how funny it was when Uncle Eugène found out the truth and almost kicked Henri down the stairs."

"Damn Henri. The lying old pig just wanted a fresh young flower to crush."

That hurt; it was too close to the truth. Henri—with his sweaty body and imperious demands. And a spanking for his young wife if she disobeyed. Charmiane blinked back her tears.

"I had to live with him, not you," she murmured. "And bury him. Shall we go upstairs?" She started up without waiting for him, but by the time they reached the landing she'd recovered some of her good spirits. "That's why I wanted to be here. To pursue Henri's claim. When Monsieur de Domfort said he thought he could arrange an invitation . . ." She shrugged. "*Eh bien.* I married once to please Uncle Eugène. I can marry again for influence and money. What better place than this to find a husband?" It was more than that, of course. She could admit it to herself, if not to Armand, who still thought of these people as the enemy. The thrill, the excitement of a formal ball had set her heart to pounding wildly the moment Domfort had proposed it. There had been so few excitements in her life.

Two couples, gorgeously dressed and laughing in lighthearted abandon, pushed past them on the stairs, making for a room from which Charmiane could hear the sounds of a waltz. She yearned to stretch out her arms to them. Take me with you! she thought.

The rush of their movements had upset Armand's balance. He teetered for a moment on his bad leg and grabbed for the banister. "Don't you dare speak to me of marriage," he growled. "I'm head of the family now, and I won't hear of it. It's one thing to use these nouveaux riches to our advantage, as they've used others. It's quite another to betray your class by marrying one of them."

She bowed her head. "Of course, Armand."

They continued their ascent. Armand's limp was becoming more pronounced with every step, and he'd begun to grimace in pain. He scowled up at the couples, who were now laughing and whispering. "Common," he muttered. "Common and ugly. You can see their lack of breeding in everything they do."

"Oh, but . . ." Charmiane had thought they seemed very like the few youthful émigrés she'd met in Switzerland.

"What good are your arts and graces to people like this? People who view money as the measure of a man or woman. They have no values, no refinements.. They have only what they've stolen. Speculators and leeches who profit from war. Lickspittles to Bonaparte. They've bought themselves titles and estates and think such trappings confer instant nobility of the soul. I'm sorry I swallowed my pride to come tonight. To see you shamed by the company of such unworthy upstarts." They reached the top of the stairs. Armand's leg quivered again; he stamped it savagely on the floor and cursed. Then he smiled, a cynical twist of his mouth. "Shall we go in and *dance*?"

Charmiane began to weep softly, the tears brimming in her gray-green eyes. How could she have hurt him so? Her dear brother. Why had she insisted on this ridiculous ball? Armand couldn't dance with his bad leg, and the awareness of their poverty next to such ostentatious wealth only brought him more pain. "Do you want to go home?" she whispered.

"Do you want to stay? To mingle with these despicable parvenus and face the scorn of the women? Whom do you expect to dance with you? The rich politicians of your fanciful schemes are looking for rich women. Not romantic innocents in shabby clothes and borrowed finery who..."

"Damn you, sir, do you put so little store upon your life?"

Charmiane whirled at the sound of the masculine voice, deep and rich and quivering with rage.

The man who scowled down at them was tall, with a chiseled, lean face and high cheekbones. His mouth—set in a firm jaw—was perhaps too straight and wide, his Roman nose a shade too long for him to be called truly handsome. But he held his head with an air of pride and arrogance that commanded attention. Charmiane pictured him upon a horse, giving orders, leading a charge, though his conservative evening dress—dark tailcoat, white knee breeches, waistcoat and elaborately tied cravat—revealed no clue to his profession. His skin was deeply tanned and weather-beaten and his dark blond hair was sun streaked. His eyes, beneath sandy eyebrows, were an extraordinary blue: pale and clear, yet edged with a smoky ring. They gave Charmiane the sense that she was gazing into a deep tunnel, wherein she might tumble and be lost forever.

And surely she *was* lost—an enchantment that had begun the moment she'd seen his face.

"*Monsieur?*" Armand's voice registered his contempt.

"I asked if you valued your life, *monsieur*. I don't waste my time with empty challenges, but a man who insults a lady in public, who brings her to tears..."

Armand inclined his head in a mocking salute. "Your pardon, *monsieur*, but this is none of your affair. By what right do you intrude?"

Charmiane trembled at her brother's recklessness. The stranger's blue eyes had become as cold as ice. If she didn't do something, the man might attack Armand where he stood. "If you please, *monsieur*," she said quickly. "Don't trouble yourself." She brushed at her cheeks. "You see? I've quite stopped."

The blue eyes focused on her face, a searching look that seemed to assess her every feature. "The man's a fool. Those vain creatures may need jewels to shine. You don't."

Her breathing had stopped. Yet how could it be so when her heart was racing, pounding, thumping with a loud haste that surely he could hear? She felt herself blushing and tried to lower her eyes, but his held her fast. She wet her lips, tried to find her voice and couldn't.

He seemed suddenly aware of the awkwardness of the moment. His intense gaze wavered, and a flush briefly darkened his tanned complexion. He cleared his throat and bowed stiffly. "Your servant, *madame*. Will you do me the honor to dance?"

To the ends of the earth with you, she thought. It scarcely seemed real, the thrill she felt when their eyes met. A stranger. Yet so known, so yearned for, all her life. Have you been waiting for me, she thought, as I've waited for you?

"*Madame?*" he repeated, and proffered his arm.

She hesitated. Would the reality of dancing with him spoil the magic? A soap bubble vanished, a bird took flight if you touched it.

"Charmiane." Armand growled her name and curled his hand about her wrist.

The stranger took a menacing step forward. "Take your hand from the lady's arm," he said softly, "or I'll knock you down on the spot."

Armand stiffened. His expression never changed, but he dropped his hand and looked toward the stairs. "I'm going, Charmiane."

"Armand..." She felt herself torn, aching, yearning. The dance. The man. The magic. *"Armand."* A heartbroken plea. Couldn't he understand?

"*Madame?*" The deep voice pulled her, tugged at her heart. But Armand was her dear brother. To lose her to the stranger would only add to his pain this evening. She wavered, tormented by indecision.

Armand shrugged. "Do as you wish. I don't intend to send the carriage back for you." He meant it as a threat and a coercion. They both knew there wasn't enough money for two carriages this evening.

"I'll take the lady home in my carriage," said the man.

Armand scowled at Charmiane. "*Bon Dieu*, I can see by your face that you've quite made up your mind. Well then, the devil with it. And the devil with you." He started down the stairs.

"Armand..." It was only a weak protest now. Her heart had already won out over her head. Overwhelmed with guilt, she watched her brother retreat, favoring his lame leg. How old he looked suddenly. How tired. She fought the urge to cry again.

"Why waste a single tear on a man like that?"

"Oh, but..." She looked up at the stranger and was lost again in those blue eyes. Her thoughts vanished, the words died on her lips. She noticed how his straight blond hair formed a gentle wave on the top of his head. She wondered if it drooped onto his forehead when he rode his horse. His long jaw ended in a strong, determined chin. She wondered if it grew in blond when he needed a shave. She started, aware that she'd been gazing at him for an immodest length of time.

"I'm sorry," she murmured. Pointless words. Sorry for what? She owed him no apology. Yet she'd wanted to speak. To make this moment last. And now—foolishly, irrationally—she felt the need to explain the scene he'd witnessed. "Don't be angry at Armand. He doesn't mean to be cruel. Pain prompts his words. That's all."

He clenched his jaw. "Curse him. To speak so to you."

"But my brother didn't mean—"

"What?" He cut in sharply. "Brother? Only your brother?" The frown vanished from his face and a tentative smile appeared. The transformation was astonishing. The smile was young, gentle, wonderful. Charmiane found it enchanting. When he frowned, he looked like a man in his thirties. When he smiled, the years melted away. He laughed his relief. "I feared he was your husband. I thought him a damnable villain on that account alone."

She was used to the subtleties of polite conversation; his directness unnerved her. She held her fan against her flaming cheek and bent her head. Why did her face always betray her? "Husband?" she whispered. "Would it have made a difference to you?"

His smile was replaced by a look of such burning intensity that she trembled. "Yes," he said softly, "a great difference."

Her knees felt weak. This is a dream, she thought.

While she struggled to recover her wits, he offered his arm. "Come. Enough of talking. We'll dance." It was more a command than an invitation. His voice was firm and assured. A man to be obeyed.

She nodded solemnly. "Yes, *sir*."

He stared, one eyebrow raised in question. "Why did you answer that way?"

She laughed gently. "You give commands. Like a general. I suspect you can be quite overbearing," she teased.

Instead of joining in her laughter, he scowled. "It's my way. Perhaps you'd prefer to go with your brother after all. It's my way."

For all the anger in his tone, she heard something else, as well. Pain? Fear that he'd drive her away with his curt manner? She tucked her hand firmly into the curve of his arm and smiled in reassurance. "You're a soldier, of course."

He sighed and relaxed. "For too long, perhaps. I beg you to forgive my brusqueness, *madame*." He stopped. "Madame...?"

"Madame Charmiane de Chevrillon de Viollet. Widowed." Why had she made a point of saying that?

"And I...Adam-François Bouchard, Baron Moncalvo, Colonel of Cavalry, Twenty-eighth Dragoons, attached to the Grand Army of Napoleon."

Baron Moncalvo. Without a "de" to his name. Baron of the Empire. One of those parvenus that Armand so despised. Yet his manners, despite his curtness, were as fine as any aristocrat she'd met. Why did Armand insist on making such foolish distinctions?

He gave their names at the door to the grand ballroom, waited while they were announced, then led her in.

Charmiane stopped, her eyes wide with awe and delight, and slowly scanned the room. I must remember every bit of it, she thought. This may never come again.

It was one of the most magnificent State rooms of the Tuileries Palace. Its paneled walls were covered with enormous eagle-crested paintings depicting the Emperor's victories, interspersed with portraits of the Marshals of France; between its soaring windows and balcony doors, draped with heavy silk moiré, were statues of Napoleon's generals and admirals. From its domed ceiling hung a giant crystal chandelier surrounded by four smaller ones.

Despite its size, the room was crowded with people: laughing, gossiping, moving from group to group, lounging on the small gilded chairs and sofas that lined the walls. Beautifully dressed women and elegant men bending attentively to them. There were no uniforms in sight except for the livery of the footmen and the gold and silver braid on the dress coats of the Senators and members of the Legislative Body. Domfort had said that Napoleon had forbidden uniforms this evening.

From what Armand had told her, Charmiane could well understand the ban. Ever since the difficult campaign in Spain, with its unprecedented French losses, the citizens of France no longer held the military in quite such high esteem. And now, in the spring of 1812, with the garrison of Paris reduced, soldiers leaving for the Rhine every day and rumors of war with Russia in the air, a ball in honor of the Emperor's wedding anniversary was not the place to flaunt a proud military presence.

Still, Charmiane thought to herself, it was curious how easily she could tell it was wartime, even with her limited experience, her recently ended exile in Switzerland. The soldiers—like Moncalvo, so recognizable as such—looked uncomfortable and unnatural in their dress clothes. Their shoulders seemed too broad for evening coats, their muscular thighs and calves too solid for tight cashmere knee breeches and silk stockings, their feet too firmly planted, demanding boots, not dancing pumps.

And the women—eager, impatient, forward of manner, frantic in their flirtations, as though tomorrow would be too late. Tomorrow they might be widowed, deserted, left to weep; tonight was the time for laughter and love and advantageous liaisons. Charmiane felt caught up by the same urgency. I want everything tonight, she thought. Life and love and the wondrous man who held her hand so tightly.

A contredanse was about to begin. Charmiane deposited her shawl and handkerchief on an empty chair and took her place beside Baron Moncalvo in the square. He was not a particularly good dancer, but each time his large hand clasped hers, burning through her glove to warm her flesh, she felt weak. And when they'd danced the final figure and the orchestra began a lively waltz, she trembled at the strength of the arms that circled her waist, at his nearness, his scent.

It was such an intimate dance, the waltz: bodies pressed close, legs bisecting the legs of the partner so that sometimes their knees touched, their thighs shared a moment of thrilling communion. Until now, she'd only thought of it as another dance. Now it made her burn, her body aflame with the sensation of his touch. She understood now why Aunt Sophie still called the waltz a scandal and had chided her dancing master for teaching it.

Moncalvo spoke little. Even when the dance was finished and Charmiane retrieved her handkerchief to dab at her brow, he seemed content just to stare at her, his blue eyes following the little fluttering movements of her hand. "Was your husband a soldier?" he said at last.

"No. He lost everything in the Revolution, as we did. We met at Lake Constance."

"Did you live in Switzerland?"

"Until a few months ago, yes."

Small talk, awkward pauses. A pretense of normality, though her racing pulse denied it. The look in his eyes denied it.

"What did he do? Your husband."

She stared in surprise. "Do? He was an aristocrat. A *marquis* under the *Ancien Régime*."

His brow darkened. "I suppose it's enough."

She silently cursed herself for being an innocent fool. She'd lived too long in her sheltered life among the *ci-devants*, the former aristocrats. To a Republican soldier, she must sound naive or snobbish or both. She fanned her face to cool the flush of shame. "And you?" she ventured at length. "Were you meant for a soldier?"

"My class had fewer choices. I wasn't meant for anything. Except perhaps to keep my mother from starving. But the army seemed a good career, especially under Bonaparte. Not like the old days, when a man had to prove four generations of nobility before he could even advance to the rank of captain."

She didn't like the reminder of their class differences. It sounded too much like Armand's bitterness. "You've been in the army a long time?" she asked quickly. A neutral question.

"I enlisted at seventeen. Half a lifetime ago." He stared at her full lips, then caught her eyes with his own. "How old are you?" he demanded.

She drew in a shocked breath. *"Monsieur?"*

He seemed not to know—or to care—how bold his question had been. "You look like a fragile child. Do you think a man of thirty-four is too old?"

"My...late husband was forty-six when we married," she stammered.

Again the long stare, the searching perusal. He scowled. "This is madness. Come and dance." He took her hand and pulled her toward the center of the room, where a new square was forming. Again he danced silently, his eyes following her even when the patterns of the dance took her to a new partner. It was thrilling and unnerving at the same time to be the object of such intense, such intimate, concern.

And yet, of course, she was studying him, as well. Each time they finished a set and retired to the side of the room, she learned something new about him. The shape of his ears—precise and small, framed by neatly trimmed hair—the whiteness of his teeth when he occasionally smiled, the gruff sound he made in his throat whenever he seemed at a loss for words.

He seemed often at a loss for words—or unwilling to voice his thoughts—as though the setting, the press of people, the reckless gaiety were part of a world to which he chose not to belong.

Schooled in the court of Louis XVI, Aunt Sophie had taught Charmiane the little games and tricks of women—the flattering looks, the coy smiles, the enticing remarks and questions. She'd had little chance to put them into practice with younger men, so scarce among their friends in Switzerland. And then, of course, after she married Henri, she wouldn't have dared to flirt.

But she hadn't forgotten her lessons. Between dances with Baron Moncalvo, she tried at first to draw him out. To no avail. She was almost glad that he seemed indifferent to her feminine stratagems; indeed, she began to welcome his reserve. It was far more comfortable to commune in silence, eyes gazing into eyes. To know that her soul was speaking to his, without the need of words, of artificial conventions.

It seemed they danced for hours, on a mystic island bathed in candlelight, warmed with music, throbbing with the beat of her heart; and yet the night was still young. Charmiane burned with impatience. He would take her home in his carriage. The night would be soft and dark, scented with spring blossoms. He'd take her in his arms, and then... and then...

She stopped in the middle of the dance, her face flaming at the wantonness of her thoughts.

Scowling, Moncalvo almost dragged her to the edge of the dance floor. "I'm a fool. You're flushed with fatigue. We've danced too long. Come. Sit down. There's sparkling wine in the Salon des Grâces. I'll bring you a glass."

"Oh, but I can go with you. I..."

"Stay here," he ordered. He seated her on a divan near a group of women and hurried to the door.

Charmiane nodded to the woman next to her and spread her fan, as much to pass the time as to cool herself. She fanned slowly, dreamily, thinking of him.

The woman next to her smiled, her eyes crinkling like a cat's. "Your escort is very handsome, *madame.*"

Charmiane examined her more closely: a woman of about her own age, beautifully dressed and coiffed, her hair looped up in elaborate curls over each ear, her white throat bedecked with jewels. The very sort of woman that Armand had said would snub her. She returned the smile with pleasure. "Thank you. I, too, enjoy looking at him."

"And well you might. My friends and I..." The woman made a graceful gesture with one languid hand, encompassing three women who sat nearby and leaned forward to listen to the conversation. They were as extravagantly dressed as she. "My friends and I have been watching him and wondering what could possibly be his relationship to you."

"*Monsieur le baron* is..." She stopped and blushed again, fanning more vigorously to hide her pleased agitation. "A friend."

"A *baron*! How fortunate for you, *madame*," murmured one of the other women. "Isn't that fortunate for her, Micheline?" This was directed to the first woman.

"Indeed," said a third. She smirked at Charmiane. "Did the *baron* bring you here for a charity? Or a church penance?"

Charmiane stared, the smile fading from her face. Surely the woman hadn't meant to be rude! "Beg pardon, *madame*?"

"What a lovely fan!" exclaimed Micheline. "May I?" Before Charmiane could stop her, she had snatched it out of her hand. She turned to her companions with a shrill laugh. "Oh, do look at this, Josine! Have you ever seen such a thing?"

Charmiane rose to her feet in indignation. "Give it back."

The laughter was now clearly mocking as the fan was carelessly passed from one woman to another. Micheline held up her own dainty fan, which was half the size of Aunt Sophie's. "Has no one told this poor creature that large fans are out-of-date?"

"She's just a country cousin. How is she to know?"

Josine, who now held the fan, spread it wide and put it before her face. "But then it's not nearly large enough! It can hide a plain country face, heaven knows. But not a plain country gown."

Charmiane clenched her fists. "Give it back." She had never brawled in all her life—a lady didn't resort to that—but she was prepared to do battle now if Aunt Sophie's fan wasn't returned.

Micheline hesitated, gauging her mood, then sighed and shrugged. She held out her hand to Josine. "Give it here." She took the fan, opened it, glanced at it with a look of contempt and snapped it shut. There was a sharp crack.

"You've broken it," cried Charmiane.

"Alas." Micheline's voice was heavy with boredom. The game no longer amused. "An accident. Do forgive me."

Charmiane trembled as she took back the fan and opened it with care. One of the delicate, carved sticks had broken in several places, and bits of ivory fell to the floor at her feet. She swallowed hard to still her emotions. It *might* have been an accident. Besides, she was too well-bred to make a scene, though she wanted to scream, to shake the woman by the shoulders, to smear her carefully rouged cheeks.

But that's how they behaved, these upstarts. No self-control. No civility. Armand had been right. She turned her head away from the simpering women, praying that her face wouldn't betray her grief.

"What the deuce has happened?" Moncalvo stood before her, a glass of champagne in his hand.

"My fan," she murmured. "It's broken."

Micheline smiled up at Moncalvo. A flirtatious smile. "I seem to have had an accident, *monsieur le baron*. Baron . . . ?" She spread her hands in a gesture of helplessness. "I'm sure we've met, though I've forgotten your name. A female weakness." She made it sound like a charming attribute.

He ignored that. "You broke the fan?" His voice was low and deep.

"It was an accident. Only look at it. So old and decrepit. It just snapped in my fingers. An accident."

Her careless indifference only added to Charmiane's pain. "It was the last of Aunt Sophie's treasures from the old days," she said.

He smiled, though his eyes flashed a warning. Then quite calmly, quite deliberately, he poured the glass of champagne into Micheline's lap.

She stared in horror at the spreading wetness of her skirt, too shocked even to cry out.

Moncalvo put down the empty glass and bowed gravely. "Your pardon, *madame*. An accident." Gently he took the fan from Charmiane, closed it and put it into the breast pocket of his waistcoat. "I'll have it repaired." He offered his arm. "And now, Madame de Viollet, do you still wish sparkling wine?"

She didn't know whether to laugh or cry, her heart so filled with the wonder of the man. She followed him obediently toward the Salon des Grâces, hearing behind her the wailing of Micheline, who had finally found her voice.

Just then, there was a stir at the door of the Salle des Maréchaux, a fanfare of trumpets from the orchestra and then the cry of "The Emperor!" followed by "Their Majesties!" As the crowd made way and bowed, Napoleon and his Empress, the Austrian archduchess Marie-Louise, swept into the salon, trailed by various functionaries and attendants.

The Emperor was in a simple woolen uniform of dark blue with white facings, unadorned except for the officers' gold epaulets at his shoulders and the several medals on his chest. Surrounded by men in splendid evening coats—many embellished with gold lace, flamboyant cravats and diamond stickpins—he was all the more striking and conspicuous for his simplicity. He was now forty-two and beginning to lose both his youthful slenderness and his hair. But the eyes in his pale, somewhat puffy face were blue-gray and piercing, and he commanded the room with his presence and vigorous stride.

His Empress, who almost had to skip to keep up with him, was so unlike him as to seem laughable. Half a head taller, half his age, she looked like nothing more than a pampered and self-indulgent child. Her sky blue eyes—large and somewhat protuberant—were vacant and lacking in intelligence, her cheeks were as plump and rosy as a well-fed country milkmaid, and her fleshy lower lip drooped, a trait of the Habsburg dynasty for generations. Only her figure—though more ample than fashion dictated—was beautiful; her low-cut pink gown displayed the whiteness of a fine, full bosom. Her dark blond hair, piled high into curls, was set off by a crown of silk roses.

Studying them carefully as they made their entrance, Charmiane had to smile to herself. It was probably just as well that Armand had left; it would have rankled him to see that the "upstart" Bonaparte exhibited a more regal presence than his Empress, for all her noble birth.

Charmiane found it difficult to share Armand's hatred of the Emperor. He hadn't been the cause of the Monarchy's fall, after all. That had happened nearly a decade before Bonaparte had appeared on the scene. A tragedy? Certainly. And the Reign of Terror was a blot on France's history. But surely this regime was only temporary. A turn of the wheel, the fall of Napoleon, and life would resume as formerly. The Monarchy would be restored, the nobles would regain their honors, their lands and titles, and she would take her place in society. A place for which destiny and her upbringing had trained her.

But, in the meantime, was it not exciting to be in the Royal presence? Charmiane watched, her eyes shining, as the Imperial party moved about the room. She was struck by the frequency with which Napoleon stopped to greet a guest with a brief word, nod at a legislator, acknowledge a scarred and grizzled campaigner. She looked at Moncalvo, standing close beside her in the crowded room. "Does he do that all the time?"

He nodded. "The man is remarkable. He remembers names. Faces. You should see him on the battlefield with the lowliest corporal. An army of half a million doesn't give its loyalty for nothing. He holds out the hope of glory, the honor of fighting under his command, his pride in France. And the men follow him willingly into battle."

Charmiane stared in awe. She should like to meet the man. "Will they stay until supper is served?"

"I doubt it. I'm sure His Majesty is here just for appearance sake. Now that the Imperial family has moved out of the Tuileries to their château at Meudon, it means a long ride. And His Majesty has work to do, I'm sure."

"Tonight?"

His eyes were solemn, and a small crease appeared between his brows. "Don't be misled by this happy scene. We shall have war again soon. With all its attendant horrors. I have no doubt the Emperor has weighty matters on his mind tonight."

"And she?"

Moncalvo laughed shortly. "Do you know what they called her—the gossips—at the time of their marriage? No, I suppose you wouldn't, living abroad. They called her the 'beautiful heifer.' Napoleon himself claimed he was only marrying a womb."

She gaped, blushing at the frankness of his words. "You mean that in jest."

"Not at all. They celebrated their second wedding anniversary two weeks ago. But I doubt that it mattered very much to the Emperor. Though I think he's fond of her, in his way, she's no longer of such importance to him. Now that his succession has been assured by the birth of his son, the King of Rome."

"But to choose a wife for such a reason . . ."

He stared at her, his blue eyes clouding. For a long, frightening moment she felt his thoughts, his soul, closed against her. "A man begins to think about leaving children behind," he said.

"Do you?" she asked softly.

He shook off his dark thoughts. "God knows how many bastards I've left behind, from Naples to the Danube. But never a one to bear my name." He scowled. "I've shocked you. I can read it in your eyes. You should have gone home with your brother."

"No. No. Not at all," she stammered, embarrassed by his stark honesty, but not shocked. She'd led a sheltered life, true enough. But not that sheltered. "I was only thinking that...you must have had a lonely life." She put her hand on his sleeve. She felt his muscles tense beneath the fabric.

"I don't dwell on it. It's a soldier's life."

"And no regrets?"

He faced her squarely. His eyes turned soft, the gentle color of bluebells growing on the hills above Lake Constance. He lifted a hand to her face, long fingers poised just beside her cheek. He didn't touch her, but his hand traced in the air the shape of her jaw and chin, the curve of her neck. His fingers were so close she could feel their warmth, and once or twice they brushed against the down of her cheeks.

She trembled. His touch felt like the kiss of snowflakes on her face. She prayed he could read surrender in her eyes.

He stiffened. "No," he growled, and dropped his hand. "No regrets." He turned sharply toward the center of the room, where the Imperial party was now surrounded by fawning courtiers, as unctuous as any Bourbon king had ever seen. "If you want to be presented to His Majesty," he said, "we should stand a little closer."

As they moved forward, Napoleon glanced up. He smiled, murmured something to Marie-Louise and brushed at the people before him as though he were scattering so many flies. The crowd parted. Abandoning his Empress, the Emperor strode to Moncalvo and nodded curtly. "Colonel Bouchard. A pleasure to see you." The voice, with its perceptible Italian accent, still betrayed his early years. He turned to Charmiane, smiling as she rose from her curtsy. "And who is this charming young woman?"

"Sire, may I have the honor to present Madame de Chevrillon de Viollet?"

"De Viollet. Do we know the family, Méneval?" He turned to one of his attendants.

"No, Sire. *Ci-devants.* The family was in exile until recently."

"Well, then." Napoleon looked pleased. Even Charmiane knew he was flattered to be surrounded by the ancient names and nobility. "We welcome your return to France, Madame de Viollet."

"Thank you, Sire."

"We note with pleasure that your name—violet—is one of our emblems. A happy omen. And we shall need all the good omens..." He stopped, musing, then turned to Charmiane's companion. "It begins again, Moncalvo. The Russians will force our hand, we fear."

"Yes, Sire."

Napoleon clapped him on the shoulder. They might have been comrades in arms, meeting on the field. "Good fellows, all."

Moncalvo bowed his head. "We do our best, Sire."

Méneval leaned forward and whispered in the Emperor's ear. Napoleon grunted and glanced back at Marie-Louise, who had begun to pout. "Her Majesty is indisposed? *Mon Dieu*, she's *always* indisposed. Tell her to throw out her pills and cures and stop eating so many cream tarts!" Despite the words, his voice betrayed a certain softness. He sighed. "Ah, well. We have our own burdens. We shall take *madame* home, Méneval. My old faithful secretary, are you up to a few letters tonight?"

When they'd gone, in a flurry of bowing and musical flourishes, Charmiane smiled at Moncalvo. "And now, *monsieur le baron*, my sparkling wine?"

He frowned. "Unless aristocratic distinctions matter to you, I wish you'd call me Bouchard. It's the name I was born with. Baron Moncalvo is an empty title, paid for with blood on the field but quite meaningless, otherwise. Unless titles matter to you."

She gazed into his blue eyes, so earnest, so filled with doubt. I call you Love, she thought. What else matters? She smiled her reassurance. "Of course not, Monsieur Bouchard."

She had thought the evening would continue as before, with her in his arms, dancing the waltz, smiling, touching. But it was not to be. The prolonged attentions of the Emperor had made her the focus of all eyes. In a moment they were surrounded by an army of young men, casual acquaintances of Bouchard, perfect strangers, ambitious courtiers. All clamoring to be presented to the divine creature who had caught the Emperor's eye.

Bouchard obliged with reluctance, but his scowl managed to drive away most of the men after they'd made their compliments. Only two or three remained, smiling in hope and longing.

One of them—a Comte de Géraud, Charmiane recalled—bowed as the orchestra struck up a fresh tune. "Madame de Viollet. They've announced the next contredanse. May I propose myself as your partner?"

Charmiane hesitated. She could scarcely tell him she didn't dance. Not when she'd spent half the evening on the dance floor with Monsieur Bouchard. And though he frowned, Bouchard was making no move to intercede with Géraud. To claim her as his own, before the world. She felt a sharp pain somewhere within her, perilously close to her heart. Perhaps she'd only imagined that he cared for her. Perhaps this whole night had been a dream, compounded of the dazzling ball, the music and her own foolish romanticism. In vain she searched his face; his eyes were clouded and distant. She forced a smile and turned. "Thank you, *monsieur le comte*," she said, and allowed Géraud to lead her onto the floor.

When she looked again to the side of the room, Bouchard was gone, and with him all the joy of the evening.

In the great chandelier over her head, a candle sputtered and went out.

Chapter Two

"They'll be announcing supper in less than an hour. May I hope that you'll allow me to escort you in?"

Charmiane smiled brightly at the Comte de Géraud and prayed that her eyes didn't reveal the turmoil of her heart. She'd danced with Géraud and half a dozen other hopeful suitors, her body moving mechanically, like a child's toy. Titled men, like Géraud, whose voices nevertheless still bore the vulgar accents of their humble beginnings. Men who leered, who stared down the front of her low-cut bodice. Young men, who surprised her with their awkwardness. Henri had been many things, but the years, at least, had given him a certain polish. She felt more comfortable with older men; perhaps that's why she'd been drawn to Bouchard from the very first.

Not that it mattered. He was gone. She'd searched for him at every opportunity, cajoled her partners to escort her into the adjoining rooms on the pretext of a stroll so that she might look for him in secret. He was gone, and her heart was breaking.

"Supper, my charming Madame de Viollet?"

"Oh." Géraud's words brought her back to reality. Only fools dreamed romantic dreams. She'd come to the ball to meet people, hadn't she? People of influence in this new society. And, in the course of an interminable monologue, Géraud had mentioned several names. A subprefect, a *maître des requêtes*—names that seemed to indicate that he was well connected to the Patron, as he called Napoleon. She sighed. There was no point in wishing for something that could never be. Whatever his reasons, Bouchard was gone. "I should enjoy taking supper with you, Monsieur de Géraud."

He smiled in pleasure and began another discourse on the wonders of Paris under the Emperor.

Charmiane tried to look attentive, though the man was a frightful bore. Over his shoulder she spied a young man and a laughing girl. Oblivious to the milling people, they were stealing a kiss behind the girl's fan. Charmiane was suddenly overwhelmed by her loss. How rash she'd been, how willing and reckless with her heart, like a gambler venturing everything on the turn of a card. And now *he* was gone, and Aunt Sophie's fan with him. Even Armand with the carriage.

She excused herself quickly, leaving Géraud stuttering, and fled down the great staircase to the ladies' dressing room. She found a dim corner and allowed herself the release of silent tears. After a few moments of weeping she blotted her eyes, scanned her face in a mirror, rearranged the short black curls and tendrils that framed her face. Witless fool, she thought. Indulging her grief. Wasting her tears. There was no reason why she couldn't persuade Géraud to take her home after supper was done. She might even allow him a kiss to ensure his continued interest.

As for Bouchard—it was clear that their meeting hadn't thrilled him in the same way that she had been thrilled. Her face always gave her away; she must have seemed an adoring puppy dog, gazing at him so earnestly. Small wonder he had vanished. She sighed. Well, perhaps the pain she was feeling now came from her wounded self-esteem, not from a broken heart.

She started back up the stairs. At the landing a woman was laughing as a man bent to kiss her hand. He straightened, slipped his arm about her waist and whispered in her ear. She laughed again.

Charmiane felt the blood drain from her face. The man was Bouchard. She hesitated, her stomach churning. She leaned into the banister for support and wondered how she might salvage her pride.

The woman on the landing disengaged his arm, blew him a kiss and hurried up the rest of the stairs alone. He stood watching her, his hands crossed against his chest, a satisfied smile on his face.

Charmiane pursed her lips in anger. She refused to concede the field to him. To turn and run. Instead, she'd snub him—coldly, proudly. He was an ill-mannered upstart, nothing more. *She* had centuries of noble blood in her veins.

He turned as she reached the landing. His eyes—so blue, so piercing—appraised her with a thoroughness he hadn't allowed himself before. His eyes raked her body from the top of her upswept hair to the delicate slippers that peeped out from beneath her hem. He smiled. "Well," he said softly. His blond eyebrows arched in question.

She kept her expression icy and regal. "Well indeed, *monsieur*." She made to continue her ascent. "You'll pardon me."

"No." He moved in front of her.

"Your behavior is tiresome, Monsieur Bouchard." She moved to one side and again attempted to mount the stairs. He moved more quickly and blocked the way. In spite of herself, her strong resolve, she felt the tears stinging behind her eyelids. Was this the man she'd lost her heart to only an hour ago? So playful, so callous, as though he hadn't abandoned her? "Why are you doing this?" she choked.

His eyes turned smoky and the laughter faded from his lips. He held out his hand. "Because I want to dance with you."

She melted. She placed her fingers in his and allowed him to lead her to the salon. The waltz had begun, and he swept her into his arms, holding her more closely than he had before. She trembled in his embrace, caught up once more in the wonder of this night, the joy of sharing the dance with him. Her foolish pride was forgotten; she was his again. His dancing had improved in the course of the evening; perhaps it took a soldier a while to lose his military bearing and stiffness. Perhaps his charming partner of the staircase was a better dancer than she and had put him at his ease. A disturbing thought. It was just one more reason to hate the unknown woman.

He smiled down at her. "You're the most beautiful woman here. Do you know that?"

She gulped. "*Monsieur*, I . . ."

"Did you ever stand at the ocean before a storm?"

"I've never seen the sea."

"A pity." He swung her in a dizzying circle. "That's the color of your eyes, beautiful lady. That stormy green. Touched with gray from the skies and the foam."

It was just as well that the dance was ending. It was easier to hide her blush in the pretense of dabbing at her cheeks. He seemed to be making a concerted effort to be charming; perhaps he'd begun to regret his earlier desertion.

"*Madame*, you promised me the next quadrille." Charmiane turned to see Géraud pouting behind her. She'd completely forgotten about him. Now what was she to do? She sent a silent plea to Bouchard.

He laughed ruefully. "Go, if you must, beautiful lady. But I warn you, *monsieur*—" he pointed a finger at Géraud "—the next dance has been pledged to me. And the next." He took Charmiane's hand and pressed it to his lips. "I'll wait for you here."

Charmiane took her place with Géraud and the dance began. She scarcely paid attention to him or to the other dancers; Bouchard consumed her thoughts. She stole glances at him whenever she could, nearly forgetting the figures of the dance in the process and managing to disrupt the other couples in the square.

Bouchard lounged against the wall, his arms crossed, a warm smile on his face. She was surprised that his smiles, his laughter, his charming attentions—while flattering—were less appealing to her than she would have thought. Somehow the undercurrent of danger, the aura of intimidating masculinity that had earlier filled her with a pulsing excitement, was lacking when he smiled.

During the last figure of the quadrille, Bouchard moved forward. The moment the dance had ended—and before Charmiane was able even to curtsy to her partner—Bouchard took her by the hand and pulled her to the door. "Come along. We'll escape him by dancing in another room." He led her to a smaller ballroom, less ostentatiously appointed but just as crowded. "You're mine again, beautiful lady." He laughed and swung her into the waltz.

They danced the next three dances together. He took every opportunity to describe her beauty, her grace, the fineness of her features, separately and collectively. Her head was spinning from the rush of compliments. "I shall never let you go," he said.

"And yet you did. I could almost have wished for a little jealousy when I danced with Monsieur de Géraud. It might have been as flattering as all your praise." She hoped she sounded coy, not anxious. But he'd made no apology for his extended absence, and his words, though charming, had a shallowness that dismayed her.

He laughed. "Jealousy? Would you have me scowling and disagreeable, ready to fight every man in the salon for a nod of your pretty head? A smile?"

"Of course not," she murmured. Her heart felt heavy. Even with Bouchard restored to her side, the night was beginning to pall after all. The wonder of the early hours was fading into a weary monotony.

He lowered his brow and turned down the corners of his mouth, but his eyes were filled with laughter. "Here you are, beautiful lady. Your frowns, your baleful looks." A mocking imitation of the forceful man who had rushed to defend her from Armand's hard words.

The magic was gone. She managed a tentative smile. "Do you mind if we stop? I've grown quite weary of the dance."

"Of course." They retired to the side of the room. He took her hand as they sat together on a divan. "You're troubled," he said.

"Mais non." What could she tell him? That the magic was gone, the spell was broken? He was as handsome as ever, but when he looked at her she felt no thrill, no jolt of recognition at meeting a kindred soul. Had she dreamed it? Or had the excitement of the ball simply worn off, like a thin layer of silver gilt on a child's brass toy?

Perhaps it was her fault. Perhaps she *had* conquered him at first. And then she'd danced with the others. He had been angry. The anger had turned to indifference, and he'd lost interest. The light in his eyes had died: that indefinable fire had been extinguished—deliberately, consciously—and she didn't know how to restore it. Now he was simply pretending with an easy charm that meant nothing.

"Such a pensive face, beautiful lady. Beautiful lady," he mused. "All these dances, and we haven't had a proper introduction."

She stared. "Was our meeting so offhand that it now distresses you?"

"Our meeting was enchanting. But I can't keep calling you beautiful lady."

"What?" Her hand went to her mouth, stifling her disappointment. He even chose to forget her name, the scoundrel! She drew herself up, anger replacing dismay. "It seems, Monsieur Bouchard, that though your dancing has improved this evening, your manners have worsened. If you'll excuse me." She rose from the divan.

He stood up in his turn. His expression had become thoughtful. "Ah, yes. Of course. I should have guessed. We danced together earlier this evening. And you told me your name."

"And you've forgotten it," she snapped. "Did you also forget the name of the lady you embraced on the staircase?" Why had she said that? It only shamed her. She sounded like a jealous lover, when it was clear she meant very little to him.

"The lady on the staircase only wanted to make her husband jealous. And I was pleased to oblige. Don't go," he added, as Charmiane gasped and turned away. "We danced earlier, *n'est-ce pas?* And was I somewhat clumsy footed upon the dance floor? All the while gazing at you with burning devotion?"

She couldn't hide the pain she felt. "Your dancing improved even as . . ." She stopped. Surely her face would give her away, if not her intemperate words.

He laughed softly and finished the thought. "Even as my devotion seems to have declined. Is that it?"

Her humiliation was complete. He knew it all. "Don't mock me." She turned to go, fighting against her tears.

He took her arm, preventing her from leaving. "Don't go," he said gently. "Circumstances mock you, not I." He reached out and touched a tear that shimmered in her lashes. "*Mon Dieu.* Have you lost your heart, beautiful lady? But surely not to me."

"Please," she whispered. "Will you let me go?"

"Only if you say my name."

"Bouchard," she answered with reluctance.

"Yes, of course. But my full name. You *do* remember it?"

She found a speck of dirt on one glove and busied herself with rubbing at it. "Monsieur... Adam-François Bouchard," she stammered. "Baron Moncalvo." She raised her eyes and stared at him defiantly. "I've forgotten the military rank."

He laughed. "So have I. In point of fact, *I'm* just a corporal."

She drew in an angry breath. "Do you now add lies to all your other...?" She was too outraged to continue.

His eyes had lost none of their good humor. "Failings? Is that the word? I am as I am, beautiful lady. But not who you think I am."

"You've taxed me quite enough, monsieur," she said coldly. "I'm sure Monsieur de Géraud will be a far more agreeable companion."

"Wait," he said. "Permit me." He bowed deeply. "You see before you Noël-Victor Bouchard, sometime scapegrace and bon vivant. And twin brother to the estimable Adam-François Bouchard, Baron Moncalvo, who, alas, you seem to prefer. Though, devil take me, I can't fathom why. I wonder your toes aren't trampled from dancing with Brother Adam."

She fell back a step, one hand going to her bosom. "Your *twin*?"

"I'm surprised Adam's here. He doesn't usually attend balls."

She shook her head. "You *are* mocking me."

"No."

"It's a cruel jest, if you are."

"How can I prove it? Let me see. At what hour did you meet Adam?"

"When I arrived. Just after nine."

"And I came at half past eleven, not ten minutes before I met you on the stairs. My...lady friend likes to come fashionably late, to appear fresh when most of the other women have begun to wilt. She only wanted an escort, as I told you, to make her husband jealous. We might ask *her* who I am. No.'' He shook his head. "I suspect she and her husband have already reconciled. It would be churlish of me to intrude on their newly rekindled love affair."

She was still finding it difficult to accept. Twins. But it would explain the changes in him that had so mystified and dismayed her. "How could I have made such a mistake?"

"On any other evening you wouldn't have. If the Emperor had decreed uniforms tonight, you would have been far more dazzled by Adam than by me. Brother Adam is absolutely splendid in his epaulets and gold braid and ribbons. Didn't you at least notice his Legion of Honor, the red *cordon* in his lapel?"

"No." She found herself blushing. She had noticed nothing except his beautiful face, his captivating eyes.

He laughed. "Well, perhaps he wasn't wearing it. Brother Adam is modest about his accomplishments."

"I still can't believe it. You're so alike."

"Not at all. Adam always scowls, and I always laugh. Which is probably why he's so much more a success than I."

"But you're a soldier, also?"

"I didn't have to be. By the laws of conscription, a man doesn't have to serve if he has a brother in the service. There seemed so many better things to do. You can't believe the vastness of America. The sun setting over the Pacific. The splendors of India. The world is wide. I think I've managed to see a good deal of it."

"But now you're a soldier."

"Brother Adam became very rich at soldiering. It seemed like a good idea. I've done everything except make money. So I enlisted five years ago. I'm still waiting to find my fortune. Perhaps I'll raise horses in America someday. *Mon Dieu*, but you're beautiful. Like a piece of Sevres porcelain, all creamy white and fragile. Damned if I know why you prefer Adam to me. I'm so much more charming."

She returned his smile. He was charming. Genuinely so. She realized it now. He'd been paying court to her as himself—Noël; she had found it grating only because it jarred with her image of Adam. "I scarcely know either of you," she said. "How can I prefer one to the other?"

"Will you tell me your name now, beautiful lady?"

"Madame Charmiane de Viollet."

"Married?"

"Widowed."

"Charming Charmiane. How fortunate for the gentlemen. A widow has so much freedom in this society. To...give her favors, as she chooses." He stared at her mouth, his expression gone serious. "I should very much like to kiss that beautiful mouth," he said. "Will you let me take you home later?"

The conversation had taken an uncomfortable turn. She laughed to lighten the mood. "Wicked sir! Did you intend to take advantage of my freedom as a widow?"

His eyes twinkled. "Only if you wish it. *Will* you let me take you home?"

"I don't know. Adam..." She twisted her fingers in helpless confusion. "I don't know."

"Perhaps it's time for you to tell me what my brother did this evening," he said gently.

"Nothing. We danced. He said he'd take me home. And then...then he went away, when Monsieur de Géraud invited me to dance." How ridiculous it all sounded, put that way. For nothing more than that her heart was breaking? "That's all," she added.

"That's far from all, I think. Your lovely face is too open and frank to dissemble."

She put her hands to her flaming cheeks. "It's stupid."

"It's charming. And I suspect Adam finds it so."

Her heart flared with hope. "You do?" she cried, and blushed again. Would she never learn to be a little more circumspect?

"My dour, tongue-tied brother never took the time to learn the social graces. He trips over his words with a woman, even when he tries to talk about the weather. He must enjoy knowing what you're thinking, without the need for conversation."

"But if he knew what I was thinking, why..." She stopped, flustered, then began again. There was no point in hiding it from Noël. Not when her face was an open book. "Why did he go away?"

"Because my brother's also a fool. Devil take it," he muttered. "Here comes that ass Géraud again. I refuse to give you up yet. There must be another room for dancing. Come along."

"Oh, but..."

He brushed her cheek with his fingers. "Please dance with me. You're an enchanting woman. I intend to sway your heart away from Adam, if I can."

She shivered. The soft caress had stirred something within her. And surely his eyes were as blue, as spellbinding. Perhaps she wasn't as impervious to the charms of Noël Bouchard as she had thought.

"Ah, Bouchard. I hear you lost your wager the other day." An ugly red-faced man with a pointed beard lolled in the doorway as they passed through. His fat fingers were bedecked with diamonds. "The lady refused, I understand."

Bouchard interrupted sharply, his jaw thrust forward in anger. "Not another word, Perrachon. Unless you intend to lose your tongue as well as your life."

"But to be refused! And by a woman who has received half the city of Paris, or so they say."

"Damn you, Perrachon!" Bouchard leaped forward. One strong hand tugged at the man's beard, jerking open his mouth. At the same moment he grabbed at Perrachon's wrist and pushed his jeweled fingers between his own fleshy lips.

Perrachon gurgled and pulled his hand loose. Fresh blood traced a line across his pouting mouth where a diamond had scratched him. "Villain!" he croaked, massaging his chin.

"My good Perrachon." Bouchard smiled, bowed low and led Charmiane through the doorway. He turned about to deliver his final shot. "Send your seconds around, if you dare." He smiled at Charmiane as though nothing had happened. "He won't." The blue eyes turned serious. "Don't frown, beautiful lady. I'm not a thorough villain. The wager was made in a rash moment. Somewhere between the ninth or tenth cognac. I can't remember now. The lady didn't refuse. But it didn't seem right to dishonor her further."

"You pretended to lose the wager, then."

He laughed. "It cost me half a month's pay. A foolish gamble. A foolish gesture. One of my many failings. And still you frown. Am I such a disappointment?"

How could she tell him that she frowned not in dismay but in confusion? Had it all been a joke, a game he used to amuse himself? *Twins*, by all the Saints? It was absurd! This was Adam Bouchard and none other. His touch had moved her as before. His temper had flared despite his pretense to insouciance. Playing the part of an easygoing twin brother, he had slipped, allowed his true nature to be revealed, if only for a moment.

What manner of wicked man was this, to play such devious games?

The orchestra began a waltz. She moved reluctantly into his embrace. She was guarded, nervous now. He frowned at her continuing silence, her somber mood. "Are you unhappy to dance with me?" he said at last.

"No, I . . ."

"Did you love your husband?"

Her eyes widened in surprise. "Monsieur Bouchard! What a thing to ask. It's only natural that a woman . . ."

"I didn't ask what was natural. I asked if you loved him."

She couldn't lie. Her face would only betray her. "Why do you ask?" A clumsy evasion.

He smiled gently. "I shouldn't like to think of you giving your love to another man. I'm jealous."

"Jealous? *Fi donc!* I don't believe you." She felt herself doubting everything he had said all evening.

His smile was warm, charming, with just the right touch of sincerity. She was beginning to hate him. "Perhaps 'jealous' is too strong," he said. "Still, it's pleasant to contemplate. Teaching you to love. A gentle tutor, an innocent pupil . . ."

"Stop!" she burst out. "Enough of your games and lies, *monsieur le baron*!"

His eyebrow arched in surprise. "*Monsieur le baron?* So that's the lay of the land. You still doubt me."

"Have I heard anything save lies this evening?"

"You've heard only the truth. At least from me. Most particularly the part about my wanting to kiss you."

She stood still in the middle of the dance floor, refusing to move another step. "Take me home," she said coldly.

He sighed and looked distractedly about the large room. Suddenly his frown of consternation became a relieved smile. "I'm saved. Come along, beautiful lady." Ignoring her protests, he swept her back into the dance, circling quickly until they'd reached the opposite side of the room. "Look, my sweet," he said. "The man seated next to the chimneypiece."

She looked and gasped. "Oh, but . . . !"

"Yes. Brother Adam himself. And scowling as usual."

Charmiane stared in astonishment. It was true. And the man who sat and frowned, his morose gaze following her as she danced, was surely Adam. Her Adam, who had stolen her heart. Even as Noël swung her away again, she could still feel Adam's eyes on her, burning her with their fervor, drawing her like a magnet.

Noël laughed. "You see?"

"I feel like a fool. To accuse you . . ."

"You're forgiven."

"But you look so very like each other."

"No. Not really. Only when you don't know us well. There are differences—little things, movements, gestures. Even individual features. It simply takes time to see the distinctions."

"But not when Adam frowns?" She wanted to laugh for joy. Adam's frowns had become loving attributes to her rejoicing heart.

Noël smiled sheepishly. "Yes. Well. I have no doubt he's frowning in particular at me. You see, I've lately seduced away a woman of his acquaintance."

She felt a pang. "He . . . cared for this woman?"

"No more than I did. Adam loves his women with the intensity of the soldier. He takes what he can. He lives while he may. We all do. But, by the degree of his scowl, I think he's especially jealous now."

"Why now?"

"Don't you know? Because of you. He's quite smitten, I think. I can see it in his eyes."

She felt happiness and pain in equal measure. "I should think he'd want to dance with me, then," she said softly. "Instead, he sits there sullen and seeming indifferent."

"You're dancing with me, *n'est ce pas?* His fiercest rival. You've wounded him. So he turns sullen. It's his way. I remember once—we were children—he saved me from drowning. My own stupidity, of course. He was as frightened as I was when he pulled me ashore. But the minute we were on land, he turned on me and knocked me down. It's his way. To hide his feelings behind gruffness. You don't really prefer him, do you?" Noël smiled carelessly.

For a fleeting moment, she wondered if he was as carefree as he seemed.

Noël shook his head. "It's a crime against nature. He's a man who'll never tell you how beautiful you are. How your hair is as dark as night, and your skin like the pale moon. Like alabaster. Only warm. Begging to be caressed. How can you choose my brother over me?" Her instincts had been right. She was sure of it. His casual manner didn't quite hide a very real yearning.

What shall I do? she thought. Despite Noël's ardent words, she wanted Adam. She longed to be held again in his arms. To feel the magic, as before. But Noël was holding her. And Noël was waiting for the answer to his plea.

Just then Adam rose from his chair. He threw her a look of anger and disgust and strode, stiff legged, to the large double balcony doors. He slammed both hands against them, pushed them open and marched into the night.

The dance was over. Adam was gone, and Noël stood smiling. And waiting, his arm still about her waist. "Well, beautiful lady. Will you choose?"

She never thought she'd be grateful to Géraud, but his appearance before her, aggrieved expression and all, was a godsend. She needed time to sort out her confused thoughts. Géraud bowed. "*Madame*, I hold you to your promise. Supper has been announced."

She disengaged Noël's arm and put her hand on Géraud's sleeve. "Of course, *monsieur*." She smiled at Noël. Now that she'd relinquished him, she wasn't sure, after all, that she wanted to lose him and his charming ways. "Will you come to supper, as well, Monsieur Bouchard?"

He smiled, his mouth twisting in a self-satisfied grin. "I'm not hungry. I had an . . . amusing supper with my friend before we arrived. I think I'll try the card room. A hand of *bouillotte* might help to pass the time." He brought Charmiane's hand to his lips and kissed the tips of her gloved fingers. "Till later, perhaps?"

Géraud chattered through every room that led to the Salon de la Paix, where supper was laid out. He nodded at men and women in the pressing crowd as if to show Charmiane how important he was. And when they reached the banquet hall, he swept his arm about the room as though he were personally responsible for the feast. Tables groaned with mutton and poultry, fruits and cakes and carafes of wine. Giant urns overflowed with flowers, and the chandeliers picked up the sheen of crystal and fine porcelain.

But Géraud's happy chatter, the laughing crowd, the lavish banquet—all meant nothing to Charmiane. With every step, every beat of her heart, the words rang out in her brain: You fool. You fool. To let him go that way. Without a word. Never to see him again, perhaps. *Ah, Dieu!* That was too painful to dwell upon, the thought of losing him forever.

She turned to Géraud and pressed her fingers to her temples. "*Monsieur le comte*, I find I'm ill-disposed to eat this evening. The very sight of the food distresses me. Will you allow me to rest while you take supper?"

"*Madame*, let me accompany you. We'll find a chaise. It would be my honor to hold your hand. To stroke the fever from your brow."

"Please. No. I beg you." She gave him a little push toward the tables. "Go. I shouldn't want you to do without on my account."

His eyes followed a footman bearing a silver platter heaped with several large joints of meat. "Well . . ."

She clasped his hand for a moment and smiled with as much warmth as she could manage. *Le bon Dieu* knew she might still need his friendship someday! "Seek for me after supper," she whispered, and fled the salon.

She sped through the State rooms, now almost empty. She stopped for a moment to look at her face in a pier glass and was appalled to read the anxiety in her eyes. Fool. Romantic fool. Whereas before she'd cursed herself for letting him go, now she wondered at the folly of her pursuit. Wasn't she asking for grief? He'd rejected her once. Walked away. Left her. What was to stop him from doing it again?

No. She turned away from the mirror. She had no choice but to follow her heart, wherever it led. She reached the ballroom with its balcony doors. She hesitated for a moment, trembling, then walked out into the night.

It was a long balcony terrace that stretched half the length of the facade of the Tuileries, set above a ground-floor arcade and reached by numerous doors. Despite the full moon, the balcony was shadowy; large potted trees and shrubs set at intervals cast patches of black velvet onto the silvered stone of floor and balustrade. The night was warm for April, sweet and mild. A gentle breeze caught at her skirt, riffled the curls on her forehead, teased her with the scents of spring carried on its breath: warm earth and new green buds and rising sap. Hyacinths and daffodils and flowering chestnut trees.

The balcony looked out upon the Tuileries Gardens with their terraces and trees and fountains, their neat flower beds. Beyond the gardens she could see the massed shadows of trees in the Champs-Elysées, and beyond that the looming shape of the new Arc de Triomphe de l'Etoile, still under construction and masked with a veil of scaffolding.

The view was majestic but deserted. She and the Arc and the sweet night were alone. All alone. Where was the joy with no one to share it?

"Adam?" she whispered. Silent tears rolled down her cheeks. She should have run to him the moment she saw him leave. She should have refused Géraud, clung to Adam as though her life's happiness depended upon it. "Adam," she said again, her voice filled with loss and despair.

A dark shadow moved from between the trees of the balcony. He stood before her, the moonlight catching the sharp planes of his face. She trembled with hope—waiting, fearful, yearning. Suddenly she was crushed against his hard chest, her breath nearly squeezed from her by the strength of his violent and impassioned embrace.

"Kiss me, Adam," she whispered, circling his neck with her arms. But she needn't have asked; his burning mouth was bending to claim hers almost before the words were spoken.

Chapter Three

His lips crushed hers. Demanding, domineering. She moaned in willing surrender, opening her mouth to the savage invasion of his tongue. She felt weak and helpless; she was his—to do with as he wished. She no longer had the strength even to cling to him, but let her arms fall away as he pressed her close to his breast. Never in her dreams, in her wildest romantic longings, had she imagined a kiss could stir her so. The night was forgotten, the dance was forgotten. Only he existed for her: his hard mouth; his possessive hands, burning through the silk of her gown to excite her flesh; his masculine scent, compounded of sun-warmed skin and horse and desire.

One strong hand dropped to her buttocks, kneading the soft mounds in a frenzy of passion. She hadn't thought there could be any space left between their two bodies, but his hand pulled her even closer, cradling and lifting her hips so their knees touched, their thighs. She stiffened in fear and thrilled surprise at the sudden and intimate feel of his hard shaft against her skirts, pressing insistently into her throbbing body.

She had never known a man could desire her so much; she had never felt such an answering desire, her body flooding with warmth and longing. Henri had merely ordered her into bed when he wanted her; though his lack of passion—even in the moment of release—made her wonder why he bothered. Except, perhaps, to reaffirm his rights as her husband, her position as his obedient wife.

But Adam wanted her. His kiss, his eager body, his arms told her so. And—God forgive her wickedness—she wanted him. When at last his mouth released hers, she still leaned against him. Willing, submissive. Only the fear of his refusal kept her from saying the words aloud. Take me, Adam. I'm yours forever.

He set her roughly away from him. "Now will you run back to my brother?" he growled.

How could he even imagine such a thing? "I thought he was you."

"And you found him more pleasant? More agreeable? He has a way with women, God knows. Surely he's your choice."

"Adam, don't. I'm *here*. Don't you understand?" Her voice trembled on the edge of a sob. Was he so blind?

He stared at her. Though his eyes were in shadow, she could feel them penetrating her very soul. At last he sighed and reached for her hand. "Come. We'll walk in the garden." He led her off the balcony and down a small staircase to the ground-floor doors. They crossed the wide gravel courtyard in front of the palace and made their way into the garden. During the day the vast Tuileries Gardens, open to the public, thronged with people and carriages. Now, with all but the main gates closed, they were deserted. Silent—save for the splashing of fountains and the occasional cooing of a dove disturbed in its rest by the drifting music that came from the palace.

Hand in hand they walked through the high iron gates, strolled over a flower-banked terrace and down several steps. The scent of hyacinths and chestnut blossoms was intoxicating. They passed into a dark grove of trees that whispered of love, their spring-budding branches stirring in the soft breeze. There was no need for words. The safe darkness made them one.

Charmiane looked up at the tall man beside her. The light of the moon, shining in the clearing just beyond the grove, made a backdrop against which his strong, handsome profile was silhouetted. He sensed her eyes on him—were they not one heart, one soul tonight?—stopped and turned.

"Charmiane," he said. Quietly, hesitantly, as though he were testing the sweetness of the word on his lips. Then he pressed her fingers through her glove and resumed walking.

"I feel as old as time," she murmured. "As if we'd walked in this garden before." She laughed softly. "In another life, perhaps we did."

He sighed. "In another life, perhaps we shall again." His voice was sad and filled with regret. It broke her heart just to hear it.

She had no response to his words. What could she say? Life itself was the sadness. They walked again in silence. Then, "Where did you go," she asked, "when I danced with Géraud?"

The sound he made was part growl, part sardonic laugh. "I thought to take a page from my brother's book. I sought out a gaming table." He shook his head. "I don't know what the deuce he sees in it."

"Were you..." It was painful to ask. "Were you so angry with me that you chose to...desert me?"

"I told you I'd see you home. I gave my word. I meant to keep my promise."

"But, in the meantime..."

His voice was husky in the darkness. "I thought you'd prefer the company of others."

"You can't have thought that!" she cried. "That I'd prefer them to you." She struggled against her tears. "Why did you leave? To break my heart?"

At her words, the anguish in her voice, he stopped and turned to face her. The moon peeped through the young, lacy growth of the trees; he pulled her into its light, lifted her chin to catch its gleam. It sparkled on the tears that clung to her lashes. *"Ma foi,"* he muttered. "Where did you come from? I should have met you a lifetime ago." He enfolded her in his strong embrace. This time his kiss was tender, gentle. A loving caress that sealed the magic bond between them and promised more. When he released her, he took her hand again and they resumed their walk under the trees.

"Noël said you were a fool for letting me go," she said.

He grunted. "Noël is undoubtedly right."

"Are you...glad you found me again?" She held her breath. Dear God, let him say what she wanted to hear.

He looked down at her. Even in the gloom she could see the whiteness of his teeth, the joy of his unexpected smile. "I'm glad you sought me out. I would have been too dunderheaded to follow *you* to the balcony."

Happiness bubbled within her breast. Her heart swooped and soared, like a bird in flight on a spring day. She wanted to dance, to throw her arms wide to the shining moon, to laugh and sing for the sheer joy of living. She tugged at his hand. "Come into the moonlight."

"Why?"

She giggled. "So I can see your scowling face."

"Am I such a monster?"

She giggled again. "Well, you're not your brother. That's certain."

Without a word he shook free of her hand and strode out of the grove. She could see the anger in the set of his shoulders, the stiff line of his jaw. She had to skip to catch up with him.

"Adam!" she cried.

He whirled to her. In the open clearing, the moon shone full and bright upon his face, picking up the hard line of his mouth, the crease between his brows. "I'm sorry I don't laugh enough," he growled.

She reached up and smoothed the frown from his forehead. "I have enough laughter for both of us," she whispered. Suddenly overcome with shyness at her bold gesture, she dropped her hand and danced away from him. "I love the moonlight. So clear and bright. I shall be Diana, the Moon Goddess."

A soft grunt. "Moon madness." The frown had returned.

"Diana's the Huntress, as well." She was bold again, at the mercy of her dizzying, changing emotions. Shamelessly she threw her arms about his neck. "Have I caught you with my silver bow?"

He hesitated, his mouth poised to take hers, then disengaged her arms and pushed her away. "You're a child. You don't know what you're doing."

Her lip trembled. "I do."

"You're too young. There's no time left."

A child? Too young? His words hurt. She thought for a moment to sulk and weep, to make him regret his harsh judgment. Then her stubborn pride reasserted itself. She forced herself to laugh. "If I'm a child, you'll indulge me tonight. Come." She pulled him to the center of the grassy terrace, where a large circular pool shone in the moonlight. In the center of the pool, a carved stone fountain shot a high jet of water toward the heavens; the droplets, as they fell, sparkled with light—dancing fireflies against the deep velvet sky. The rim of the pool was a low stone wall. Charmiane pointed to it. "Help me up." With Adam's hand steadying her, she climbed onto the wall and began a slow progress around the pool.

"Madness," he muttered. "You'll fall and soak yourself."

"*Fi donc!* No such thing." She let go his hand and danced recklessly along the edge of the pool. Foolish bravado. The wind had freshened and now tugged at her skirts, making her balance precarious. She had just about decided to ask his help to descend when a sudden sharp breeze caught the fountain and swung the full force of its spray in her direction. "Oh!" she cried, and toppled from the wall into his arms.

He set her on her feet, though he seemed reluctant to let her go. He shook his head. "Madness."

She began to laugh. "Look at me." Her face, her bosom, her arms were drenched. She stripped off her long taffeta gloves—wet and no doubt ruined beyond hope—and tucked them into the sash at her waist. She started to wipe her face with her fragile lawn handkerchief, but he stopped her.

"Wait." He pulled out a large linen square and dabbed her forehead and cheeks. She closed her eyes, transported by his nearness, the gentleness of his touch, the bewitchment of the scented air. His hand moved down and pressed the cloth against the exposed flesh of her bosom. She felt herself trembling.

Without warning, the movement stopped. She opened her eyes. His face was in shadow, but she saw the perceptible rise and fall of his chest, heard the tortured rasping of his breath. She pulled the handkerchief from his lax fingers and guided his hand down to the rounded swell of her breast. He shivered and tried to pull his hand away, but she held it fast, knowing her nipple was growing hard beneath the warmth of his palm.

"Damn it," he growled. "Do you know what you're doing?"

"Yes. Yes, I do."

"So be it!" He pulled her roughly toward him, lifted her in his arms and carried her to the whispering shadows of the grove. He set her on her feet and kissed her hard, his lips overpowering hers, his tongue seeking out the sweetness of her mouth. His impatient hands ranged her body, squeezed her trembling thighs through her skirts, played wildly along her spine. No part of her was free from his possessing touch.

Her head was spinning. Her legs buckled beneath her. She clung to him dizzily—balance gone, reason gone. "I'm falling...I can't..." she stammered, and sank to the cool grass.

He dropped to his knees and arranged her unprotesting body before him. A vulnerable body, but willing and eager for whatever might befall.

His movements were quick, strong, demanding. He tugged at the bodice of her gown, releasing her breasts from their thin coverings, and bent to the soft orbs. Curling his mouth around one nipple, he sucked sharply. Charmiane cried out as a jagged flame raced through her body. She tore at the grass beneath her hands, helpless and quivering under his violent assault. And when he turned to her other breast and repeated his tantalizing kisses, she thought she'd go mad. She writhed with desire and lifted her hips, twisting and straining, as though the movement alone could ease the painful ache that sprang from her loins.

He seemed as impatient as she. He rose to his knees and pushed up her skirts, sliding them carelessly to her waist. With a rough pressure of his hand he separated her legs, seeming unaware that she opened for him willingly.

She trembled in an agony of longing. Now, she thought. Now! Heart pounding, she watched as he unbuttoned the flap of his breeches and released his manhood. She felt a moment's uneasiness. Unlike Henri, he was frighteningly large. But they'd gone too far; she hadn't the courage to stop him. She gulped and closed her eyes. Would he hurt her?

I don't care, she thought. Only let it be now!

She heard him swear, and opened her eyes to see him still kneeling before her. Even in the gloom she could see the fierce scowl on his face, the frightening, looming hunch of his shoulders. She trembled. "Adam?" she whispered.

His voice was an angry growl. "Will you persist in this, *madame*? Do you want a fatherless child?"

"I want you," she said. "That's all I know." She closed her eyes to hold back the tears.

"God forgive us both." He poised himself above her and thrust with all his might.

She gasped in shock at the savagery of his attack and tossed her head from side to side, swept by raging waves of feeling. He thrilled her with his power, ignited her by his fierce passion. She was an untutored bride again, facing the unknown. For surely those nights of unpleasant tedium with Henri, his lackluster performance, had not prepared her for this. The wild thrusts, the hard slap of his flesh against hers. Adam rode her like a madman, panting with each pulsing stroke, stirring her body to ever greater heights until she thought she couldn't bear another moment of such exquisite joy. She had no thoughts; she was pure sensation—floating, soaring, burning in a red-hot fire, then shivering and trembling. She threw her arm across her mouth to stifle her cries of ecstasy. She felt a welcome release, a rush of feeling; then Adam cried out and collapsed against her, burying his face in her tousled hair.

At last he stirred. "Damn it," he muttered, "what kind of an impetuous fool are you? Inviting your own ruin."

She didn't answer. There was nothing to say. She hadn't been impetuous. It was as though she'd always known him, always wanted him. From the first moment she'd seen him this evening, the signals had flashed from every part of her body to her brain, like bonfires on a May eve flashing from village to village. From her eyes, which couldn't stop looking at him; from her madly racing heart; from the quivering in her vitals when he spoke; from the heat that burned her fingertips each time he held her hand. All the signals, all the sweet signs—flashing, shouting, crying out to her brain.

This is the one.

She lay with her eyes closed, unable to move, to speak. She mistrusted the stability of her legs. Even her voice. And when he rose from her, she still lay uncovered, welcoming the cool breezes against her burning thighs. She heard the soft movements that indicated he was straightening his own clothing, and then there was silence. After a few minutes, she heard him beside her.

"Charmiane?"

She opened her eyes. He knelt at her side, holding his handkerchief. He had moistened it in the fountain, and now he gently sponged her thighs, the dark patch of hair, the tender throbbing core of her that still tingled with the memory of passion. When he was finished, he pulled down her skirts, modestly recovered her breasts and helped her to her feet.

She leaned against him. "I can scarcely stand," she said. "I'm shaking too much."

"I'd best take you home."

She felt her topknot; her combs were still in place, but several long strands of hair had come loose. "I must look a sight," she said. "How can I . . ."

He kissed her softly, then slipped a supporting arm around her waist. "Come to the edge of the garden. Near the Place. I'll bring my carriage around for you."

She waited, seated on a bench just inside the iron fence, and gazed out at the Place de la Concorde. She felt an odd sense of loss and sadness. The end of a strange, mystical, enchanted evening. She'd given her heart to a man she knew so little of. She'd made love with a stranger, a phantom. And now it was ending, and it scarcely seemed as though it had been real in the first place.

She shivered. She was suddenly aware that it had turned cold, with a touch of lingering winter in the air that had come with the rising wind. *Dieu!* She'd left her shawl in the ballroom. Looking the way she did—with her unruly hair, her creased skirts—she could scarcely retrieve it now. She felt for her gloves, tucked into her sash. Alas. They were still damp from the fountain; they'd chill her more than protect her. If she'd owned an evening cape, she would have worn it tonight. April was such a changeable month.

She heard the clip-clop of horses. A splendid carriage appeared just outside the gates. As it stopped, Adam leaped from it before the footman had even lowered the steps. He hurried to her. "The deuce!" he said. "You're shivering."

"My shawl. I left it inside."

"I'll send for it and have it delivered in the morning. Come." He bundled her into the carriage and put his arm about her to keep her warm. His footman waited outside the open carriage door, a look of expectation on his face. Adam bent to Charmiane. "Faubourg Saint-Germain, of course?"

She smiled. "Of course." All the discontented Royalists and émigrés lived in that particular suburb. Would her family have chosen any other? "Number six, rue de la Planche." She felt a twinge of shame at the thought of him seeing their modest apartment. "It isn't very grand, you understand. But we have hopes."

The footman nodded. "Rue de la Planche. Very good, *madame*." He closed the door.

Charmiane sighed and leaned against Adam as the carriage made its way across the Place and toward the Concorde Bridge. Too soon, she thought. Too soon! Oh, Adam. Don't let me go.

He cleared his throat. "Do you go home by way of the Concorde Bridge?"

Was it ended for him so soon? she thought, anguished. A moment of passion and then he spoke of bridges and routes as though they were the most important matters in the world. "No. We use the Pont Royal. That is, the Pont de la Réunion, I think you call it now. The Pont de la Concorde isn't on the maps *we* have, from the old days."

"Of course. They built it after you must have left France. From the stones of the old Bastille, after they tore it down."

How could they be talking like this? As if they were two strangers who'd met half a moment ago. As though they hadn't made love in a scented garden beneath the moon. She slipped from the circle of his arm, leaning forward to stare out at the lantern-lit streets. He made no move to pull her back. "The Bastille. Yes," she responded, matching his matter-of-fact tone. "The fourteenth of July, in '89."

"I'm surprised you'd know the date of that bloody uprising."

"Quite by coincidence, I was born that day. In our *hôtel*, here in Paris. Papa heard the shouting in the streets as they were bringing me forth."

"*Mon Dieu,*" he muttered. "You're twenty-three?"

"Not until July."

"Damn. So young." He closed his eyes and leaned his head back against the cushions of the coach. With the gesture, he seemed to have closed her off, as well. They rode in silence, with only the sound of the ringing cobblestones to mask the heavy thud of her heart.

The carriage stopped. The door was opened by the attentive footman. Charmiane could see her apartment behind him. He lowered the steps and held out his hand. *"Madame?"*

"Wait." Adam leaned toward the door. In the light of the lamp that hung above number six, his brow was a changing map of perplexity and irresolution. "What time is it, Darnaud?" he asked.

"Well after three, I think, *monsieur le baron.*"

Adam scowled at Charmiane. "I'm hungry. Did *you* have supper?"

"No, I . . ."

"Do you want supper?"

"If you . . . yes," she stammered.

"Darnaud, does that little cabaret near les Halles still stay open all night?"

"I think so, *monsieur.*"

"Take us there," he ordered. He leaned back and closed his eyes again as the carriage retraced its path across the river Seine.

Charmiane trembled. His silence was frightening, reminding her again that he was a stranger. But a stranger she had loved. "Are you angry, Adam?" she ventured at last.

He opened his eyes. "Why should I be angry?"

"Because . . . because of what happened in the garden."

"God knows it was madness."

She bit her lip. "I'm not sorry."

"You're a little fool! Too young to know anything." His voice was a harsh bark.

"You *are* angry," she choked, and covered her eyes with her hand.

He grabbed her roughly by the shoulders. "No! It shouldn't have happened, that's all."

She felt a moment's cold terror in the pit of her stomach. "Are you *married*?"

A dark laugh. "No. There was never time." He stared at her, at the soft trembling of her chin. "Charmiane, don't cry." He kissed her gently, then pulled her into his strong embrace as though he would hold her forever. His kiss deepened—eager, hungry for the sweetness of her mouth.

Charmiane clung to him, lost once again in the passion of his demanding kiss, the fire of his ardent mouth. She felt a rapid pounding of a heart and could scarcely tell if it was hers or his, so closely was her bosom pressed against his hard chest.

They remained locked together, sharing kisses until the carriage stopped and the footman rapped discreetly on the window.

Then they reluctantly separated and descended, leaving the coach to await their return.

Les Halles was a rambling collection of low buildings, open sheds and crowded alleyways—the central markets of Paris, where wholesalers came to display their wares and shopkeepers to haggle over prices. Interspersed between the markets were wineshops and cabarets that accommodated the late-night carousers and the dawn-rising farmers who came to sell their produce.

At this hour, neither night nor dawn, the cobbled streets were filled with an odd mixture of people. Sleepy country peasants in wooden sabots and loose smocks were beginning to straggle into their various places, pushing barrows of spring vegetables, hay and sides of mutton. They rubbed shoulders with the patrons of the *guinguettes*—noisy, music-filled halls for drinking and dancing—who were being turned out by tavern keepers eager to close up shop and go home to their wives. A yawning broom merchant stopped to speak to a knife grinder who had just positioned his stone near the butchers' market.

Adam led Charmiane to a narrow, crooked building set between two arcaded markets. The lantern light from its windows spilled golden pools onto the pavement. They climbed a twisting staircase to a small room set with only two tables. The walls were finished with coarse stucco and stenciled with passages from merry drinking songs. From a similar room on the floor above could be heard the happy laughter of several men and women. As they seated themselves at a cozy table that overlooked the square, the other patrons came staggering down the stairs. Two recruits in plain uniforms with faces as young and unrazored as children waved drunkenly in at them, then continued their descent. Their companions, three painted *filles de joie*, giggled and followed after.

Adam grunted. "Let them enjoy themselves while they may." He scowled at the door. "Innkeeper!"

After a long wait, a little man came shuffling in, wiping his hands on a large apron. *"Monsieur?"*

"A simple meal, if you please. What have you?"

The man smiled slowly and scratched his head in thought. "Good honest leek soup, sir. My own daughter made it. A nice piece of boiled beef. Yes. I think there's still beef." He nodded. "I'm sure there's beef. Some fresh bread and butter and radishes."

"Good. We'll have that." Adam hesitated, then looked askance at Charmiane. He cleared his throat. "That is, if you wish it." It seemed an unfamiliar concession to him, to ask for another's approval.

"Of course."

"And wine. Have you Burgundy?"

The innkeeper deliberated for a long minute, then bobbed his head. "Yes. Yes, *bien sûr*. And cake for dessert. And dried apricots. If I can find them. For the grand *monsieur* and his beautiful lady." He beamed at them like an indulgent father.

"The deuce," growled Adam. "Then go and fetch it all. *Tonight*, if you please. And take your cheerful face elsewhere."

Charmiane smiled as the innkeeper made a slow and stately bow, moved with dignity to the door, then bowed again before exiting. "I liked his face," she chided gently.

Adam rubbed his eyes and sighed. "I'm not a fit companion for you. Filled with bile and black humors tonight."

She put her hand over his. "You're all the companion I want tonight."

He stared at her, his intense blue eyes searching her face. He shook off whatever thought had clouded them for a moment, then laughed mirthlessly. "It could be dawn before you arrive home. Nothing, I suspect, will hurry our merry host. Will I be greeted at your door by an irate brother, prepared to challenge me to a duel?"

"Not at all. Armand doesn't live with us."

"Parents? An uncle? A cousin?"

"I live with Aunt Sophie. And she sleeps soundly. The rest of the family is dead and gone."

"And Aunt Sophie. Does she hate the Emperor's nobility as much as your brother seems to?"

"Yes." She blushed for shame. "I suppose they think they have their reasons. I was too young when it all began. I never knew what was at stake. But they lost everything."

A cynical smile. "And so they wait for the Emperor to fall, *n'est-ce pas?*"

She looked surprised. "Well, it must happen, sooner or later, Armand says."

"And then what?"

"Why then the aristocrats will be restored."

"You think it's as simple as that? To cancel out the past twenty years?"

She nodded. "Of course. Why do you think we came back to France? Someday..."

"Damn it, there is no 'someday.' God help us, there's only now."

The despair in his voice brought tears to her eyes. "Adam," she whispered.

He stared, then groped for her hand and brought it to his lips. "Don't leave me tonight."

The magic had returned, shining in blue eyes filled with devotion and longing, echoing in the song her heart sang. "No. I won't." There were no words left. Nothing more to say. If their union in the garden had not joined them fully, now the press of his lips on her palm sealed the unspoken vows between them.

Supper was served. Charmiane could scarcely remember eating it. They existed alone together, on an island in time. Absorbing each other with their burning eyes, sighing, smiling in shy communion.

The candle on their table began to sputter. For the first time Charmiane became aware that the small patch of window had turned dawn gray and the cries of hawkers drifted up from the streets below. "We should go."

"Yes," he said reluctantly.

"Why are you looking at me that way?"

He reached out and stroked the line of her jaw. "To memorize your face."

"Flowers? Pretty violets?" A wrinkled crone stood in the doorway, holding out a basket filled with flowers. "Violets for the lady, *monsieur*?"

Adam nodded. He paid for the flowers, blessed them with a kiss, handed them to Charmiane. He paid for their supper and guided her down the stairs to his waiting coach. The mists of dawn were rising from the Seine when they crossed the Pont Neuf and turned toward Saint-Germain.

Charmiane lay in Adam's arms, savoring the sweetness of his embrace, the thrill of his touch, the warmth of his lips. There seemed no way to hold back the day, to prolong their last moments together.

Suddenly Adam reached up and rapped on the roof of the coach. "We'll walk the rest of the way," he announced firmly. "The deuce." He looked abashed. "That is . . . you'll forgive me . . . do you *want* to?"

She smiled in tenderness. His momentary discomfort had made him seem, for a brief second, like an awkward young boy. "I want to. Yes."

"Follow us with the carriage, Darnaud," he ordered, and helped Charmiane down from the coach.

It was chilly on the brightening street. A lone lamplighter stopped to rub his hands together before he extinguished a corner lamp. He tipped his hat as he passed them. Adam pulled off his coat and draped it over Charmiane's shoulders. The coat was warm and faintly scented with his cologne.

Hand in hand they made their way slowly down the rue des Saints-Pères. From within a half-timbered cottage that jutted over the narrow street they heard the cry of a baby. The rest was silence.

At the corner of the rue de la Planche, Adam stopped and kissed her. The first rays of the dawning sun glinted gold on his hair. He looked about to speak. Then he frowned, shook his head, led her to her door, a heavy paneled rectangle set into a high stone wall. He rang the bell for the concierge.

"Zut alors!" A muffled curse from within.

He rang again.

"Yes, yes! I'm coming, by all the Saints! Could you not wait for the cock to crow? To disturb my rest . . . a poor woman who works her fingers to the bone by day . . . a pox on you and your . . ." The door was pulled open. A frowsy woman, her greasy brown-gray hair falling over her eyes, stood before them in a grimy chemise and shawl. She yawned loudly and scratched beneath one ponderous breast. "You and your accursed . . ." She stopped and blinked, her eyes opening wide. "Madame de Viollet! What an hour. *Mon Dieu.*" Her eyes lit on Adam, then returned to Charmiane with Adam's coat about her shoulders, her fragrant bouquet of violets. She smiled and gave a sly wink. *"Mon Dieu,"* she said again. This time the words—purred low—held a different meaning.

Adam cursed under his breath and fished in his waistcoat pocket. "Here," he said. "For your trouble. And this—" the second coin placed more deliberately in her fleshy palm "—for your silence. Now let us in, and be quick about it."

The concierge clinked the coins in her hand and grinned. "Still as the grave, *monsieur*." She opened wide the door and ushered them into the open courtyard of the apartments. A prowling cat scratched at the coarse gravel.

Charmiane looked up quickly to the dormer windows just under the roof. Thanks be to God. Not a light showing. Aunt Sophie was still asleep.

Adam scowled at the concierge, who had closed the door behind them and now stood watching with unabashed curiosity, her fists on her fat hips. "Since we disturbed you," he growled, "you'd best go back to bed."

There was a small box on the ground beside the door. She plopped herself down on it, legs spread clumsily, and leaned her hands on her knees. "I can wait, *monsieur*, while the gentleman concludes his business."

"His business will include planting a foot in that fat backside of yours if you don't vanish at once! Do I make myself clear?" The commanding voice of a military man.

The concierge jumped to her feet. Charmiane almost laughed aloud, half-expecting to see her salute like a green recruit. The woman scurried to the door of her ground-floor apartment. At the last moment she turned, made a final attempt to reassert her authority over the building. "*Monsieur*, I . . ."

"Go!" he barked. "I'll see myself out."

She vanished, the cat scampering after her.

Charmiane pointed to an inner door. "There. We live in the top apartment."

He put his arms round her. "Then I'll say goodbye here." He kissed her fervently, his arms holding her tight.

She returned his passion in equal measure, then pulled his coat from her shoulders and handed it to him. "Good night," she whispered.

Without a word, he slung the coat over one arm and turned to go.

"Adam!" she cried. Aunt Sophie would be horrified at her brazenness. "Will you call upon me later today? Please?"

He looked at her, his eyes dark with pain, and said nothing.

She was too desperate, too devastated by his continuing silence, to remember her pride. "Tomorrow, then," she ventured with a tentative smile. "It will be soon enough."

He grabbed her fiercely by the shoulders. "Damn it, don't you understand yet? This was all we have! I report to my regiment this morning."

She felt the blood drain from her face. "This morning?"

"I'm a soldier. I go to war. I have no time for courtship or niceties." The words were brutally abrupt.

"Of course. I understand." She clenched her jaw to keep her chin from trembling and recovered her tattered pride. He would never know her pain. "I thank you, Monsieur Bouchard, for a pleasant evening. I, too, enjoy an amusing diversion from time to time." She held out her hand—the regal aristocrat—for his farewell kiss.

At the haughty words and gesture his eyes went cold. He clicked his heels and bowed sharply, took her hand and barely brushed his lips against her fingertips. "Your servant, *madame*."

She laughed gaily. She wondered if it sounded as hollow to him as it did to her own ears. "Will I have the company of your brother, Noël, perhaps, while you're away?"

His mouth twisted into an ugly smile. "Even my brother can't avoid this campaign."

"Alas. I wish you both well." The pretense was becoming too painful, too difficult to maintain with her revealing face. She opened the door and fled into the apartment, hurrying up the four stories by ever-narrowing staircases until she reached their dingy rooms at the top. She tiptoed into the small sitting room. She could hear Aunt Sophie's snores and soft gasps as she slept. She moved quietly through Sophie's tiny room, still untouched by the morning sun, to her own smaller room at the back.

She undressed quickly. It wasn't until she stood shivering in her chemise, staring at the few crushed bits of grass that clung to its hem, that she realized the enormity of her loss.

After the long years of exile, the impermanence of her life—even with Henri—she had thought she was home. But it was only a bitter dream. Her life was still a prelude, waiting to begin.

She trembled violently and clung to the back of her small chair for support. The trembling became deep, heaving dry sobs that shook her from head to foot.

Gone. He was gone.

"God help me," she murmured. With a muffled cry, she surrendered to her grief and collapsed onto her bed.

Chapter Four

Charmiane awoke to the late-morning sun with her eyes still puffy from weeping and a surprising tenderness at her inner thighs. She rolled over in her bed, sat up and pulled back the hem of her chemise. Her pale skin was mottled with several large bruises, attesting to the violence of Adam's lovemaking. She frowned. Had it been necessary for him to be so rough? It was a stark awakening, a less-than-perfect postscript to what had seemed a magical night: swollen eyes and battered flesh.

And her head was pounding. The sunshine pouring through her curtainless window only made it worse. She shut her eyes and leaned back against her pillows. What in the name of the Almighty had she done? Made love with a stranger in a garden! A stranger she would probably never see again. Do you want a fatherless child? he'd asked. *Ah, Dieu!* She felt a thrill of fear. Had he left her with more than just a fleeting memory? Her monthly cycle was usually preceded by a headache, but still...

She lifted herself reluctantly from the bed and moved toward her small washstand. She paused at the clothes that lay on the floor in the heap she'd left last night. Hastily she pulled off her chemise and dropped it beside her gown. She scarcely wanted to be discovered still in last evening's clothing! She found a nightdress, slipped it on and returned to examine her clothes with care. The grass of the Tuileries Gardens had only stained the hem of her chemise—an innocent stroll might have produced the same results. But her satin gown was more seriously compromised. Telltale green smudges covered the back of the skirt and the shoulders; though she might manage to wash them out, the pale yellow fabric would never be the same again. And how was she to explain it away?

She folded the gown into a drawer of her small commode, away from prying eyes, until she could decide what to do with it. With her bare toes she stirred the remaining clothes on the floor—stockings, lace-trimmed petticoat, delicate dancing slippers, sash. She bit her lip. Even with her hair combs and jewelry added, it seemed such a little pile. The shawl was gone, and the fan; she could only pray that Adam . . . that Colonel Bouchard would see to their return. And one of her gloves seemed to be lacking its mate. She'd need another plausible lie to explain the missing items, her carelessness.

What *have* I done? she thought again. She turned away from a watercolor of the Chevrillon château that hung on her wall. The windows were like eyes, filled with dark accusation. She'd never had to lie to Aunt Sophie before. But then she'd never behaved in so shameless a fashion before. In all her life, she'd never let any man make love to her except Henri. No matter what others did, she'd been a faithful wife, a chaste widow. Respected and respectable, like all the Chevrillon women.

Until last night. She must have been mad last night! Intoxicated with the glitter, the music, the moonlight. A handsome face she now had trouble recalling.

She could scarcely blame *him*. She blushed to remember her actions. She'd thrown herself into his arms, begged him to make love to her. And he was a soldier. Taking what he could, when he could. Wasn't that what his brother Noël had said? Why should he have told her he was leaving, when her manner, her eyes, her intemperate words begged for her own ravishment?

Still, he might have resisted her, knowing he'd be gone in the morning. But perhaps he was used to satisfying his desires, with no thought for anyone but himself. "No time for niceties," he'd said. She snorted in disgust. No indeed! Not when a silly, romantic fool was offering her virtue, her willing body. Not in a society that thrived upon sexual favors given and received.

Her eyes lit upon the bunch of violets, now wilted, lying on the small table near her bed. A less than fervid thank-you for the surrender of her favors! She scooped them up, pushed open her dormer window and tossed the flowers down into the dim, trash-filled alley that backed their apartment. The sooner she forgot him and the whole shameful evening, the better.

She started, hearing a clatter just beyond her door. She pulled shut the casement and scurried to her bed, managing to burrow under the blanket and emerge, yawning, as the door opened.

"Good morning, Madame de Viollet."

"Good morning, Jeanine. What time is it?"

The little maid, a pert girl not yet out of her teens, maneuvered her tray through the door and set it on the table. "Well after ten, *madame*. I should have let you sleep a little longer, but *madame*, your aunt, is bursting to hear your story of the ball!" She plumped the pillows behind Charmiane, poured a cup of coffee and handed it to her mistress. She giggled. "She wanted me to wake you directly I came in this morning, but I kept her busy by curling her hair."

"How good you are to her. To us both."

The girl curtsied, her eyes shining. "Oh, how I should have liked to serve you in the old days. It must have been grand! To live in a fine château, and dress my ladies in beautiful gowns...."

Charmiane laughed and shook her head. "I don't know. I don't remember."

As she sipped her coffee, she watched Jeanine bustle about the room, letting in the morning air, laying out fresh towels, tossing yesterday's cold water into the alley and refilling the brass ewer from a hot kettle she had waiting outside the door. She stooped to Charmiane's clothes, then straightened, frowning. "*Madame*, where's your gown?"

"I... put it away myself, last night."

Jeanine made a face, her lips pouting in annoyance. "*Madame*, it's not your place. Not your place at all! To fetch and carry like a servant. What am I to tell the other maids when we meet at the market? That *my* lady does for herself?"

Charmiane suppressed a smile. The lower orders were just as aware of class as the born aristocracy. "I'm sorry," she said. "I put it away out of habit. My maid in Switzerland didn't have your... sensibilities."

"Hmph. No pride in her work, *sans doute*." She picked up Charmiane's slippers, turned them over and smiled her approval. "You've quite danced them through. It must have been a wonderful ball. I'll throw them out. You'll replace them for the next time, *n'est-ce pas?*"

If there ever was a next time. "Yes. And, Jeanine—" she tried to sound offhand "—do you know a skillful dyer?"

Jeanine bobbed her head. "My last lady used to go to Monsieur Gachot on the rue de Miromesnil. Number twenty-five, I think. Shall I do it for you?"

"No, thank you. Now don't frown. It's for me to do. I must consult with Monsieur Gachot on the color." Thank the good Lord that problem could be solved. Despite her headache, she was beginning to feel a little better. But she could see that Jeanine, busy putting away her garments and accessories of the night before, had a perplexed look on her face. In a moment, heaven knows, there'd be a new round of questions and the need for more lies. She put down her cup and tossed back her blankets. "Finish that in a while, Jeanine," she said. "For now, fetch me my dressing gown while I wash my face and brush my teeth. Aunt Sophie will be turning purple with impatience if I don't put in an appearance!"

Fifteen minutes later, her cheeks glowing, puffy eyes reduced with the help of a bit of astringent and hair freshly brushed and pinned up, she presented herself for Aunt Sophie's cross-examination.

Aunt Sophie was a pink dumpling of a woman, with huge, helpless eyes and an air of trembling fragility. Her soft mouth perpetually alternated between a bemused smile and a child's pout, as though the problems of her world were more than she could deal with. Even her graying brown hair—though freshly curled by Jeanine—seemed beyond her control: stray ringlets drooped onto her forehead, and she constantly pushed them back with plump little hands. Her faded but once magnificent dressing gown scarcely managed to contain the round, uncorseted body beneath, which insisted on bulging in the most unlikely spots. She sat enthroned on a threadbare sofa in the sitting room, her feet resting on a brocaded footstool that filled the distance between the soles of her tiny slippers and the floor. Before her was an oval table set with the remains of breakfast. She put down her cup and looked at Charmiane. "I couldn't wait for you, my dear. I've eaten all the sweet cakes."

Charmiane pulled up a rush chair and sat beside her. "It doesn't matter, Aunt Sophie. I'll have bread."

Aunt Sophie fluttered her fingers in the air. "Jeanine. Jeanine! Fetch some bread for *madame*'s breakfast. And fresh *café au lait*." She turned mournful eyes to Charmiane. "It isn't like you to make me wait for my breakfast. It was very thoughtless."

"I'm sorry. Truly. Next time you must wake me earlier." It really had been thoughtless of her, after all that Aunt Sophie had done for them. For her. A motherless child almost from the moment she was born. Papa would have engaged a nursemaid and gone away to ease his sorrows: three children dead of the fever and then a wife, exhausted by a difficult labor and drained by her own grief. Papa would have abandoned Charmiane and Armand to an uncaring household staff. But Aunt Sophie wouldn't

hear of it. She and Uncle Eugène were unhappily childless. Was
her brother-in-law blind to his blessings, despite his misfortune?
Let him return with his motherless children to his elder brother's
château—the splendid home of his own youth—and let there be
no more nonsense about raising children in a small manor house
on the limited income of a second son. Uncle Eugène was won
over. Papa was agreeable. And Armand, just come into his teens,
was thrust into a life of luxury that he'd only dreamed of. All too
brief. Poor Armand.

"Well?"

Charmiane looked up from stirring her coffee. "Well what,
Aunt Sophie?"

"After all my waiting, am I to hear nothing about the ball?"

"Of course, *Liebchen*. Where shall I begin?"

Aunt Sophie settled herself more comfortably into the sofa.
"With the clothes, I think."

"Quite showy. It seems to be the fashion. Trimming upon
trimming. Laces and brilliants and ribbon bows. I thought
that . . ."

"Oh, I know what you mean. Not like in my day, when good
taste reigned."

"In point of fact, I thought some of the women looked rather
handsome. After the years of plain white robes *à la grecque*. And
the profusion of jewels . . ."

"Hmph. It's just their way of making themselves important. I
prefer to stay at home in retirement rather than acknowledge the
upstart Corsican and his friends! I met Madame du Barry's
seamstress in the street the other day. A little mouse who used to
sit in a corner, squinting over her needle. She's a baroness now.
Can you believe it?" Aunt Sophie sniffed. "I trust she's still
practicing her arts. She'll need them when the King sits on the
throne again."

"I've never seen so many jewels in my life. Such diamonds!
The men as well as the women. On shirtfronts and fingers. Tiaras
and earrings and . . ."

"What do you expect? They've plundered the world. Stolen
from every God-fearing household." Aunt Sophie's voice shook.
"Sometimes, when I pass a jeweler's shop, I fancy I recognize a
ring or a brooch in the window. A little treasure that belonged to
some dear old friend who paid for the accident of her birth with
her blood."

Charmiane reached forward and patted Aunt Sophie's hand. "Ill-gotten or not, they make a dazzling show. Particularly against the dark gowns."

"They're wearing dark?"

"Oh, yes. As often as pale colors. As a matter of fact—" she prayed her face wouldn't give her away "—I think I'll have my ball gown dyed. A dark gold, perhaps. I should like that."

Aunt Sophie shook her head. "No. Plum. It must be plum. To set off your coloring."

"Well...of course. If you think so, *Liebchen*," she added quickly, to forestall the pout that had begun to form about Aunt Sophie's lips.

"And whom did you meet at the ball?"

"You'll never believe it! The Emperor himself."

"*Gott in Himmel!* That devil." Aunt Sophie made the sign of the cross. "Well, I suppose it does no harm. It might be useful at a later time, to claim an introduction to the upstart."

"I found him charming."

"As charming as a man can be with the deaths of innocents on his conscience!"

"*Mon Dieu*, Aunt Sophie. *He* wasn't part of the mobs in the streets."

"He's as guilty as the rest. All of them who profited by the misfortunes of our class."

Charmiane sighed. She could almost have wished they hadn't returned to France. It had stirred up bitter memories for Aunt Sophie so that now the stories of the old days were clouded with an anger that hadn't been apparent in Switzerland. Ah, well. How could she begin to understand what it had been like for Aunt Sophie and Uncle Eugène, for Armand and Henri and the rest? They had lost not merely their homes and possessions but their friends, their homeland, their sense of permanence. All the certainties of life that gave meaning to the existence of even the humblest peasant. Lost. All lost. For Charmiane, raised in exile and nurtured on expectations, life was a grand ball waiting still to begin. For the remnants of the old aristocracy, living with penury and ghosts, the dance was long over. She sighed again. "I danced all evening," she said to change the subject, and forced a smile. "With a score of well-connected men who might be helpful."

Aunt Sophie brightened. "You weren't a wallflower, then. Good! And did you enjoy yourself?" She chuckled. "You're blushing. Of course you did."

Charmiane looked away. Strange that the heat of the blush could bring tears to her eyes. Strange that his face kept rising up before her, though she tried to cast it from her memory. "It was a wonderful ball," she whispered. "I'll never forget it."

"Despite a brother who did everything he could to spoil your evening?" Startled, Charmiane looked up. Armand stood in the doorway of the sitting room.

Aunt Sophie threw up her hands. "*Gott in Himmel!* What shall I do with that girl? You ought to have been announced! Jeanine!"

Armand laughed. "You're not in Switzerland anymore, Sophie. Let your curses be good French oaths. It's my fault. I told the girl not to bother." He limped into the room. "I hope you don't mind. I've brought Bertrand."

Aunt Sophie beamed and leaned over to tug at the sleeve of Charmiane's dressing gown. "Of course we don't mind, do we, my dear?"

Charmiane smiled thinly. "No. Of course not. It's always a pleasure to see Monsieur de Domfort. And after his kindness... the invitation..." While Armand bent to kiss Aunt Sophie, Charmiane held out her hand in greeting to the man who had followed Armand into the room.

Bertrand de Domfort was a tall, graceful man with deep-set and soulful eyes. Though he was a year or two younger than Armand, he appeared older, owing to his perpetually somber expression and a full, striking head of snow-white hair. He had lost his entire family to the guillotine, Armand had said, and had himself been thrown into prison during the Terror; only the death of Robespierre and the end of the madness had spared him the same fate as his noble father. When he had emerged from the Conciergerie prison—a young man of eighteen—his hair was turned to silver and his face was etched with a permanent grief.

Charmiane murmured a greeting as he bowed and kissed her hand. She really couldn't understand why she didn't like him better: since Armand had introduced him two months ago, the man had never ceased to be charming, thoughtful, courtly. Henri had often said she wasn't a very good judge of people. Maybe it was so.

"Madame de Viollet," he said. "You're looking particularly beautiful this morning. May I presume so much as to take a little credit for that glow of pleasure in your eyes?"

"You may indeed, Monsieur de Domfort. I'm in your debt for a joyous evening."

"For you, fair one, it would have been worth stealing the invitation, if necessary."

Armand snorted. "Oh, do stop sounding like a cavalier in a bad play, Domfort. Sit down and have some breakfast." He drew up two rickety chairs to the little table.

"You'll forgive me," said Domfort as he and Armand sat and waited for Jeanine to bring fresh cups. "But when your sister manages to look so charming so early in the morning..."

Armand smiled. "And so she does." His dark eyes turned serious. "I *am* sorry for last night, Charmiane. I don't know what could have put me into so foul a mood." He sighed. "Too few innocent balls, I suppose. Too many casual liaisons. A sense of loss. Of growing older. I hope I didn't ruin your evening."

Charmiane felt a tug at her heart. But for the Revolution, what might Armand's life have been? A dukedom, property and ease, a wife to comfort his old age, heirs to carry on the Chevrillon tradition. Instead, he'd become a lonely wanderer through the years, not just an exile. He had stopped to visit them in Switzerland now and again. A week here. A few days there. Cloaked in a kind of poignant isolation, he had touched Charmiane's soul but never allowed himself to be touched. She smiled in love and understanding. "Dear heart, how could you ruin my evening? Ever."

"I'm glad." He raised a questioning eyebrow. "But I trust the meddlesome gentleman's dancing was better than his manners."

Aunt Sophie leaned forward, her large eyes shining. "What's this? What's this? What gentleman?"

Charmiane fiddled with the lace on her sleeve. "He was...an agreeable companion but not a very good dancer. No."

"A gentleman?" Aunt Sophie's voice held a sudden sharp edge.

"A *baron*. A soldier."

"But a gentleman? One of ours?"

"No."

"But he turned your head. I can see it in your face." The accusation was now unmistakable.

"Aunt Sophie, please. I..."

"Don't be absurd, Sophie," Armand cut in sharply. "She just had a nice time. Have you forgotten what it's like to be young?" He stared down at his hand. On the little finger was a small ring. A filigreed medallion set upon a golden circlet. During his infrequent visits to Lake Constance in the early days, he'd allowed Charmiane to try it on. The medallion had proved to be a secret locket, containing—beneath a round of clear glass—a curl of hair in a beautiful shade of deep red. He'd never explained it; Charmiane had never had the courage to ask. He glanced up at Charmiane now. His eyes were filled with pain.

"Do you intend to be maudlin this morning, Chevrillon?" Domfort leaned forward and put down his cup.

"Go to the devil, Domfort." Armand rose abruptly and crossed to the window. His hands were shaking at his sides. He clenched them into fists to steady them.

"Yes, yes. Of course." Aunt Sophie's voice was a soothing murmur. "I'm sure the girl only had a nice time. What harm in that?"

What harm, indeed? Unless Adam had left her with child. She silently cursed her recklessness. "A pleasant evening. Yes. I met several influential men. And the *baron*...was very kind. He saw me home in his carriage, as he'd promised."

"*Gott in Himmel!* You didn't return with Armand?"

"No, Aunt Sophie. Armand left early."

"And this...*baron*...of yours? Was it very late when he brought you home?"

"N-no. Just... Not late. As soon as we finished supper." It wasn't a total lie.

"A woman can't be too careful of her reputation, you know."

"I know."

Armand turned from the window and scowled. "Nevertheless, I don't want you to see the *baron* again. I didn't like the way he looked at you. Altogether too hungry and possessive."

She bit her lip. "You needn't worry. Baron Moncalvo has returned to his regiment. With scarcely a thought for me, I'm sure."

Domfort shook his head. "I refuse to believe that. A man would have to be a blind fool to forget you. To forget a single moment in your presence."

"Name of God, Monsieur de Domfort. It was only a ball, not an assignation!" The words came out more sharply than she'd intended, fueled by her guilt, her shame. Her painful sense of loss. He would forget her, *sans doute*.

Armand's eyes blazed in sudden fury. "How dare you use that tone with Bertrand? The man is my friend. He saved my life. Don't you forget it!"

Domfort rose from his chair and put a restraining hand on Armand's shoulder. "Come, Chevrillon. Your sister meant nothing by it, I'm sure. There was no offense." He persuaded Armand to return to his chair and have another cup of coffee.

There was an awkward silence. Charmiane felt the prick of her conscience. Monsieur de Domfort hadn't deserved her rudeness. "We didn't know," she ventured at last. "That is . . . that Monsieur de Domfort had done you such a great service. You never told us, I don't think. *Nicht wahr*, Aunt Sophie?"

Armand leaned back in his chair and allowed his stern expression to soften. "No. Perhaps you didn't know. It's so long ago. I thought I'd told you, but . . ."

"Of course you didn't," said Aunt Sophie, her round mouth puckered in a *moue* of disapproval. "Whenever you visited us at Lake Constance, you were far more concerned with discussing your affairs with Eugène than with me!"

"I don't think I told Eugène, either," he said mildly. "I probably forgot to tell you after the long months of recuperation. . . ." He slapped at his crippled leg.

Aunt Sophie interrupted again. "Of course. You were wounded in the fighting. I used to tell Marthe, my dear companion in Switzerland, who used to be the Comtesse de Granville and then disgraced herself by marrying a Swiss cheesemaker, that my nephew was serving in the Army of Condé with great distinction."

"Sophie, *chère tante* . . ." Armand's gaze held a gentle reproof.

Aunt Sophie fluttered like a young girl. "Of course, *Liebchen*. Not another word."

"Well, then." Armand paused, his expression darkening. "It was the spring of 1804. It was clear by then that no army of émigrés could ever defeat the Tyrant. And so . . . several of my friends and I determined to rid France of him. We returned to the country with forged papers. Bonaparte was attending the opera one evening. We rode up, sabers drawn, and surrounded him as he alighted from his carriage. We managed to kill his aide-de-camp, but the Corsican must have had a presentiment. He was more closely guarded than usual. We were attacked by fusiliers. I watched my companions being slaughtered. I was shot myself but managed to make for a dim alley." He stilled his trembling leg, his eyes dark with remembrance. "They shot my horse and it fell on me. Crushed my leg. But Bertrand . . ."

Domfort looked apologetic. "As luck would have it, I had just come from a visit with a charming soprano. Pure luck. Nothing more."

"And courage, my friend. The horse, in the throes of death, released my leg. In the gloom, Bertrand dragged me to the darkest recess of the alley, then directed the troops to seek me beyond the next corner. A stranger to me. Yet he risked all."

Domfort inclined his snowy head. "Your face was unfamiliar to me, *mon ami*. Your cause was not."

Aunt Sophie crossed herself. "*Gott in Himmel.* To think my own nephew nearly saved France!"

Armand sighed. "A futile gesture, perhaps. But I wear my injury as a badge of honor."

Charmiane jumped from her chair to throw her arms around him. "And well you might, dear heart." She smiled at Domfort, resolving to be more generous in her thoughts of him. "And you, *monsieur*. We're in your debt."

Domfort looked pleased. "I had thought to ask you to dine with me, in thanks for the invitation to the ball. But, upon reflection, it seemed too calculating—to exact your company in payment for such a little favor. Now, seeing your gratitude for Armand's life, I dare to ask for more."

Aunt Sophie giggled and held her hand up to her face. "Oh, Monsieur de Domfort! That sounds quite bold. Are you flirting with my niece?"

"Yes." His eyes were an intense gray and very direct. Serious, friendly. Yet clearly asking for more than mere friendship. Charmiane found it disconcerting.

"What more would you ask of me, *monsieur*?" She hoped her voice didn't betray her unease.

He laughed. "Put away your fears, *madame*. I should only like to take you dancing. The Hôtel Frascati has a charming public garden and dance hall. Will you . . . ?"

Aunt Sophie giggled again. "Of course she will! It sounds quite enchanting."

She had thought to turn him aside. After last night she never wanted to dance again. But Aunt Sophie was waiting, her face wreathed in smiles. And Domfort *had* saved Armand. It would be ungracious to refuse. She bowed to the inevitable. "Of course. But if you wanted to dance with me, you should have come to the ball last night."

"Alas. I had a previous engagement. I'll call upon you on Friday at half after four? We'll dine first." He smiled when she nodded her assent.

Armand had been fidgeting in his chair. Now he stood up and scowled at Domfort. "Shall we go? I'm weary of sitting."

Charmiane gazed at him, her eyes filled with love and sympathy. "Will you never cease your wandering, *cher* Armand?"

He touched her gently on the cheek. "It helps to fill the empty time." Then he turned briskly to his aunt. "Sophie, do you need money?"

Aunt Sophie pursed her lips. "Armand, *Gott in Himmel*. Not in front of Monsieur de Domfort!"

"We have no secrets, Sophie, Bertrand and I. Our fortunes have risen and fallen together in the past eight years."

Domfort sighed and shrugged. "Mostly fallen, more's the pity. So close. So close." He sighed again and inclined his head toward Aunt Sophie. "I had hoped to have my title back by this year. But it takes money in this society. To bribe the right officials. To reach the right ears. And even then, a man must have a provable income and maintain it. Land. Something." He smiled ruefully at Armand. "I should have bought that estate two years ago. Before last year's bank failures wiped out all our gains."

"How can you buy an estate that belonged to someone else?" growled Armand. "I can't be content unless I recover the Chevrillon lands."

"I do whatever I must."

Armand's voice was harsh with bitterness. "Yes. Bribe a prefect if you must. Lick the boots of an upstart if you must."

"New times demand new ways."

"I'll never bow to them."

Domfort kissed Aunt Sophie's hand and made for the door. "Then you'll break, my friend."

"I agree with Monsieur de Domfort," said Charmianc with some spirit. "Wasn't that why we went to the ball?"

Armand managed a smile. "Yes. Yes, of course. I'm being pigheaded again. Forgive me. If you should hear from any of the men you met last night—and they can be helpful in the matter of Henri's affairs—encourage them. By all means." He limped to the door and turned, his scowl returning. "But only for advancement and nothing more. Do you understand? And I forbid contact with the hungry-eyed *baron*. I don't intend a Madame de Plasse in this family! Sophie, I can spare ten francs at the end of the week. I'll send them around to you."

When they'd gone, Aunt Sophie made a sound that was half sigh and half moan. "Ten francs. There was a time I'd give a boy ten francs just to deliver a love letter for me. And now it keeps us from starvation. Alas! A woman needs a man to keep her life in order. I'm so grateful for Armand and his strength."

Charmiane moved toward her room. "We'll manage well enough, Aunt Sophie. Unless you need Jeanine now, I'll have her help me bathe and dress."

"Of course, my dear. I think I can spare her for a little."

On the threshold, Charmiane turned, frowning. "Sophie, who was Madame de Plasse? That Armand spoke of?"

"Oh, my dear. You were quite young at the time. I thought to shield you. But it was dreadful. Dreadful! She was a widow. Quite indiscreet. The scandal of Constance. She thought to amuse herself. She had a fondness for a uniform, particularly on a man who was off to war. 'Dead men tell no tales,' she used to say. Which was so for a while. It saved her reputation, except perhaps among her intimates, who knew better but said nothing."

"Then why was she the scandal of Constance?"

"She grew careless. The gossips had it that she was languishing in her bed. Suffering from the morning sickness. When she came to Mass one day, the priest turned his burning glance upon her and sermonized on the wickedness of debauchery. There was not a salon after that which did not speak of her in disapproving tones. And when the exiled king, Louis XVIII, visited from Coblentz, Madame de Plasse was not invited to be received."

Charmiane found herself trembling. "*Mon Dieu.* What happened to her? To her child?"

"When she could no longer go into the streets without people staring at her swelling body, she threw herself into Lake Constance." Aunt Sophie made the sign of the cross. "To add the sin of suicide to her other crimes . . . *Ciel!* Her mother was a friend of mine. But I couldn't bear to look her in the eye after that."

God save me from the same fate! thought Charmiane. She was careful to climb in and out of her tub without Jeanine's assistance, to keep her bruises hidden from the maid's curious eyes—earning instead the girl's frown of disapproval at her independence.

Dressed in a simple muslin gown of blue printed with pink rosebuds, she returned to the sitting room and the small desk where she did her work. She pulled out pen and ink, a thick stack of papers—some covered with her precise handwriting—and a small, leather-bound book. She opened to the page she had left off the day before and began to write.

Aunt Sophie, powdered and perfumed and freshly coiffed by Jeanine, came into the room, sat down and pulled out her needlework. "Will you finish that by next week, do you think, *Liebchen*?"

Charmiane nodded. "I hope so. Monsieur Mafflu has promised twenty-five francs. And more work, as soon as I'm ready for it." She didn't know what they would have done without Monsieur Mafflu. He owned a small printing shop on the rue Gaillen. When he'd learned, through Armand, that Charmiane had done some translating in Switzerland, he had been eager to employ her. The poet and playwright Heinrich von Kleist had become something of a failure in his native Germany after a few modest, early triumphs. But since his dramatic suicide the year before—preceded by the killing of his dying lover, out of mercy, it was said—there were those who had begun to show some interest in the man's work. A specialized taste, of course. Not worth a costly, scholar's translation. But enough to make it worthwhile for Monsieur Mafflu to hire Charmiane and put out a small edition of Kleist's greatest success.

Charmiane worked for some time, trying to concentrate on the words, their meanings, the clarity of each sentence as she translated it. But the plot kept intruding on her consciousness. It was a romantic fairy tale of a woman drawn to a mysterious man by an irresistible love. Not reason, not common sense, not supernatural dangers could keep her from loving him. It was a good play, but like so many of the German works she'd translated in the past few years, it concerned itself almost solely with love. Heartbreaking, soul-consuming, fiery and passionate love.

She put down her pen and stared out of the window with unseeing eyes. What a fool she'd been. How blind. Fed by this sickly sweet molasses for so long, she'd lost all sense of reason. Small wonder that she'd fancied herself in love with Colonel Bouchard from the moment she'd met him! But she'd clearly read more into the evening's adventure than ever was there.

He must have seen it in her face—how easy it would be. His little kindnesses had been meant to soften her, to seduce her with words and actions, for his own ends. How it must have added to his pleasure when she threw herself at him! How simple it was for him to pretend that *she* was at fault. Conspiring in her own ruin. Isn't that what he'd said? As though he had no part in it.

Well, if she should be carrying his child, it would be wise of her to encourage Domfort. God knows she might need a husband in a hurry. She scarcely saw herself as the self-sacrificing Madame de Plasse!

"Madame de Chevrillon, there's a messenger at the door."

Aunt Sophie put down her needlework and smiled in pleasure. "What a happy distraction! Like the old days. Show him in, Jeanine."

The "messenger" was no more than a young boy who carried a bulky package and shifted uneasily from one foot to the other as he stood before Aunt Sophie. "*Madame?* Madame de Viollet?" he piped, and thrust the package into Aunt Sophie's hand.

Her smile turned to a pout of disappointment. She dismissed the boy with a wave of her fingers. "Jeanine, give the lad five sous for his trouble."

Jeanine looked for confirmation to Charmiane, who nodded in agreement, though her heart sank at Aunt Sophie's careless extravagance. Every centime was spoken for, and there was scarcely a spoonful of tea left in the canister. Ah, well. They'd have to make do with coffee until the end of the week, when Armand's ten francs arrived.

Aunt Sophie held out the package to Charmiane. "Well, open it. Open it! I'm bursting with impatience."

Charmiane knew what it was even before the last wrappings fell away. "It's only my shawl, Aunt Sophie. I left it in the palace by mistake, and *monsieur le baron* promised to return it." She might as well dare more before Aunt Sophie's questions proved difficult. "Your fan should be arriving in a few days. Baron Moncalvo noticed a fragile stick where the ivory seemed about to snap. He insisted on having it repaired." *Dieu!* She was becoming quite adept at lying to Aunt Sophie this morning.

"He sounds very kind and thoughtful...for an upstart. What does Armand have against him?"

"I don't know. Armand seemed tired last night. Perhaps..."

"Nevertheless, he is the head of the Chevrillon family now. We must obey him."

"Name of God," Charmiane snapped. "The *baron* is off to war, I told you. And if he weren't, I'd still have no interest in seeing him again. I . . . Oh!" She stared in surprise at the package in her hand. Beneath the folds of the shawl lay her missing glove. "I wondered where that had got to. I must have dropped it in his carriage. Jeanine . . ." About to hand the items of clothing to the maid, she stopped. There was a peculiar crackling at the palm of the glove, as though something were inside. "Jeanine," she said smoothly, rising from her chair, "I'll put these in my room for now. When you go to market, you may return the shawl to Madame de Lesparre, with my thanks." She hurried to her room, closed the door and thrust her hand into the glove. She withdrew a small piece of paper.

"Madame, if you will, please come to the Fontaine Grenelle at two o'clock this afternoon," it said. That was all. No signature. No expectation of her refusal. She frowned and tucked the note into the bodice of her gown, then returned to the sitting room. How dare he order her about! She picked up her pen and resumed her work.

But despite her annoyance, two o'clock found her in the curved stone niche beside the rue de Grenelle, staring up at the splashing fountain as though she were one of the American tourists she had seen so often since her return to France.

"Madame de Viollet?" A servant in livery stood at her elbow.

"Yes." She knitted her brows, recognizing at length Colonel Bouchard's footman. "Darnaud, is it not?" she asked.

"Your servant, *madame*. Will you step into the coach?" He pointed to where Bouchard's carriage awaited, its door ajar.

Her heart began to pound. Could he...? Would he...? She permitted Darnaud to usher her into the carriage, blinking her eyes against the dimness after the sun-filled street. She felt a distinctly physical jolt of disappointment to see that the man within—his hair and mustache the color of steel and a large black patch over one eye—was not the one she'd hoped to find. He smiled and guided her into the seat opposite. "Madame de Viollet, my name is Charles Bazaine. I am Monsieur le Baron Moncalvo's—" he shrugged "—what you will. Adviser, secretary, steward, majordomo...and confidant."

She smiled in turn. "Aren't you sure?"

"As to that, an Austrian saber put an end to the position I was most suited for—Colonel Bouchard's personal aide in the field. Now I do what I can to serve him." He stroked his mustache in satisfaction. "Well, to business. *Monsieur le baron* has put your welfare into my keeping. I do apologize for this melodramatic meeting. But Baron Moncalvo led me to believe that your family would perhaps not allow a more open communication."

"Yes, I'm afraid so," she said, remembering that she had sneaked out today under Aunt Sophie's very nose, guiltily defying Armand's interdiction.

"The fact that you're here shows me that you received the shawl and the glove this morning. I've also seen to the repair of your fan. Do you wish me to send it to your home, or would you prefer a more covert arrangement?"

"Since my aunt is aware that *monsieur le baron* has kindly offered to repair the fan, I see no reason for secrecy. My home will do."

"Still, there would be no harm in making some arrangement for you to communicate with me—and by extension with Monsieur Moncalvo—should you wish to do so."

She bit her lip. So it had occurred to Moncalvo to have a little concern for the possible consequences of last evening! Well, she didn't need him, no matter what happened. "It isn't necessary," she said firmly.

"*Monsieur le baron* was quite insistent about it. Do you go to church nearby, *madame*?"

"Really, I . . ."

His voice was very soft but very firm. "Do you, *madame*?"

"Yes. Twice a week. To Saint-Sulpice."

He frowned in thought, then nodded. "Yes. Good." He pulled out a small notepad and pencil and wrote one or two lines in a neat, precise hand. "Now. There is an apothecary shop on the Place Saint-Sulpice. The proprietor is a Monsieur Vernis. A sergeant major—and a good one—before he lost half his foot at Jena. I'll arrange it with him. Should you wish, for any reason, to reach me—" he coughed discreetly "—leave a message with Monsieur Vernis."

"I told you, it isn't necessary. If you have nothing further to add, I'll go now."

"One more thing, *madame*. From *monsieur le baron*." He held out a long, narrow box.

Charmiane took it from him, her hands suddenly grown unsteady. Within the box was a fan: small—in the current fashion—pale sea green silk and net, trimmed with golden spangles in the shapes of leaves and delicate blossoms. It was the loveliest fan she had ever seen.

She caught her breath, overwhelmed by the rush of recollection. His face was before her again, clear and strong and beautiful. And she was in his embrace once more, their souls entwined as surely as their clinging arms. She was his, and he cared for her, and the sweet gift of the fan—was it only an accident that it matched her eyes?—told her as surely as if he'd spoken the words. She closed her eyes and leaned back against the seat of the carriage.

Bazaine's soft voice disturbed her sweet reverie. "May I tell *monsieur le baron* in my next letter that you're pleased, Madame de Viollet?"

She nodded in silence. What was there to say? That she knew herself to be loved? That her heart rejoiced once more in the memory of a magic night? Her eyes flew open. What had Bazaine said? "You write to Colonel Bouchard?"

"Indeed, yes. *Monsieur le baron*'s affairs require constant correspondence, even when he's campaigning with the Emperor. There's the matter of his lands and holdings, his investments, his *hôtel* here in Paris. And then I've encouraged him to consider buying an estate in the country. Constant correspondence, you see. But I have many friends in the army. Old comrades in arms who can be persuaded to include our letters in the official dispatches and pouches that travel from Paris to the outlying garrisons and back again."

She twisted her fingers together. "Monsieur Bazaine...do you think...is it possible...to ask him to write to me? Tell him I implore him to...No." She had her pride. She turned her head away, fighting in vain against her tears. "Only if he wishes it."

"My dear Madame de Viollet," he said gently after a moment's silence. "Dry your eyes. I'm sure I can phrase it in such a way that he'll wish it."

She made her way home in a warm cloud of renewed love. They belonged to each other, now and forevermore, whatever the future held. As she reached the gate of her apartment, she was struck by a sudden thought. The violets. His violets. By some chance might they still be in the back alley?

She picked her way through the castoffs and debris that had been thrown into the alley, ignoring the concierge's cat, which prowled underfoot and meowed loudly. She saw a blur of purple, half-hidden by the shards of a broken dish. She scooped up what was left of her dear bouquet, dismayed to see that a stray dog or cat had torn it apart, leaving only a few sorry blossoms.

Cradling them in her palm, she hurried up the stairs to her room, grateful that Aunt Sophie hadn't yet awakened from her afternoon nap. She looked at the beautiful fan once more before finding an empty spot on her bookcase shelf where she could mask it behind books that Jeanine never disturbed. She pressed the few violets between the pages of a book, whispering "Adam" as she did so. And then "Adam, my love."

She felt a sudden warm trickle between her legs. Her menses had begun. There would be no child. Strangely, she felt not relief but a sagging disappointment.

It was romantic, fanciful, foolish. But she would have been proud to be carrying a part of him within her body.

Chapter Five

"Bouchard, you damned idiot, get down off that horse and come and have a drink!"

Bouchard swung himself from the saddle and handed the reins to a young trooper. "You see, Callot? Treat her like a woman, with gentleness and care. She may not keep you warm at night, like a good whore, but she'll save your life in battle." He turned toward the man who lolled at the opening of a small campaign tent—an officer in a scarlet Hussar's uniform with bright blue breeches. "I'm damned! Hautecoeur, you reprobate, what the devil are you doing in Cologne? I thought you'd be singing with the angels by now." He snorted. "Or cavorting in Hell is more like it." He ducked into the tent and pounded Hautecoeur on the back.

"Your mother was a camp follower," said Hautecoeur cheerfully. He smacked his fingers against his lips in an exaggerated kiss that was as good-natured as it was meant to be insulting. "Do you think those damned Spaniards could stop the Ninth Hussars?" He gestured with his chin at the retreating trooper. "Have you taken to wet-nursing babies?"

Bouchard sat down at a small table and helped himself to a cup of wine. He took a long draught, then frowned. "They're calling up children now. That one's fresh out of school. A smallpox inoculation, a week at the depot for training and equipment, and he's sent to the front. If I can teach him a few things in these weeks before we march, he might live through his first engagement."

Hautecoeur twirled the ends of his bushy mustache, as glossy black as the two side braids and back queue that many of the

Hussars affected. "We were all young and fresh once." He grinned. "I heard you were in Paris."

Bouchard unbuttoned the top of his green uniform tunic and loosened the neck of his shirt. He leaned back in his chair and gazed out at the blue of the May sky. "Yes," he said softly. "For a week or two."

"You sly dog. And did you meet anyone interesting?"

"Why should I tell you?"

"By God, you did, and no denying it. I can read it in your eyes. Come. Tell me."

"Not that it's your concern—" he rubbed at his chin, his eyes thoughtful and faraway "—but I met the most beautiful woman in the world."

Hautecoeur snickered. "Above or below her girdle?"

Bouchard leaped to his feet, upsetting the chair behind him. His blue eyes glowed like burning sapphires. "When you insult the lady, you insult me."

Hautecoeur looked startled. "Peace, my friend. I've never known you not to ride an agreeable wench when you could!"

"This was a lady."

"And so you bowed and kissed her hand before you . . ." He made an obscene gesture with his finger.

Bouchard roared and lifted him bodily from his chair, his hands hooked under Hautecoeur's armpits, his scowling visage only inches from Hautecoeur's face. "There will be no more talk of the lady," he said through clenched teeth. "You understand?" At Hautecoeur's frenzied nod, he set the man on his feet. Then he sighed and extended his hand. "Peace, indeed, my friend. How were you to know that a woman could touch me so deeply?" He laughed in self-mockery. "*Mon Dieu*, I scarcely believe it myself!"

Hautecoeur seemed about to go for his saber. Then he shrugged, smiled sheepishly, took the proffered hand. "*Zut alors.* Life is too short. Come, refill your glass. I've wine enough to fox us both today. Tomorrow . . ."

A shrill female voice interrupted him. "Yes! Drink yourself senseless, you snake! You rat! Without a thought for me." At the entrance to the tent stood a young woman shaking her fist at Bouchard. Her red-gold hair tumbled in curls over shoulders laid bare by a low-cut bodice and swung against the creamy flesh of her bosom as she stamped her foot in annoyance. "Must I forever seek you out?"

Bouchard grinned and strode to her. "You're an impatient little filly, aren't you. Well, if you can't wait..." He pulled her into his arms and kissed her firmly on the mouth.

She struggled furiously in his embrace. "Let me go! You don't care about me. You..." Her words were cut off by another kiss. By the time he released her from the second kiss, she'd stopped fighting against him. She shook her head. "You really are a bastard." Her deep blue eyes were warmer than her words.

He laughed. "Yes."

"You only want one thing from a woman, damn you."

"Yes," he said, his finger tracing a line across her flesh just above the bodice of her gown. "And you're so good at it."

Hautecoeur cleared his throat. "Am I not to have an introduction, Bouchard?"

"Of course. This is Mademoiselle Martine Rollin. My companion since we left France."

Hautecoeur clicked his tongue. "You have my sympathies, *mademoiselle*. If you should ever tire of that lout, you'll find I'm far more worthy than he." He slapped at the breast of his flamboyant Hussar's uniform with its rows of gold buttons and braid.

Martine tossed her head. "Hmph! They say that laurels cover a great many faults. Do men ever seem more attractive than in wartime? Or think themselves so? Besides, *Monsieur le Hussar*, I'm Bouchard's woman."

Bouchard slipped his arm around her waist and kissed her neck. "At least until we reach the Polish border. Then you'll go back to France."

"I will not!"

He turned her about and pushed her toward the entrance. "Wait for me in the tent," he said. "We'll speak of it later." The words were accompanied by a firm slap to her bottom.

"But..."

"Go!"

"Damn you," she muttered, and flounced away.

Hautecoeur laughed. "I trust that nymph of the night—beautiful though she may be—isn't your lady from Paris."

Bouchard righted his chair, sat down and refilled his cup. "No," he said softly. "I lost *that* beautiful lady to my brother Adam. I kept hoping she'd come back to me that night, but..." He shrugged. "Come. Let's finish your wine. If I'm lucky at cards tonight, you'll drink as well on me tomorrow."

"I didn't know you had a brother."

Noël absently fingered his corporal's chevrons. "An officer. A colonel. Brother Adam is an exemplary fellow. Commander of the Twenty-eighth Dragoons."

Hautecoeur shook his head. "Be damned. The Twenty-eighth came into camp last night."

"*Hein!* To pick up supplies?"

"No. I don't think they'll move on until we do."

Noël tapped a finger against the edge of his cup, musing. Adam here. In the same camp. Of all the campaigns, to be together on this one. To die together, perhaps. He frowned. It might be well to make his peace with Adam while he could. There'd been bad blood because of that Fleury woman. He'd been shameless in his seduction of her, stealing her from under Adam's very nose.

Now he wondered if Adam had had the last laugh. If he'd spent the night with *her*. Charmiane. Even her name was beautiful. Damn! What a mischance. If only he'd met her first, before Adam. If only he'd followed her when she'd left the supper room, abandoned that ass Géraud. He'd searched for her after supper, filled with a sense of desolation to find her gone. "Where's the Twenty-eighth?" he asked. "I ought to pay my respects to Brother Adam."

Hautecoeur glanced down at the gold braid of his own lieutenant's stripes, then eyed Noël's insignia. "Your brother's a colonel, you said. Yet *you* still wear the woolen epaulets of a *brigadier*—a corporal of cavalry. Good God, man. What's the matter with you? No promotion yet? We fought at Wagram together, you and I. You're not lacking in manly accoutrements."

Noël touched his forehead in a mocking salute. "*Merci mille fois.* Thank you very much. But I'm lucky they haven't cashiered me by now. A man can use his . . . equipment for more than just bravery."

"You didn't! That major's wife . . . ?"

Noël grinned. "I was confined to quarters for a month. And worth every minute of it. She was exquisite." He put down his wine. "Now, before I get too blind to see, point me in the direction of the Twenty-eighth."

With Hautecoeur's directions, he made his way across the vast plain on the outskirts of the city of Cologne that had become one of the supply and assembly garrisons for Napoleon's Grand Army. He knew from camp gossip that regiments and divisions were converging on the site every day in preparation for war with Russia; everything he saw about him confirmed that gossip.

He passed groups of grenadiers in close drill, troopers wheeling their horses to shouted commands, men loading food and guns and ammunition into covered wagons. But there were signs of impatience and boredom, as well. From the many clusters of tents came the sounds of raucous laughter, drunken singing, the oaths of quarreling soldiers with nothing to do but wait. And there were the women: the wives and lovers—some with suckling babies—who had refused to leave their men; the whores who found in the lonely recruits an unending source of money; the old, frowsy *vivandières* with their stores of tobacco, brandy and wine, who followed every army and supplied the troops with whatever necessities the whores couldn't provide.

Noël shook his head. So many men. Probably twenty thousand already assembled here. And who knew how many more in the other encampments strung out on the German borders, along the Rhine and the Elbe rivers? And for what? There were those who were beginning to whisper that the Emperor had overreached himself. That too many victorious campaigns had made him blind to the appalling loss of men. Noël had really been surprised to see Hautecoeur alive; most of his regiment of Hussars had been wiped out in the victory at Valencia in January. Noël's own regiment of *Chasseurs à Cheval* had been brought up to strength only by the addition of untrained youths. And he'd heard reports that of this year's class of conscripts, more than a quarter had failed to report for duty. The patriotic fervor that had fired French armies for a score of years was on the wane, despite the triumphant force of the Emperor's personality.

And now they were going to Russia, and few seemed to want it except Napoleon himself. The marshals and the senior officers had grown fat and contented from looting. The old campaigners were dead or maimed or burnt out; the green conscripts yearned for home and mother. Only the younger officers, inspired by honor, glory and the promise of adventure and personal gain, chafed with impatience.

Noël sighed. It was not the life for him. He should have stayed in America. At the very least, he should have left the soldiering to Adam. Still…he felt an inexplicable surge of pride. It was his country that he fought for. His France. He had nothing but contempt for those men who turned their backs when their country needed them.

He chuckled softly. *Dieu.* He was beginning to think like Adam, all sober duty and responsibility. Better to think of the sweet future—of riding free someday, a wild horse under him, the blue sky above.

Reaching the Dragoons' encampment, he found a young trumpeter who pointed out the field tent of Colonel Bouchard; the boy stared in openmouthed surprise at the Colonel's double who had asked the question, then backed away, his eyes wide as saucers.

Noël heard Adam before he saw him. "Damn it, you tell the Major when I give an order I expect to be obeyed! What the deuce does he mean by sending you in his stead?" Adam's voice resonated with such authority that Noël imagined he could almost see the tent shake. He couldn't hear the response, only a soft murmur. But it obviously displeased Adam, for his voice rang out again, more dictatorial than before. "In one hour! *Here.* You tell him that."

A white-faced adjutant came scurrying out of the tent. He glanced at Adam's orderly, who waited just outside, rolled his eyes heavenward in despair and hurried away.

Noël ambled forward and addressed the orderly. "Is Colonel Bouchard alone?"

"He won't see anyone. He..." Again the gasp, the stare, the disbelief. "But you...your face..."

Accustomed to this reaction, Noël smiled. "My twin. He'll see me." He pushed aside the tent flap and went in.

Adam sat at a small folding desk strewn with papers and dominated by a large map. Behind him was his camp bed, with its muslin drapings; it bore the imprint of a body on its top blanket, as though its owner had been too harried to turn down the covers and sleep between the sheets like an ordinary man. His quill pen scratched furiously on the paper before him, slowing only for a moment at the sound of Noël's entrance. "Get out," he said coldly, without raising his eyes from his work. "I will see no one."

Noël laughed. "Not even me, brother?" Then, as Adam looked up, startled, he snapped to attention and saluted. "Colonel."

Adam acknowledged the salute with a curt nod. "*Brigadier,*" he responded stiffly. "You were a *brigadier* the *last* time I saw you in uniform. I should have liked to see you promoted by now." A small frown creased his brow. "But if you go about with your tunic unbuttoned...with no pride in your regiment... Does it really content you to be a *brigadier*, Noël? A cavalry corporal at forty sous a day?"

Noël shrugged and reached for a stool from the side of the tent. "May I?" He sat without waiting for an answer. "You have a hundred times that, Brother Adam. Does it make you happy? All your wealth? Perhaps I'm still a *brigadier* because I like it. Is that so bad? I get to ride as much as I want. And I have my choice of horses above the troopers."

"If you were an officer, you could own your horses."

"Ah, but then I'd have to make decisions. To sit and frown all day. As you do, brother."

Adam snorted in disgust. "You always were irresponsible. Leaving the burden to others."

"I never remember you complaining. Not when Mother rejoiced in her good, dependable Adam. Her rock and mainstay."

"Did you resent it?"

Noël laughed. "I? Why should I care? It gave me more time to play. Have you a cognac?"

Adam turned toward the tent opening. "Foullon!" he barked.

Immediately his orderly appeared. "Sir!"

"Bring out the cognac. And two glasses. Does it still look as if it will rain?"

"More than ever, sir," Foullon replied as he fetched the cognac.

"The deuce! I hate when it rains the first day in a new bivouac. It saps the men's spirit to be knee-deep in mud in a strange place. See that my horses are dry and fed."

"Sir." Foullon saluted again and left them.

Noël chuckled as he took the glass of liquor from his twin. "Now you rail against the weather, brother? Do you never grow tired of it? The orders, the commands, the burdens?"

Adam passed a hand across his eyes. "I've forgotten what it's like to be carefree. I should take lessons from you. But it's probably too late."

"That sounds pessimistic even for you, brother."

Adam rose from his chair and moved to the entrance of the tent. He pulled back the flap and stared out at the darkening sky. "Do you smell it?" he asked softly.

"Smell what? The rain?"

Adam shook his head. "Death. Futility."

Noël stared at his brother's back in surprise. It wasn't like Adam to show his doubts. It made him uncomfortable. He forced a laugh. "Don't be an ass. This camp may stink, but they're entirely human smells."

"I'll be dead within the year. I feel it in my bones." Adam resumed his seat but kept his eyes averted from Noël's.

It was an awkward moment for both of them. They had never been enemies but never close enough to bare their souls. Noël cleared his throat. "This is excellent cognac," he said at last.

"I can afford it."

"Of course, *monsieur le baron*. I'd quite forgotten." There was gentle mockery in Noël's tone.

Adam glared at him. "I *like* money. I like having it. I like spending it. I like throwing it in the teeth of those snobbish aristocrats who still think that their birth makes them superior!"

"Are you still so bitter after all these years?"

"What did you know of it then? You didn't have to take off Father's boots, put him to bed after a night of drinking. Hear the shame behind his mumbled stories and drunken rage. Father was only a clerk. De Jaurès was the land surveyor. And an idiot. But an idiot with a *vicomte* for an uncle and generations of nobility behind him. An idiot who delighted in humiliating those who weren't of his class. I might have been only ten, but I swore I wouldn't settle for a life of struggle and shame, as Father did. That if ever the chance came, *I'd* be the one with the title, force the old aristocrats to welcome me. Even if the words stuck in their throats."

"Well, you've certainly come up in the world."

Adam stuck out a belligerent chin. "With no apologies."

"I'm delighted for you, brother. I'm not quite sure how you did it. Perhaps I'm envious."

"What did you expect? While I patched his broken heart and kept up *Maman*'s spirits, off you went to charm Monsieur Mansel. To gamble with him and ride his horses. And, later, to seduce his maids."

Noël laughed. "And his wife. I never told you that!"

"You never took your fair share of the burden."

"I didn't need to be at home all the time. They had you." He poured himself another cognac. "They'd be proud of you now, if they were alive."

"And you?"

He grinned. "I can hear *Maman* now: 'That Noël. Always a trial to me! If only he were more like Adam...'" It was odd how the memory could still tear at him after all this time. Deliberately, he turned the conversation away from the past: there were too many ghosts. "I was surprised to see you at the ball in the Tuileries last month."

"I hadn't intended to go. But...I told you. This odd premonition. This sense of my own mortality. It seemed my last chance to attend a ball. I was surprised to see *you*. Were you in Paris long?"

"Several weeks."

Adam frowned. "You should have stayed at my *hôtel*, as you usually do. Bazaine was quite put out when I told him I'd seen you. He misses your games of cards together."

Noël looked shamefaced. "I...didn't think you'd want me this time. Because of Fleury."

"Fleury? *Mon Dieu*. I've forgotten her. Do you still see her?"

"No. I should have guessed that a woman who was so easily led into betrayal could do it again. You should be flattered that I was your rival, brother. My rival was a fat old banker from Chartres. With a wart on his nose, a faded wig and a lisp. And he giggled."

Adam leaned back in his chair and chuckled. "A fat old..." The chuckle became a guffaw.

"You don't laugh enough, brother," said Noël softly. He felt a surge of relief. Adam's laughter had cleared the air, and the cloud of hostility that had hovered since the Fleury incident was dispelled.

The scowl returned to Adam's face. "What is there to laugh about? The endless campaigns? When will I enjoy what I've earned?"

Noël hesitated, then plunged. It was the perfect opening, and he had to know. He had to. "Didn't you enjoy yourself at the Tuileries? With the beautiful lady? Madame de Viollet."

Adam looked at him sharply. "Why do you ask?"

"The beautiful lady told me you'd promised to take her home. Did you?" He wondered why his heart had begun to beat so rapidly.

Adam stared at the tip of his boot. "Damn it, I told Foullon to take a brush to this." An awkward silence. Then, "Bazaine says she wants a letter from me."

Then she *had* lost her heart to Adam. Noël forced his mouth to curve into a smile. "A letter? She'll be fascinated, I'm sure, with descriptions of redoubts and campaigns and strategies."

"It's scarcely cause for laughter! What the deuce am I supposed to say?"

"True. You can hardly translate clumsy stammers into written words! Still, the anonymity of a letter..." He tried to sound offhand. "*Will* you write to her?"

"I don't know. I've hesitated for weeks."

"Hesitation? How unlike you, brother. Are you unsure of the lady? Didn't she give you . . . proofs of her affection?"

Adam glared at him. "I'm sorry you find it so amusing." He began to straighten the papers on his desk. "I have work to do. If you can get away, have dinner with me in Cologne tomorrow night. There's an inn that does mutton well. I see you're still with the Sixth Chasseurs. I'll send Foullon with the details for our meeting."

Noël stood up and made for the tent flap. "It's got under your skin, hasn't it, brother. The thought of having to write a letter to the beautiful lady. Now, if I were to write to her, I shouldn't be at a loss for words. It's a pity that I don't have more of your money and you don't have more of my charm!" Laughing, he went out into the gray afternoon.

It was beginning to rain. By the time he reached his small tent he was soaked through and shivering, and his boots were spattered with mud. He ducked inside to be greeted by Martine. He had expected a shrew; he was met by a purring cat.

"You poor dear," she murmured. "I kept watching the sky and hoping for your return. And now you're drenched. Let me help you."

The tent was small. Almost too low for Noël's height. And unlike an officer's tent, there was no room for table or chair—only a small folding cot and a battered service chest that saw duty as a table, bench or candle stand. Now it held a tallow candle and a bottle of wine. Noël kissed the girl lightly and gestured toward the bottle. "Where did the wine come from?"

"Never mind. I have my ways. It's for you. Now, out of those wet clothes this instant." She began to strip off his uniform. She pulled off his boots, then tackled the pewter buttons of his tunic. It was of dark green, like all the Chasseurs' uniforms; its yellow piping and stiff collar of the same shade identified it as belonging to a soldier of the Sixth Regiment. And the red epaulets of a *brigadier* on the shoulders—while the humble wool of the lower ranks—identified Noël as a member of an elite company. Other noncommissioned officers had to be content with shoulder straps.

After Martine had untied his black neckerchief, she stopped to kiss his neck before handing him a towel for his hair. He raised a quizzical eyebrow but said nothing.

She knelt before him and began to work on the fastenings of his tight breeches. "You've a button missing," she said. "I'll re-

82 *Stranger in My Arms*

place it." Her voice was husky, and her hands caressed his flanks as she worked.

He fought the familiar urge; the little minx was only trying to soften him up. "I'll do the breeches," he said. "You can pour me some wine." He pulled off his breeches and sat down to remove his wet stockings. He laughed softly. Martine was determined to play out the game. While he drank the wine, she toweled his feet, turning the simple act into seductive foreplay until he felt his loins stirring with desire. He stared at the top of her head, the tawny, silken curls that were the color of a leopard's coat. *Dieu*, but she was a tempting little devil!

And devious, lest he forget. "I won't change my mind," he said dryly. "You'll go back to France when our marching orders come."

She pouted up at him. "Where shall I go? To Strasbourg, where you found me?"

"Name of God! And if I'm killed in this campaign? Then what? What is there in Strasbourg for you? To be a lady of the garrison again? To beg as well as whore?"

Her soft blue eyes were unreadable. "Do you care?"

"I'll give you what money I can. Go home, for God's sake. Your people are in la Ferté-Milon, *n'est-ce pas?* Go to them."

She laughed bitterly. "Do you know what my mother sees when she looks at me? For twenty years she has seen a *marquis* in a powdered wig who beat her until she screamed in pain and then raped her. She was fourteen. And when the Terror came, she went to watch him die and stood close enough to the guillotine to hold me up before him. The foul product of his villainy. She told me we were splashed with his blood when the blade fell. She kept my little gown and pointed out the stains whenever she cursed me. 'Bad blood. Bad blood.'"

"Martine..."

"I only go home when I'm starving and there's nowhere else to turn."

"Martine," he said again, and reached out to stroke her hair.

"The devil!" she said, rising to her feet. "Don't be so damned sentimental. It doesn't suit you. Take off your shirt so I can hang it up to dry." When he stood up, she unbuttoned his shirt and helped him out of it, then rubbed her hands against the taut muscles of his chest. "God's teeth, but I like your body." She dropped her hands lower. "You'd best take off your under-breeches," she whispered. "The rain..."

It took all his willpower to hold her at arm's length and quiet her arousing hands. "I can't take you to war with me," he said. "It would be madness."

"I know that. I just want you. Want your body. There'll be few enough times for a merry ride before you abandon me." She saw the sudden angry flash in his eyes. "Send me home," she corrected herself.

"Send you home for your own good," he growled.

She ran her tongue across her lower lip. "Dance the jig-a-jig with me now," she purred, "as only you can. My cavalier of the bed sheets." She took one of his hands and placed it against her full breast. "Come. Dance."

Dance. The last time he'd truly danced it had been with an angel. Not a dance of the flesh with a good-hearted but foul-mouthed camp follower who aspired to nothing more than the giving and taking of pleasure. But a glorious waltz. With a raven-haired angel with sea green eyes. Adam's angel. He felt a sharp stab of jealousy. Lucky Adam. To write to her, to touch her heart. If only...

"Rat!" Martine pounded at his chest. "What are you thinking of? Who are you thinking of?"

He laughed. "Nothing. No one. Only you, my sweet." He lifted her fingers to his lips and kissed them with mock fervor.

"Damn you. Do you love me?"

"I don't love any woman. I can't be bothered. But you'll do, for now."

"O-o-oh!" She tried to slap him, but he caught her in his arms and pressed his mouth to hers. Her lips were sweet and yielding. Again he felt a stirring of passion. And perhaps something else. "Will you be safe in Strasbourg?"

She clung to his naked shoulders. "Don't concern yourself with me. I can take care of myself."

"Will you wait for me in Strasbourg?"

She pushed herself out of his arms and danced a turn about the small tent. "Maybe yes. Maybe no."

He shrugged his indifference. "Maybe I'll look for you, maybe not." He shivered. Perhaps it was the cold. And perhaps Adam's dark premonition had touched him, as well. They were twins, after all. Joined by more than a mirror image. "If I survive," he added softly.

"Damn you, Noël. What a blasted stupid thing to say!"

Yes. Stupid. Mad. Unacceptable. How could he die without seeing her again? Charmiane. With his bones left to rot in some strange land. Never to know her smile again. No. No! He felt as he had as a boy of ten, when Monsieur Mansel had sold his favorite mare. Perilously close to tears, for all his pretense of unconcern.

"Noël." Martine frowned and touched his cheek. "What?"

He laughed and pulled her down to the cot. "Come on, woman. Dance with me. Show me how a woman's body can erase the past—and blot out the future. One more dance before you go."

Chapter Six

Charmiane hesitated on the steps of Saint-Sulpice, her gloved hand shading her eyes from the glare of the noon sun. Mother of mercy, it had turned hot since the beginning of Mass! Her peaked straw bonnet would shield her cheeks from the burn of the sun, of course. And her long gloves, reaching up to the short puffed sleeves of her muslin gown, would do the same for her arms. But, oh, it would be nice to own a parasol to protect herself from the June heat that baked her shoulders. Nicer still to be back at Lake Constance, now that summer was coming. Aunt Sophie did nothing lately but complain about the heat, remembering with bitterness that Paris was always stifling in July and August, fit only for the poor in *her* day. Now the émigrés remained behind with the poor in their sour enclaves of the Faubourg Saint-Germain, while the rich bourgeoisie escaped to the country estates that they'd bought for a song during the troubled times.

Charmiane sighed. She was beginning to wonder why they'd ever returned to France. It cost money to pursue Henri's claim, money they didn't have. And—after more than sixteen years—there might be no records left, even if they could afford the painstaking search for documents. She was just beginning to realize what a fool Henri had been. Forced to flee the country, as had the Chevrillons, Henri at least had had the time and the opportunity to arrange for the transfer of his vast holdings—country château and lands, Paris *hôtel*, even a small village in Anjou—into the possession of his trusted valet, Troche. It was widely believed that the assets had been confiscated by the state and acquired cheaply by the servant as a kind of revenge; Henri—in Switzerland—had done everything he could to encourage this fiction, confident that he'd reclaim his holdings as soon as the

Revolution was over. But his trust in his valet had been built on shifting sands and too few signed documents: when old Troche had died, his children had claimed everything as their inheritance. And how was Henri to prove otherwise?

Yes. It would have been more sensible—and far cooler—to stay at Lake Constance. But with Uncle Eugène gone nearly four years and Henri two months in his grave, she and Aunt Sophie had begun to feel rootless and lost in Switzerland. Strangers in a foreign land without a man to lean on. Every day general amnesties were being granted to returning émigrés; Armand himself had been in France legally for several years. It had seemed a wise decision last January. To return home. Now she wondered. In some ways, France was more foreign to her than Switzerland ever had been.

She sighed again. But perhaps her malaise these past weeks had less to do with her yearnings for Lake Constance—and Aunt Sophie's complaints—than with her disappointment in Colonel Bouchard. All this time—and no letter from him. She had allowed herself only a few discreet inquiries at the apothecary shop; to send a note to Monsieur Bazaine, repeating her plea—her request—for a letter, was something her pride prevented. If he no longer cared for her, what was she to do?

Well, once more. She descended the steps of the church and started across the Place Saint-Sulpice toward the apothecary shop. She felt a perfect fool. Monsieur Vernis must be tired of seeing her. She glanced in the direction of his shop. Vernis, a mountain of a man with a red face, stood in the open doorway. He must have been waiting for Mass to be over: at the sight of Charmiane he grinned and held up a white square of paper.

Charmiane felt her heart thump in her breast. A letter! Sweet heaven, it must be a letter from him. Oh, why was the Place so crowded? The shop so distant? "I beg your pardon," she said impatiently as several sweating merchants loomed in front of her, blocking her way.

"*Madame!* Charmiane. Where are you off to in such a hurry?"

She whirled to find Monsieur de Domfort smiling down at her. "What . . . Bertrand," she stammered. "What are you doing here?"

He tipped his hat and bowed. The sun was bright on his snowy mane. "Madame de Chevrillon told me I might find you coming from church."

Aunt Sophie the matchmaker, she thought, feeling trapped. "And so I am."

"And hurrying where?"

"Why . . . nowhere."

"With such a frown of concentration, my charming lovely? And such a firm step? Where were you going?" He clearly meant to persist.

She swallowed her disappointment. The letter would have to wait. "I was only hurrying to get out of the hot sun. It's most uncomfortable." She blushed. Would she never learn to lie convincingly?

"And well it might be for such a tender blossom as yourself." His gray eyes scanned her face with warm concern. "You're quite flushed. You should have hidden your charms beneath a parasol." He brought her hand to his lips and brushed them lightly against the pale silk of her gloves. "Then my heart would have been my guide to you, rather than my eyes."

"Oh, Bertrand. Don't be silly." She suppressed a smile. As usual, it was obvious that he'd spent many an hour at Court in the old days, playing the gallant: his speech still preserved the flowery language of those times. "Why *did* you come looking for me?" she teased. "I've already dined with you thrice in the past two months, and danced once."

"And gone to see the illuminations, which paled beside your beauty."

She laughed. "An extravagant compliment. But it was too dark to see my beauty."

His eyes were solemn. "And never let me kiss you."

"Please, Bertrand," she whispered. "Don't."

He sighed, his expression deepening into its customary melancholy. "I had thought I was beginning to win you over. Was I mistaken?"

"Bertrand, I . . ." What could she say? She *had* begun to enjoy his company. The modest dinners, where his gallantry made up for his meager purse. The strolls along the Seine, while he told her of the Paris of his youth; a Paris she had never seen, that was no more. Prompted by Aunt Sophie's hints, she had secretly begun to consider marriage with him, should he offer it—despite her wretchedness as Henri's wife. But that was before Monsieur Vernis had waved the letter. Adam's letter. "You were . . . premature, perhaps. It's still too soon after Monsieur de Viollet's death."

"You wear no mourning." His eyes were dark with accusation.

"A choice I made when we left Switzerland—and the past— behind us. It doesn't mean I don't think of Henri."

He sighed in resignation. "Then let me take you for ices on this hot day. The reason I sought you out to begin with."

He led her to a small café in a cellar, just off the rue des Aveugles. It was dim and cool, with round marble tables and tarnished gold chairs. A curly-haired waiter, looking bored, held out the bill of fare to them. He shifted from one foot to the other, brazen hips jutting alternately, as though the effort of awaiting their decision were beneath him. His large apron was stained with food. "Your pleasure, *monsieur*?" He barely managed to suppress a yawn.

Domfort waved away the menu. "I'll have a large cognac. Ices for the lady." He inclined his head toward Charmiane. "With a little maraschino on top?"

"*Kirschwasser*, I think. If you don't mind."

The waiter shrugged. "No *kirschwasser*."

"Maraschino will do," she said quickly, seeing the look on Domfort's face. As the waiter shuffled away, she put a restraining hand on Bertrand's sleeve. "I like maraschino."

He relaxed visibly and even managed a smile. "What an angel you are. It never seems to bother you. All the insults to our class."

"I never bore the title of *marquise*, for all of Henri's posturings. And the only dowry I brought to him was a catalog of the jewels and gold that *would* have been mine, had the Revolution not come. I'm far more accustomed to rude waiters than you are."

"It's not right," he growled. "Armand and I think we've found one of Troche's sons. A *vicomte* now, damn his black soul. He claims to have sold his share of Henri's estate to buy his title. If only we could see the records! He had no power to sell in the first place. No clear title of ownership. It *must* have been a forged bill of sale. But without bribes to the right clerks, the papers might as well be on the moon!"

"Bertrand, why do you suffer so on my behalf?"

"Two years ago we had money, Armand and I. Almost enough to buy land. Almost enough to recover our titles. Six months more. That's what we swore to each other. A few thousand francs more." He rubbed his hand across his eyes. "And then the banks failed. And we lost everything."

"Oh, my dear . . ." Her voice shook as she felt his pain.

He stared at her, his gray eyes filled with longing. "It was only a small disappointment, I told myself. A setback. I'd begin again, that's all. And then I met you. And wished I had all the gold of the Indies to lay at your feet. Now I hunt down petty officials who might hold the key to Henri's secrets. If I can help you reclaim what's rightfully yours, I'll be content."

She felt a pang of guilt. "You mustn't care so deeply for me, Bertrand. I told you my heart isn't free." Let him think she meant Henri's memory.

"But..." He scowled as the waiter put down their order, spilling the cognac on the already stained marble of the table. By the time it had been wiped up and the drink replaced, Charmiane had sorted out her confused thoughts.

No matter how kind he was, how devoted to her, any liaison was out of the question unless she could free her heart from Adam's possession. That is, if she wanted to free her heart. She resolved to turn Bertrand aside each time he strayed into the realm of Love. She removed her gloves, spooned up a taste of the ices and smiled brightly. "Delicious! What a clever idea on such a hot day." She tried not to notice how he frowned at the retreating waiter. "But then, I think you're very clever. How did you and Armand manage to get so much money?" She remembered her brother's visits in Switzerland: sometimes he came bearing gifts and a small purse to help them out; sometimes he looked exhausted, with threadbare clothes, dragging his crippled leg as though all the miseries of the world tugged at his heel.

Domfort stirred in his chair, cast down eyes fixed on the cognac before him. "Your brother and I... there are ways..."

She smiled uneasily. "That sounds so ominous. Honest ways?"

He lifted his head and stared at her. A direct gaze. Almost a challenge. "Would it distress you if I said no? Would you think less of me? Of Armand?"

After all they'd suffered? "No. No. Of course not."

"We do what we must to survive. And sometimes, if we're fortunate—" his eyes caressed her face "—a rare jewel crosses our path and makes it all worth the effort."

Oh, dear. It was time to change the subject once more. She laughed, seeming to be carefree. "And perhaps Bonaparte will fall, and things will return to normal. And none of us will ever have to worry again. I heard gossip in the church, before Mass. There are many, certainly, who think as we do."

"What are they saying?"

She shrugged. She really had very little interest in politics. But if she could keep Domfort from courting her...

"They're hoping that the latest unpleasantness between Great Britain and the Republic of the United States of America doesn't result in war. It would only strengthen Bonaparte's hand to have Britain retire from the ranks of France's enemies. The more enemies, the sooner Bonaparte will fall. Or so they say."

"Such open gossip, and in church? Perhaps it's a good sign."

"It was more open, even, than that. I heard a dowager whisper—to nodded approval!—that *Le Glaive en Feu* is calling for a coup d'état. This very summer, while the Tyrant is away in Russia."

His mouth twisted in an unexpected smile. "The Flaming Sword?"

She lowered her voice. "He's a writer for a secret newspaper. *La Voix.* The Voice. No one knows much about it. I only heard of it myself at a small soiree in Madame de Lesparre's rooms. Someone was trying to raise a subscription to keep the newspaper afloat."

"Yes. The richer conspirators of the Faubourg Saint-Germain are always willing to pay handsomely for calls to treason. It costs them money, but nothing more."

"Treason? What a thing to say!"

"Well, it is treason, my dear Charmiane, to call for Napoleon's overthrow. Though it might fulfill *our* deepest wishes."

"Then long live the Flaming Sword and his kind of 'treason'!"

He laughed. "Are you busy this afternoon?"

She hesitated. She didn't want to go home yet. Adam's letter still waited for her. And, once at home, she'd be hard-pressed to find a suitable excuse for going out again today. "No," she said.

"Good." He put a handful of coins on the table and waited while she donned her gloves. "Come with me," he said, rising from his chair and offering his arm.

She began to feel uneasy when they left the bustling rue des Aveugles, wound their way through twisting side streets and finally reached the rue du Paon, a dim cul-de-sac crowded with dingy little houses. She had never felt uneasy in Domfort's presence—at least not after she'd begun to know him better; but now her original misgivings returned. What did she know of him, after all? A landless émigré. He spoke of the past only in the most general terms. He never spoke of his family—the family he had lost to the guillotine. And there was desire in his eyes when he looked at her. She was sure she didn't imagine it. His words were always civil, charming, respectful. But sometimes his eyes told a different story.

"Come," he said, pulling her to a grimy, recessed doorway. "Here." When she hesitated he frowned. "Haven't I earned your trust?"

She felt the heat rise in her cheeks. She had given her trust—and her willing body—to a stranger in a garden. Domfort didn't deserve her suspicions. "Lead on," she said.

The dirty little room they entered seemed scarcely to be lived in. A small table with several books, a chair drawn up to a bare fireplace, a half-empty cupboard with one door hanging by a hinge. In one corner—and quite incongruous in the barren room—was a music stand piled with sheets of music, and a dented brass trumpet. Beside the fireplace was a huge paneled armoire that had seen better days: the carvings were cracked, several panels were missing, and the empty shelves that could be glimpsed through the partially opened door were warped and battered.

To Charmiane's surprise, Domfort strode at once to the armoire, opened wide the door and thrust his hand to the back of one of the shelves. There was a soft click; then he gave a firm push and the rear of the armoire, shelves and all, opened before them. Beyond, Charmiane could see a staircase with a sputtering candle on its newel post.

"Mind your bonnet," said Domfort, indicating the opening to Charmiane. He followed her through, pulled shut the outer armoire door and closed the back of the cabinet.

As they mounted the stairs, Charmiane heard the murmur of several voices from the room above, then one voice that burst out, louder than the rest. "No more ink? We're cursed! What are we supposed to do?"

Charmiane gasped and stared at Domfort. "That's Armand!"

Domfort smiled, nodded and opened the door. The room beyond—windowless and candlelit—was festooned with half a dozen lines of thick string over which were draped small printed sheets of paper. The floor was littered with crumpled bits of paper, several broken quill pens, an apple core and a rag splotched with black ink. In the center of the room was a small printing press. Three men stood before it: a scrawny young man with sad eyes, a fat man whose rounded belly was echoed in the curve of his bald pate, and Armand. He was in shirtsleeves, his gray-touched curls tousled, his cravat hanging loose about his neck. He had never looked more haggard to Charmiane. He pounded his fist against the press. "Whose responsibility was it to buy enough ink, damn it? You, Georges?"

The fat man shook his head. "No. But it will take a day for Jean-Pierre and me to set the rest of the type, anyway. And by that time . . ."

"By that time, we could all be dead," growled Armand.

Domfort laughed softly. "Leave off, my friend. Don't you remember? Gaston is bringing more into Paris in the morning."

"Not in wine barrels this time, I hope! The last delivery leaked. The old busybody in the alley was far too interested in it."

"Stop worrying so much. Do your own job and leave the rest to the others."

"*Morbleu*, Bertrand, I . . ." For the first time, Armand raised his head to look at his friend. His eyes narrowed at sight of Charmiane. "Why did you bring *her* here?" he demanded.

"If you're going to bark," said Domfort in a weary voice, "let's go into your office."

Armand grunted and led the way into a tiny cell nearly filled by a large, paper-strewn desk. He turned on Domfort, his eyes dark and angry. "Why is Charmiane here?"

"Because she's old enough to be trusted, dammit. Your sister isn't a child, Armand, though you seem content to treat her so. I thought it was time she knew." He turned to Charmiane, his voice taking a softer edge. "Permit me to introduce you to the Flaming Sword." He gestured toward Armand.

"Armand! You?"

His mouth twisted in a sardonic smile. "Who better?"

"Does Aunt Sophie know?"

"No. And she's not to be told. You understand?"

She shook her head. "The Flaming Sword. I can't believe it!"

"Why not? What are *you* doing to save France from the Tyrant? You and all the rest. Wishing for the old times while you fritter away your lives. Well, I want to make it happen."

Charmiane bent her head and turned away, stung by her brother's reproach. If only she had Armand's passion! France and its problems seemed unimportant to her next to the daily business of living. It was all she'd ever been taught, all she'd ever seen. In Switzerland politics had been discussed with a certain dispassion. Long ago. Far away. Other people and other times. Someday it would all change. But in the meantime . . . weren't the strawberries of Geneva tasty this year? As shallow as that. But

Armand dared to live his convictions. "It's dangerous for you, dear heart. Isn't it?"

"*Mon Dieu!* Get her out of here, Domfort!"

"Damn it, Armand . . ."

Charmiane turned toward the door, choking back her tears. She had never felt more useless in her life. "Don't bother, Bertrand. I'm going."

He put a comforting arm around her shoulders and guided her out of the tiny room. "He doesn't mean it. He's been working too hard. Georges—" this to the fat man "—how many broadsides can I have next week? I think I've found a Royalist magistrate who'd be willing to distribute *La Voix* in Nantes. For a price, of course. He said he could take a hundred or so."

"It can be done."

Domfort turned to the young man, who had been gazing at Charmiane, an awed expression on his face. "Isn't it time for you to practice, Jean-Pierre?"

"What?" Jean-Pierre blinked, dragged his eyes away from Charmiane and managed to focus on Domfort. "Oh. Yes. I'll come downstairs with you." He blushed to the roots of his hair. "That is, if the lady doesn't mind."

"No." She was still upset from Armand's words. What made people risk their lives for a cause? And what was lacking in her? "Why do you do this?" she asked Jean-Pierre as they descended the stairs. He seemed too young to be an émigré, too unrefined to be the child of an aristocrat.

He smiled at her. His eyes were the saddest she'd ever seen. "I want to see peace," he said. "But there can't be peace while the Tyrant rules. His armies swallow everyone up. My father fought and died at Jena. My brother went down with his ship at Trafalgar. My two cousins never came back from Spain. And my best friend was conscripted and died at Barrosa. And still the Corsican calls for more. More men, more blood, more lives. I wouldn't go when I was called up. My mother would have died at another loss. I ran away from my village. *Maman* is waiting for me to come home again, when this is over. And I will!"

"Amen," murmured Charmiane, her heart going out to him. So young. So thin—did he even get enough to eat?

They had reached the outer room. Jean-Pierre went to the music stand and picked up the trumpet. Domfort smiled at the quizzical look on Charmiane's face. "The printing press is noisy. Jean-Pierre practices the trumpet every day for several hours. That's when Georges does his work upstairs."

Charmiane listened while Jean-Pierre played an air by Lully, then nodded. "That's very good. Perhaps you should do it for a living."

His eyes blazed with the same passion she had seen in Armand. "If I'm good enough, maybe I'll play for the Tyrant's funeral someday!"

Out on the street, Domfort offered his arm. "I'm sorry. Perhaps that was unwise of me. Shall I take you home?"

"Yes." No! She'd almost forgotten about Adam's letter. What to do? "No, I'll go to the apothecary shop in the Place Saint-Sulpice first. I . . . need a headache powder."

He nodded in sympathy. "I understand."

Monsieur Vernis, the chemist, took a long time to wrap her package: by its size, she guessed that he had discreetly folded in the letter. She bid Domfort a hasty *au revoir* at her gate, begging his indulgence for her abruptness. A little nap, a cold compress on her forehead... She assured him she'd be quite herself in a day or so, even promising to take a stroll with him in the gardens of the Champs-Elysées in two days' time. She sped up the stairs, tiptoed past a napping Aunt Sophie, threw herself down on her own bed and opened Adam's letter.

Charmiane,

Shall I begin by reproaching you? Why did you ask me to write? Don't you know how futile it is to cling to the commonplace, the normal, when the world is in turmoil? And one small letter—the traffic of mortals—is a snowflake in the whirlwind, too easily swept away.

I dreamed I saw my grave last night on some windswept hill in a foreign land. I awoke in terror, trembling like a child. Not in fear of death, but because I knew that I should never see your sweet face again. That thought has haunted me all day. A deep sadness overwhelms me. My heart is desolate.

I move through the camp here. I tell no one of my despair. They see only the face I present to the world. And yet—why should it be so?—now I find myself writing words that my lips would never utter. Telling you of my fears and dreams. Is it the safety of writing that frees my soul, here alone in my tent tonight? Or is it the memory of you? Of your soft eyes so filled with sympathy and understanding?

The Greek Paris went to war to keep fair Helen. Noble sentiments, ridiculous sentiments, for another time. I go to

war and fear to lose you. Fear more to ask you to wait. Not
when the certainty grows on me day by day. We shall all die
in this brave adventure.

God alone knows what the future holds for me. I only
know that life has never seemed more sweet and precious—
because of you. Never have I clung more desperately to it,
though I feel the inevitable hand of Death upon my shoulder.

For your own good, my fair Helen, turn your eyes away.
Live out your life as though we had never met. Forget me.
In God's name, forget me.

Adam.

The letter fell from her hand as she stifled a sob. Hot tears
coursed down her cheeks to stain the gloves she had not even
bothered to remove in her haste. She wept for the pain in his letter, the desolation. For her own yearning to see him again, to kiss
away his pain. She wept long and silently, her heart filled with a
dull ache. It was only when she heard Aunt Sophie stirring in the
room beyond that she managed to dry her tears. She took off her
gloves and bonnet, hid Adam's letter with the fan he'd given her.
She even attempted a smile as she opened the door to Aunt Sophie's room. She would read Adam's letter again tonight, after
Aunt Sophie had gone to bed. That sweet thought managed to see
her through the rest of the day. It eased the loneliness that had
often been with her, but never so poignantly until now.

It was almost a week before she was able to answer him. She
couldn't move pen and ink from her desk in the sitting room
without facing a score of prying questions from Aunt Sophie; and
to write in Aunt Sophie's presence—with her telltale face—would
have been madness.

But there came a morning when Aunt Sophie awoke sneezing
and coughing and decided to remain abed all day. Between her
aunt's petulant demands on Jeanine and the sleep-inducing
medication she took so freely, Charmiane was largely overlooked at her little desk in the corner. Murmuring a prayer of
gratitude, she took pen in hand and began to write.

Dearest Adam,
Forget you? Never, my beloved. I don't know how I lived
until your letter arrived. Your Monsieur Bazaine's kindness—and the lovely fan, thank you so much—cheered me

a little. But how could I be sure that our meeting in the Tuileries was not—for you—merely a chance encounter, best forgotten?

Then your letter arrived, and I read between the lines to discern the sweet devotion that I had found the night you held me in your arms. Only the pain in your words broke my heart. Oh, Adam, my dearest! For me, for yourself, tear your thoughts away from darkness. Think instead of the future. Our future.

You fear to ask me if I'll wait for you. How foolish. They say the desert doesn't bloom until it rains. And my heart is a desert, parched and empty, waiting for your return.

Write to me again, for pity's sake. When you write, it's as though I hear your voice. Speak to me with your letters. Whether you're happy or filled with despair, I need the nourishment of your words.

Whatever life brings us, I am, and always will remain, your loving Charmiane.

It was the beginning of August before she heard from him again—half a dozen thick letters that Monsieur Vernis placed into her hands with a triumphant smile. With his shattered foot and his beefy, war-scarred face, he seemed an improbable go-between for lovers. But Charmiane was so filled with happiness that she stood on tiptoe and planted a kiss on his cheek. His face turned even redder than usual.

Despite the summer heat, she hurried to the nearby Luxembourg Gardens and found a tree-shaded bench. She raced through Adam's letters helter-skelter, devouring the words like a starving creature. Then she sorted them according to their dates and allowed herself a more leisurely reading—savoring each word, picturing the dear man who had penned them. It was clear from his words that he had received very few of her letters yet, though she had managed—despite Aunt Sophie—to write almost every day since that first time: Monsieur Vernis had chuckled to see her so often, letter in hand.

Adam's letters were long and filled with details and descriptions—the commonplace observations of an intelligent man, the pride of a soldier in his country, his fellow Frenchmen. But here and there, within the spare paragraphs of the several letters,

Charmiane could feel his heartbeat, hear his anger, his pain, see the flashes of wonder and tenderness.

...We received our marching orders on the twenty-ninth of May. They say it's the largest army ever assembled. More than half a million men. Generals and marshals, and their servants and women and carriages of personal supplies. Far too many unnecessary people. I wonder if Marshal Ney's chef will know how to fight, should the need arise....

...Your few letters—but so welcome!—are filled with optimism, fair Helen. A sunny morning warms me less than the rereading of your words....

In a strange coincidence, my twin brother and I find ourselves thrown together. Our regiments have been assigned to the same corps of cavalry, General Grouchy's Third. It will be like our school days together, one watching the other for a sign of favor, an unfair advantage. Which one of us shall earn the first medal, I wonder?

...We hear constant reports of looting and pillaging by the soldiers of the line. Not content with stripping the fields bare of grain as we pass, and tearing the thatch from cottage roofs to feed their supply animals, they've stolen everything of worth except the crucifixes from the churches. We haven't even reached the Russian border yet. What must the Poles, our allies, think of the rape of their territory?

...We crossed the Niemen River into Russia on the twenty-fourth of June. The roads here are wretched, the men already beginning to tire. The days are hot and dusty, the nights cold. And when it rains, the primitive roads are impassable. The horses stumble; we lose precious wagons of supplies in the mud.

I thought of Paris today. Do the children still play in the Luxembourg Gardens? Do children still play at all? Have you ever seen the coast of Brittany? I should like to have a house there someday, near where we grew up....

Our first objective, Vilna, is still a day or two away, and we've already begun to lose men through starvation and dysentery. When we reach Vilna, God willing, our supplies will catch up to us. But in the meantime conditions are frightful. There's no water to be had. The Russians have poisoned the wells with dead horses. Men die shivering and exhausted. Carts and equipment, even cannon, lie abandoned along the roadsides to join the dead, the dying, the stragglers. The cavalry alone has lost five thousand horses. They were fed green rye from the fields. How can men be asked to fight under these conditions?

We reached Vilna today. At last. We captured it with almost no fighting. The Russians have abandoned it and made off with most of the stores. . . .

I rode to the outskirts of Vilna today, on a scouting mission. We found a beautiful little farm, miraculously untouched but deserted. The inhabitants must have abandoned it in a hurry. They had taken away most of the stores, but there was fodder for the horses. And a small vegetable garden that the hungry men fell upon with great joy. I wandered into the house alone. A pretty little cottage. In the corner was a cradle, still bearing the soft impress of the child's body that had lain in it. I thought of you. . . .

We set off yesterday toward Vitebsk. The cowardly Russians still run before us, avoiding a battle. . . . Someone struck up *Malbrouk* on the march. I sang as robustly as the next man. I don't know whether my starving horse cared, but it brought me some cheer. . . . Much of the land has been picked over or set afire by the Russians. . . .

God help us all. A fusilier struggled back to the line today, one arm horribly hacked from his body. He had been caught in a field by some peasants while he was trying to dig for a potato. If he doesn't die on his journey back to France, perhaps he'll be the lucky one.

I begin to wonder about the nature of our enemy. The raiding Cossacks are savage and fight to the death. The serfs give us no quarter. They glare at us with fear and hatred as we pass, then send their sons to swell the Tsar's army. They fight for God and Mother Russia. It's hard to see—amid the misery of this endless march—the purpose for *our* being here. . . .

His last letter, dated the nineteenth of July, nearly broke her heart.

We made our way through a marsh today, fighting the insects, the heat, the smells. The stench of rotting horseflesh was everywhere. And on the other side, where we'd hoped to find a village and food and rest, we found smoking ruins.

The Russians had been there first. I saw a young trooper sink to his knees, sobbing. I tried to lift him up, to hearten him, but he only begged me to let him die. I wandered through the rubble of the village, kicking at smoldering logs, blackened trees. And then, beneath the charred ruins of a wagon, I saw a flower growing. And I thought, Is the human spirit as resilient as that, to blossom through adversity? I couldn't think so. Not then. I confess only to you, my dear fair Helen, my sweet Charmiane, that I wept. And then I noticed that the flower was yellow. The yellow of the gown you wore that night in the Tuileries. And I knew that my future was brighter than this desolation. How I should like to see you in that gown again someday. With all the yearning in my heart, I remain your Adam.

She closed her eyes. Yes, Adam. Always mine, though misfortune keep us apart.

Chapter Seven

She sat for a long time in the Luxembourg Gardens, thinking of Adam. Then she roused herself. There had been a small note besides the letters, written in Monsieur Bazaine's somewhat prim hand.

Madame,
I have learned that you translate scholarly works for a living. A modest occupation, with modest recompense, I have no doubt. Should it be insufficient to your needs, you must tell me, and I shall augment it. This is Monsieur le Baron Moncalvo's wish.

She frowned. She didn't know whether she resented or welcomed his almost paternal superintendence of her life. *Dieu!* What was that? She raised her head. Could that be the church bells already sounding the hour? She'd lost all track of time. Aunt Sophie had asked her to invite Armand and Monsieur de Domfort for dinner tonight. Nothing extravagant. Soup and a main dish. It was the most that any émigré could afford. Perhaps a few hands of whist later. But she'd spent so long with Adam's letters that Armand would have left his modest garret room by now. She could leave a message with his concierge, of course, but . . .

She guessed he'd be at the secret print shop. She felt an odd curiosity, remembering his passionate devotion to his cause. Adam's letters had filled her—for the first time—with an anger against the Empire, Bonaparte and everything he represented. Perhaps now she could view Armand's endeavors with more sympathy.

She found the rooms on the rue du Paon without much trouble: she could hear Jean-Pierre on his trumpet before she'd even rounded the corner. He glanced up in shy surprise as she entered, and stopped playing. *"Madame."* He blushed and stared, at a loss for further words.

She smiled gently. Perhaps he was eighteen. Nineteen. No more. "Don't you have a sweetheart?"

He looked away. "Yes. In my village. We plan to marry when this is over. She said she'll wait."

She sighed. Adam's dear face was before her. "We all must wait. Until this is over. May I go upstairs?"

He looked at her. His large sad eyes seemed to accept the implied rejection in her words. "Monsieur de Chevrillon's sister is always welcome here." He showed her how to release the catch in the armoire, then returned to his playing.

Only Georges was in the room above, pulling down the handbills from their lines as they dried and stacking them in neat piles. He informed her that the two gentlemen were expected shortly, offered her a chair and resumed his work.

Charmiane took one of the handbills and scanned it with interest. It was crudely written and scattered with coarse phrases and curses, as though the Flaming Sword were one of the common folk, calling his compatriots to arms.

How long must the people of France endure the Tyrant, the Dictator? How long must we allow him to hold France by the throat? Our brave sons go off to war in the service of a godless man and his kind. His brothers rape the treasury and grow rich on corruption, stealing the bread from your mouths. His sisters fornicate like animals, like whores in the street, while you struggle to teach your daughters the chastity that is God's commandment. His false nobility piss on the Holy Church and tear up your Bibles for paper to wipe themselves. Return France to God! Disobey the Tyrant's laws. Refuse to send your sons to their deaths. Take to the streets and let France live again! *Vive le Roi!* Long live the King!

There were half a dozen pages in this vein. Though she blushed at some of the words, Charmiane was struck again by the passion that leaped from every page. And still it escaped her. Armand's rage was as foreign to her as Adam's devotion to his duty

and his Emperor, which shone through the darkest passages of
his letters. She felt torn, caught between the two men she loved
most in life.

"What a pleasant surprise. To find you here." Domfort stood
in the doorway, a broad smile on his face.

"I'm here to ask you and Armand to come tonight for dinner
and whist."

"That would be delightful. I'll tell Armand later."

"Isn't he expected?"

"No. He's spending the afternoon with several Senators.
They've promised a donation of five hundred francs for *La
Voix*."

"Senators?" She held out the paper she had been reading.
"Why should they work toward the overthrow of the government?"

"They're Royalist sympathizers, with connections to the *Ancien Régime*. As Senators, they have power now. But they're
prepared to jump either way, whoever wins or loses." He
shrugged. "Most of us are. It doesn't hurt, in these troubled
times, to have friends in both camps."

She wasn't sure his practicality sat well with her. "It does to
Armand. His hatred is a singular polestar. What keeps *you* going,
Bertrand?"

He smiled. "My hopes for the future. My tender devotion to
you and your cause. Far easier to live with than hatred."

"I thank you for your devotion . . . to my cause." She hoped
he'd notice the distinction. "I wish Armand had someone."

"Yes. I worry for him. In the past—you'll forgive my frankness—he had a woman sometimes, to bring him solace. Now he
has no interest even in that."

She sighed. "Ah, well. Perhaps we can cheer him this evening. At five?" She allowed him to kiss her hand, then went out
into the street.

Armand arrived late for dinner that evening, irritable and
downcast. Everything seemed to set him off. When Aunt Sophie
whined that Jeanine would expect a few extra francs for staying
later than usual, he dug into his pocket but glared at his aunt as
he handed her the coins. When Charmiane, noticing the threadbare quality of his shirt, suggested that she could find a tailor to
turn the collar and cuffs, he frowned. "I'm not all that desti-
tute. I simply forgot to buy a new shirt this week." And when
Domfort made an attempt to hearten him by telling of a prefect's secretary he'd befriended who might be willing to support

a request for a restitution of their titles and lands, Armand turned morose, his eyes filling with tears. "It will never happen. Titles, lands, possessions and honor. We're all doomed."

"Armand. Dear heart." Charmiane rose from her chair to put her arms around her brother.

He smiled sadly. "I seem always to make you unhappy." He touched her cheek. "Do you know how much you look like *Maman*? Let me go tonight, so you can smile again." He stood up and took his hat from a side table. "I'll see you tomorrow, Bertrand." He was gone before they could stop him.

There was an awkward silence, then Aunt Sophie laughed nervously. "Well, so much for whist. But perhaps another game?"

"No." Domfort rose and took her hand. "It's time I left, as well. Thank you for dinner, *madame*." He kissed her fingers and turned to Charmiane. "Will you see me out?"

She nodded and walked with him to the tiny vestibule of their apartment. But at the outer door he turned, took her chin in his hand and bent to her lips. "Sweet Charmiane."

A kiss? No. Not with the memory of Adam's words still fresh in her heart. She turned her head aside and caught the kiss on her cheek.

He dropped his hand. The sad gray eyes had turned cold. "Your stubbornness only makes me want you more." He gave a stiff little bow— "Your servant, *madame*" —and clattered down the stairs.

Aunt Sophie was waiting to pounce when she returned to the sitting room. "Did you let him kiss you?"

"Why should he want to kiss me?"

"Oh, *Liebchen*! He stared at your mouth every time you spoke this evening. If he didn't try, it means you're not encouraging him. And you won't get a better offer of marriage."

"Perhaps I will."

"Not from a man of better lineage than Domfort! I want you to encourage him. Lead him to a proposal."

"And if I don't want to marry him?"

Aunt Sophie sighed and lifted herself from her chair. "If you choose to disappoint me, I suppose there's nothing I can do. Come and help me unhook my gown."

Charmiane was treated to an injured silence as she helped her aunt prepare for bed. At last, unable to endure another moment of Aunt Sophie's reproach, she patted the older woman on the hand. "Very well. I promise I'll begin to think about marriage again," she said, and was rewarded by a forgiving smile.

Consider marriage? she thought as she pulled down Adam's letters from their secret niche and settled herself for a leisurely rereading. Marriage? Yes. But not with Domfort. Thank God, as a widow, she had some say in her own future.

Later, in the dark, her mind and heart overwhelmed by Adam's presence, which seemed to vibrate in the air around her, she hugged her pillow and thought again of Aunt Sophie's words. Marriage. Madame Bouchard. Madame la Baronne Moncalvo. She whispered it to the night. How sweet it sounded to her ears.

Marriage. She frowned. Why did she remember Henri? Why, at this moment, with Adam's letters still warm from her kisses, did the thought of Henri have to intrude?

She still remembered those days. She'd been eighteen—an innocent child. Aunt Sophie, all beaming pride, had announced to her that marriage arrangements had been concluded with Monsieur le Marquis de Viollet. A man of pedigree. With a small income from the sale of his family's jewels, and more waiting for him in France, if their return could be arranged. Uncle Eugène had been pleased with his negotiations.

It wouldn't have occurred to Charmiane to disobey. This was the way it had always been done, particularly among their class. If she had had a moment's unease at meeting Henri—a large man of forty-six years, heavyset and frighteningly imposing—she had swallowed her doubts and assured Uncle Eugène that he couldn't have made a finer choice for her. That she was more than young enough to be Henri's daughter disturbed her less. Hadn't she always been the child among older people—Aunt Sophie, Uncle Eugène, Armand?

As a bride, she had found it somewhat unpleasant when Henri made love to her. She had expected to feel cherished, not used. But she learned to endure and to nod dutifully when his evening greeting was accompanied by the curt order, "Tonight, *madame.*" He was demanding in other ways as well, critical of her management of their small household. But, after all, he had been a great noble with exacting standards, and his mature years gave him an understanding of life that was quite beyond her. A young and inexperienced girl who needed his guidance. She trembled when he frowned and raged, but resolved to try harder. To earn his approval.

They had been married nearly eight months when he first spanked her. A hot summer's evening. He had come from the coffeehouse, where he spent his days with other émigrés, regretting the past. He took off his hat, mopped his brow, brushed his lips against her cheek. "Tonight, *madame.*"

She smiled thinly. He was large and bulky, and he sweated profusely in the heat. The thought of his body on hers tonight . . . "If you please, Henri, I . . . should prefer to wait for a cooler night." She avoided his eyes, sure that her humility would win him over.

Instead, she found herself dragged to her room, pulled across his lap, her skirts tossed back to expose bare flesh. He spanked her long and savagely, his hand a burning fire across her buttocks. She struggled in vain and bore it in silence. When he released her, she fought against her tears, nodding dumbly in agreement to his renewed command, "Tonight, *madame.*" Dinner was an agony of lingering pain and humiliation. When he came to her room later that night, she submitted to his lovemaking with cold anger, which earned her another slap on the bottom for her "sullenness in receiving me, *madame.*"

In the morning, she went to Aunt Sophie and Uncle Eugène. She hadn't seen them much in the past few months, not since Henri and Uncle Eugène had quarreled violently over Henri's misrepresentation of his fortune. Uncle Eugène wasn't feeling well and was still in bed. Charmiane sat with Aunt Sophie over their coffee and hesitantly told her story.

To her surprise, Aunt Sophie nodded in satisfaction. "Well, of course he punished you for your waywardness, child. It's how he shows his love, to mold you into perfect obedience. You had no right to refuse him."

"Have I no say in the matter?"

"My dear, your husband's desires take precedence over yours. Always! He has a right to chastise you until you learn your duty to him."

"Did Uncle Eugène . . . ?"

"Oh, yes! Half a dozen times, when we were first married. Until I learned to please him. Cheerful obedience in all things. That's what's expected of a wife."

She felt an unfamiliar stirring of rebellion. "I don't care. I won't bear it! I want to come home to you and Uncle Eugène."

Aunt Sophie began to cry softly. "You can't. You can't. Eugène is dying. Wasting away. I didn't want to tell you yet. The doctors say he won't last the year."

"Oh, Aunt Sophie!"

"We have almost no money left. When Eugène is gone, I'll have to move in with you and Henri. I'll need his protection and his financial support. You see how important it is for you to keep him content? Go back to your husband now."

She shook her head. The memory of her humiliation was too fresh. "No. I can't."

Aunt Sophie's voice rose in an accusing wail. "Will your willful disobedience of me, of your husband, destroy us all? After all we've done for you?"

She began to weep. "Aunt Sophie. Please. You're the only mother I've ever known."

"Then don't disappoint me. See your duty clearly, and go home where you belong."

In the end, she returned to Henri. She learned to please him, to avoid punishment as often as possible. Sometimes, despite her best efforts, she failed. "We need a game of *paumèle* this evening, I see," he would say coldly, after some minor transgression of hers—referring to a spanking game that the children played. But she soon learned to wail and beg his forgiveness after the first hard slap, realizing that her stubborn refusal to cry or show contrition that first time had only fueled his anger. The spankings were frequent, though not very severe after that first time. And when she saw Armand at Eugène's funeral, she was too ashamed of herself to tell him of Henri. It was her duty to please and obey her husband; surely she only got what she deserved.

Aunt Sophie had been living with them for more than two years when Henri, irked at the cost of maintaining the expanded household, found a small position for Charmiane with a publisher. Her days became exhausting. Hours of translating in a cramped little office, then hurrying home to supervise the preparations for dinner, for Aunt Sophie had become more and more helpless with their few servants, then fearfully scanning Henri's face, in dread that she'd displeased him in some way.

And then, last November, after four and a half years of marriage, she had killed him. As cruelly as if she'd taken a knife to his bosom. Killed him with her willfulness, her unwifely lack of respect.

They were sitting at dinner, the three of them. When Henri criticized the cut of beef, Charmiane excused herself by saying that the price had gone up and she'd been forced to buy a lesser cut.

He scowled. "I saw you dawdling in the street this morning, before I went to the coffee shop. Chatting with that stupid woman across the square. If you spent a little more time on your translations and less on idle gossip, you might earn enough to buy a decent cut of meat!''

She began to tremble. "Please don't be angry, Henri. I only stopped to talk with the woman because her child has been sick.'' She managed a smile, hoping to soothe him. "Surely you can understand that. With your good heart.''

His eyes were cold. "At least she has a child.''

Charmiane cringed. It was just one more way that she'd failed him. "I work as hard as I can,'' she said. "But Monsieur Conradi can't afford another franc. Perhaps if you made an effort to...'' She regretted the words even as they escaped her lips.

His eyes bulged and he slammed down his fork. "If I *what*?'' he demanded.

She gulped. It was too late to back down now. "If...if you could get employment,'' she whispered. "I know some of the other émigrés teach dancing or fencing.''

He rose from his chair. His face was turning red. "You think I'm no better than a peasant—to sell myself?'' he roared.

Her heart sank. She could see she'd already earned a beating tonight. But somehow that emboldened her. She had nothing to lose now. She too stood up, facing him across the table, her voice strong and accusing. "You sell *me*. My work. And it doesn't shame you. You could work, if you weren't so lazy!''

He pounded his fist on the table. The dishes shook and rattled. "I see I've been too lenient with you all this time, *madame*! To your room at once! Tonight I take a horsewhip to you!''

She gasped. "You wouldn't!'' She turned to her aunt, her hand stretched out in supplication. "Aunt Sophie...!''

The older woman rose unsteadily. "This is none of my affair.'' Her voice shook. "You have no cause to cross your husband. He keeps us both by his good graces. You owe him an apology.'' Her large eyes begged Charmiane's forgiveness. "I'm sorry, *Liebchen*.'' She scurried to the safety of her own little room.

Henri advanced around the table toward Charmiane. "Your apology won't save you tonight, my dear wife. I intend to raise welts on your backside!''

She stood her ground. "No! You won't beat me again. I won't endure it! Not ever again.''

"By God!'' he choked. He reached for her, his large hands closing around her arms. She pushed against him in a frenzy of terror, pounded at his chest, writhed within his savage grasp. He choked again, his face purpling. He released her and staggered back, hands pressed against his breast, eyes wide with surprise. His heart had stopped beating before his limp body reached the floor.

She had buried him on a snowy hillside, consumed with self-reproach at his death. If she'd been a dutiful wife—as Aunt Sophie had admonished her—he would still be alive. And yet, when she considered it, she was glad that she'd never had his child.

She stirred now in her bed, her thoughts returning to Adam. She loved him. She knew it with a certainty. But did she really want marriage again? To be once more under the dominion of a man, owing him perfect obedience?

The golden leaves of September had begun to drift across the Place Saint-Sulpice before she heard from Adam again. Another batch of letters, stained from travel and written sometimes with a careless hand, as though he'd penned them in a hurry, between engagements.

The Grand Army had finally met the enemy in a small skirmish near Ostrovno. A brief engagement in which the cavalry had distinguished itself. It had seemed the prelude to the long-desired major battle. Overjoyed, the Emperor had deployed the bulk of his troops, massing them against the Russian army across the plateau, and rested his men for a day. In the morning, they had discovered only a single Russian soldier remaining, asleep under a tree. The enemy had gone. A force of eighty thousand men, gone like phantoms in the night.

What bitterness I feel, my dear Charmiane. To have come this far, drawn deeper and deeper into this miserable land, and for what? The Emperor will not rest until we have won a decisive battle. But men die from small skirmishes and disease and starvation with as much ease as from a great victory....

I think of you often now. You said you write almost every day, but so few of your letters reach me....

I dreamed I kissed you and held you in my arms. Then you vanished, and I awoke with tears on my pillow. I remember your eyes are green. Your hair black and fragrant. Sometimes I imagine I can smell your perfume. I have the strangest longing: to see your hair unbound. I imagine to myself that it reaches to your waist. That it covers you like a shiny black veil. And then it reminds me of widow's weeds, and I wonder if you'll mourn for me when I'm gone. . . .

We have been at Vitebsk for a week now. All our spies report the movement of Russian troops, converging on Smolensk. And still we sit here and wait. A few wagons of supplies and stragglers and reinforcements have caught up to us, and the men have full bellies again. But best of all, my dear, fair Helen, has been the arrival of a few of your letters. You're like a magical chalice. I fill you with my bitter tears and find them returned to me as sweet nectar, to sustain my spirit for a little longer. . . .

I write to you this night from Smolensk. After three days of fighting, it's ours. It was a clashing, savage battle. I was horrified to discover that death and bloodshed no longer had the power to move me, that the sight of men without arms and legs had become so commonplace as to leave me indifferent. Perhaps we learn from our Commander. Watching the bombardment fires consume the city in a great hellish conflagration last night, the Emperor proclaimed it a fine sight. But I have found there's a spark of humanity left in me still. For today I wept for Smolensk. After the Russians had gone, we marched in this morning, in proud and triumphant ranks, our trumpets blaring. There were no witnesses to our glory but ourselves. The city was still a smoking ruin. The ditches, the riverbanks, the streets were crowded with the dead. Blackened, shrunken corpses, shriveled and charred beyond human recognition. Twisted, as though they had died in agony. In the Cathedral, women and children who had escaped the fires huddled in frightened groups around the altar and trembled at our approach. Families in rags, with horror in their eyes. Weeping, starving, bleeding from raw burns and hideous open wounds. Have we done this? In the name of France's glory?

Oh, Charmiane, my beloved. I pray your letters reach me. In the midst of this interminable war, you're my only reality. Your sweet, loving words my only shield against despair. You're my beacon of hope and sanity in a world gone mad.

Through a haze of tears, Charmiane stared at the children playing happily in the Luxembourg Gardens. She felt old and wise. And very sad. Who had she been—that simple creature of the Tuileries? Mindless, innocent, she had given her heart to a stranger. She had known nothing about him, and, upon reflection, she guessed that his handsome face had done as much to capture her that night as anything else about him. How could she have known of the beautiful, the precious soul that lay within him? That spoke to her through his letters, open and unashamed and trusting.

Adam, she thought. My dearest Adam. I love you. I love you.

A happy shout roused her. Several people were gathered about a nearby tree to which a municipal officer was tacking a handbill. Curious, Charmiane joined the crowd. The handbill was a copy of a report that Napoleon had sent to his Minister of Foreign Affairs. With Adam's heartrending letters clasped to her breast, Charmiane scanned the few lines and felt the bile rise in her mouth.

We have captured Smolensk, the Emperor reported, without the loss of a man.

"Colonel Bouchard, I can go no farther."

Adam scowled and tugged at the tight chin-strap of his yellow copper helmet. "Foullon, what kind of a soldier are you to complain so? The Emperor is waiting for my report at the Kremlin."

Foullon slumped in his saddle. Only by tangling his fingers in his horse's mane did he keep from tumbling onto the cobbled street. "I'm sorry, sir. My wound has opened again."

Adam scanned the long street. They were passing a magnificent house, which a swarm of French troopers was busily engaged in looting. The pavement was already piled with gilded furniture, sacks of grain, silver platters and urns, fur throws and bolts of bright silk. Beyond the house, from distant streets, rose wisps of smoke—small fires that had begun to appear mysteriously throughout the captured city of Moscow. Adam swore loudly. For a moment, the troopers stopped in midplunder, glancing with unease at the mounted senior officer, so resplendent in his silver epaulets and leopard-banded Dragoon's helmet. Adam averted his eyes and the troopers resumed their thievery.

He sighed. The Emperor had forbidden pillaging, a futile order. If he prevented one act of vandalism, what effect would that have on the thousands of other looters swarming throughout the deserted city like bourgeois housewives on a shopping expedition? And, after the bloody battle at La Moskva—which the

Russians called Borodino—could he blame the men for wanting recompense? He turned to his orderly. "There's a small house at the end of the street, Foullon. We'll find a place for you to lie down for a few minutes."

"But your report, sir..."

"What the deuce is there to report that he doesn't know already? That the Russians are gone? That we're in possession of an empty city? Come." He moved down the street, his eyes on the tottering Foullon, and guided their horses through an open gate into the courtyard of the house. A wagon with one broken axle, a servant's muslin cap and a torn and abandoned oil painting attested to the haste with which the inhabitants had fled. He dismounted and found a side door that gave way easily to a sharp blow of his shoulder. Except for a few bare spots that must have held a valuable painting, a precious piece of furniture, the house was in order. He helped Foullon from his horse and carried him to a neat little drawing room, placing his orderly on a brocaded sofa.

"My boots, sir," protested Foullon.

"The lady of the house will be fortunate if a muddy sofa is her only concern. Let me look at your wound, and then I'll try to find us some wine." He unbuttoned Foullon's green tunic and pulled up his shirt to expose a thick bandage across his ribs. "It hasn't bled through the wrappings. I'd just as soon leave it until a surgeon can look at it. Rest for a while." In a sideboard he found a decanter of wine and two glasses. While Foullon slept, he poured himself a second glass, found a comfortable chair, propped his spurred boots on an inlaid desk. The wine was good. The glass was fine crystal. They lived well, these Russians. He hadn't seen so delicate a glass since he'd left Paris. He stared at the ceiling. God, he was tired. This past week...

On an impulse, he reached into his breast pocket and pulled out a piece of paper. Her letter. The only one he'd managed to save from his saddlebag when his horse had gone down, screaming, in that first charge at Borodino. He unfolded the letter. It was crumpled and stained. The dark spots of blood were from the horse; the sweat was his. He stared at the words—the one line, strangely, where the ink hadn't run—and laughed sardonically. "Dearest, dearest Adam. How precious you are to me," she had written. Good God, he thought. She doesn't even know me. Who I am, what I am.

Would she have called him dearest at Borodino? That charnel house, that field of mutual slaughter? Thirty thousand of their men killed and wounded at last count. More than that of Russian losses. How many had gone down under his saber alone? They were fanatics, these Russians. Animated by religion and patriotic fervor, they fought for their homeland to the death, dragging themselves back to the line again and again. What had inspired the Grand Army that day? God? His mouth curved in a bitter smile. No French chaplain had even crossed the Niemen into Russia to follow the troops. No. They had fought with savagery because the Emperor's order had come down that no wounded man was to be removed from the field until the battle was done. He had seen men crawling over the bodies of their dead and maimed comrades to find a sheltered spot in which to reload their muskets.

And afterward. The chaos. The sea of corpses. The moans of the wounded beneath an icy September rain. The stench and the horror and the waste.

But Grouchy's cavalry had distinguished itself again and again, despite heavy losses. And on the trek to Moscow afterward, Adam had looked for Noël among the remnants of the Sixth Chasseurs. He'd been heartened to see his brother's cocky grin. It was the only thing that had cheered him all week.

There had been no joy in their bloody victory at La Moskva; it was marginal at best. There had been no formal surrender. And though the Russian Army had retreated, leaving the road to Moscow open, they'd removed the signposts, destroyed bridges, fired the towns that might have provided food and shelter for the scant hundred thousand men who remained of the glorious Grand Army. Men in ragged uniforms and boots worn thin as paper. They had floundered for a week on muddy tracks and back roads before sighting the golden domes and cupolas of Moscow. A deserted Moscow. Another hollow triumph. The Emperor and his staff had taken possession of a silent, empty Kremlin. The nobility and the middle classes had evacuated weeks before.

Adam finished the last of his wine and flung the glass into the bare fireplace. The crashing sound roused Foullon. Adam stood up and replaced his helmet on his head. "It's time we were going. It will soon be dark." He stopped, listening. In the courtyard, a horse had whinnied.

He sprang from the room and dashed outside to find a Russian soldier attempting to mount his horse. He growled a curse, took the man by the shoulders and threw him to the ground. The Russian struggled to his feet with his sword drawn. Adam dodged the first wild thrust and drew his saber. Before the Russian could strike again, Adam swung his blade in a whistling arc, nearly decapitating the man with the blow.

"Damned thief," he muttered. He turned at the sound of a labored grunt from the doorway. Foullon stood there, clutching his side. Adam wiped his bloody saber on the Russian's tunic and sheathed it. "Can you ride again, Foullon?"

"I think so, sir. I . . . oh, God, look!" He pointed to the evening sky behind Adam. Against the deepening blue, the fires had increased in numbers and intensity, patches of glowing red that seared the few low-hanging clouds.

"The bastards!" Adam kicked the corpse at his feet. "Can you ride, Foullon?" At his orderly's nod, he swung himself into the saddle and waited for the other man to mount. "The Emperor will have to wait for my report. I want to be sure that the regiment is safely bivouacked in its quarter of the city."

The fires were spreading rapidly. The house they had passed earlier in the day was now engulfed. A few remnants of booty still remained on the pavement before it. The next street was burning from one end to the other. Every house was a torch, with sheaves of flame that reached to the heavens. Adam shielded his face from the intense heat and urged Foullon to make haste. All around them were whistling noises, explosions, sharp cracks as walls fell, windows heated and shattered, tongues of flame roared from one rooftop to the next.

"Damn it, man!" shouted Adam. "Hurry! Do you want to be roasted alive?"

"Colonel. Sir. I can't . . ." Foullon's gasping words could scarcely be heard above the noise. His face was twisted in agony, and his tunic had begun to turn bloody.

Adam leaped from his horse and pulled Foullon from the saddle. With one blow of his fist he rendered the young man insensible to further pain. He threw the orderly facedown across the saddle, tied his hands and feet together beneath the horse's belly and remounted his own horse. He took Foullon's reins in his hand, spurred his own horse and raced through the fiery streets, dodging showers of sparks and flying embers, until he'd reached the safety of his own encampment in an orchard that remained untouched by the fire.

"Sir! Thank God you're safe!"

Adam slid from the saddle and threw off his helmet. "Lieutenant, get Foullon here to the surgeon major." He rubbed his smoke-darkened face. "Get me something to drink. Where's Major Tranié? I want him to find out if the Emperor is safe."

"He took some prisoners. He wants to know what to do with them."

"Bring them here." Adam sat on a hastily fetched camp stool, gulping great draughts of water from a canteen while the prisoners were paraded before him: a frightened peasant who'd been caught looting, four bearded Russian troopers in long heavy tunics and two men in rags who glared at Adam out of the corners of their eyes.

He waved away the peasant, who smiled his relief and vanished. "Damn it, why do you waste my time, Tranié? Find me a man in this accursed city who *hasn't* stolen something as yet! What about those four? Were they armed?"

"They threw down their weapons when they saw us."

"Let them go, then."

"But, sir . . ."

"The deuce! Don't argue with me, Tranié! You just earned your promotion at Borodino. Do you want to lose it so soon?" he barked. "These are deserters. Can't you see it? Their officers beat them to keep order. The wretches only want to go home. Until the Emperor orders us to do so, we're not taking prisoners. Let them go." He pointed to the two in rags. "What about these gallows birds?"

"That's the word, all right, sir. As far as we can tell, the Russians opened their prisons before they left. We found these devils with sulfur fuses in their hands, setting fire to some of the houses. What shall we do with them?"

Adam rose from his seat and stared out toward the burning northern and western quarters of Moscow. Except for the Kremlin, with its thick walls, the whole city seemed now to be engulfed in flames. The sky was bloodred, with pillars of black, choking smoke. Even from this distance he could hear the occasional screams of looters and unfortunates, trapped by the fires in flaming houses and burning streets.

He turned to Major Tranié. The fire lit up his face in a satanic glow, but his eyes were hard and unblinking in the light.

"Shoot them," he said.

Chapter Eight

"God, Bouchard, I'm going!"

"Don't be a fool, Captain. We've come so far. Hold on!" Noël pushed against the bodies that crowded him from every side in a desperate effort to reach Captain Luisat. "Let me through!" he shouted. It was no use. The press of humanity on the fragile trestle bridge moved him along in a shuffling lockstep, taking him farther away from his struggling captain. He heard a pitiful cry from Luisat, submerged up to his neck in the frigid waters of the Berezina River and clinging to the edge of the low makeshift bridge with all the passion of a lost man.

"Bouchard..." A final gasp, and Luisat was swept away to join the hundreds of other bodies that choked the ice-filled river.

Noël felt the unexpected rush of scalding tears on his face. Why the devil should he care about one man? By the time they finished this retreat across the Berezina, there'd be enough corpses in the icy waters—horses and men, women and children—to make another bridge for the attacking Russians to walk across. Thank God he hadn't let Martine follow him into Russia. He'd seen too many camp women and their children fall along the way, victims of the cold, of starvation, of the savage marauding Cossacks.

He kept his eyes on the rough planking of the bridge. He wasn't about to allow a misstep to plunge him over the side. The man in front of him, his Chasseur's uniform augmented by a fur-lined ladies' cape, stumbled for a moment, then regained his balance. From one corner of his cartridge case, slung across his shoulder, protruded the bottom half of a golden chalice. Stolen from a Moscow church, no doubt, thought Noël. Damned fool. To risk his life for useless treasure!

That was half the reason they were in this fix now. All that greed. They'd stayed in Moscow for five weeks after the fires had gone out. Five weeks, waiting for a surrender that never came from the Tsar at Saint Petersburg. And Moscow had been a carnival of looting, where precious goods were cheap and hearty food was dear. Soldiers set up shop in every ruined square and traded silks for bread and gold plate for a bit of dried herring. They had fed on horse meat and fueled their fires with priceless furniture. Meanwhile the weather turned cold, and the Cossacks harassed without respite, attacking the troops on the outskirts of the city and occasionally even venturing within the walls.

They'd left Moscow on the nineteenth of October. Noël had never been much for campaigns and strategy—he'd ridden fearlessly into battle on many an occasion, but he'd been far more concerned with encouraging the troopers behind him than seeing the whole picture. He'd leave the grand design to Adam and the other officers. But even *he* could see that the strategic withdrawal from Moscow had been badly handled from the very beginning.

A line of march that stretched for sixty miles had moved out of the city. Behind the army—still close to one hundred thousand men, with reinforcements—had come wagons loaded with plunder and personal belongings, Muscovite servants and whores who'd been persuaded to throw in their lot with Napoleon's troops, horses and cannon, baggage carts with food and fodder and guns and ammunition, the sick, the wounded, the dying. Chariots, berlins, cabriolets—carriages of every description, numbering in the thousands and thousands. Sixty miles of chaotic humanity! Too large and unwieldy a force to fight, if they had to; too loaded with treasure to move with speed out of the country before winter set in.

The first snows had fallen in the beginning of November.

Swallowed up by blizzards and whistling winds, they had struggled on. Food was scarce, and animal fodder even more so. Even then, the hay and grain were reserved for the use of the cavalry horses, the senior officers and their retinues, the gun teams and pontoon-wagon animals. The rest were fed on pine bark. Starving, exhausted, the dray horses collapsed in the snow, to be hacked up for food before they were even dead.

At night, clustered around sputtering fires, men sat huddled in groups, gnawing on bloody, half-cooked horseflesh, their faces blue with cold. If they sat too close to the fire, their frostbitten noses and fingers would turn gangrenous and lead to certain death; if they sat too far away, they'd be found lifeless in the morning, frozen like statues, their eyes open and staring, their beards and mustaches weighted with icicles.

As the army's morale crumbled and food became dearer, the wounded were left behind, the camp followers abandoned to fend for themselves. The roadsides were littered with dead horses and men, vanishing into soft white mounds under the steadily falling snow.

Bundled against the cold with an overcoat and a woolen rag he'd pulled from a corpse, and urging on his exhausted horse, Noël found himself hallucinating as the days dragged on. The snowy mounds that hid their ghastly secrets became clouds to his tortured mind, and he imagined himself on the coast of Brittany, staring at the billows in the sky. The snow on his face became the spray of the sea, and the moans of his fellow unfortunates shrieking gulls, wheeling in the wind. He had to imagine the green of the sea—for there was nothing in this stark landscape of snow and black pines to remind him. And then, of course, that reminded him of her green eyes—the beautiful lady of the Tuileries. That always brought him back to reality, with a tug of regret at his heartstrings.

Sometimes they stopped the march for a skirmish, fending off the attacks of a Russian division or a Cossack horde. The losses were appalling, as frozen, starving, haggard men threw themselves once more against the enemy. But it was better to die in battle than to suffer the long march or endure the horror of becoming a straggler. The Cossacks and the peasants were merciless to captured stragglers: they stripped them bare and forced them to march in the snow until they died, or burned them alive, or smashed their heads with rocks.

They had found a brief respite amid the ruins of Smolensk, with food supplies and reinforcements that had been brought from depots in Germany and Poland. But the pressing Russian army and their indefensible position had forced them on. It was no longer being called merely a withdrawal. The word *retreat*, unheard of under the Emperor until now, was whispered more and more by the disheartened troops. They were reduced to forty thousand men when they left Smolensk; the cavalry down to three thousand, with half the men already on foot. Noël had tended his sickly horse with care, but the poor beast had died a week out of Smolensk.

A soldier beside Noël sighed and collapsed onto the bridge. The man was a tattered ghost, with a piece of carpet tied over his hat and thick cloth bindings on his feet in place of worn boots. His face was gaunt and white with frostbite, half-hidden by a ragged beard. He looks no different than the rest of us, thought Noël. "Have a care!" he cried to the men behind, who would have stepped over the fallen soldier. With the help of a burly trooper, Noël raised the soldier to his feet. But the dull look in the man's eyes made him wonder if he'd even make it across to the other side of the river.

They'd reached the Berezina two days ago, thirty-five horror-filled days since leaving Moscow. They had expected to cross easily over the solid ice of the river. The main Russian forces had been diverted above and below their chosen crossing, and the small Cossack patrol nearby had been defeated.

And then the weather, which had been their enemy on the long, terrible march, betrayed them once again. The days turned imperceptibly warmer, and the frozen river began to melt. The pontoons for bridges had been long since abandoned, seeming unnecessary burdens for the exhausted horses. But the corps of engineers had moved in and, miraculously, had built two rickety trestle bridges, one for the pedestrians and one for the carriages, cavalry, wagons and gun caissons that still remained.

Noël sighed. They'd been crossing for two days now. What was left of Grouchy's cavalry had gone over the first day, but he'd stayed behind to wait for his captain and to help a sobbing whore bury her dead child under a mound of soggy leaves and snow.

From somewhere behind him on the bridge he heard shrieks, and then a Russian shell exploded in the water nearby. A savage cry, almost in unison, echoed over the water: *"Houra! Houra! Houra!"* It chilled a man's marrow to hear it.

Damn! thought Noël. The Cossacks were attacking again. The shouts and the bombardment threw the occupants of the bridge into a panic. Up ahead, Noël could see a ragged Hussar, saber drawn, cutting a bloody path through the wretches who kept him from the far bank and safety. Bodies surged forward, screaming, shouting, jostling. Women fell to their knees and were trampled; a dozen men, pushed into the water, were forced back into the swirling current again and again as they tried to remount the bridge. Noël felt himself swept along in the mass of struggling humanity, kept upright as much by the bodies that hemmed him in on every side as by his own agility.

By some miracle, he found himself on the far bank at last. There were shells exploding here as well, and officers shouting to the cavalry to repulse the enemy. He saw an officer of the Grenadiers shot from his horse, nearly beheaded by a Russian shell. Without a moment's hesitation, he leaped for the animal. With a horse, a man had a chance to survive the exhausting marches that killed so many of the troopers whose mounts were dead, or eaten, or both.

He wheeled about to join other horsemen forming into an attacking wedge to charge the enemy. He saw a familiar face, as gaunt and haggard as his own, with eyes as blue as his own, bloodshot from exhaustion and the smoky camp fires. "Adam!" he cried. "My God, Adam!" He began to sob for joy. He hadn't seen Adam since they'd left Moscow; it was a miracle that they'd both got this far. He guided his horse to his brother, leaned over in the saddle and pounded Adam on the back. He grinned through his tears. "Still here, brother? I should have known you'd be too tough to kill!"

Adam stared at him, his expression frozen and unreadable. Then he scowled and cleared his throat. "Why aren't you with your regiment, *Brigadier*?"

Noël was undaunted; it was enough that his brother still lived through all this horror. He shook his head. "Poor Adam. How hard it must be for you. To be a soldier instead of a man."

"Why won't you say yes? I have your brother's permission. I have your aunt's permission."

Charmiane frowned and picked up her gloves. "I didn't come here to quarrel with you, Bertrand. Not again. I came to find Armand. We haven't seen him since Christmas."

Domfort ran his hand through his white hair. His shirt was stained with ink from the printing press. "He's not here. I sent him home to rest. We've been working like dogs to turn out enough handbills. But don't you see, Charmiane—" his eyes were bright with hope and enthusiasm "—it can't be long now before the Emperor falls! And we'll be a part of it." He lowered his voice and glanced at Jean-Pierre and the others working in the cramped room. "We've sent letters to England, Armand and I. To France's true King. When Napoleon falls, Louis will remember our loyalty and restore our titles. I want you to be my wife by then."

"For my title, or yours?" It was a cruel remark. Domfort would be only a *baron*; through Henri, Charmiane was a *marquise*.

A cruel remark. But she'd wanted to hurt Bertrand. He had badgered her for months, pressing for an answer to his proposal, enlisting Aunt Sophie and Armand as his allies so she never had a moment's peace from their accusations of selfishness, their appeals to her sense of duty to the family. And all the while she lived in agony, not knowing if Adam lived or not. She'd had one letter from Moscow at the beginning of October. One letter that had managed to make it through the attacks on the messengers that were said to be cutting the lines of communication with the Grand Army. One letter. Then nothing. After awhile, she'd stopped writing, too.

And then, in the middle of December, the Emperor had appeared in Paris, racing home to respond to an attempted coup d'état, and his Twenty-ninth Bulletin had been issued and printed in *Le Moniteur*. All of Paris was talking about it. It presented— for the first time—an honest account: a tale of horror, of brave deeds and battles canceled out by cruel Nature, of an army reduced to starvation and agony in the bitter cold of the Russian winter. With a loss of lives that was staggering. The Emperor admitted only to a loss of fifty thousand men. But of the half million who had marched into Russia—had it only been last June?—it was now being whispered that no more than thirty thousand would come out alive. That France would never recover from such a disaster.

And Domfort and Armand had gloated, reprinting the more devastating passages of the Bulletin in *La Voix*. She wanted to scream, to cry out to them: one of those dead soldiers whose death you celebrate might be the man I love!

Domfort's eyes were hard. "Do you think I want you for your title? For Henri's lands and holdings? Do you think the Domforts have no pride?"

She turned away from his accusing eyes. "Oh, Bertrand. I'm sorry. Please don't press me for an answer yet." She pulled on her gloves and buttoned her redingote. "When you see Armand, tell him to visit soon."

"I do love you dearly, Charmiane. Give me a few minutes to finish here, and I'll walk you home."

"No, no. You're busy, and I need the solitude of a long walk to clear my head. There's so much to consider."

He kissed her gloved hand. "If your considerations result in the answer my heart longs to hear, I'll rejoice."

She went down the stairs and out into the street, hunching her shoulders against the cold winter air as she walked. What was she to do? Surely Adam was dead, lost somewhere in the snows of Russia. And she was a fool to wait and hope. Oh, Adam! She stood on the busy corner of the rue des Aveugles, suddenly unable to move. Her heart was so filled with despair that the simple act of crossing the street had become too much to deal with. She feared she would begin to cry in a moment.

"Madame de Viollet?"

She looked up, startled, at the man who stood at her elbow. A black eye patch. A gray mustache. She hadn't seen him since April. "Monsieur Bazaine."

He gestured toward a small café. "You look chilled, *madame*. Perhaps a cup of coffee?"

He was being too kind. She dreaded to ask why. Her heart had gone cold. Silently she followed him into the café and took the seat in a sheltered corner that was offered. "How did you find me?"

"You frequent a dangerous neighborhood, *madame*. The rue du Paon is no place for you alone."

"You dare to follow me?" Really, it was too much.

"For your own safety, *madame*."

"Today? Or always?" she demanded.

He ignored her question and nodded to the hovering waiter. "Two coffees." He removed his gloves and leaned back in his chair, studying her with his one good eye. "Don't you want to know the purpose of this meeting?"

She hesitated. "I think I can guess," she said at last. "A note wouldn't do to tell me that . . . he's dead."

"No. Not at all, *madame*. He's very much alive."

She cried out and clapped her hand to her mouth. Alive. Thank God! Adam . . . alive! Her own dear love. "Safe and alive?" she whispered.

"Very much so. He's sent me to propose marriage to you." He humphed. "Though I'm far too old, it seems to me, to play go-between for an affair of the heart." He reached into a pocket. "Would you like a handkerchief, *madame*?"

"Thank you, no." Her voice shook. "I'm . . . too happy. Perhaps later I'll cry, but now . . ." She took a steadying breath. Her heart felt ready to burst for joy. He wanted her for his *wife*. "Why didn't he write to me and ask me himself?"

"It's been months since he's had a letter from you. He wasn't sure you would still be . . . amenable to a proposal."

With all my soul, she thought. "And he's well?"

"Yes. He's garrisoned on the German frontier at the moment. He's not sure how long he'll have to stay. The remnants of the army are still straggling in from Russia and Poland. It is *monsieur le comte*'s responsibility to take charge of them and assign them to new regiments, if necessary."

"*Monsieur le comte?*"

Bazaine allowed himself a pleased smile. "*Monsieur* has been honored by the Emperor for his bravery at La Moskva."

"Le Comte Moncalvo?"

"The Emperor has seen fit to further reward him. His title has not only been advanced from *Baron* to *Comte*, but he has been granted the right to add the honorific *de* to his name. I shall be pleased to call you Madame la Comtesse de Moncalvo, after your marriage. There's also the matter of a heritable estate, as required by the Emperor if he's to bear such an exalted title. To...ahem...pass on to your sons. It has been arranged for *monsieur le comte* to purchase a large château and lands just outside of Paris, where..."

She began to giggle. "Stop. No more. I shall die of happiness. That he's alive." The laughter caught in her throat and became a sob. She covered her eyes with her hands. "That he's alive, dear God."

In the silence, Bazaine cleared his throat. "You might be pleased to know that *monsieur*'s brother, Monsieur Noël, also survived the Russian campaign."

She dabbed at her cheeks and smiled. "I'm pleased. I remember how charming he was. Monsieur Noël."

"Yes. A jolly companion. And quite *monsieur le comte*'s equal in strength of character."

The enormity of Bazaine's news suddenly overwhelmed her. Adam, alive! She was blessed a thousand times over. To be his love. To be his wife. To feel herself in his arms again. She closed her eyes. "I think I should like to go home now," she whispered. She was still trembling.

"I understand. Will you write to him?"

"Of course. I'll leave a letter tomorrow with Monsieur Vernis."

"I shall inform you of *monsieur*'s plans, as I receive them. And of course there's the matter of a trousseau..."

"No more. Tomorrow." She needed time to adjust to the reality of her joy. She left the café, weeping for happiness. On the corner of the rue des Saints-Pères, she suddenly began to laugh. She hadn't even said yes to the marriage proposal! But Bazaine probably knew from her face. The reluctant go-between. And Adam. It was curious that the man who had been so eloquent in his letters had lost his voice at this crucial moment and had relied on his attendant to propose.

She paused at the entrance to her apartment. Aunt Sophie would know her happiness. She couldn't hide it. And how was she to explain Adam? Perhaps she'd wait until after dinner. Jeanine had bought a sweet cake for dessert. That always put Aunt Sophie in a good mood. She opened the door and stepped into the sitting room. If she could reach her own room unhindered ...

An outraged cry. "You deceitful creature!" Aunt Sophie and Armand sat before a small table. Adam's letters were spread out in front of them.

Armand stood up. He was shaking with fury. "Did I not forbid you any traffic with this man?"

She trembled in turn at his wrath. "They're ... only letters, dear heart. I never saw him again after that night."

"And how did you get the letters?"

She swallowed hard. "Through Monsieur Bouchard's secretary."

Aunt Sophie pouted like an aggrieved child. "Do you care that you've dishonored yourself, disgraced the family? And disobeyed your brother?"

"What disgrace? We exchanged letters. That's all." She took a deep breath. "I love him," she said with firmness.

"And your love is more important than the heartbreak you give to us? *Liebchen*, forget this man, I beg you. He means you no good."

"He wants to marry me, Aunt Sophie."

Aunt Sophie sagged in her chair. "*Gott in Himmel*, Armand. What are we to do?"

Armand pressed his hands against his temples. "My head explodes with such madness! You'd marry one of *them*? When Domfort waits to honor you with his family name?"

She smiled bitterly. "I had the honor of Henri's name. Now I want happiness."

"It's necessary to know how to choose, at your age, between pleasure and happiness," sniffed Aunt Sophie. "Happiness lies in doing your duty and remaining faithful to your class. Shame. Shame!"

"Adam has just been invested with the title of *comte*. I see nothing to be ashamed of in that."

Armand threw himself back into his chair. "Did it ever occur to you, little fool, that the man might want the prestige of marriage to a *true* aristocrat? To elevate himself in the Tyrant's eyes?"

"He's not that crassly ambitious! He loves me!"

Armand slapped at the stack of letters. "I saw no declaration of love here."

Her face flamed. "You read them?"

"Every word. I think *La Voix*'s subscribers might like to hear how their army has suffered in Russia because of the Tyrant."

She sank into a chair, fighting back her tears. "How could you be so cruel, dear heart? To read his letters. To use his words as weapons." She turned to her aunt. "Aunt Sophie, I appeal to you."

"We must obey Armand in this, Charmiane."

She tried another tack. "Adam is very rich, Aunt Sophie. It will mean an easier life for you. Please take my part in this," she added, seeing her aunt waver.

Armand pulled his watch from his pocket and threw it across the table. "If you want money, pawn my watch. It will bring you five hundred francs! Or, if you must—" his shoulders sagged, and his voice took on a tremor "—sell this, and finish killing me." He stared at the ring on his little finger and opened the tiny locket to touch the red curl within. When he looked at Charmiane, there were tears in his eyes. "She was only sixteen. Her hair was like the sunset, as fine as silk. She waved to me from the window of the prison at Tours. They screamed curses at her in the tumbril, and when she mounted the steps to the guillotine. Only sixteen, my God! What were her crimes against the common people? Pure and good and innocent. Why couldn't I save her?" He buried his face in his hands and began to sob. "Oh, God! Why couldn't I save her? They hacked off her hair to make it easier for the blade. I had to bribe... Dear God. I should have killed myself then. It shames me still to live."

"Oh, Armand. Oh, my dear." Charmiane hurried to him and cradled his head on her bosom. "Don't cry, dear heart."

He raised his tear-ravaged face to her. "Then give him up. Don't stain her memory with an unworthy alliance."

"But Adam isn't unworthy. He's brave and honorable and..."

Armand pushed her away from him. "Was he born to his title? Or was he an opportunist, feeding on the misery of others? What will happen to his grand title when the Tyrant is defeated and the King returns?"

"And what will happen to us if the Empire persists? Adam has earned the right to his honors, to his title."

With a growl, Armand tore himself from his chair and towered above her. "I see the man's Republican thinking has begun to poison your mind!" He turned to the table and gathered up Adam's letters. Before Charmiane could stop him, he had hobbled to the porcelain stove, flung open the door and tossed the letters to the flames.

Charmiane cried out in dismay. She had begun to waver—her loyalty to her family, to her class, a strong determinant. But to destroy Adam's letters, his dear words... "I don't need your permission," she said boldly. "Not either of you. I intend to marry Monsieur Bouchard as soon as he returns from his garrison."

Armand limped to the door of the sitting room and pulled the key from the lock. "Sophie, I want her kept locked in this place until she comes to her senses."

Aunt Sophie scampered to him and took the key. "Of course, my dear. If you're going now, I'll lock it this very minute."

Armand nodded, picked up his hat and tucked it under his arm. "This is for your own good, Charmiane. You know nothing of the man. Of his lineage. It would be madness to marry."

"But, Armand..."

"I'm doing this because I love you," he said gently. "Try to understand and forgive me." With a nod at Aunt Sophie, he was gone.

Chapter Nine

The following weeks were a torment. Armand didn't return, and Aunt Sophie was a cruel and reproachful jailer. Long hours of cold silence were followed by sighs, accusing glances, appeals to her reason, her common sense. Monsieur de Domfort, a man of honor and true nobility, was only waiting for her acquiescence. She had but to say the word and her imprisonment would cease. The day of her release would be her wedding day.

In vain she railed against her aunt or begged to be allowed to go to church or conspired with Jeanine to let her out. At the very least, wouldn't the girl deliver a message to Monsieur Vernis when she left for the day?

"No, no, no, *madame*. You should marry your own kind. It's only right. I'd be ashamed in front of the other maids in the faubourg. To tell them that *my* lady chooses to marry beneath her!"

She wondered what Bazaine must be thinking, with no word from her since the day he'd offered the marriage. Perhaps he assumed she'd changed her mind, and he was even now writing to Adam, advising him that her silence meant renunciation.

In desperation, she slipped a note into her last translation, which Jeanine was to deliver to Monsieur Mafflu. She begged him to go to the apothecary shop on the Place Saint-Sulpice and tell the proprietor that Madame de Viollet was steadfast but helpless. At the last moment, alerted no doubt by Charmiane's telltale blush, Aunt Sophie searched Monsieur Mafflu's papers and found the note.

"Wicked girl!" she cried. "Quite beyond redemption!" She reached forward and slapped Charmiane's fingers.

Charmiane fled to her room in tears. The sting of Aunt Sophie's rejection hurt more than the humiliation of being treated like a naughty child. She went to bed early that night torn with guilt, frustration at her helplessness, longing for Adam. She had memorized some of his letters; the remembrance of his loving words lulled her to sleep at last.

She awoke, coughing, to find her room filled with smoke and Aunt Sophie bending above her, tugging at her nightdress. "*Liebchen!* What shall we do?" A helpless bleat.

She jumped out of bed, alert at once. The room was gray; it was surely near dawn. "Is there fire?"

"Not here. But the smoke . . . I'm frightened. Oh, Eugène! He was always my strength!"

Charmiane ran to the window and pushed it open to get air. *Dieu!* That would never do. The alley below wafted up great blinding billows of smoke. She pulled shut the casement and groped for her aunt's pudgy hand. "Come! The stairs! They may still be clear."

"Yes. Of course. Oh, the key! *Gott in Himmel*, where did I leave the key?" Aunt Sophie rummaged in a small commode, all the while letting out helpless gasps and squeaks. But the key was found and they hurried out the door, meeting on the staircase other tenants of the building who had been awakened by the thick smoke. Charmiane had had the presence of mind to stop and find slippers for herself and Aunt Sophie; otherwise, the race through the gravel-paved courtyard—as smoke filled as the back alley— would have been painful.

It was freezing on the street. They huddled together, shivering in their nightclothes, as the street filled up with curious onlookers and chattering neighbors. The smoke and the predawn light made vision difficult.

Charmiane frowned. The crowd was really becoming quite unmanageable. She felt herself pushed farther into the middle of the street, separated from Aunt Sophie by the press of people.

"*Madame*. Come!" At the same time that Charmiane heard the urgent command, she felt herself wrapped in a warm, hooded cloak. She looked up. Monsieur Bazaine stood beside her. "Come," he said again.

"But, *monsieur* . . ."

"Do you wish to marry *monsieur le comte*?"

"Of course! But the fire . . ."

"There is no fire. Merely a great deal of smoke that—alas!— will dispel in a few moments. At which time, we *must* be gone."

"My clothes. My books . . ."

"We'll send for them. Or buy new. Come, *madame*. Yes or no?"

Ah, Dieu! What a cruel dilemma. She could never go back. Her life, as it existed, would be over. The memories, the friends, the love of her family. All finished. Done. But Bazaine was waiting. And her future with Adam. She nodded.

"Good. I thought it must be against your will, when no letter appeared and you seemed to have vanished." He pulled up the hood to shield her face and bundled her through the crowd to his waiting carriage. "I've left a servant to wait out the hubbub and then inform your aunt that you are safe and quite where you wish to be. It is so, *n'est-ce pas?*"

"Yes. Yes, of course." She wished she felt as certain as her words.

He took her to Adam's *hôtel*, a magnificent house off the rue Saint-Honoré, on the Grande rue de Verte. She was dazzled by the splendor of it, its walled gardens, soaring windows, superb furnishings. She was taken in hand by half a dozen servants, led to a beautiful suite of rooms and dressed in clothing that had been hastily bought in preparation for her arrival.

She had known that Adam was rich, of course, but the extent of his wealth astonished her. Within a day, *couturières* and other dress merchants began to arrive at the *hôtel*, along with milliners, linen drapers, cobblers, ribbon and lace sellers. They spread before her an array of fabrics and clothing of a richness she'd never dreamed of. Shawls, capes, chemises. Fans and gloves and lacy handkerchiefs. Furs of all descriptions. And if she hesitated, reluctant to indulge herself with a particularly fetching trifle, Bazaine was always there to nod his approval, snap his fingers, insist on a timely delivery of the goods she ordered. He even arranged for her to have a few simple necklaces: delicate gold chains, linked ovals of carved amethyst surrounded by tiny pearls, an enameled pendant.

"I'm sure," he said, "that *monsieur le comte* will wish to give you more costly jewels, *madame*. But I hope these will do in the meantime." She nodded in agreement; indeed, she felt she had no say in the matter. Bazaine seemed to be in total control. And with Adam's blessing. Each day's post brought a fat letter for Bazaine with detailed instructions on the furnishing of Bonneval, the château that Adam had bought to the north of Paris, near the forest of Chantilly.

She felt a stirring of resentment toward Adam that she tried to suppress. But it was difficult. Daily letters for Bazaine. Two or three stiff, oddly impersonal notes for her, dashed off between staff meetings and troop reviews. In the face of his coolness, his infrequent notes, she found it impossible to respond with more than brief letters herself. He had time for the material details of his life, but no time for her. Or so it seemed.

To make matters worse, Bazaine had begun to travel back and forth to the new château, leaving her alone in a strange house with unfamiliar servants. She had felt abducted at first; now she felt abandoned. Aunt Sophie and Armand had refused to release her possessions to her. She had neither the comforting familiarity of her own things nor the work from Monsieur Mafflu, which would have helped to pass the weary time. She took short walks on the nearby streets, vaguely aware that someone watched her at all times. She was desperate with loneliness, longing for a spark of love from someone. Anyone.

At last she confronted Bazaine. "I want to see my family."

He frowned. "*Madame*, is it wise? What's to prevent them from spiriting you away? Putting you under lock and key, far from *monsieur le comte*'s control? No, no, *madame*. *Monsieur le comte* would be in a fury if you were lost to him now."

She was beginning to feel like a possession. Adam's possession, like his château, his *hôtel*, his lands and holdings! What had happened to her lover of the letters? She pursed her lips in anger. "Am I a prisoner here, as I was with Aunt Sophie? Monsieur Bouchard's prisoner?"

Bazaine looked uncomfortable but held firm in his insistence on caution. Finally he agreed to communicate with Aunt Sophie and Armand. To arrange a meeting. "But in an open place, *madame*, where your safety can be assured."

He chose the Palais Royal, a covered arcade of fashionable shops and restaurants that surrounded an open garden on three sides. In one corner there was a café with large windows; Charmiane was instructed to take a table in the front of the café, easily seen by Bazaine and Darnaud the footman, who waited outside, sheltered from the chill January wind by the covered walkway.

She hadn't long to wait. Fluttering in agitation, Aunt Sophie came into the café, followed by Armand and Bertrand de Domfort. Charmiane was almost sorry she hadn't let Bazaine sit with her, as he had at first proposed. They seemed so imposing, so formidable, the three of them, arrayed against her across the café table.

Aunt Sophie began at once, her voice filled with condemnation. "Well, ungrateful child," she said, pouting, "what have you to say for yourself?"

"I've missed you, Aunt Sophie, dear. How have you been getting on?"

"How should I be getting on? I returned the work to Monsieur Mafflu. He paid me for the pages you'd completed." She scanned Charmiane's velvet redingote, quilted bonnet and fur muff. "*You* don't seem to need the money," she sniffed.

Charmiane reached into her reticule. "I have money for you."

"Keep your money," growled Armand, who had been staring at her with eyes that glowed with rage.

She sighed. "I thought surely you'd understand, dear heart. You loved *her*. That's how I feel about Adam."

"You speak of them together in the same breath? Curse you!" He closed his eyes and pressed his hand to his forehead. "I've had nothing but nightmares since the day you left." He lifted his head; the grief and anger on his face made her cringe. He seemed drawn and tired, as though the pain of her betrayal had worn away at him. He sneered. "Has he returned yet, that pig of a man you choose to marry?"

"Stop, Armand. He's good and noble and brave."

For the first time, Domfort spoke up. "Did he tell you that his château, Bonneval, was stolen from a family that went to the guillotine? After the infant and heir had had his brains bashed out against a tree?"

"*Ah, Dieu!* Don't reproach him for sins committed by others, Bertrand!"

His eyes were cold. "I don't even speak for myself, though you've driven a knife into my heart. But look at your brother. Your poor aunt. How they suffer. You should be praying for the fall of Bonaparte and the return of the Royalists. Not deserting your own kind. My friends and Armand's. They suffered and died. Sacrificed to the madness. And for what? A better France?" His lip curled. "No. So that upstarts with no talent and no expectations could rise and rule. And you wish to be a part of it. A *comtesse*, with no right to the title! Bah! There's more corruption and evil now than there was in the worst days of the *Ancien Régime*."

"Thieves. All of them," said Aunt Sophie sourly. "Not like the old days."

Charmiane held up her hands as if to ward off the assault of their words. "Not Adam."

"Really?" Armand leaned forward and curled his hand around Charmiane's wrist. She could feel the tremor of his anger through her glove. "Do you know how he got his money? Your Adam?"

What had Bazaine told her? "He . . . was honored by the Emperor . . . when he got his title. Baron Moncalvo. Years ago."

"His title, perhaps. But not his money. Because you're dear to me, to Sophie, I made inquiry. Something you should have done before you behaved so rashly. Your 'noble' lover came back from the Italian campaigns with millions in diamonds. Millions! God knows where he keeps them. But every time there's an investment to be made or a piece of land for sale, he sells another jewel. The town house you're staying in cost him a quarter of a million francs five years ago. Bonneval was a bargain; since its confiscation and plunder during the Revolution, it's lain empty. All he had to do was pay the taxes on it."

Aunt Sophie's voice was a whine of resentment. "And now it's to be yours. Will you rest easy, living with the ghosts of martyrs?"

Charmiane felt besieged, forced to defend Adam. "But if he bought it fairly . . ."

Armand snorted. "And did he buy the diamonds that came from Italy? Or did he steal into some great house, like a thief, and kill the inhabitants? And come away with bloodstained booty?"

"Stop!" she cried, sick at heart. "No more. I can't bear it!"

Armand rose unsteadily to his feet. "Then choose the path of honor and come with us now."

How could she go back? She had known Adam's love. She shook her head. "No," she whispered.

Armand's eyes filled with tears. "Then the Chevrillons disown you. You're no longer a part of this family. Sophie, Bertrand. Come away."

She watched them go—Armand limping painfully, Sophie shrunken and old in her shabby cloak, supported by Domfort—and felt the life drain from her heart. She buried her head in her folded arms. Adam, she thought, agonized. How much I sacrifice for your love!

Bazaine was at her side. "Come, *madame*. We might as well go. You can't reach them. They're in eternal mourning for a France they cherished and have lost forever."

"Is there nothing we can do?"

"If you wish, I'll arrange to have a banker pay your aunt's bills."

"But won't Adam . . . Monsieur Bouchard . . . ?"

"*Monsieur le comte* gives me great latitude in these matters," he said smoothly. "It isn't necessary to consult with him. As for your situation . . . I'll be spending much of my time now at Bonneval. I think it's wise for you to come there with me." Like his master, Bazaine gave commands even when he seemed to be deferring to her. She nodded in agreement. She wouldn't have known how to refuse.

Bonneval—a few hours' carriage ride from Paris—was an elegant and formal château, built in the Italian style that had characterized many a building in the previous century. A long line of trees led to a wide gravel courtyard that fronted the building and its two side wings. A low stone terrace, reached by half a dozen steps, ran the width of an imposing facade; on the garden side, tall windows looked out upon symmetrical flower beds, clipped hedges and a large, man-made lake.

It was clear that Bazaine had spared no expense for his master: hundreds of workmen swarmed within and without the château, mending plaster, retiling roofs, painting and gilding and polishing. Adam's suite had already been completed in the classical Roman mode that had become so popular under the Empire. The walls were papered a deep red and gold in a printed imitation of swagged velvet; there were gilded chairs and a canopy bed, chiffoniers and commodes overlaid with marble and gilt bronze, sofas and chaise longues. There was a separate study lined with books, a bathroom with a deep copper tub, washbasin and shaving stand, and a sitting room for visitors. Charmiane smiled in pleasure at the lavish splendor of the suite, already anticipating the cheering effect that furnishing her own rooms would have on her low spirits.

"Will you look at your suite now?" asked Bazaine. "It's just down the passageway." He led her across the hall and pushed open a door with a flourish, like an artist making a presentation. "There you are. Almost done."

Her heart sank. She hadn't even been given any choices in the rooms that were to be hers. A suite furnished very much like Adam's, with rather heavy furniture and drapings, more suited to a man's taste than a woman's. Only the colors were different. Instead of the reds and golds of Adam's rooms, her suite was done in deep green with touches of gold, white and a pale salmon color. The heavy carved mahogany bed was adorned with golden sphinxes and set in an alcove framed with Corinthian columns of dark green malachite. Craftsmen were busy hanging green velvet draperies.

"I hope it pleases, you, *madame*."

She swallowed. What was done was done. "Yes, of course."

"I chose the color because of your eyes. Monsieur de Moncalvo was quite taken with the color of your eyes at the Tuileries. I remembered that quite distinctly when I chose the fan."

Ah, Dieu. Was she to be left with no illusions? "*You* . . . chose the fan?"

"Upon *monsieur*'s orders, of course. 'Buy her the most beautiful fan in the place,' he said."

But Bazaine had chosen the color, not Adam. She sighed. "Where shall I stay this evening?"

"I've been promised that your suite will be ready for you tonight. Would you care to see the rest of the château in the meanwhile?" He led her from room to room, pointing out half-finished carvings, furniture in large crates, swatches of fabric and wallpapers. "It will be quite splendid when it's done, *madame*. Don't you agree?" There was a long gallery, several drawing rooms, a ballroom, a reception room for great parties. A buffet room for dining, a music room, servants' quarters on the upper story. One of the side pavilions was the stable, with an enclosed courtyard; the other, containing several modest suites, simply furnished, was for guests who might visit.

Charmiane found it difficult to think of it as her house; indeed, as the days wore on, she felt like a stranger in every way. Bazaine, directed by Adam's constant notes, made all the decisions. The servants were hired by him from the nearby villages, and he ordered them about with all the skills of a military commander. Still, unlike Jeanine, who had served other émigrés, they had no sense of the elegant way of life of the old Monarchy, which had been ingrained in Charmiane since her childhood. And when she tried to speak to Bazaine, he looked bewildered. "They do their jobs, *madame*. Isn't that so? What more do you want?"

How could she explain it? That they were a little forward, a little insolent, a little careless and indifferent in their attentions? Perhaps she was to blame. Perhaps she was the one who didn't belong in this new society. She yearned for Adam's return—to drive away her growing doubts and fears.

She began to ride on pleasant days. It was easier than staying inside the château, feeling useless and in the way as the renovations progressed. She hadn't ridden in years. Not since the early days in Switzerland, when Eugène, thinking that they'd soon return to France and their estates, was still spending money freely.

She came in from a ride one blustery February day to be greeted by a smiling Bazaine. "A letter from *monsieur le comte, madame*."

A letter from Adam! She read it quickly, then sighed in disappointment. It was more like a note one would dash off to an indifferent friend, a distant relative. He was coming home to France at last. The Emperor had charged him with escorting Russian prisoners to Paris, after which he'd be free to take an extended leave. He expected to arrive toward the end of the month. He had already instructed Bazaine to arrange for the priest on the twenty-sixth. He had waited long enough for a wife, he said; he trusted that she didn't expect a courtship at this late date.

She refolded the letter and frowned at Bazaine. "Not until the end of the month! You've made the marriage arrangements?"

"The village curé will come here to Bonneval's chapel. Do you wish me to send an invitation to your family, *madame*?"

"Alas. I fear they won't come. But I'll write to them myself." How sad, how lonely her life had become. "Were you ever married, Bazaine?"

"Briefly, *madame*. I trained to be a country lawyer but found a lack of adventure in the calling. When I joined the army, my wife left me."

"And you never married again?"

He shrugged. "I like the challenge of my work with *monsieur le comte*. Love is too imperfect, too haphazard for control. Perhaps it's the soldier's point of view."

"Is it Colonel Bouchard's point of view?"

His expression was bland. "I speak only for myself, *madame*."

Still vaguely troubled, she sat at the desk of her study and composed an answer to Adam's letter.

Beloved, it grieves me to learn that I won't see you as soon as I had prayed. But if your duty keeps you away, who am I to blame? I must be content with knowing that you'll be here. That I'll be in your arms. That I can whisper at last the words I've longed to say: I love you, Adam. I love you.

She stared at the words for a long time. Did he love *her*? He had never told her so. When she thought of what she knew of him from his behavior, she realized that he had never really shown love or tenderness. The night of the Tuileries, so long ago? She thought of his moody silences, his domineering manner, his crude haste in the garden. He'd been a soldier on leave, satisfying his desires with a willing woman. The gift of the fan? Bazaine's thoughtfulness. For Adam, perhaps, merely payment for the night in the garden. No. No! She mustn't think that way! She must remember the letters that had touched her heart, revealed a different Adam.

But the letters were ashes now; even the memory of the words had begun to fade. And she was left with nothing. No family. No certainty. Only the uneasy awareness of a stranger who had grown rich, God alone knew how! Who wanted a wife. And had neither the time nor the social graces to search one out. And hadn't she proved herself pliant and agreeable? Willing to give up her family, to defer to him and his overbearing majordomo in all things?

She snatched up her letter and tore it into pieces. Only time would tell whether she'd made a mistake. But she wasn't ready to confess her love to him. Not yet. Nor to give him more power over her than he already held.

It was scarcely more than a week later that, standing at an upper window, she saw him gallop up the large drive. It was a mild afternoon. He had taken off his overcoat and helmet; his uniform tunic was a bright patch of color against the stark line of leafless trees, the dull gray of the gravel. His dark blond hair fell in a boyish wave across his forehead. And though his deep tan had faded in the harsh Russian winter, his face was as strong and handsome as she had seen it in her dreams.

Her heart swelled with love, all her doubts fading away at the sight of him. She turned and flew down the staircase, reaching the outer terrace just as he leaped from the saddle and bounded up to meet her. She threw herself into his arms and lifted her head for his kiss. He smiled a warm greeting—how could she have questioned his feelings for a single minute?—and took her mouth with his. His lips were sweet, the kiss less impassioned than she would have expected or hoped for, but the thrill of his being home at last was enough.

He drew away from her, his blue eyes drinking in the sight of her with an intensity that made her tremble. "My God," he said softly. "Just as beautiful as I remembered you."

Several grooms ran out from the stables to calm his horse, which was still snorting and stamping and pawing the ground after its wild race up the drive. The commotion brought Bazaine to the door that Charmiane had left open.

Bazaine smiled and held out his hand. "Monsieur Noël! What a pleasant surprise!"

Chapter Ten

"Noël?" The word emerged as a soft croak. Charmiane stared in disbelief.

He grinned. "Pity I didn't fool you for one kiss more! Bazaine, you one-eyed devil, why did you have to spoil things?" He clapped the older man on the shoulder. "How are you, *mon vieux*?"

"As well as can be expected. You're still in one piece, *monsieur*?"

"Hale and hearty. And luckier than I ought to be."

Charmiane was still struggling to absorb the reality. "Noël?"

"Yes, beautiful lady. Now will you greet me as myself?"

Her face flamed. "I think one greeting is enough. But how did Bazaine know you?"

Noël laughed. "He'd remember a man who beats him at cards and takes him for every sou he has. Besides—" he pointed to the two chevrons on the cuff of his dark green tunic "—that's the insignia of a *brigadier*. Brother Adam's an important man. A colonel."

Bazaine stepped away from the door and motioned them inside. "Come to the small drawing room, where it's warmer." When they'd settled comfortably before the fireplace and Noël had been furnished with a large glass of cognac, Bazaine turned to him. "You've seen *monsieur le comte*?"

"I stopped at his garrison on my way to Strasbourg."

Charmiane couldn't stop gaping at him. She felt like a fool. And when he smiled at her, his eyes twinkling in delight at her consternation, she blushed again. "You...had a reason for going to Strasbourg?" she ventured, just to say something.

The twinkle became even more pronounced. "I thought I did. But after a week of my company, the bird flew the coop." He laughed at the look on her face. "I think I'll keep you blushing for the rest of the day!"

Bazaine cleared his throat. "I'll see to your rooms and a bath. Do you mean to stay for any length of time?"

"We marry on the twenty-sixth," murmured Charmiane. "Adam and I."

Noël's eyes were serious, lingering on her face. "Yes, I know. Adam told me."

"Will you stay until then, Monsieur Noël? I'm sure *monsieur le comte* would wish it."

"No. Only for a few days, Bazaine. I've been discharged. I intend to enjoy civilian life again. I thought I'd go back to Brittany. Rent a cottage by the sea for a month or so." His mouth twisted in a rueful smile. "Not quite as elegant as this place. But then I never had Brother Adam's talent for making money." He shrugged. "I'd hoped Adam would be here by now."

"Is there a reason you wish to see Monsieur de Moncalvo?"

Noël laughed. "What a snob you are, Bazaine! I think that 'de' pleases you more than it does Adam. And yes, you old paper-pusher, there's a reason to see Adam. He owes me money for a favor."

"I think I can see to the funds. But on one condition. That you not gamble at cards while you're here." Bazaine allowed himself a smirk. "I don't want to win it back."

How surprising, thought Charmiane. It was the most human, the most amusing thing Bazaine had ever allowed himself to say. There must be something in Noël that inspired such lighthearted-ness. Indeed, at dinner that night, seated across the table from him, she was struck by the way he joked and laughed with the footmen who served the meal and welcomed the flirtations of the little maids who followed them into the drawing room afterward and handed them coffee.

Charmiane shook her head as the maids retired giggling and casting glances back to Noël, who lounged against the chimney-piece. "You're quite wicked, you know."

His smile was warm and disarming. "Of course. But you knew that the first time we met. At the ball. When you succumbed to my charm."

She looked away. "I thought you were Adam," she said defensively.

"Not all the time, beautiful lady." He sighed. "Ah, well. You might have been mine if I'd moved faster than Adam."

It made her uncomfortable to remember. She had indeed found him attractive. It seemed such a disloyal thought, with Adam not here to claim his own. She played with the lace cuff of her green velvet gown, aware that he was watching her intently. It was too intimate a moment. He would be her brother-in-law. She should begin to sound like a sister. Concerned but impersonal. "We were so glad to hear you were safe, after Russia. It can't have been pleasant."

"Pleasant? God's teeth!" He slammed down his cup with such force that the coffee spilled into the saucer.

She stared at him. His face was contorted in anger. "You look just like Adam at this moment," she said. "All frowning."

He relaxed visibly. "Sorry. Russia was nothing to joke about. Not even for me."

"Yes. Adam's letters . . ."

"You were . . . pleased with Adam's letters?"

"Pleased?" The memory of his beautiful and heartbreaking words brought tears to her eyes.

"Mon Dieu," he said. "Lucky Adam." He rattled his cup. "Is there more coffee?" He came and sat beside her as she poured a fresh cup. "Bazaine says you ride. Shall we ride tomorrow?"

She nodded and rose from her seat. She found his closeness disconcerting. She crossed to a window and gazed out at the night. "I'm sorry you won't stay for the wedding."

He laughed. "No. I'm too jealous of Brother Adam."

She turned. "Nonsense. You don't mean that."

"I'm afraid I do," he said softly. His eyes were a smoky blue. She trembled. "You mustn't say such things."

"Why not?" He stared at her while the color rose to her cheeks. Then he laughed and turned away. "In truth, I'm easier to like, and we both know it. I shouldn't want Adam to be overshadowed on his own wedding day!"

He left three days later, bidding her farewell on the same terrace where he'd greeted her. Charmiane felt more alive and lighthearted than she had in weeks. They had laughed and ridden and played cards. There had never been a serious moment between them after that first night. She knew she'd miss him.

He bowed and kissed her hand. "Goodbye, beautiful lady. Are you sure I can't persuade you to give up Adam and marry me?"

She clicked her tongue. "Then what would all the maids do when you couldn't flirt anymore?"

He laughed. "I said marriage, not purgatory!"

She giggled. "You'd brazenly threaten faithlessness even before the marriage?"

"Of course. Man wasn't meant to be monogamous!" His carefree smile faded. "My God, you're beautiful." Before she could stop him, he had swept her into his arms. This time his kiss was hot and hungry, his mouth moving over hers with an urgency that took her breath away.

She pushed against him and broke free of his embrace. Shaken and confused, she could only stare at him dumbly.

Noël grinned. "Lucky Adam." He saluted her, leaped to his horse and disappeared down the drive.

Charmiane glanced at the sky and shivered. A hard and gray light, with a cold stillness that matched the winter-dead landscape. She should have listened to Paterne, one of the grooms, who had warned her a storm was brewing. She wheeled her horse about and made for the woods that stood between her and Bonneval.

Despite the ominous certainty of the sky, she prayed that it wouldn't snow. It was already the twenty-fifth of February, and Adam hadn't yet come home. If the roads became impassable...*Ah, Dieu,* she couldn't bear the waiting much longer!

The first large, soft flakes of snow dotted the plum velvet of her riding coat as she emerged from the woods. By the time she reached Bonneval, the gravel drive was covered in a thin layer of white, and the air was thick with swirling snow. She was surprised that Paterne or one of the other grooms wasn't waiting on her return, standing at attention in front of the stable: Bazaine was quite rigid as to their duties. But the wide gate that led to the stable yard was open. She slid from her horse and led the animal through, brushing at the cold flakes that touched her face.

There was an unfamiliar coach in the yard and, more surprising, a dozen idle grooms and servants standing about. Coatless, hatless, in tight-knit groups, they hugged their shirtsleeves and shuffled their feet against the cold, but otherwise they seemed to be rooted where they stood. She followed their gaze and nearly cried aloud for joy.

This time there was no mistaking the uniform. It was bright green, where Noël's had been dark, and the silver epaulets and braid and buttons were the trappings of an officer.

"Adam," she whispered, and made a move to run to him. Then she stopped, peering through the snowfall to take in the whole scene.

She was aware suddenly that Adam's scowling face was bent to a man lying at his feet. Charmiane gasped aloud. Paterne! Both his eyes were swollen shut, and blood poured from a torn and ragged lip. His shirt was open; Charmiane could see red welts and bruises around his ribs and flabby belly. My God, she thought. What had happened to him? An accident with a horse? Why was no one helping? Even as she stared, bewildered, Adam reached down and hauled Paterne to his feet. Had the groom been able to stand, he would have been dwarfed by the other man, who towered above him. Adam held him erect with one hand, curled his other hand into a fist and smashed it into the groom's face. The sound of Paterne's howl didn't quite drown out the loud crack of the bones in his nose.

"Adam! *Mon Dieu!*" Horrified, Charmiane dashed forward. "Stop! In the name of God, stop!"

At her words, Adam released Paterne and swung around to her. His eyes glowed with fury. "Damn it to hell!" he barked. "What the deuce are you doing here?"

"Adam, I . . ."

"Get out of here, woman!"

"But, Paterne . . . Adam, please. Stop!" Her voice shook.

He took a menacing step forward. His voice dropped to a growl that was more frightening than his roar had been. "Get inside and wait for me. This is none of your concern."

Trembling, she fled into the château. She started up the stairs to the refuge of her suite, then changed her mind. No. For her own safety, she mustn't cross him. She had known he was a strong man, a determined man, even a man of dark moods; she hadn't been aware of his terrifying temper. Now she could imagine him storming into her rooms and dragging her out by the hair. Meekly she went into the small drawing room, where a cheery fire blazed. The snow on her riding coat had begun to melt and soak through, but it would have to wait. Her first duty was to try to placate him. She rang for a maid and ordered coffee to be brought, then called the girl back and had her fetch some cognac, as well.

She had managed to compose her turbulent emotions by the time Adam found her. He was wrapping a handkerchief around his bruised and bloody knuckles. He shook the snow from his tunic and silently allowed her to help him out of it. His expression was guarded, and as cold as the day beyond the high windows. When she would have turned away to put down his tunic, he stopped her, his hand a brutal clamp on her arm. "I don't intend ever again to be countermanded in front of inferiors. *Do you understand?*"

She took a steadying breath. "Yes, of course. But why Paterne?"

"The man is a rogue and a villain. That's all you need to know."

"But it seemed so cruel..."

His eyes narrowed. "Must I be crossed in private, as well?"

She was finding it hard to hold back her tears. "Please," she said, pulling away from him. "My jacket is damp and cold." She stripped it off and went to stand before the fire, gazing disconsolately into the blue-tipped flames. She felt his hands on her arms, unexpectedly soft and caressing.

"This was not the kind of homecoming I anticipated," he murmured in her ear. "I'm sorry you had to see that scene."

"Adam." She turned around. Instead of giving her room, he pressed even closer so that she would have had to step into the hearth to avoid him. He rested his arms lightly on her shoulders. His physical presence was so much larger, stronger, more overpowering than she remembered. The contrast to Noël, so insouciant and nonthreatening, was remarkable. Even the way he stood before her, giving no quarter, was intimidating. But his eyes were soft and focused on her lips; perhaps the scene in the stable yard had made her misjudge him. She reminded herself that she loved this man. She managed to smile. "Why didn't you write to me? After Russia?"

His expression was bland. "I did."

"No, but... they weren't the same. After."

He frowned. "*Bon Dieu.* You asked for letters. You got them. What more did you expect?"

"But your letters from Russia..."

"What about them?" He looked bored with the whole matter.

"Nothing." What could she say? He was being deliberately difficult and obtuse. She felt an odd sense of loss, almost sorry to have poured out her heart in her letters. Clearly *he* regretted it.

"Do you yet have them?" he asked sharply.

She gulped away her grief. It still hurt. "No. Armand burned them when he found them."

He shrugged. "Well, after all, they were just words."

"But such sweet words," she whispered.

"Words are a waste of time," he growled. His arms tightened around her and his mouth captured hers. It was a hard kiss, possessive and demanding; as he moved his lips against hers she could feel the rough scratch of his unshaven chin on her face. And he'd been drinking. There was the sour tang of alcohol in her mouth when he thrust with his impassioned tongue. She stiffened in his embrace, feeling strangely violated, and waited for him to release her.

He let her go at last and strode to the table that held the cognac. She studied him as he poured himself a glass and tossed it back in one swallow. She hadn't noticed that he needed a shave until he had kissed her; now she saw that his hair was straggly and unkempt, as well. He looked tense and exhausted, and his waistcoat hung on a frame that seemed thinner than she remembered. His cravat was carelessly tied, and his white pantaloons and Hessian boots were splashed with mud—and Paterne's blood.

She shivered. Everything about him was rough, coarse, crude. His kiss, his beard, the hard, angry expression on his face. She found it impossible to reconcile the gentle man of the letters, her sweet Adam, with the brutish man who had returned to her.

He poured himself another glass of liquor. "Have you finished your examination?"

She laughed uneasily. "Examination? Really, I'm not . . ."

He sighed in exasperation. "Spare me your denials. You've examined me. And now you're disappointed."

"Of course not, Adam. Why should I be?"

His eyes swept her body, lingering on her face, then dropping to the curve of her bosom beneath her snug riding waistcoat. "I'm not," he said. His voice was thick with desire.

She tried not to show her dismay. Was that what he had come back for and nothing more? Her sexual favors?

His lip curled in a mocking smile. "*That* hasn't changed. Not a bit. That face of yours that tells everything. My God. I don't disappoint you. I can see that. I disgust you! *N'est-ce pas?*"

Why did her face always betray her? She clasped her hands together and stared down at her entwined fingers. "It . . . it will take time. To learn to know each other."

"I have no time," he said coldly. "I want the life I've earned with my blood and tears. I want you, willing and loyal. I want children. Can you live with that? Or do you want to go home now, and tell me it was all a mistake?"

"Name of God, Adam. Have a little pity."

His voice softened momentarily. "The curé is coming tomorrow. I only want you to be sure you've made the right choice." His eyes glinted with a sudden, dangerous light. "But if you choose me, know who I am. And what I am. *And never look at me that way again!*" He whirled to the fireplace and tossed his glass against the andirons. The cognac flared up with an explosive burst.

Her lip trembled. She *would* go home. There was nothing here for her. Only a hard stranger. She glared her defiance. Let him read that on her face! *"Monsieur,"* she began coldly. The word was like a challenge. And he knew it. She could tell by the way his jawline tightened. Well, let the battle be joined here and now. And then she'd go.

"Ahem." Bazaine stood at the door, a small portfolio in his hands. *"Monsieur le comte.* Letters to sign. That property in Normandy. Will you do it now or later?"

Adam never took his eyes from Charmiane's face. "Later. Go away."

"I've had your carriage emptied and the trunks unpacked. Will you bathe now?"

"Damn you, Bazaine!" growled Adam. "Are you deaf?"

Bazaine held his ground. "I may be blind in one eye, but there's nothing the matter with my hearing. Or my sight. *Monsieur le comte* has had a long and tiring journey," he said pointedly. "Sometimes, a strategic withdrawal . . ." He shrugged and allowed himself a small indulgent smile. "Will you bathe now?"

Adam wavered, then conceded, dragging his angry glance away from Charmiane's face. He sighed and rubbed at his eyes. "Sleep first. It *was* a long ride." He strode to Charmiane and took her hand in his, then pressed it to his lips in an unexpected kiss. His touch, his voice were gentle, a reminder of that long-ago Adam. "Perhaps we can start again at dinner."

She watched him go, wondering whether she should call him back, end it now. Go home to Sophie, her pride in her hands. Beg to be returned to Armand's good graces and make a life as Domfort's wife.

Fool! What was she thinking of? It must have been as uncomfortable and difficult for Adam as for her, their meeting. To come home to a strange house, a woman he scarcely knew, the trivial and unfamiliar life of a country gentleman after the excitement and danger of war. Bazaine had been wiser than either of them. She wondered if his interruption had been purely accidental.

It was a changed Adam who took his seat opposite her at dinner. Shaved, his hair trimmed, the tenseness clearly eased away by a bath and a nap. The severe uniform had been replaced by handsome evening clothes that gave him an air of elegant informality. He even managed to smile in that awkward way that she had found so endearing at the Tuileries.

She tried not to notice that his fist was bruised, that the knuckles that had beaten Paterne so savagely were covered with small scratches and scabs where the flesh had split from the force of his blows. The maids had gossiped as they helped her to dress. Paterne had been dismissed, sent back to his village this very night—no matter the storm nor his own terrible injuries. No one seemed to know what had driven the master to it; but there was general agreement, below stairs, that this Bouchard twin was a man to fear.

Adam cleared his throat, and a pale-faced, quaking footman was immediately at his elbow. "*Monsieur le comte*. Sir?"

"The glasses are empty. They are *never* to be empty at this table." Adam waited for his wineglass to be filled, tasted the wine appreciatively, then finished the whole glass. It was immediately refilled. He nodded his approval and looked across at Charmiane. "Are you pleased with Bonneval?"

"Very much. Aren't you?"

"I bought it for you. To remind you of the old days."

She smiled gently. "I don't remember the old days."

"A vestigial memory, then. Common to your kind. Bonneval seemed fitting for a *comtesse*. Who should have been a *marquise*, except for people like me. Parvenus. Upstarts. Wasn't that your brother's word?"

She bit her lip, turned aside his sarcasm. "I would have hoped you bought Bonneval to please yourself."

He shrugged. "I've slept on snow and bare floors." He looked about the lavishly appointed dining salon. "But I do like it. Yes." He lapsed into a silence that persisted until the first course had been served then cleared. Once or twice Charmiane tried to engage him in conversation, praising the cook's skills, deploring the still-falling snow; but he only nodded in response. He began on the soup, watching her intently as though he wished to speak. At length he put down his spoon and motioned his bowl away with a sweep of his fingers. "Bazaine tells me you visited rooms on the rue du Paon. Several times. From the comings and goings, he suspected that there was something not quite legal happening there. Or, at the least, dangerous to you. Is that so?" he demanded.

She felt her cheeks redden. "Of...of course not. I knew some people there. That's all."

"Your brother, among others, Bazaine said." His eyes bored into her while she tried desperately to think of a convincing lie. Mercifully the next course was being served. She waited, staring at her plate, until the servants had withdrawn; then she picked up her fork and pretended to find her food of interest.

He cleared his throat. "No matter," he said quietly. "But I forbid...that is, I don't wish you to return to the rue du Paon. Is your aunt pleased with her subsidy?"

"I don't know. She hasn't answered any of my letters."

He drank from his wineglass and laughed sharply. "That hasn't kept her from taking the money, Bazaine tells me. So much for the honor of the *Ancien Régime*."

"Will you judge us all by one unfortunate old woman?"

"No. Nor your brother, who's probably enjoying my largesse, as well."

She shook her head. "Not Armand!" Her voice rose in her brother's defense. "He has only the highest principles. That's why he's still poor today. Because he couldn't bend. Not like some of the other old aristocrats, who take positions in the new government just to get their titles back. And toady to..."

He laughed at her sudden silence. "To men like me. Upstarts. Isn't that what you were going to say?"

"Oh, must we talk politics? It matters very little to me." She lifted her chin proudly, defiantly. "Just don't speak of my dear brother in that voice."

He leaned back in his chair and stared at her. A look so strange, so still and secret, that it made her stir uncomfortably. He took another drink of his wine, dabbed at his lips with his napkin and folded the square of linen with deliberate hands. "Let's speak of *my* dear brother, then."

Her eyes shot to his face, then she looked away. "There's nothing to speak about," she said quickly. Too quickly, she thought. It made her sound guilty. "He visited for a few days, and then he went away."

"But not before you greeted him with a kiss. Very... impassioned, I'm given to understand."

Ah, Dieu! She didn't want him to be jealous of his own brother! Not when there was no reason. "Adam, my dear," she said gently. "I thought he was you."

He cocked a mocking eyebrow. "Really? Then who did you think *I* was when you suffered my kiss this afternoon in the drawing room?"

She covered her eyes with her hand. Why was he so cruel? "This afternoon I was upset about Paterne, and you, and...name of God, Adam, don't start again."

He swore under his breath. "Not tears. For God's sake, not tears! A woman's ultimate weapon."

Sobbing, she fled the room. He followed after her and caught her at the foot of the grand staircase. "Let me go," she cried, struggling in his arms. "My tears weren't meant to soften you."

"I'm a fool," he said, and pressed her to his broad chest. His arms were warm and strong; for the first time since his return she felt cherished. She sighed and relaxed in his embrace. "I meant to give you your wedding present as soon as you sat down," he said gruffly. "Perhaps I should have. I seem to have said the wrong things every time I opened my mouth. Here." He held her away from him, reached into his waistcoat pocket and pulled out a flat velvet box.

She opened it with trembling fingers and gasped in wonder. Within was the most magnificent diamond necklace she had ever seen: a dozen huge stones linked together with silver and gold mountings and supporting in the center an oval diamond pendant the size of a robin's egg.

"Oh, Adam!" She brushed away her tears. "Oh, Adam, it's beautiful. Put it on me." She turned her back to him and smiled to feel his hands fumbling with the catch. If she only remembered that he was a soldier and clumsy with women, she could avoid awkward, angry scenes. In his own way, he needed to be soothed and indulged quite as much as Henri. She turned around and put her arms about his neck. "Can my thank-you kiss be a proper welcoming kiss, as well?"

"Charmiane." He pulled her close, and when their lips met, the anger, the rancor, the long bitter months of separation melted away. His mouth was sweet—exploring, not demanding. Waiting until she parted her lips before his tongue claimed sweet entrance. Timidly she touched his tongue with her own and felt his hard body tremble. A passionate quivering that matched her own unsteadiness. At last he pulled away, only to bury his lips at her neck and press frenzied kisses onto the soft flesh of her shoulders. He groaned. "Charmiane," he whispered again. His arms tightened around her, touching the back of her bodice where the deep V met her bare skin.

"What are you doing?" She stiffened in surprise and wrenched herself out of his arms, her fingers searching at her back to find the hooks he had begun to open.

He looked around the open vestibule and made a gruff sound in his throat. "I'm sorry. We'll go to my rooms."

"Your rooms?"

"It was stupid of me. I should have realized you'd want privacy," he muttered.

"Adam, no. Not your rooms."

"Then where?" he growled impatiently, reaching for her again.

Did her face show her dismay? "Nowhere! We're not even married yet. This isn't right." It didn't feel right, his ugly haste.

His expression registered surprise, then annoyance. "I don't remember that those were your sentiments in the Tuileries Gardens!"

"The Tuileries . . . !" His words struck her like another insult. She felt a burning shame for having submitted to him in the Tuileries. A regret that was deeper now than the morning after the ball. She fought against fresh tears. "Have you so little regard for my honor?"

The blue eyes glittered as hard and cold as a winter sky. He drew himself erect—even without the uniform he was a soldier—clicked his heels and made a little bow. "As you said this afternoon, we need time to understand each other. I trust this sudden reticence is a passing thing. The nervousness of a bride."

For all his icy stare, she thought she saw a flicker of pain and bewilderment. "When we're married, dearest, I won't lock my door to you," she said to soothe him.

Her words had the opposite effect. His face darkened. "If ever you contemplate it—locking your door—you'll regret it." It seemed less a threat than the bravado of a man needing reassurance.

She reached up and touched his cheek. "Not my door, and not my heart, Adam. I swear it."

He stared, the frown lines relaxing between his brows. Then he took her hand in his, turned it over and pressed his lips to her palm. "Until tomorrow." He turned on his heel and strode away.

The snow was a white blanket in the morning, covering the fields with its thick silence. But the sun shone brightly, its warmth challenging winter's grip; by the time Adam rode out with Bazaine to inspect his new estate and meet his tenants, the snow had already begun to melt. Charmiane stayed in her suite in morning dishabille, receiving a steady stream of reports from her maids. Before he had gone out, Monsieur le Comte de Moncalvo had spent hours touring his château, poking into every corner, asking questions, making demands. It was impossible to know if one pleased him; it was only painfully apparent when he was dissatisfied. More than one chambermaid had been reduced to tears this morning, and *monsieur*'s own valet begged to be released from his duties in favor of his cousin, who had a stronger disposition.

"As though his money gives him the right to be high and mighty and treat people like dung," sniffed Yvonne, the young girl who had been assigned by Bazaine to be Charmiane's personal maid. She smiled nervously at Charmiane. "You won't tell him I said that, *madame*?"

Charmiane frowned. "If you think he shouldn't hear it, you shouldn't have said it to begin with." She was beginning to find Yvonne entirely too free with her opinions. It was a line that Jeanine would never cross.

"Well, it's only that . . . it's hard to believe that he and his brother can share the exact same face and yet be so different! I swear that not a soul could tell them apart if *monsieur le comte* weren't such a monster!"

"Yvonne . . ." There was warning in Charmiane's tone.

The maid bobbed a curtsy. "I'm sorry, *madame*. But Monsieur Bazaine is the only one I know who can abide the one brother as easily as the other!"

"Monsieur Bazaine has known them both for years. Enough chatter now. Help me bathe and dress for my wedding."

The gown she had had made for the occasion was in deep yellow satin with thick bands of silk roses at the hem. She'd chosen it to remind him of her Tuileries gown; now she was almost sorry. Yvonne dressed her hair in a braided coronet with ringlets at the temples and forehead. Over it, instead of a veil, she wore a triangle of sheer embroidered muslin tied under the chin with its point grazing her forehead. The diamond necklace was almost too much, overpowering the delicacy of the dress with its large stones. Stolen from some unfortunate Italian matron? she thought. She forced the ugly notion from her brain. Today was her wedding day. She should be full of joy.

Bazaine bustled into her sitting room and smiled his approval. "You look sunny and gay in that gown, *madame*. *Monsieur le comte* is waiting in the chapel, with several guests who have been invited. The gentry who live nearby. It seemed an opportunity to meet your neighbors." He offered his arm. "May I escort you?"

She hesitated. "My . . . aunt isn't there, is she?"

"I'm sorry, *madame*. Only *monsieur*'s guests."

She tried to smile. "I'm sure it's only because the snow made the journey impossible from Paris."

"Of course, *madame*. Shall we go?"

Adam was waiting at the altar, standing stiffly in his dress uniform. Glittering braid and epaulets, polished boots, officer's *chapeau bras* under one arm, elegant ceremonial sword. He had put on all his decorations, his campaign ribbons, the gold star and red ribbon of the Legion of Honor. It made him seem all the more distant from Charmiane; the great officer condescending to take a bride.

She sighed in resignation. She had burned her bridges behind her, and she would have to find enough in this moody and reserved man to fill the emptiness left by her lost life.

They knelt together, they listened to the curé intone the words; and when at last the ceremony was over, Adam bent and kissed her formally on both cheeks. Bazaine ushered them into the reception hall, which had been arranged for dining with a long table, upon which sat a large, tiered wedding cake. They were presented to the company, "Monsieur et Madame Bouchard, le Comte et la Comtesse de Moncalvo," and the guests crowded around to be introduced and to welcome them to the parish.

The wedding feast was long and tedious. With the purchase of Bonneval, Adam was now the ranking aristocrat in the district. The curé fawned over him, and the locals—several *barons* and minor officials, recent appointees to judge by their appalling manners and gaudy, tasteless dress—smiled and bowed and made much of *monsieur le comte* and his bride. The wives were even worse, plucking at Charmiane's gown to admire the latest style and fabric from Paris and inviting themselves to some future tea—along with their seamstresses, who would be delighted, if it pleased Madame de Moncalvo, to copy one or two designs from her wardrobe. For the first time she understood what Armand had meant: these were not her kind. She'd be hard-pressed to find a friend among them who could bring her the same companionship as Sophie or Bertrand or any of the other émigrés of the Faubourg Saint-Germain.

Adam sat opposite her at the end of the long table, silent and withdrawn. His few responses to their guests were curt and sharp, so they began to recoil from him almost as much as the servants did and turn at once to their neighbors to pass an innocuous remark.

Sometimes Charmiane caught him staring at her with his smoldering gaze. She remembered the Tuileries again. He had looked at her in just that way on that long-ago night. She had thought then it was a look of burning devotion, the communion of a kindred soul. But perhaps her innate romanticism had clothed the look in beauty. For surely what she saw now was only lust, the hungers of an impatient lover.

At length he cleared his throat. "*Monsieur le curé*, Bazaine tells me it has begun to snow again. You're welcome, of course, to stay here. But I mark that you said you wished to return to the village tonight, so you can work on your sermon tomorrow. And the snow will be impassable if you delay much longer." It was an adroit dismissal, if abrupt.

The curé nodded and rose to his feet. "Yes, yes. I do like a full Saturday to collect my thoughts. Will we see you in church, *monsieur le comte*? It would be our honor. Such a grand gentleman."

Adam smiled, his eyes distant. "Why don't I send you in my coach? It will be more comfortable than your horse." He held out his hands to the other guests in a gesture that clearly invited them to leave the table. "If you follow behind in your carriages, the path through the snow will be easier. Bazaine, see to my heavy coach for *monsieur le curé*." He stood at his place, barely concealing his impatience, as the guests bid *au revoir* and filed out.

But when he was alone in the room with Charmiane, he suddenly seemed ill at ease. He cleared his throat, ran his finger along the carved back of his chair and cleared his throat again. "I have a few dispatches to write this evening, *madame*," he said at last. "I'll join you in your rooms in a little while." He inclined his head in a little bow, reached across the table for the decanter of wine, picked it up along with his glass and went out of the room toward his library, which looked out onto the gardens.

Charmiane had her maids prepare her quickly for bed: her black hair hanging loose and full down her back as he had longed to see it, her modest white muslin nightdress covered with a pale blue silk velvet dressing gown that accented her womanly curves. She wanted to please him tonight. If his attraction to her was based largely on their sexual encounter in the Tuileries, a passionate and satisfying wedding night was not such a terrible way to begin to build a marriage. And though it seemed improbable, she wondered if his story about the dispatches was just that: a story to cover the fact that he was as unsure of her tonight as she was of him.

Indeed, as the time ticked by, marked by the bronze and malachite clock on her mantel, she became more than ever convinced of it. Her maids had been dismissed and sent to bed, the noises in the château had died down, and still Adam didn't appear. She had been sitting in bed, propped against the pillows, concentrating in vain on the book of poetry in her hands. Now she threw off the coverlet, put on her peignoir and mules and went in search of her husband.

The corridor was dim, with only a few candles to light the way; she could hear the whisper of the snow falling beyond the dark windows at either end. A footman stood outside of Adam's suite, leaning tiredly against the wall but ready to spring to attention should the master appear. That meant that Adam was still in his library downstairs. She accepted the salute of the footman, passed him without a word and descended the broad staircase.

She heard noises as she neared the library. Loud voices, the crash of furniture, the unmistakable crystal-sharp sound of breaking glass. Two servants stood outside the door, their faces white with fear. At Charmiane's approach they shuffled nervously and closed ranks, blocking her way.

"Open the door for me," she ordered.

The footman's voice shook. "*Madame.* Begging your pardon, but we've been forbidden. *Monsieur le comte...*"

A loud cry from behind the door, a drawn-out cry of agony, interrupted him. Then there was silence, as chilling as the cry had been.

Charmiane trembled. The voice, familiar and well loved, had turned her blood to ice. "Step aside!" she shrilled, and pushed past the servants to open the door herself.

The room was in shambles, furniture overturned, papers scattered about. In the center of the room, Bertrand de Domfort knelt amid the chaos, cradling Armand in his arms. An Armand whose coat front bubbled blood like an underground spring rising to the surface of the earth. An Armand who gasped, moving his lips to form words that refused to come forth.

And above this ghastly tableau loomed Adam, his sword drawn and still dripping gore, his face set in an evil scowl, as though the mortal blow he'd just delivered weren't enough to satisfy him.

"Armand!" Charmiane shrieked and dropped to her knees before her brother. It seemed a useless gesture, but she lifted the hem of her nightdress and pressed the muslin against his wound.

FREE BOOKS!

FREE GIFTS!

PLAY THE "LUCKY 7" SLOT MACHINE GAME !

AND YOU COULD GET FREE BOOKS, A FREE VICTORIAN PICTURE FRAME AND A SURPRISE GIFT!

NO COST! NO OBLIGATION TO BUY!
NO PURCHASE NECESSARY!

PLAY "LUCKY 7"
AND GET AS MANY AS SIX FREE GIFTS...

HOW TO PLAY:

1. With a coin, carefully scratch off the silver box at the right. This makes you eligible to receive one or more free books, and possibly other gifts, depending on what is revealed beneath the scratch-off area.

2. You'll receive brand-new Harlequin Historical™ novels. When you return this card, we'll send you the books and gifts you qualify for *absolutely free*!

3. If we don't hear from you, every other month we'll send you 4 additional novels to read and enjoy. You can return them and owe nothing but if you decide to keep them, you'll pay only $2.89* per book, a savings of 36¢ each off the cover price. There is *no* extra charge for postage and handling. There are no hidden extras.

4. When you join the Harlequin Reader Service®, you'll get our subscribers' only newsletter, as well as additional free gifts from time to time just for being a subscriber.

5. You must be completely satisfied. You may cancel at any time simply by sending us a note or a shipping statement marked "cancel" or returning any shipment to us at our cost.

This lovely Victorian pewter-finish miniature is perfect for displaying a treasured photograph— and it's yours absolutely free—when you accept our no-risk offer.

PLAY "LUCKY 7"

**Just scratch off the silver box with a coin.
Then check below to see which gifts you get.**

YES! I have scratched off the silver box. Please send me all the gifts for which I qualify. I understand I am under no obligation to purchase any books, as explained on the opposite page.

(U-H-H-12/90) 246 CIH YA32

NAME

ADDRESS   APT

CITY   STATE   ZIP

7 7 7	WORTH FOUR FREE BOOKS, FREE VICTORIAN PICTURE FRAME AND MYSTERY BONUS
🍒 🍒 🍒	WORTH FOUR FREE BOOKS AND MYSTERY BONUS
● ● ●	WORTH FOUR FREE BOOKS
🔔 🔔 🍒	WORTH TWO FREE BOOKS

HARLEQUIN "NO RISK" GUARANTEE

- You're not required to buy a single book—ever!
- You must be completely satisfied or you may cancel at any time simply by sending us a note or a shipping statement marked "cancel" or returning any shipment to us at our cost. Either way, you will receive no more books; you'll have no further obligation.
- The free books and gifts you receive from this "Lucky 7" offer remain yours to keep no matter what you decide.

If offer card is missing, write to:
Harlequin Reader Service, 3010 Walden Ave., P.O. Box 1867, Buffalo, N.Y. 14269-1867

She looked wildly at Domfort, desperate to read denial in his face, denial of the evidence of her own eyes.

Bertrand blinked at his tears. "Charmiane, I'm sorry. I tried to keep him away."

Armand groped for her hand with bloodstained fingers. *"C'est fini,"* he whispered.

"No, dear heart," she sobbed. She looked up at Adam, her face twisted in grief and hatred. "Assassin! Will you send for a doctor, at least?"

He stared at her, then dropped his sword and turned away. "It won't matter. On a night like this..."

"Upstart! Hireling of the Tyrant!" cried Domfort. "He never had a chance, Charmiane. With his crippled leg." He glanced around the disordered room, at Armand's bloodless sword, which lay at his feet. "But he fought bravely. Like a true nobleman."

Armand had begun to wheeze, his mouth opening and closing in a helpless attempt to speak once more. He lifted one trembling hand, the hand that held his ring with its precious contents. "Take... take..." he gasped.

Charmiane slipped the ring from his finger and put it on her own hand. "I'll wear it always, dear heart. I swear it. Do you see?" But her words were in vain. With a final gasp, Armand twitched violently, then sagged in Domfort's arms, his eyes squeezed tight against a world that had brought him so much pain.

Charmiane stared at her hand: at Armand's ring, smeared with his blood; at Adam's ring next to it. She rose unsteadily to her feet and glared at Adam's back.

"Look at me!" she shrieked. "Look at me, you murderer!"

He turned. "Charmiane," he began, "will you listen to me?"

"To hear what? How you killed a cripple? Here. Here!" She fumbled with her wedding ring, tore it from her finger and flung it at him. "Let me tell the world that your bride curses you. That she'll never forgive you. That she wishes you dead for the evil you've done tonight!" She couldn't bear to look at Armand for another minute, at the way he lay so still, his thin face twisted in its final agony. She felt as though she'd choke in this room. With a wail, she rushed to the glass doors leading to the garden and thrust them open. She dashed out into the night, ignoring Adam's warning cry behind her. Her nightdress, where it had soaked in Armand's blood, was cold and wet against her legs; in a few moments the rest of her clothing was as wet, pelted by the icy snow, which was turning to sleet.

Adam was suddenly there, reaching for her. "No, no, no!" she screamed. She tore herself from his grasp, raised her arms in supplication to the sky that covered her with its icy tears and collapsed into insensibility at Adam's feet.

Chapter Eleven

It was three days before she felt well enough to lift her head from her pillow; a week before she allowed Bazaine to speak of arrangements for Armand's funeral and burial. A simple service in Paris, with a weeping Aunt Sophie refusing to speak to her, a pathetic, lonely burial—far from the lost lands and tombs of Chevrillon—in the little cemetery of Saint-Jacques, then back again to Bonneval and the welcome isolation of her suite.

Adam had left Bonneval the morning after Armand's death; now Bazaine told her he had gone to stay at his *hôtel* in Paris until Charmiane should recover from the shock of her brother's passing.

"His murder, you mean," she said bitterly.

"*Madame*, I wasn't there. Nor were you. I feel sure that *monsieur le comte* is burdened with regret at what happened."

"Does he know I never want to see him again?"

"I don't know *monsieur*'s thoughts on the matter. But let me urge you, *madame*, to put this behind you."

She paused, unsure of how to proceed. "Do you…think he'll let me divorce him?" she said at last.

Bazaine looked shocked. "*Madame*, you were married in the Church!"

"Bah! The Upstart allowed it, when he wished to throw over his Josephine!"

"*Madame*, whatever the Emperor granted himself, I think *you* had better put it out of your mind." His words held a finality, as though he had no wish to pursue the subject.

"Why?" she demanded. She would give him no quarter.

"Because—" he rubbed at his one good eye "—*monsieur le comte* has already told me how he wished to deal with the matter if you raised it." He shrugged in apology. "He forbids a divorce. And the laws of the Empire give him that power."

Her heart sank. She knew it was so, that her only hope of being free of Adam was if *he* permitted it. Under Napoleon's code, wives had far less control of their own affairs than they'd enjoyed under the Monarchy. And now she was trapped—bound to a detested husband who made Henri seem almost benign. She glared at Bazaine. "What *am* I allowed?"

Bazaine looked insulted. "*Madame*, you're not a prisoner. You have the freedom of Bonneval and the parish."

"And Paris?" she persisted.

"Not the *hôtel* when *monsieur le comte* is there. But at other times."

"I wasn't thinking of that. But if Aunt Sophie will forgive me, I should like . . ." She gulped back tears of misery. "I should like to see her sometimes. And my old friends."

"Of course, *madame*," he said gently. "I'm sure an escort . . ."

"No! I don't want your people spying on me. Do you understand?"

He nodded reluctantly. "Will there be anything more?"

"Money. Has Adam made any arrangements?"

"A clothing allowance of fifty thousand francs a year, and ten thousand for your own purse. I will continue to oversee the households, so that you need not be bothered with those expenses. And Madame de Chevrillon's allowance is to be maintained."

"I want it doubled," she said boldly. "Without Armand . . ." Her grief overwhelmed her and she buried her face in her hands. Dear Armand. Dear heart. And now she was forced to share her life with the man who'd killed him. She lifted her head, staring angrily at Bazaine through her tears. Her life, perhaps. But not her bed. "I have the freedom of Bonneval, you said. Very well. I wish to move my rooms. Put me into the east pavilion. One of the guest suites will do very well for me."

Bazaine scowled—just like his master, thought Charmiane—and shook his head. "*Madame*," he said, his voice edged with warning, "do you understand what you're doing?"

She took a deep breath. Damn Adam, forever and ever! "Yes," she said icily. "I hope my husband understands, as well."

It took several weeks of notes to Aunt Sophie before a reconciliation of sorts was effected. Adam still hadn't returned: Bazaine said his letters indicated he was spending a great deal of time with the Emperor and his general staff at Saint-Cloud, preparing a new offensive. It seemed a good time to visit Aunt Sophie. Charmiane penned a letter begging her aunt to receive her and was glad to get an answering assent.

It was a blustery March day. Armand had been dead for nearly a month. Charmiane dressed in a somber gray gown. She hadn't ordered mourning clothes; they seemed an unnecessary show to the world. She'd always mourn Armand in her heart.

Number six rue de la Planche looked much the same—the slovenly concierge, the slightly seedy old building. The scrawny elm tree in the courtyard had begun to swell with spring buds. Charmiane nodded at Darnaud, who had escorted her into the courtyard, and bade him go away and return for her in three hours' time.

"But, *madame* . . ." he protested.

"I don't plan to flee from Monsieur Bazaine's clutches," she said with sarcasm. "Find a café where you and the coachman can have something warm to drink. I'll expect you here at five." She went inside and climbed a broad staircase to the first-floor apartment, where a small card on the door, embossed with the Chevrillon crest, announced the presence of Aunt Sophie. Jeanine, handsomely costumed in a servant's uniform, let her in and took her redingote.

"Right this way, *madame la comtesse*," she said grandly. "Madame de Chevrillon is in the drawing room." She allowed herself a satisfied smirk. "I live here now, you know. In my own room." She flung wide the double doors to the drawing room and curtsied as Charmiane passed through. Forever the snob, thought Charmiane, surprised that she could find it so amusing. But a bit of humor at least would make this difficult meeting more endurable.

Aunt Sophie sat in regal splendor upon a brocaded sofa, in a large, high-ceilinged room with gilded paneling and heavy, fringed-silk draperies at the windows. Everything in it—from the elaborately carved mirrors to the Sevres porcelain vases and candelabra to the Aubusson carpets on the floor—recalled the elegance of the old aristocracy, if not the vast sums of money. A young footman in livery with a powdered wig and silk bows on his knee breeches was handing around cups of tea to the dozen or so guests who paid court to Aunt Sophie. Charmiane hurried forward to kiss her aunt on the cheek.

She was greeted with a sigh and a tear. "How are you, *Liebchen*?"

"As well as can be expected, Aunt Sophie." She cast her eyes around the drawing room. "This is lovely. I'm so glad you were able to move downstairs to these fine rooms."

"Oh, well. We manage as best we can, my dear. Not like the old days, but it will have to do." Sophie waved a pudgy hand about the room. "It's all secondhand, of course."

Charmiane felt a pang of guilt. "Isn't it enough? The money?"

"Hmph! Eight thousand francs! Armand used to say it was barely more than the villain's annual stipend for the Legion of Honor! But I suppose if it's all he can spare..."

"I've asked them to give you more."

Aunt Sophie dabbed at her eyes. "Well, if it will ease your conscience to have it so..."

"Sophie, please." She straightened, forced a smile. "I'm not sure I know all your guests. Will you introduce me?"

It was clear that Aunt Sophie's new financial position had given her the opportunity to expand her social circle. Whereas before she had avoided the more well-to-do émigrés, uncomfortable that she couldn't return their hospitality in kind, now the names she presented to Charmiane came from some of the finer old families of the *Ancien Régime.*

But whether they were proud and fortuneless members of the Royalist opposition, as Armand had been, or quite comfortable with their titles newly restored through judicious cultivation of the Upstart, they all shared one point of view: a deep contempt for the new aristocracy. It was in their witticisms, their sly gossip, their use of birth, not money, as a measurement. Each time one of them sneered Charmiane's name— "Madame la *Comtesse* de Moncalvo" —she felt like a betrayer of her class. What could she say, moving among them in a gown that most of them could never afford: "I'm one of you? My marriage was a horrible mistake?"

The talk turned to the war. The Emperor, it was said, was running out of men after the Russian debacle; he was already calling up the Class of 1814 for conscription. Fifteen- and sixteen-year-olds that they scornfully called "Marie-Louises," after Bonaparte's Empress. But perhaps the circumstances of war would prove favorable to *madame la comtesse*'s husband? Did she anticipate being addressed as *madame la maréchale* someday? A title, at least, that would be earned on the battlefield.

"Of course," sniffed one of the women, "perhaps *monsieur le comte* chose marriage so he could claim exemption from military service. I'm given to understand that the number of claimants has doubled this year alone!''

Charmiane felt the need to defend herself, if not her husband. "I don't think that's what Monsieur de Moncalvo had in mind.''

"Oh,'' Sophie moaned softly and dabbed at her forehead with a black-edged lace handkerchief. "Will you kill me, *Liebchen*? Don't ever mention that man's name in this house. He has ended the Chevrillon line.''

I should never have come, thought Charmiane miserably. She had already decided to send for her redingote, when Bertrand de Domfort appeared. She smiled in gratitude, welcoming the first friendly face she'd seen all afternoon. But after he'd kissed her hand and remarked on how grand she looked, he pulled her into the embrasure of a window, where they could be alone, and his voice changed. "Are you happy,'' he said coldly, "with the man who killed your brother?''

She closed her eyes in pain. "Oh, Bertrand, not you, as well! I'm desperately unhappy. But what can I do?''

"I'm sorry,'' he murmured. "I should have guessed. Perhaps I spoke from my grief at having lost you. Lost you to a man who...my dear, I'm glad you weren't there to see it. Armand hobbling about the room, trying with all his limited strength to evade... God! He never had a chance!''

She collapsed into his arms, weeping afresh for Armand's death. And perhaps a little for the loss of this dear man who comforted her now. She should have married him when Armand wished it instead of playing the romantic fool. At last she sniffled and dried her eyes. "Dear Bertrand. How goes *La Voix*?''

"Struggling. With the voice of the Flaming Sword stilled...''

"I can let you have money, if it will help. Two hundred francs a month. More, if I can manage it without arousing suspicion.'' She laughed bitterly. "The Tyrant's minions are as meddlesome and repressive as the Tyrant himself. How are the men?''

"Georges is as fat as ever. Gaston comes and goes, bringing supplies, paper and ink. We dare not ask from where.''

"And Jean-Pierre?''

"He asks for you. I think he's in love with you. They... we all miss Armand.''

"Bertrand,'' she whispered. "Please don't. It's my fault he's dead. If it weren't for me...if I'd had your faith in the restoration of the Monarchy...''

His eyes, normally so sad, glittered with zeal. "Then take up his pen! Let the Flaming Sword speak again! You have the skills.''

She shook her head. "No, no! Not I. I couldn't do it."

"Are you afraid of the danger? Because it's treasonous? Or are you afraid of that murdering pig you've married?"

It was too much to bear. She had never felt more abandoned in her life. With a sob she turned away from him, motioned Jeanine for her redingote and escaped into the cold afternoon without even waiting to say goodbye to Sophie.

She wandered the streets of Paris, her mind in turmoil. Her brother was dead for a cause he believed in; she couldn't even find the passion in her—despite Adam's evil—to speak out.

Without realizing it, she found herself in an unfamiliar and vile section of the city—old and dirty, crowded with beggars and prostitutes, the narrow streets filled with refuse and filth and horse droppings. Concerned now, afraid she might be lost, she crossed a narrow plank set in the street to aid pedestrians and stopped to ask directions of a one-legged veteran in a shabby uniform that barely kept him from shivering with cold. She pressed a franc into his hand and turned down the alley toward the rue de la Planche, as he had directed.

She heard shouting from the next corner. Several street children, a drunken sailor, a knife grinder and a pedlar with a pack stood in a rough circle, crying encouragement to two boys engaged in a savage fight.

"Come on, Antoine. Hit the little beetle again!"

"*Cafard!* Cockroach, cockroach!" A singsong taunt.

Charmiane scowled. Antoine was a large boy, around fourteen or fifteen, with a stocky body and a stupid smile on a brute's face. He held a length of chain, some ten inches long, which he swung in the direction of the other boy. The one the gamins called Cockroach was half Antoine's size, perhaps ten years old, with a thin body and the worn-out, old face of someone who has seen too much, suffered too much. He gripped a wooden ax handle in one hand, with which he was attempting to ward off Antoine's attack with little success. The chain had already split open his cheek, and blood dripped on his ragged coat; even as Charmiane watched, horrified, Antoine struck him again, across one shoulder. She could see fear in the child's eyes. But he was game and stubborn, and he parried with his stick as he tried to dodge the next swipe of hard iron.

"Stop it!" shrieked Charmiane, elbowing her way through the passive bystanders to plant herself firmly between the two boys. *Mon Dieu,* she thought, as Antoine raised the chain in one hamlike fist. What am I doing? But it was too late to regret her rashness, too late to back away. She glared at Antoine and drew herself up. Perhaps she could intimidate him with an air of authority. "Put down that chain and get out of here!"

"Hey! Stupid whore! Leave the boys alone." The sailor shuffled forward, one obscene finger expressing his contempt.

She prayed—just once, dear God!—that her face wouldn't betray her. "My coachman has already gone for the police!" she lied. "Now begone, before I see to it that you're all arrested!"

They scattered at that. Even Cockroach would have vanished down an alley if Charmiane hadn't caught him by the collar. "Wait," she said. "Someone should attend your face. Where do you live?"

He studied her expression, as though he were wondering whether to trust her. Then he pointed to a space between two buildings, no wider than perhaps a foot and a half and stuffed with rags. "There?" she asked, incredulous. He nodded. "Where's your family? Your people?" she went on. He shrugged and wiped his grimy sleeve against his bloody cheek.

"*Fi donc!* Not your dirty sleeve. Use this." She handed him her linen handkerchief. "Can't you speak?" His answer was to unwrap the tattered scarf about his neck, lean his head back and point to his throat. His neck was scarred, the Adam's apple dented in a peculiar fashion. He read the question on her face and made a kicking gesture with one foot.

"Oh, alas," she murmured. "Come. We'll see to your cheek." As he followed her to the rue de la Planche, she managed—by dint of a one-sided conversation and his gestured responses—to learn that he was eleven, an orphan for the past two years and a pickpocket from the age of eight, when a kick to his throat from a cow had made his father decide that a boy with no voice was no longer of much use in an honest trade.

She found herself taken by him; there was a gentleness in his demeanor for all his street toughness that was quite appealing. She would take him home. She would turn him into a pageboy if he proved honest and as quick as he seemed. "I shall name you Prosper," she said, "so you can grow and thrive."

She realized it was past five when they reached the rue de la Planche and encountered a Darnaud frantic with worry. But he was quickly placated when she praised his loyalty and competence and announced that she was putting Prosper under his direct care—with a suitable raise in salary—to be taught to serve in as fine a manner. As soon as they reached Bonneval, Darnaud took the boy off for a meal, a bath and a few stitches to his cheek.

Charmiane had just finished a quiet dinner when loud shouting and the slam of several doors announced to her that Adam had returned. She had dreaded this moment. She found herself trembling, whether from hatred or fear she wasn't entirely sure. But there was no time to wonder how to receive him; the door to the dining salon crashed open and he stormed in. The footmen in attendance at the table jumped in alarm.

Adam's eyes blazed blue fire. "Bazaine has told me of your adventure in Paris today," he growled.

She swallowed the fear. "Welcome home, my husband." Her voice dripped sarcasm. She wondered if he could read the hatred in her eyes. "I saw my aunt in Paris. Is that forbidden?"

"I have half a mind to sack Darnaud for letting you wander about alone in the slums! That is certainly forbidden! If I must put you on leading strings to keep you safe from your own folly, I'll do so." The air crackled with his anger; Charmiane fought the urge to flee.

"Your rooms are being prepared, *monsieur le comte*." Bazaine stood at the door, his voice a soothing balm.

"I don't want that valet you gave me the last time. He was a damned idiot!"

Bazaine remained unruffled. "He's already been replaced, *monsieur*. I think you'll be pleased. Have you had dinner?"

Adam seemed to make a conscious effort to cool his temper. "I wish to speak with my wife. Alone. You can serve me something to eat in her sitting room."

The room stilled at once. A trembling hush. The young footman who had been clearing the table dropped a fork; the sound echoed across the coved ceiling. God save me, thought Charmiane. It was clear that no one had told Adam she'd moved her suite. She felt a surge of anger toward Bazaine. He might have spared her this.

Adam looked about at the white faces, the quaking footmen. "What the deuce is going on?"

Bazaine cleared his throat. "It seemed unimportant until your return, *monsieur*. *Madame* is now in the east pavilion."

"What?" Adam's roar was like the rage of thunder in a storm. He pointed toward the door. "Out. Out! Every one of you! Except—" he whirled around and his finger stabbed the air in Charmiane's direction "—*her!*" He waited until the servants had scurried out, and then he pointed to a spot of carpet in front of him. "Come here," he ordered.

In spite of her terror, she found her voice. "I'm not one of your soldiers," she quavered, but took a few timid steps toward him to ward off the next storm.

"Why did you move your rooms?" he said more calmly.

"I said I'd never lock my door. Moving my suite seemed the only way to tell you how I felt about you."

His eyes narrowed. "I'm your husband, damn it. You have a duty to me. I can claim my rights. Demand my rights!"

"You can tie me to the bed, too," she snapped. "If you want to claim your rights, like the savage you are."

"Damnation! Little bitch!" He lifted his fist as though he'd strike her down, his eyes shining with an unnatural light. She cringed, throwing up her arm to ward off the blow. The gesture seemed to bring him to his senses. He took a deep breath. "Will you defy me if I order you to my bed?" he demanded.

She hesitated, filled with fear of this man she'd married. If she said yes to his question, he might beat her with all the savagery of which she knew him capable. But if she said no, she'd be forced to submit to him. It had been easy to submit to Henri—coldly, passively. He didn't seem to care most of the time. But she suspected that if she was cold to Adam, his fury might be greater than if she refused him outright. But she had one weapon. The one thing she'd realized from the first. He didn't understand women very well. Perhaps her silence would confound him. She turned away, refusing even to answer his question.

And surely he was confounded and confused. He made a low growling sound in his throat, stomped to the table, poured himself a glass of wine. "Do you intend to stay in the east pavilion?" he said at last.

"Yes." She turned and faced him, challenging him with her words. "Your hands are covered with my brother's blood."

"We must speak of that night, sooner or later."

"There's nothing to be said, ever, about Armand's murder."

He flinched at the word but shook his head. "Charmiane . . ."

She brushed at the tears that had begun to flow. Would she ever think of Armand without weeping? "Do you deny that your sword took the life of a crippled man who couldn't have been your equal? Do you deny it?"

His face reddened and he turned away. "No." She had to strain to hear the word. His shoulders sagged, as though she'd put a great burden on them. "Go to your suite, *madame*. I'll leave you in peace."

* * *

He was silent and withdrawn after that, which was almost as frightening as his rages. He would wander into her sitting room unannounced as she sat with Prosper and tried to teach the boy to read. Adam would stare morosely at her, glaring from beneath beetled brows, until she began to feel as she had with Henri—the guilty urge to scream "What have I done?" But of course it wasn't what she'd done. It was what she refused to do. Her duty as his wife. She tried to tell herself she had a right to refuse, because of Armand. And if Adam was too stubborn to seek a divorce . . .

Prosper was a source of delight to her. He had a delicate face, quite pretty and round now that he was eating well, and a shock of straw-colored hair. The cut on his cheek had left only a small scar. He wasn't as bright as she had hoped—the reading and writing sessions went slowly—but his sweet nature and his devotion to her warmed her heart. She had needed someone to love. She enjoyed petting him, fussing over him, sending him on little errands that pleased him as much as they helped her. He was her only joy. She hadn't the courage to face Sophie, Bertrand or the other émigrés again.

After Adam's return, she had stayed in her rooms as much as possible, hoping to avoid seeing him except at dinner. But he had discovered she played the piano. Now he insisted that she play for him in the music room every afternoon, when he came in from his ride. Prosper would stand beside her, in the little suit of livery she'd had designed for him, and turn the music pages.

She wondered why she didn't rebel against this daily ritual; Adam never seemed to be paying much attention to the music. There were constant interruptions that he tolerated: Bazaine with messages from Paris, the head groom to discuss the horses, even his valet, a retiring little mouse, to decide on which coats were to be taken to the tailor and copied. It was even worse when the servants came to consult with her. Adam would behave as though she weren't even in the room. He would motion them to his chair, stare at them in the way he had that made them shake with fear, then demand to know why they had come. He would make his decision, and they would scurry away. And always at his elbow was a bottle of brandy.

She couldn't pretend to herself that her fear wasn't as strong as her hatred; he made Henri's domineering ways seem mild by comparison. Even Bazaine, she noted, was respectful and correct, if not afraid.

She sighed and settled herself at the piano. It was a mild April day, with the doors thrown open to the terrace, but it might as well have been wintry November from the chill nod with which Adam had greeted her when he strode into the music room, tapping his riding crop against his boot. He'd been at Bonneval for nearly three weeks, and she didn't know how much longer she could live this way—swallowing her anger, fearing his very presence—without exploding from the strain.

"Turn the pages a little sooner today, Prosper," she said, and smoothed back the boy's yellow hair.

"You make too much of a fuss over him," growled Adam. As usual, he had set his armchair so that he faced her; there was no avoiding his burning glance each time she lifted her head to the music.

"He's a sweet boy. Why shouldn't I?"

"Boys grow into men. Enjoying the privileged access to their ladies' boudoir."

The words were so cruel, so surprising, that she stared at him, openmouthed. She wondered if Prosper had understood and been hurt. She patted his hand. "Prosper, go now. I'll not need you."

"Prosper, stay." Adam's voice was like edged steel. "Your mistress manages to be so much more charming when you're in the room."

"Name of God, Adam . . ."

He seemed indifferent to her distress. "I never told you the disappointing news. Noël, my dear brother, had planned to visit us, but he was recalled to service. I was looking forward to seeing how much charm you could show to *him*."

She moved away from the piano, pacing angrily in the center of the room. "A great deal of charm! He's not a murderer. He's not a parvenu, pretending to aristocracy! An artificial noble of the Empire." She spat the words, her lip curling in disdain.

"Ah. Are we to have Armand's class arguments now, *madame la marquise, ci-devant*?"

"The title I was born to, the title I married in Henri, were legitimate! When I'm with my kind, I feel like a bastard *comtesse*."

He scowled. "At least it's not a phantom title. As dead as your kind is dead. When will you learn to live in the present?"

"Curse you! Someday . . ." She bit back her tears.

He laughed, an ugly sound. "Someday you'll be a *marquise* again? I meant to tell you. I had Bazaine look into your late husband's affairs. You were hoping to reclaim his fortune, I understand.''

"You pursued it?" She felt like a fool. It hadn't occurred to her that between Adam's money and Bazaine's bureaucratic skills the matter could be resolved.

"Ah. That makes your eyes dance at last. The thought of Viollet's fortune. Before you anticipate too much, let me remind you that it would belong to *me* now, as your husband. But . . ." He shrugged. "The family Troche will keep it all."

"All?" She felt a twinge of pity for Henri. How the truth would have hurt him. "Bazaine found no documents, then."

"*Au contraire.* There were records, if one knew where to look. But I've decided to let Troche's family keep what they hold, particularly Troche's daughter."

"*You've* decided . . . !" She whirled to him. "What can *you* do if there are papers to prove the estate is still Henri's?"

"Not anymore," he said tiredly. "I had them destroyed."

She felt trapped everywhere she turned with this man. She stamped her foot in fury. "How dare you! By what right did you destroy what was mine?" What she had earned in the misery of her life with Henri. She felt cheated by this . . . this . . . Angry tears sprang to her eyes. "You upstart, with your peasant ways! You lowborn mercenary, selling your sword to live like a nobleman! You don't even know enough to stand when a lady is standing in a room!"

Her words brought him to his feet like a shot. "Now, by God, you sharp-tongued bitch . . . !" He moved toward her.

She stood rooted to the spot, too terrified to move. She could feel the rivulets of sweat running down her back. She had gone too far, said things a wife had no right to say to a husband. She was sure he'd strike her. But Prosper darted forward and kicked Adam in the shins. He was rewarded by a savage cuff to the side of the head, which sent him sprawling. Charmiane gasped.

Adam's voice was a low growl. "Get out, boy." When Prosper had gone reluctantly, still fearful for Charmiane, Adam turned on her. "It troubles you, *madame*, that your husband kills people for a living?"

It seemed so stark, put that way. "No, I . . ."

"You don't mind spending the money, though. You and your kind. You just don't like to talk about it. I've watched you these past weeks. Taking so readily to the life I've paid for. The difference between your kind and mine is that you pretend that money doesn't matter."

"And what matters to you? Armand said you married me for the prestige. But I think it was to bring me down to your level."

"No," he said softly. "I married you to prove I was better than you. A tribute to a poor clerk who ate the dirt of an aristocrat for too many years." A light tap sounded at the door. "Yes?" he barked.

Yvonne came into the room and curtsied. "*Madame*, you never told me what gown you wish to wear for dinner."

Charmiane was still struggling to absorb what she'd heard. He'd married her for revenge against the aristocracy. For his father, perhaps? And capped his revenge by killing her brother. It was all of a piece, his behavior. From the coarse animal in the Tuileries to the brute who'd stormed around for weeks, frightening and intimidating her with his rage. Only the letters didn't fit.

"Which gown, *madame*?" The girl's voice held an edge of insolence that set Charmiane's teeth on edge.

"The green velvet."

"No," Adam cut in sharply. "The yellow. That *madame* wore on her wedding day."

"Oh, but . . ." She hated that dress because of him.

"The yellow gown," he repeated.

Yvonne bobbed in Adam's direction. "Very good, *monsieur*. The yellow. And the diamond necklace?" She smiled at his nod of agreement.

Charmiane's face flamed. It was enough that the girl was insolent and he didn't even see it. But to be contradicted, ignored, shamed before her servant, was almost more than she could bear. She feigned unconcern, sat at the piano and played with the keys until Yvonne had left the room. Then she turned. "Am I now to be under your control even in the matter of my own wardrobe?"

"I had a reason," he said. "It's my last evening at Bonneval. The Emperor plans to leave for Germany on the fifteenth. I'm going back to war. To do the job you find so contemptible. I thought it would be nice to see you in the yellow once more." He laughed softly, ironically. "What a pleasure, after all these weeks. To see the hatred in your eyes turn to relief at my going." He threw himself back into his chair and picked up his glass of brandy. "Now get out of here before I start remembering all the spiteful things you've said today."

Chapter Twelve

"Will there be fighting in Germany?" Charmiane picked at her cream tart, then put down her spoon and fork.

Adam nodded. "Yes. The Russians have crossed the Elbe and occupied Dresden. Prussia has declared war. Austria has decided on neutrality and will no longer help us. And Hamburg has rebelled against French rule. Between our enemies and the crumbling of our alliances, we shall soon stand alone."

"What would you do, if you were your great Emperor?"

He smiled, a distant smile, and stared up at the chandelier. "I'd sue for peace. I much prefer a treaty of peace." His gaze lowered to fasten on Charmiane's face. She stirred uncomfortably at her place, aware of his searching eyes.

It had been such a strange dinner. He had greeted her with a bow, rising from his chair when she entered the room. *"Madame,"* he had said solemnly, "you look very beautiful this evening." He had waved aside the footman and seated her himself. There had been a small velvet box at her plate. Within had been a pair of diamond-and-emerald earrings that he had entreated, not ordered, her to put on. And then dinner had begun, with his customary silence broken only by the occasional compliment, so awkward and so flowery that she wondered what was in his thoughts tonight. She had raised the topic of the campaign—humdrum, impersonal, comfortable for him—as a means to dispel the strange aura that hung between them.

"A soldier?" she said. "And craving peace?"

"When the battle is futile, why not?"

"A peace treaty, not a surrender, nor even a retreat?"

"A soldier wants honor and respect even from his enemy."

Why did she feel they weren't speaking of the Emperor any-more? "And peace, no matter the soldier's barbarity?"

He sighed and rubbed a hand across his eyes. "Even a small truce would be welcome." He lapsed into silence, then tried again as the footman served the fruit course. "You should wear yellow more often. It becomes you."

Why his preoccupation with compliments tonight, so foreign to his nature? She pursed her lips. "I ought to be wearing black or gray. Yellow is for happiness."

He swore softly, hacked at a pear with his knife, then snapped his fingers for more wine. The drink seemed to calm him; he managed a tentative smile. "Shall I write to you from Germany?"

Dieu! she thought. His letters had lied to her before, painting a picture of another man. "If you do, I won't read your letters. It's best to send your instructions through Bazaine."

"I lost your letters in battle. I'm sorry about that."

There was unexpected tenderness in his voice. She felt hurt and confused. "Why?" she asked. "They were just letters, you said."

"Charmiane..." He stared at her, then abruptly rose from his seat to stand near a window, out of the glow of the candles. His face was shadowed, his voice low and strained. "I want a wife before I go."

She stiffened. "Of course. I should have understood. The compliments, the gift of the earrings. Clumsy bribes."

"Are even my kindnesses suspect now?" he growled.

She felt contempt for his obvious maneuver. "Only your motives, my dear husband. You want a wife. How charming. Willingly? Or unwillingly?"

He came toward the light. Now she could see the scowl on his face. At least it was more natural than his artificial flattery. "I've known camp followers more generous than you," he said.

"I'm sure you have. On every battlefield, in every garrison, every frontier village!" She was suddenly weary of their fencing. She sagged in her chair. "Oh God, Adam. Why don't you let me divorce you?"

"No." Cold and final.

"Why?" she begged.

"Why can we never speak of your brother's death?"

"Armand." She clapped her hand over her mouth to stifle her cry. Why did grief always creep up unawares, clutching at her before she had time to protect her fragile heart? The bitter tears flowed on her cheeks.

"Stop that," he muttered.

"I'll cry if I want to, curse you!"

"Damnation!" He swung his arm across the table, a wide arc that cleared half the platters in one sweep so they fell in a great crashing heap of porcelain and silver and glass. "He was just one man!" he shouted. "One man against the thousands killed! Against the hundreds I've killed myself. With sword and bayonet and pistol! What does it matter that one more man is dead?"

Aghast, she rose from her seat, trembling, staring in horror. "You have no heart. You have no soul!"

He laughed cynically and made a little bow. "I knew that long ago. What I have, in abundance, is hunger. *And I want a wife tonight.* Go to your rooms and prepare for bed. Then wait for me."

She shook her head. "No." Her own bravery astonished her.

He strode to her and clamped his hand about her wrist. He looked around at the several footmen who hovered in the shadowy corners of the room, silent and terrified witnesses. *"Madame,"* he said quietly, through clenched teeth, "I'm quite capable of spreading you on that table and having you in front of the servants." He gave an ugly laugh as she cringed. "Alas, *madame,* my class hasn't the sensibilities of yours. Now, will you choose our battlefield? Or shall I?"

Somehow she had thought this would never happen. That his respect for her honor would prevent it. She bowed her head. "I'll be in my suite."

Yvonne helped her to dress for bed, brushing her hair out and tying it back with a silk ribbon. She hadn't the courage to look at her reflection in the mirror, knowing what she'd see: a stupid woman, so filled with her sense of duty that she'd submit to a monster. Or perhaps just a frightened woman. Neither image would bring her much cheer. She sighed and stood up from her dressing table. "You may go to bed now, Yvonne. I won't need you for the rest of the night."

"Of course, *madame.* I understand." The girl's mouth twisted in a knowing smirk, and she glanced at the wide bed.

Charmiane frowned. Why must she endure these servants? They had no shame, no sense of what was proper. Even if the servants in Switzerland had been aware of when Henri came to her bed, they had always behaved as though they knew nothing. All of Bonneval, of course, would have learned that *monsieur le comte* had never shared his wife's bed, even on their wedding night. Unlike the châteaus of the old kings and queens of

France—as Sophie used to tell—there were no hidden stairways here to aid a secret midnight tryst. Still, it was distressing to think of Yvonne sharing her gossip with such delight, after the scene the footmen had witnessed in the dining salon.

Though she had anticipated it, Adam's appearance at the door filled her with fresh dread. He had obviously been drinking a great deal since he'd left the dinner table: his casual stance as he leaned against the doorway of her bedroom was decidedly un-soldierly. His coat was gone, and his stiff collar and cravat. His ruffled shirt, opened almost to the waist, revealed a muscled expanse of chest. His ankle-length, tight pantaloons clung to legs grown hard and powerful and sinewy from years in the saddle; without the visual distraction of coat and waistcoat, the bulge at his groin loomed frighteningly large. He meant to use her to-night; she had no doubt of it.

He locked the door behind him; the key squeaked softly, like the iron sound of a cell closing. He put the key into his fob pocket and advanced to her, a mocking smile on his face. "I thought you'd be waiting in bed for me, wife."

"You make me feel like a common whore." God, why did her voice have to shake?

He laughed. "Common? Scarcely common! Do you know what a whore in the Tuileries costs? A man can pick them up by the dozens during the day." He paused and studied her face, which had flamed red with the mention of the gardens. "A *common* whore can be had for seven francs for two hours. During which time a man will feel desired and cherished. And then—" a cynical laugh "—providing she hasn't left him with more than moral apprehension for his soul, he can go back the following night and expect as warm a welcome for another seven francs. That's a *common* whore, *madame*. But you…do you know how many Russians died to pay for your pretty yellow dress?"

"And my diamonds?" she said, remembering Armand's story of Adam's Italian venture. "Who died for them, you mur-derer?"

"An old man," he said coldly. "My life is littered with corpses. And all for your pleasure. So you can eat my food and wear your beautiful clothes and care for that parasitic aunt of yours. And feel free to give me your hatred and your contempt. And every venomous insult that passes, unchecked, from your pretty lips. You're a very expensive whore in every way. I wanted a wife. You made this choice, not I."

"Wife?" she sneered. "You wanted an aristocratic jewel for your sword hilt, peasant!"

"Enough!" he growled, taking her by the shoulders. "Tonight I want what I paid for."

She turned her head aside. The liquor on his breath made her sick.

He released her and stepped back, his eyes raking her body. "Now, my little *fille de joie*, let me see what I've bought. Take off your nightclothes."

She gasped. "Now? Here?"

"Yes."

"Please." She trembled. Not even Henri would have shamed her so.

"If I tear them off you, I won't mind. I've paid for them, as well."

To strip before him? She had her pride. "Am I a horse you plan to buy?" she said haughtily.

"You're a horse I plan to *ride*, and ride well tonight. Now take off your clothes, *putain*." His eyes were cold and implacable.

With shaking hands she undid the buttons of her dressing gown and nightdress and let them fall at her feet. He was determined to humiliate her, she could see. He took a candle from a table, held it before him and slowly circled her naked form. His steps were unsteady. His eyes were dark with lust, and he ran his tongue across dry lips. He reached out and pulled the ribbon from her hair, then stroked one long tress from the crown of her head, across her shoulder blades and down her back. He circled her again, his eyes so thorough that she felt robbed of every secret. This time, when he reached out, his hand cupped one rounded breast and played with it like a child with a new toy. She bore it all in silence, staring straight before her. Though she felt nothing but cold hatred for this man who had killed Armand, he was clearly aroused by her.

The candle began to shake in his hand. He put it down and pulled her, unresisting but passive, into his arms. "Kiss me," he said.

She closed her eyes. He pressed his mouth against her lips. She held them rigid and tightly clamped. She felt the urgent push of his tongue and resisted all the more. He kissed her so hard that her teeth hurt, and she thought her jaw would crack. But still she denied him the satisfaction of a response.

With a growl, he pushed her away, stormed to the fireplace and pounded his fist in frustration against the mantel. At last he

turned and looked at her. "Damn it, this isn't what I wanted."
He ran his hand through his hair. "Charmiane—" his voice was
husky "—be my lover tonight."

"Your lover?" All the rage and grief that had been building for
weeks, all the guilt she felt for having betrayed the Chevrillon line,
defied the only family she'd ever known, burst from her in an
agonized shriek. She forgot the shame of her nakedness. She
forgot everything but her hatred. A kind of madness possessed
her, carrying her beyond reason, beyond her fear of him.

"Your *lover*? Monster! Assassin! Murderer! From the moment I met you, I made poor Armand suffer. Even at the Tuileries. I broke his heart when I chose you. I lied to Sophie as I never
did before. I cut myself off from all I held dear for your sake.
And how did you repay me? By murdering my brother! A poor
crippled man who had suffered so much from your kind. And
now you want a *lover*?" She cast her eyes wildly about the room
until they lit on a pair of scissors sitting on her dressing table. She
snatched them up and lunged for him. "This is my kiss, you assassin!"

"*Mon Dieu!* You're as mad as your brother! Put down the
scissors." He dodged her assault and grabbed at her arm and her
waist, twisting her naked body close to his and holding her hand,
with its weapon, above her head. Their faces were so close that
she could see the dark pools of anger in the depths of his eyes.
"Put down the scissors," he said, his voice tight with the effort
at control.

She knew he'd overpower her in a moment, and the thought
only added to her hatred. "Murderer," she said softly. "How do
you sleep at night with your hands drenched in blood?"

"Damn you, bitch!" he exploded. With a violent shove he
threw her to the floor. While she lay gasping, he knelt to her and
pulled the scissors from her limp fingers. "You want to play with
scissors? I have a game!" He caught a lock of her hair in his fist;
the scissors flashed and the long tress lay on the carpet beside her
head.

"My God, Adam . . . !" Somehow she must stop this. Their
passion had carried them both beyond the point of sanity and
reason. He'd already had too much to drink before he came to
her. She cursed herself for having goaded him, for having attacked him in her madness, for having turned this night into the
horror it had become. "Please, Adam," she whispered. Soothing. Conciliatory.

But it was too late. She could see it on his face. His rage had transformed itself into the icy, distant menace that she found infinitely more terrifying. This was the man who had beaten Paterne nearly to death, then had coldly demanded that she mind her own business. She trembled in fear as he bared his teeth in the mockery of a smile and reached for another lock of hair.

"No, Adam, please!" she cried, struggling to rise. "What must I do?"

He leaned back on his heels. His eyes were as chilling as a frosty day. "Get on the bed, whore." Shaking, she did as she was told, sitting on the edge of the bed with her hands folded in her lap, like an obedient schoolgirl waiting for her lesson. He stripped off his clothes. His body was hard and potent. Frightening. He followed the focus of her eyes and laughed sharply. "Take a good look, *madame*. It's your master. As I am. One way or another, you'll satisfy us both tonight." He pushed her roughly onto her back, spread her legs and lay down on top of her.

She was aware of how heavy he was, his weight suffocating, enveloping. Had it been so in the Tuileries? But everything had been different in the Tuileries, from the trembling thrill she had felt at his kiss to . . .

"*Dieu!*" She screamed aloud as he thrust into her. She had been aroused, ready for him at the Tuileries. Tonight she was tense and dry, and every movement he made, every savage plunge of his cruel weapon brought pain. She writhed beneath him, her face twisted in agony, and prayed for an end to the torment. At last, in a final burst of frenzied movement, he found his release.

"Will you go now?" she choked, as he lifted himself from her.

He stood up, sighed and stretched. "No. I might want you later. Get into bed while I put out the candles."

It was absurd, she thought, watching him padding around the room, casual in his nakedness, extinguishing the lights. They might have been a happily married couple, turning in for the night. Instead, she was a violated woman, treated like a whore by the husband who had vowed to honor and cherish her less than a month and a half ago.

In the dark he climbed in beside her. She tried to move away from him but he pulled her close and tangled his fingers in her long curls. She waited until she heard his breathing slow, grow deep and rhythmic. Then, carefully, so the movement wouldn't bring pain from her trapped hair, she turned her face to the pillow and gave way to wrenching sobs that tore at her body, no matter how she tried to stifle them.

She dreamed of Switzerland, of lying on the grass of the mountainside. It was spring, and the air was filled with blossoms. They touched her body, soft and caressing, stirring her senses so she trembled and moaned. They were on her face, drifting across her lips. Only now there were no blossoms. There was a man—she couldn't tell who—kissing her softly. She put a languid arm around his neck. His kisses were gentle and seductive, rousing her passions, filling her with an aching need. There was throbbing within her. There was desire, a blooming wetness. There was . . . oh, God! A man. The hardness of a real man! Her eyes sprang open to find Adam above her, within her, possessing her. "Adam!" she cried, and felt her desire vanish. She struggled beneath him. "Curse you, villain, let me go."

His face was tense with passion. "Keep still until I'm finished," he warned. "You're still my whore."

She stared at him with renewed hatred. It didn't hurt this morning; her dream had made his entrance painless. But the thought that she had responded to him in her sleep, had made him believe that she wanted him, filled her with disgust. She lay stiffly and allowed him his lust.

He satisfied himself quickly, then withdrew. He sat up and moved to the edge of the bed, his back toward her. "I should have known it was too good to be true," he said.

"I was dreaming," she said with contempt. "Surely you didn't believe that I welcomed you."

He shrugged. "Of course not. But you looked so tempting this morning. And I was too drunk to appreciate you last night." He turned to her, his eyes cold. "You might make a passable whore if I had the time to train you."

She turned her head away. The bastard!

He stood up and silently began to put on his clothes. "No tears this morning?" he said at last.

She had lain in bed, avoiding the sight of him all the while he dressed; now she sat up, the sheets pulled around her, and felt for the spot where her hair had been cut away. The memory of last night, the pain and degradation, was an ugly wound that would never heal. But a private wound. "You'll never see me cry again," she said coldly.

He buttoned his pantaloons and tucked in his shirt. "Pray God a Prussian bullet makes you a widow, *madame*."

"Amen to that."

He laughed sharply. "Perhaps we'll meet in Heaven someday."

"I doubt that. Unless there's a place for common, drunken upstarts," she said scornfully. "All the diamonds in the world would never make you a *comte*. All the diamonds in the world haven't made you a *man*."

His eyes narrowed and he drew a sharp breath through his teeth. He strode to the bed and stared at her while his jaw worked in anger. Then he lifted his hand and slapped her savagely across the face. Once, and then again.

She gasped and fell back against the pillows, then watched him, her cheeks burning, as he unlocked the door and threw it open. He almost tripped over Prosper, who lay, sleeping like a loyal puppy, just beyond the door. He prodded the boy awake. "Get up," he growled. "Your mistress survived me." He turned to Charmiane, clicked his heels and saluted. "A rich widow, lest you forget, *madame*," he sneered. Then he was gone.

Prosper scampered in, his eyes wide with fear. He stooped to the cut tress on the floor and held it out to her, blinking against his tears. With a cry, Charmiane clutched him in her arms, holding him tightly and sobbing out her heartbreak.

"Here, Darnaud. Take this note around to Monsieur de Domfort's rooms at the address I told you, then bring him here in my carriage." Charmiane stepped from her coach and entered the Café Frascati, asking for a table in a secluded corner. Fearing Adam as she did, she dared not disobey him and go to the rue du Paon lest he should learn of it. The Café Frascati was one of the few places in Paris where an unescorted lady was admitted. Charmiane took off her gloves, dismissed the hovering waiter with an order to come back when the gentleman arrived, and looked around the room. Painted women who laughed too loudly, strutting men with flashing diamond rings. This was the new society of Paris, enjoying foolish pleasures while their world crumbled. And the rightful King, in his English exile, waited to reclaim his throne. Well, by heaven, if she had anything to say about it, it would come to pass!

Self-consciously she tucked a stray curl into her toque. It had been very difficult this morning, while Yvonne dressed her hair, to pretend that she didn't notice the girl's questioning looks. She sighed. Ah well, her hair would grow back, and the less the servants knew, the better. It had been a night of losses: her long tress, her pride, her last shred of feeling for that brute of a man, her hope that the future would be anything but misery, should he return alive from his next battle.

But she had gained something in the course of that night of horror. Passion. The passion that had fired Armand, that inspired so many of the émigrés to hope, traveling from capital to capital in search of foreign support for their cause. That led a young innocent like Jean-Pierre to risk his life. It was so simple she wondered why she hadn't realized it before. The passion was ignited by hatred, a hatred of the injustices one suffered. Until Adam had come into her life, she had had nothing, no one, to hate.

"Charmiane, I'm so glad you sent for me." Domfort bowed, took her hand and kissed it with fervor. "I was planning to visit you, to tell you how sorry..." He sat down, ordered coffee for them both and reached into his pocket. "Sophie and I both regretted making you so unhappy at your last visit. She wanted to make amends. I was to give this to you when I came to Bonneval." He pulled the green fan from his pocket. Adam's gift.

She stiffened. "I don't want it. Give it to someone you care for."

"Dearest Charmiane, you're the only 'someone' in my life. And always will be."

"Oh, Bertrand, I should have married you."

He patted her hand. "Perhaps you may, someday. The man's a soldier. He can't live forever. Not the way the Tyrant throws his troops at the enemy's guns. There'll be a better future, I promise you."

She reached into her reticule. "Let me hurry it along. Take these—" she put her diamond-and-emerald earrings into his hand "—to feed *La Voix*."

His sad eyes lit up. "Charmiane!" He took her hand and pressed kisses into her palm. "And the Flaming Sword?"

"You'll find someone. You..." She looked up. Georges was hurrying toward them, mopping his bald head. He looked about to cry.

"Domfort," he said, "we're finished! The soldiers came...the presses and everything..."

"My God, what?"

"They smashed the presses, destroyed everything. I was able to get out, but Gaston was arrested."

"Damn! And Jean-Pierre?"

Georges shuddered. "Killed. A bayonet to the stomach. Horrible!"

Charmiane gasped. Dear Jean-Pierre with the village sweetheart who waited for him. She'd wait in vain now. "How could it happen?" she cried.

"I don't know." Georges fell into a chair and put his head in his hands. "I don't think they'll come looking for me or Domfort. They didn't seem to know any names. Just the address."

Domfort pounded a fist into his palm. "Damned bastards! Souls of slime! How did they find the place?"

Someone told them, thought Charmiane. Someone who wished to leave her with one last cruel memory. Adam. Her eyes blazed. "Then we'll begin again! Bertrand, can you find a new place?"

"Maybe not inside the city. Beyond the gates. It might be safer to do the printing there and smuggle the papers into the city."

"Will my jewels bring in enough to get you started?"

"But of course."

"Good! Send word to me when *La Voix* is ready to speak again. The Flaming Sword will be one of the voices!"

"Colonel Bouchard, we've been within the sound of the guns for two hours now! Will we never get our orders?"

Adam leaned forward in the saddle and patted his horse's neck to calm the pawing animal. He scowled at the young mounted soldier beside him. "Patience, Rousselot. You have time enough to taste smoke and fire." He saw that Rousselot had begun to fidget again. "God! That tree must be withered by now!" He watched in disgust as Rousselot dismounted, moved among the trees to a well-trampled spot and undid the flap of his breeches. He shook his head. The young fool could piss for half the day and it wouldn't take away the fear. He missed Foullon. There had been an orderly a man could depend on. Poor Foullon. With his wounds, he hadn't survived that first week's retreat from Moscow.

And now they gave him men like Rousselot. Young, scared, untried. And at that he was lucky. It was a tumbledown army that the Emperor had assembled for this campaign. After the winter of 1812, there weren't many good men left in France. Discharged men—like Noël, who'd served his five years—had been recalled, the National Guard mobilized, even pensioned invalids who could still hold a musket had been called up to join what was left of the "glorious" Grand Army. And then there were the young conscripts. They were disheartening to watch. Schoolboys with down on their faces, and so hastily and poorly trained it would be a miracle if they didn't shoot one another during the battle. The army outnumbered the combined Russian and Prussian forces, but it would still be a hard-fought campaign.

The cavalry was the worst off. So many experienced troopers had perished in the Russian debacle that the Emperor had only managed a cavalry of eight thousand, even with the regiments of Dragoons who'd been recalled from duty in Spain to serve in this army. And the horses! Was there a decent horse left in all of France? Too many men and gun teams were reduced to relying on draft horses and nags and animals put out to grass. There weren't enough mounted troopers to send out a proper reconnaissance patrol; and even if they won the battle today, there wouldn't be enough cavalry to exploit the victory. Without horses, how could they pursue the fleeing enemy or take prisoners?

He wheeled his mare around and moved among his troops beneath the stand of trees. He greeted them, exchanged pleasantries, slapped a tight-lipped trooper on the back for encouragement. How the deuce was he supposed to mold a fighting unit out of this motley collection of old men, babies and tired veterans? The spirit of the Grand Army was gone; that sense of fierce pride, loyalty and glory that had buoyed them on the start of the Russian campaign was gone. Now they were just a rabble, waiting to die.

From the vantage point of the hill that held his regiment, he looked across the battlefield of Lützen. If they took the field today, Leipzig lay just beyond, and then Dresden. A few decisive victories, as in the old days, would make the Prussians eager to come to the negotiating table. He prayed it might be so.

A massed battery of some eighty guns had been pounding the enemy for an hour now, and the air, even up here, reeked of smoke and gunpowder. He could only hope they'd softened the enemy line; their sketchy reports had it that the combined Russian and Prussian cavalries were three times the number of theirs.

"Sir! Message from the marshal!" A young aide-de-camp rode up and slapped a paper into Adam's glove.

Adam scanned the orders, then passed the commands on to his subordinates. He tightened the chin strap on his yellow copper helmet, drew his straight-bladed saber, signaled to the standard-bearers and the drummers. At the cadence, the regiment began to move out from the trees, a long undulating line, moving like the sweep of the wind across grain. They trotted down the hill, tricolor flags waving proudly, and skirted an old stone farmhouse. They picked up speed, moving at a canter toward the booming guns. The drums pounded, the pace increased. Occasionally a man would scream and go down with his horse as a stray enemy cannonball found a target.

They slowed just behind the guns—an intake of breath before a flow of words, the hush of a sky awaiting the first violent thunderclap. The tension among the men was palpable. The guns fell silent. Adam raised his saber, smiled grimly at Rousselot and gave the signal to the trumpeter. At the sound of the last sharp, brassy note, a cry arose that seemed to come from a hundred throats. With a roar and pounding hooves, the regiment charged past the guns and into the enemy lines.

The ground shuddered with the shock of colliding troops. The air was filled with the acrid smoke of bursting shells. Holes opened in the ground before Adam's horse. Deep, gaping chasms, like scars on the field. He turned and dodged, deep in the enemy's midst now. The sounds of gunfire and cannon were deafening here, blending with the agonized shrieks of men as they fell. The dust and the rubbish thrown up by the shells was suffocating. Adam felt the sting in his eyes. He hacked at a Russian Hussar who had suddenly loomed before him and tumbled him from his horse to fall in a bloody heap. He felt a sharp pain and knew he'd been hit, but he ignored it. There'd be time later. The fighting grew in savagery as they closed on a Prussian gun emplacement. Everywhere was the flash of bayonets, the bark of a pistol, the whistle of cannonballs. Adam's voice was hoarse from screaming encouragement to his men. The field was already littered with the dead and dying, with blood and severed limbs. Rousselot had taken a musket ball to his forehead; his horse rode beside Adam's, its rider hanging grotesquely from the saddle.

They passed through the first enemy line, leaving devastation in their wake, and reassembled for the next charge, massing with the remnants of the several other regiments that had charged with them. Adam started at the sight of one of the riders, at some distance down the line. Even in the heat of battle he could feel a momentary shock at having recognized Noël through the smoke and the dust. But as he stared, half-minded to go to his brother, a shell exploded in a great burst of shrapnel and Noël went down with his horse.

He choked back the involuntary cry of grief and rage at seeing his brother fall. There was no time to mourn. No time for anything except the charge. He signaled his men and they galloped toward the enemy line. This was where he belonged. He was a soldier. And men were meant to kill, and be killed.

The shot was so sudden it took him by surprise. One moment he was dashing through the enemy line, saber slashing; the next minute he was on his back on the ground, his body racked with pain. He struggled to rise and was hit again. He managed to get to his knees, then looked up to see a Cossack bearing down on him, his pike poised to strike. A dead lancer's horse lay beside Adam, half its head blown away. Adam dragged himself to the saddle and fumbled with the pistol case. He groaned. His body was drenched with blood and sweat, his exhausted muscles refusing to function. He managed at last to wrench the pistol from its case, turn and fire as the pike cut into him. The Cossack fell, screaming in pain.

Panting, Adam lay back against the dead horse. So this was how it would end. With his body ripped to pieces in a blood-soaked field. God! How he would have liked to leave a son behind, to keep the Bouchard name! His last homage to *Papa*. Maybe Noël was more fortunate than he and would survive this day. And have the sons *he* should have sired long since. He had waited too long to marry. He thought of her. Charmiane. She was too young, too fragile. He should have married a breed sow, as the Emperor had. And now it was too late even for regrets.

He closed his eyes, feeling the lifeblood draining from his gaping wounds. "Father," he whispered, "I commend my soul to you."

Here at last was Death. And welcome.

Chapter Thirteen

It was a robin. Surely it was a robin whose spring call sang so merrily in the stand of trees. Charmiane slowed her horse and guided it toward the leafy shadows. The May sun was warm on her back—it would be cool and pleasant under the trees. She rode slowly, eyes turned upward, following the bird, which paused only long enough to sing a beckoning trill before taking wing again and flitting farther into the woods. Her horse nickered. She lowered her gaze from the leafy bower. Before her, set in tall grass, was a ramshackle hut, perhaps a shelter for hunters in the old days, when Bonneval boasted a true aristocratic owner and the pleasures of hunting came with the land. There was a horse in front of the hut. A poor sorry animal, drooping with exhaustion and lathered white from a hard ride.

Charmiane frowned and slid from her mount. The grass was bent and crushed in a path that led to the door. The rider must be inside the hut, perhaps as spent as his animal. She moved forward and through the door, which was ajar, hanging by a hinge. It was dark within; too late she realized how foolish, how incautious, she was.

She felt the clamp of a hand around her ankle. She screamed in shocked surprise. "Let go!" The hand was a filthy claw, and now it tugged at her riding skirt, its owner trying in vain to haul himself to his feet.

"Help me." A croak that was barely human.

She stared. "Oh, my God! Adam?" She bent to him, horrified at the sight. Even in the dimness she could see that his clothes were stained with mud and dried blood. The dark shadow of a week's growth of beard was on his face, and his eyes, ringed with purplish circles, were unnaturally bright with fever. He smelled of horse, sweat and putrefied flesh. He seemed more dead than alive. She knelt in the dirt of the hut. "How did you come here?"

At the sound of her voice he began to laugh. A weak staccato that left him gasping. "Is it you? Are you real? Or am I in Heaven with the angels?" He reached up to touch her face. "So beautiful. So beautiful." His eyes were misty with tears, and his smile held a warmth and a charm she hadn't seen since...

For the first time she noticed his tunic beneath the pelisse jacket thrown over his shoulders. *Dark* green, with yellow facings. One sleeve had been completely cut away to accommodate an arm that was swollen grotesquely beneath his grimy shirt; but the insignia on the other sleeve was clearly that of a noncommissioned officer. She looked again at his face. She should have seen it at once—the softness around his mouth, the gentle look in his eyes, the sweet smile, for all his suffering. *"Dieu!"* she cried. "But you're Noël!"

The smile grew broader, mixed with a grimace of pain. "I'm not dreaming, am I? Of all the luck..."

She stroked the tangled hair from his forehead. His flesh was hot and feverish. "Foolish Noël. Where did you come from? Why did you come here? Surely a hospital..."

His voice was beginning to falter. "Lützen. We whipped them. Doctors wanted to... amputate my arm. Wouldn't let them. If I die, want to be a whole corpse. Thought to see you...before..." He groaned. "Would have made it. But I fell. Two days ago. Damned arm...broken again..." He gingerly touched his swollen left arm; it was as wide as a man's thigh above the elbow. And the dark patches on his shirt that Charmiane had at first taken for dirt and filth were the deep crimson brown of dried blood. His eyes searched her face. "Beautiful. It's good to die with the tender gaze of... beautiful..." He sighed and closed his eyes.

"Die? Nonsense. I'll get help. I have a bottle of water in my saddle. I'll leave it with you."

He opened his eyes and managed a lopsided grin. "There's a flask of cognac in mine. If you don't mind."

She brought him the liquor, supported him as he gulped from the flask, then made him comfortable on the ground, mounding his pelisse for a pillow. "I'll be back with help as soon as I can."

"Wait." He clutched at her arm, his eyes grown serious. "If you shouldn't return in time..." He smiled sadly. "Give us a kiss, beautiful one. To see us over to the other side."

"Noël." She felt an inexplicable tenderness. She bent to his mouth and brushed her lips against his, then straightened and

hurried out to her horse. She raced for Bonneval and dashed in
to pour out the whole story to Bazaine.

He frowned. "Poor Monsieur Noël. If they planned to amputate, the bone must have been severely broken. And he fell, you
say? I'd best send to Mortefontaine for a surgeon. Lützen. I
wonder if *monsieur le comte* was in that battle. The first reports, just reaching us, say the casualties were heavy."

How could she tell him that she didn't care if Adam survived?
"*Mon Dieu*, there'll be time for that later! Noël..."

Bazaine nodded and began to bark orders. While he sent a
messenger for the surgeon and saw to the preparation of rooms
for Noël, including a large linen-draped table for the surgery,
Charmiane directed a wagon with two litter bearers to the spot
where she had found Noël. He was barely conscious as they
bundled him into the wagon. But when they reached Bonneval,
lifted him out and carried him inside, he managed to rally. "Bazaine, you devil," he muttered, as the man hurried forward.
"Hasn't Brother Adam sacked you yet?"

Bazaine stared in surprise at the mock insult, then raised a
scornful eyebrow. "*Monsieur le comte* would be helpless without me. Now, Monsieur Noël, save your strength for what's
ahead." He turned to Charmiane. "*Madame*, if you wish to assist, I would suggest that you change to more appropriate attire
while *monsieur le comte*'s valet and I get Monsieur Noël out of
these filthy rags."

Charmiane put on a simple cotton gown, wrapped a large
apron around herself and hurried to Noël's suite; Bazaine had put
him into the east pavilion, just across the corridor from her
rooms. Noël was already stripped of his clothes and lay on the
table that had been set in the center of the room, beneath a lighted
chandelier. He was naked except for his soiled bandages and a
small cloth draped across his loins and thighs. Charmiane cringed
as Bazaine took a scissors to the dirty bandages and carefully
peeled them back. Noël had sustained two more wounds besides
the injury to his arm: a bullet to his side—just above the hip—
that seemed to have been hacked at by butchers from the look of
the torn flesh around the bullet entry, which was blue with powder burns, as well; and a slash across his breast, like a saber cut,
some three or four inches long. Both wounds had begun to close,
but the lack of clean dressings during his solitary ride from Germany had allowed the injuries to fester. The skin was raw red and
beefy, with patches of blackened, dead flesh and oozing green pus
whose sickly sweet odor almost made Charmiane gag.

His arm was the worst. Bazaine had had to cut his shirt off at the shoulder. The slow seepage of blood through bandage and sleeve as his arm swelled had produced a thick red "plaster" of fabric and dried blood, impossible to remove without tearing the flesh from his arm. In preparation for the surgeon, Bazaine set it in a basin of warm water to steep off the hard coating and reach the torn skin and bones beneath. A parade of footmen came and went, changing the basin as the water cooled and turned bright red.

Bazaine shook his head. "Was it a clean break the first time, Monsieur Noël?"

"No. The ball shattered the bone. And then, when I fell...stupid. Asleep in the saddle."

Charmiane felt helpless. "What can I do? Have you eaten at all?"

"Not for a day. I stopped at several garrisons the first few days. But when I fell...afraid they might amputate if I should grow too weak to stop them." He tried to rise, his eyes darting frantically about the room. "Bazaine, they mustn't...!"

"No. Lie back. The arm is probably too swollen now for that."

"But if you haven't eaten," said Charmiane with some concern, "let me send one of the servants..."

Bazaine's voice was unexpectedly sharp. "No!"

"But if he's hungry..." She could scarcely contain her anger.

Noël held up his hand. "Trust an old military man. He knows what he's doing," he said. And then, in answer to Charmiane's puzzled frown, he smiled ruefully. "Men sometimes vomit when they're in pain. And I suspect my friend the surgeon will be none too gentle." He ran his tongue across his lips. "Damn, but I am thirsty."

Charmiane fetched a pitcher of water, but at Bazaine's warning glance she contented herself with dipping a cloth into it and pressing the moisture to Noël's lips. She had already sent for soapy water and towels; now, while Bazaine supervised the bringing up of more candles and bandages and water to wash the wounds, she attempted to clean those parts of Noël that weren't injured. She washed and dried his face, then began on his good arm and shoulder, his legs and feet—discreetly avoiding the area beneath the draped sheet. She worked slowly and gently; his body must be racked with pain, and the less she disturbed him the better. Her eyes strayed to his face and she blushed to find him watching her, a bemused smile playing at his lips.

He laughed. "I haven't been so tenderly mothered in years."

She fought the urge to turn away and hide her embarrassment. She had been very conscious of his nakedness as she worked, his strong masculinity, his long, beautifully formed limbs. Curse her open face, he must have seen it! "Really," she snapped in as impersonal, as motherly a tone as she could manage, "if you had any sense, you would have stayed in the hospital. I'm sure they would have tended you with as much care."

He snorted. "Have you ever seen a military hospital? Not enough beds, not enough doctors, not enough food or medicine. And the surgeons' assistants have little enough tenderness, God knows! Most of them are unwilling conscripts, forced to help in the medical service because they refused to fight." He put his hand near the wound to his side. "Some damned orderly worked on me to take out the bullet. If I'd had two good arms, I would have throttled him as he carved me up." The effort at speaking had exhausted him. He closed his eyes.

The surgeon arrived, a bustling little man with pink cheeks and a large nose. He introduced himself as Dr. Hébert. He looked at Noël's wounds, clucked his tongue, motioned the footmen to stand by to fetch and carry and proceeded to wash his hands.

"What shall I do?" asked Charmiane.

Bazaine stared at her across Noël's inert form. "I shall assist the doctor, *madame*. I've had some experience in the past. It would be best if you simply try to keep Monsieur Noël comfortable and distracted. It will be a long afternoon, I fear." There was a world of meaning in his sharp glance.

Noël's arm still hadn't soaked enough to be free of its cement-like fabric coating; Dr. Hébert began instead on the other wounds. He washed them thoroughly, squeezing water from a dripping sponge and blotting at the festered sores; the linen cloth under Noël turned dark with blood and corruption as he worked. Noël kept his eyes closed; Charmiane thought at first he was asleep. But when Hébert pulled out a scalpel and began to scrape at the dead and blackened patches of flesh around the wounds, Noël's eyes sprang open in pained surprise and he began to twitch. Bazaine shot Charmiane a warning look. Distraction. That's what Noël needed. She smoothed back the hair from his forehead. "How long were you on the road from Germany?" she said quickly.

He grimaced. "Five days, I think. Maybe . . ." He winced in pain. "Maybe six."

"You should have stopped to rest. It was foolish of you."

"I thought I was dying. Men die of gangrene, too, you know. Eh, doctor? And I wanted to die among my own." He grunted as the doctor cut away a large chunk of dead skin from his chest. "Have a care, Hébert!" He reached for Charmiane's hand. His fingers were strong as they closed around hers, but hot and feverish. He stared at her with pain-filled eyes. "I remember you," he whispered, "on the night of the ball."

"When you first called me beautiful lady."

"A fitting name. Then . . . and always." He closed his eyes. "I see you still in my mind's eye. From across the room."

She laughed softly. "What am I doing?"

He opened his eyes and grinned, but it seemed a forced smile. "Breaking my heart every time you're not with me."

She lapsed into silence, flustered, while the doctor finished cleaning his chest and side wounds and wrapped them in fresh bandages. She watched Hébert carefully: it was a chore she'd be sharing with Bazaine, she knew, and teaching to the maids. "At least twice a day," Hébert said, "until the wounds stop discharging."

He turned his attention to Noël's arm. The "plaster" was now softened enough to peel away. Hébert clicked his tongue at the sight of the raw, oozing flesh beneath, the dark bruises, the spots of blackened tissue. He felt for Noël's pulse at his wrist, then squatted down and sighted along his arm. He shook his head. "It's clearly twisted, of course. No pulse. Luckily, the swelling has kept the misalignment to a minimum. And there's no infection." He nodded briskly to several footmen. "I'll need help to hold him down."

"It won't be necessary," growled Noël.

"I'll hold your shoulders, Monsieur Noël. That should be enough," said Bazaine smoothly.

Hébert shrugged. "Whatever you wish. If you're fortunate, you'll lose consciousness," he added cheerfully.

With Bazaine standing behind Noël, pushing down on his shoulders, and Charmiane holding tightly to his good hand, Hébert began his work. He felt for the shattered bones, pressing deep into the swollen muscles and tendons. Noël gnashed his teeth. Then, one hand on the injured upper arm and the other on Noël's elbow, Hébert began to reposition the bone. He tugged at the limb, extending it as much as possible, then twisted it from side to side. Charmiane winced to hear the grinding, crunching noises that came from the arm. Noël was now clutching her hand so tightly that her fingers ached. Hébert jerked on the arm and a strangled cry escaped Noël's throat. His face was twisted in agony, his eyes squeezed shut as though that response alone could fend off the pain. As Hébert let go of the arm, Noël sighed and relaxed.

Charmiane blotted at the perspiration that had beaded up on his forehead. "It will soon be over."

He opened his eyes. They were filled with tears. "Charmiane." He turned his head aside.

"You needn't be ashamed of your tears," she murmured. "There's a limit to suffering, even for brave men."

His eyes were warm with gratitude. Then he shook off the moment of weakness and even managed a laugh, looking up at Bazaine, who hovered over him. "But I should never hear the end of it from this devil." He glanced at the doctor, who had begun again to sight along the arm and feel for his pulse. "Hébert, you flesh tailor, are you done yet?"

"Alas, no, *monsieur*. A little more. Be of good cheer." Again the manipulation, the grinding of bones, the struggles of Bazaine to keep Noël from throwing himself off the table in his distress. But at last it was over. Hébert felt for the pulse, which had returned now that the bone was in its proper place, declared himself satisfied and began to bind the arm.

Noël lay exhausted, his eyes beginning to glaze from fever and pain. His mind was clearly wandering. "Must reach Bonneval," he mumbled. He focused on Charmiane's face. He released her fingers and touched the side of her cheek with a trembling hand. "If I should die . . ."

"No, no. You mustn't talk that way."

"If I should die . . ." He closed his eyes, then opened them again. His finger moved across her cheek to stroke her lips. "My God, I wanted you at the ball . . . on the stairs, when I first saw you . . ."

Bazaine shook him gently on the shoulder. "Hush, Monsieur Noël. Save your strength. You'll need it for playing cards with me."

Noël stared at Bazaine, then nodded and flashed the shadow of a grin. "Get me to a bed, you old devil, and let me sleep."

"Madame la comtesse," said Bazaine, "go and change your clothes. You've done enough here."

Charmiane did as she was told. She was worn-out but bewildered, as well. When she'd seen Noël at the ball, and again when he'd visited before the wedding, she'd known he was attracted to her. But there had been a lightheartedness about his wooing, a certain flirtation, as though he weren't quite sure whether he took his own emotions seriously. But the Noël who had looked at her today, held her hand, said he wanted her, had revealed a depth of feeling that surprised and shook her. Perhaps it was the effect of the fever that had loosened his constraints, made him say things that they both might regret when he'd recovered. He was her husband's brother; she must remember that. She prayed that the fever would blot all memory of the afternoon from his mind.

The fever lasted for three days. He tossed and shouted in his sleep and clutched wildly at Charmiane and Bazaine when they came to change his dressings. They kept his arm bound close to his body; still, fearful that he might fall out of bed in his wild ravings, they tied him down, leaving only his good hand free.

There came a morning when Charmiane, exhausted by her constant bedside vigil, had slept late. She awoke at last and rang for Yvonne. The girl was slower than usual today. When she finally appeared, carrying Charmiane's breakfast tray, she was humming. "Monsieur Bouchard is awake at last, *madame*."

"Good!" Charmiane smiled in relief. "How does he feel?"

"Hmph! He pinched Suzanne."

It sounded more like jealousy than a complaint. Charmiane smothered a laugh. "And you?"

"Well, he did say I was a saucy little thing," purred the girl. "And he didn't say it to Antoinette."

"*Mon Dieu!* How many of you have been in to see him this morning? Just to change his bandages? Help me to dress. I see we'll have to put a stop to all this coquetry before the man has a relapse."

Dressed in a bright printed muslin, she hurried into Noël's suite to find him lying in bed, surrounded by half a dozen twittering chambermaids. She clapped her hands together sharply. "Out, out! Have you nothing better to do?" She watched them depart, waving their fingers in Noël's direction, then turned on him, hands on hips. "Really! You ought to be ashamed of yourself! Barely out of your fever and . . ."

He grinned. "I can't help it if I like women."

"Oh, tush! Do be serious." She put her hand on his forehead. "How do you feel?"

"Tired and thirsty. And can I be untied now?"

"Of course." She loosened the ties, put another pillow behind his head and gave him a sip of water. "Do you want anything more?"

He rubbed his cheek. "A razor, a toothbrush, a bath. Some food."

"All in good time. I'll send in one of the maids with a toothbrush and a bowl of broth. The sponge bath and shave will wait until tomorrow."

"Will you send in one of the maids for the bath? I rather fancied Suzanne."

"I'll send a footman," she said dryly.

He looked disappointed. "And the shave?"

She relented. "I'll do it myself."

"Did you shave Brother Adam?"

The joy was gone from their banter at the mention of Adam's name. "No," she snapped. "But sometimes my first husband."

He studied her face, his blue eyes grown serious. Then he shrugged with his one good arm. "It's none of my concern, beautiful lady. I . . . Damn! How did you get those bruises?"

She looked at the blue finger marks on her arms. She should have worn long sleeves this morning. "It's nothing. When you were delirious . . ."

He lifted her arm and brought it to his lips, planting a soft kiss on the bruised flesh. Then he looked at her with a look that was so intense that she wasn't sure, after all, that he'd forgotten what had happened during his operation. "I'll never hurt you again," he whispered.

She brought Prosper with her the next day to help with the shave. Noël's health seemed to have improved dramatically even in one day. He had been given a sponge bath and a pair of underbreeches. He sat up in bed, his still-swollen arm supported by a sling. He grinned at Charmiane. "I'd hoped you hadn't forgotten."

"Of course not. Prosper, put the washstand over here."

Prosper scurried forward and put down a brass tripod near the bed, then set a basin on top of it. He left the room and returned with a brass ewer of water and the shaving tools. He set them down and jumped back as though he thought Noël would bite.

Charmiane noticed Noël's frown. "The boy is mute," she explained.

"But why does he look at me that way?"

"He's . . . he's afraid of Adam. I wish you wouldn't scowl when he's here."

Noël muttered a curse but managed an artificial smile in Prosper's direction. "Tie that napkin around my neck, boy."

Charmiane took the napkin from Prosper and put it around Noël's neck. "And don't give orders, please. We have quite enough of that when Adam's home."

His eyebrows shot up in surprise. "The beautiful lady has spirit, I see."

Not when Adam is around, she thought bitterly, remembering her cringing obedience. Ah, well. She perched on the edge of the bed and began to lather Noël's chin. His face was craggy and lean, with sharp angles to his jaw and high cheekbones. But for all the haughty splendor of his features, so like Adam's, there was a world of difference. His face seemed so much younger, softer. And the eyes held a vulnerability that touched her heart. Perhaps it was Adam's cruelty and rancor that made him seem ugly in comparison. She took up the razor and began the shave. After a moment, Noël laughed softly, his body shaking so she had to stop her work. "What is it?" she asked.

"You do the strangest thing with your nose when you're concentrating. You pull it in, like a little rabbit."

"Oh, dear." She touched her nose self consciously. "I had a nursemaid who did that. A silly habit that I can't seem to lose." *Dieu!* She was blushing.

He searched her face, his eyes warm with approval. "It's charming. Everything about you is charming."

She blushed again. "You're as wicked as ever, Noël."

"Will you kiss me, as you did the last time I visited?"

She bristled at his presumption. "No! That was a mistake. And I wasn't married then." She resumed her work, making a conscious effort to keep her nose still.

"Tell me about your first husband," he said at length.

"There's nothing to tell. We were married for more than four years. He was much older than I. He died. That's all."

"Did you love him?"

She couldn't look him in the eye. "I honored and obeyed him."

"But did you love him?"

"Really, Noël." She was becoming quite agitated. Must he dig at her with his prying questions? Her hand shook and the razor nicked his chin. She frowned and stanched the blood, putting all her concentration into the act. But still he stared with those searching blue eyes, waiting for an answer. "Of course I loved Henri," she lied.

He laughed, a dry bark. "A veritable love match."

She colored again. Her face had betrayed her, as usual. "What does it matter if I loved him or not?" she said with bitterness. "The heart is no better a guide than the head!"

"Ah." He nodded in understanding. "Tell me lies about your *second* husband now."

She turned away. "My silent husband. What is there to tell?"

"It's Adam's way. Does it bother you, his silence?"

"Yes," she admitted. "Especially when he can tell what I'm thinking. I feel at such a . . . disadvantage."

"You make it sound like a war. Why do you think he married you?"

"Why does any man marry? To have children. To perpetuate his name. To puff up his pride."

He grunted. Prosper, hovering nearby, jumped. "His pride?" said Noël. "Because you were born to nobility and he wasn't?"

"It's what he said himself."

"That doesn't sound like Brother Adam. Perhaps he spoke in anger."

She snorted. "And maybe he wanted an aristocratic bride! Your Emperor chose the same path to legitimacy."

"He had a dynasty to found," he said dryly. "I doubt that Adam had such a vainglorious view of himself. Nor Napoleon's Empress such an inflated sense of her worth."

It was a sharp reproof and she flinched. It had sounded snobbish, though she hadn't meant it. She finished his shave in silence and wiped his face clean of lather. She felt the need to defend herself so as not to leave him with the impression that she was at fault if he suspected trouble between her and Adam. "Oh, why does *any* man marry?" she burst out. "For the convenience. To be the master of his own little domain, with an eternally loyal subject in attendance!"

His eyes widened in surprise. "Name of God! Is that what a husband is?"

"Isn't he?" she sneered. "The lord and master, expecting a dutiful wife?"

He frowned in dismay. "If you truly believe that, then why did you marry Adam?"

She was fighting her tears now. "Must we talk of this?"

"No. I'm sorry." He rubbed at his chin thoughtfully, then laughed. "You missed a spot." He scratched at a bit of bristle.

She was glad of the chance to resume the shave. It gave her time to put her emotions under control again. She relathered the spot, scraped at it with the razor. He chuckled and reached out to touch her nose. Unconsciously she had tucked it in again. Their eyes met and they laughed together. The air was clear. She had no quarrel with Noël. If she let it happen, his warmth and goodness could replace for her a little of that brotherly love she'd lost when she lost Armand. She finished the job and patted his cheek. "There. Now try to sleep."

She started to turn away, but he grasped her wrist. "Whatever else your husbands were," he said, "they probably didn't deserve you. Maybe someday you'll tell me the truth."

She fled from the look in his eyes. Perhaps "brother" wasn't what he wanted to be.

His strength grew as the days wore on. It was impossible to keep the chambermaids from him, and Charmiane would often find them, when she went to change his dressings, gathered around his bed flirting outrageously. And then, when she'd chase them all away, he'd tease her, tell her she was jealous, until she blushed and laughed together. He seemed determined to restore his body as quickly as possible; he spent hours with a sponge in his left hand, squeezing it to exercise the muscles, until the sweat broke out on his forehead from the pain and the exertion.

There had been no word from Adam. But Bazaine had heard reports of continual fighting in Germany. He felt sure that Monsieur de Moncalvo was quite safe and would communicate with them as soon as he could.

Or perhaps he's dead, thought Charmiane. Then suffered pangs of guilt for wishing it was so.

May was nearly over. The garden bloomed with spring flowers. Charmiane sent Prosper to the gardeners to cut her a basketful of blossoms. The boy had a knack for communicating in silence, and his sweet nature and open, trusting face smoothed away any misunderstandings.

With the windows thrown open to the bright day, Charmiane stood in the music room, arranging the flowers in a tall *jardinière*, a painted porcelain vase set on a gilded tripod decorated with winged beasts. She stepped back, surveyed her handiwork, then shook her head. "Prosper, fetch me another pink peony. I think I need..."

"He's gone. I sent him away so I could be alone with you."

She whirled. Noël stood in the doorway, grinning. He was wearing Adam's clothes: a loose shirt that covered his bandaged arm, a brocaded dressing gown thrown over his shoulders and a pair of pantaloons and slippers.

"*Fi donc!* What are you doing up?" she demanded.

"I missed your company." He shuffled slowly into the room and lowered himself into a gilded armchair. Charmiane hurried forward to put a small footstool under his feet. "And since you wouldn't come to me," he went on, "I decided to come to you. I sent my valet to get me some of Adam's clothes, and . . ."

Still at his feet, she looked up sharply. "Your valet?"

"Fouché. Adam's valet. The man had nothing to do, so I appropriated him the other day. And Adam's wardrobe today."

She rose stiffly and returned to her flowers.

He swore under his breath. "What have I done?" She busied herself with rearranging several bright yellow tulips. "Come now," he said at her continued silence, "aren't we friends enough for you to tell me?"

She turned, unwilling to meet his eyes. "You're . . . a guest here. A welcome guest, to be sure. But the disposition of the household is not in your hands. You should have asked me first."

He smiled sheepishly. "I never thought of it. Forgive me for treading on your toes."

She didn't know why it should have annoyed her so. "I'm quite capable of making decisions myself," she said with some heat.

"Do you make the decisions when Adam's here?"

That was why she'd reacted with such anger. Because Noël had usurped what little power she had. If he'd asked her for the valet, she'd only have gone to Bazaine for his approval anyway. "I'm Adam's wife. I follow his lead," she said in defense.

"Of course. Your lord and master. Isn't that what you said the other day?"

"You don't understand. You haven't been married. A wife has a duty to give her husband cheerful obedience, Aunt Sophie always said."

"*Le diable!* That sounds like schoolgirl cant. Did you give Henri cheerful obedience?"

"I dared nothing else!" she said, then blushed for shame. She hadn't been a good wife to Henri. She had obeyed out of fear, but her heart had been in constant rebellion.

He gazed at her, searching her face. "My God," he said at last, "did he *beat* you?"

How could she lie, with him reading her face like a book? Yet she hadn't the courage to turn away. She began to stammer excuses. "You don't understand. He . . . was much older. I was young and willful. Henri knew what was best for us both. I...had no right...to cross him."

"God," he growled. "He sounds like a bully."

She stared, openmouthed. It was such a revolutionary thought. "But my duty..."

"You have a duty to yourself, as well."

Her mind teemed with thoughts of the past. Henri. The days in Switzerland. But everything was changed now, as though a bright light had been suddenly focused on a picture she'd seen a thousand times. Henri the bully. Too weak and useless to do anything but brutalize her. She began to laugh softly. "Yes, I suppose he was a bully. And I was too young to realize it." She laughed again. She felt incredibly free. "The damned villain!" She looked at Noël, her chin set at a new and defiant angle. "I didn't weep when he died, you know."

He smiled warmly. "He doesn't seem to have destroyed your mettle."

"Squashed for a time, I suppose," she said. "But I think I forgave him when he died."

His eyes were dark. "And Adam. Will you forgive him?"

She stared out at the lawns, dappled with sunlight. "I'll curse his name though he be in the grave."

"Charmiane..."

She turned to him, her eyes filling with tears. "He killed my brother, you know."

"Yes. Bazaine told me. But perhaps..."

"Will you defend him?" she challenged.

"Not if it does no good."

She buried her face in her hands. "I shall never stop seeing him as a monster. Not just because of Armand." She thought again of the horror and shame of that night. Of Jean-Pierre's death through betrayal. "He's a cruel stranger. A man I'll never learn to know. To like. To feel anything but hatred and contempt for." She looked up. Noël's face was stricken, a mask of dismay. She ran to him and threw herself at his feet. "Oh, forgive me! I shouldn't speak of him this way to you. He's your brother, whatever he's done."

"A well-loved brother," he chided gently, "and not without reason. And my friend, as well."

"Friend?" It seemed inconceivable to her that this man—so kind and warmhearted—should find anything to like, to love, in Adam.

"A good friend." He leaned back in his chair and closed his eyes. "We used to swim together in the ocean, growing up in Brittany. And wrestle in the sand. And then go to school with our hair wet and plastered down and pretend to the schoolmaster that we'd been studying. I suppose we took each other's beatings many a time. There's a peculiar bond between twins. I never grow used to it when we're together. It's all unspoken, but . . . I know he feels it, as well."

She crossed to her flower arrangement and pinched off a dead blossom. "Do you think Adam's alive?" She tried to keep her voice neutral. She wasn't sure what she wanted to hear.

He hesitated. "I think I'd know it if he were dead."

"You weren't such good friends at the ball. I remember how he scowled at you."

He laughed. "Yes. I'd forgotten. Some woman. I don't even recall her name now. We've been rivals, I suppose, in some ways. It's natural. Too often we've wanted the same things." He stared at her. "Like you."

She was saved from the awkward moment by Yvonne's entrance. The maid curtsied. "Antoinette said that you were complaining about your linens this morning, *madame*."

"Yes. I thought I told you that I wanted my best laces to be sent to Neuilly for bleaching and ironing."

The girl pursed her lips. "There's nothing the matter with our laundress, *madame*."

"It's an indulgence I allowed myself in Paris. I should like it to continue. The laundresses at Neuilly have the most delicate hands." After much grumbling, Yvonne was persuaded to do her mistress's bidding. With a sigh and a sidelong glance at Noël, she left the room. Charmiane shook her head. "That girl. She only came in here to flirt with you. Oh, well. I think it's time for you to return to your bed. Do you need help?"

"Let me stay a little longer. Play the piano for me. You *do* play?"

"Yes." She seated herself at the piano and played a sonatina, then closed the instrument firmly and turned to Noël. "Enough now. To bed."

"Will you help me?" He stood up and waited for her to come to his side, then put his good arm around her shoulder. Together they made their way up the stairs to his rooms. Charmiane was conscious of his weight, his scent, his closeness. And when she helped him out of his dressing gown and slippers, she was grateful that he was content to go back to bed in shirt and pantaloons without undressing further. His presence was too disturbing, even clothed.

As she tucked the blanket around him, he reached up and played with a curl of her hair. "Beautiful lady," he murmured. "And you belong to Adam. Did you play the piano for Brother Adam?"

"I don't think he ever listened," she said with annoyance.

"What? Never listened?"

She felt as though she had an ally, for all that he was Adam's brother. He had shown himself to be a sympathetic and understanding listener. "There was always a parade of servants when I played for him. In and out. With questions and problems. It never seemed to bother him. To make his decisions while I was playing. He even made *my* decisions!"

He frowned. "The devil you say! Perhaps he never realized it. Why didn't you tell him?"

"Are you mad?"

"I don't understand you. You didn't like Adam making decisions for you. You didn't like playing the piano for him. You clearly don't like your own maid. What else don't you like about Bonneval? The château? The rooms? The furniture?"

She shrugged. "I don't feel as though it's mine. Bazaine saw to all the decorations."

"Poor Charmiane. In a strange house and married to a stranger." He reached for her hand and kissed it. "Perhaps when I'm well, we'll run away together."

She blushed and pulled her hand away. "I never know when you're just teasing me."

He grinned. "Even better, if Adam never returns, I can stay here and take his place. Who would know?"

She laughed. "Oh, you *are* a devil! I wonder it only took a few Prussian bullets to put you down!"

"You should laugh always," he said. "It makes your eyes sparkle." His voice was a husky growl in his throat, and his eyes were on her lips. "Now go away and let me sleep. If you stay, I'll have to kiss you."

Chapter Fourteen

"Noël, you can't possibly escape that trap."

Hand on chin, Noël frowned at the chessboard, then looked up at Charmiane. "You have the tactical advantage, sister-in-law. How can I concentrate with you staring at me with those beautiful eyes?" He sat back in his chair and grinned.

She felt herself blushing, a hot stain that suffused her face and neck. It was nearly a month now since he'd been at Bonneval, and the compliments had become more and more lavish, the flirtations more outrageous, the invitations to share a kiss more frequent. And the worst of it was, she wasn't sure if he was joking or not. His smile was lighthearted, but there was something in his eyes. It seduced her, but frightened her, as well. As his strength grew, she found herself trying to avoid the intimacy of being alone with him. She'd taken the care today to have the chessboard set on a table on the terrace overlooking the gardens, in plain sight of half a dozen gardeners and servants. And still he pursued her shamelessly. With his words. With his eyes. "Tush!" She waved away his flattery. "You simply can't admit defeat."

He grimaced and tugged at the sling on his arm. "Lord, I'm getting tired of this. And my chest itches." He rubbed at Adam's waistcoat.

"Oh, Monsieur Bouchard! May I help you?" One of the maids came flying out of the drawing room to bend solicitously to him. "I couldn't help but notice how uncomfortable you seemed."

He smiled up at her. "Suzanne, isn't it? Well, Suzanne, you can retie it, if you will. Give me a little more play in the elbow." As she finished adjusting the sling, he let his hand rest for a moment on hers. The maid giggled and blushed.

"That will be all, Suzanne," said Charmiane impatiently. *Dieu!* she thought. She sounded as snappish as a jealous rival! Which was absurd. But Noël was so obvious, so unsubtle and brazen when he flirted with the maids, that it rankled her. She pushed away the chessboard; his hand on Suzanne's had put a shadow across the joy of the game. "I concede to you," she said.

"*Le diable!* Why? When you have the advantage?" If he had meant to pursue the issue—which she prayed he wouldn't, since she'd find it impossible to hide her feelings toward Suzanne—he was prevented from doing so by the appearance of Bazaine.

"*Madame.*" Bazaine bowed in her direction. "The head groom tells me you've asked about a cabriolet."

"Yes. I thought it would be pleasant to drive myself to some of the villages hereabouts."

"*Madame*, that's very foolish and dangerous. To go out alone. I think you ought to reconsider." There was finality in Bazaine's tone.

Charmiane sighed. She'd hoped to find a way to visit Bertrand de Domfort in Paris without anyone at Bonneval knowing of it. It was difficult enough for her, having to hide her articles for *La Voix* in the letters she sent to Aunt Sophie. She was always sure, when Bazaine hefted the sealed letters she handed him, that he suspected more than just gossip was in the heavy packet. If she could go to Paris unattended sometimes... But Bazaine objected to the idea of the cabriolet, that was clear. She tried once more. "I won't be alone. I'll take Prosper with me."

He shook his head. "No, *madame.*"

She saw Noël watching her with interest, curiosity, an edge of disapproval. This was her decision, and she had a right to make it. She was the mistress of Bonneval, wasn't she? "I want a cabriolet for my use," she said firmly. "Is there a comfortable one in the stables?"

Noël grinned his satisfaction. "Why don't you have him buy a pretty new one? Brother Adam can afford it."

She smiled. "Yes. Yes, indeed! Gray, I think. And a team of horses to match. Good mares, with springy steps."

Noël nodded. "Good for you! Oh, and, Bazaine, Madame de Moncalvo and I will go and choose the horses together." He smiled at Charmiane. "That is, if *madame* is agreed."

"Of course."

Bazaine cleared his throat angrily. "Monsieur Noël, you may take it upon yourself to spend your brother's money in a reckless manner and encourage *madame la comtesse* to do so. But *I* am responsible for your care, and I won't have you dashing all over the parish to buy horses! Not until you're fit enough!''

Noël scowled and rose to his feet. "Now, by God, Bazaine..."

Bazaine's one eye narrowed threateningly. "Monsieur Noël, you have no right to play the tyrant in your brother's house. As for the matter of your health, only a jackass would take as little care as you've taken since you've been here. Up and around and dancing attendance on the servant girls as though you hadn't been near to death! Ah!'' Bazaine shook his head in disgust.

Noël stared in disbelief at this tirade, then laughed ruefully and subsided into his chair. "Bazaine, you martinet, you should have been a village grandmother. You have the sharp tongue for it.''

Bazaine bowed in deference, but he couldn't quite hide the smirk of victory that made his mustaches twitch. "If you wish, *monsieur*, I'll have several horses brought here to the stables, so you and *madame* can make your choice.'' With another bow, he left them alone.

Noël patted Charmiane's hand. "I was proud of you, sister-in-law. The way you stood up to Bazaine, the old devil.''

"Oh, Noël, you're teasing again. You...'' She stopped, flustered. His eyes were clear and intense, filled with genuine approval. Admiration. Hidden thoughts she couldn't begin to fathom. She remembered the night of the Tuileries ball. Even then she'd suspected that his lightheartedness hid far deeper emotions. Though he seemed often to make a conscious effort to be bright and cheerful, she was more than ever convinced that beneath the easy charm lay a sensitive, serious man.

And surely there was a deeper side to him, for all his insouciance. Only this morning, rising early, she had been surprised to find Fouche, Adam's valet, coming out of Noël's rooms as she passed his door. Fouche had seemed embarrassed to be discovered, but upon her questioning he had admitted that he sometimes spent the night beside Noël's bed.

"But what for?'' An odd thing to do, since Fouche had a wife.

"Monsieur Bouchard has bad dreams,'' he had said reluctantly. "And he won't let me tie him down at night. I worry sometimes. His arm and all. So I spend the night, to see that he doesn't hurt himself.''

What a dismaying surprise, she had thought. "How often does he have these nightmares?''

Fouche had sighed. "Almost every night, I think. Though he doesn't always remember in the morning. A good man. He seems to suffer in his sleep. I do what I can."

Now she stared at Noël, smiling so warmly at her, and thought of Adam and his cruelty and cold rages, and wondered how a mother could produce two sons so different one from the other.

A moonbeam woke her. The weather had turned warm, and though Yvonne had grumbled about the unhealthiness of it, she'd had the maid leave her windows wide to the night air. And the moon had crept up in the sky, peeked in her window and danced on her closed eyes until her sleep had been disturbed. Now she sat up in bed, wide awake. She heard the song of a nightingale. On an impulse, she got up, threw on her dressing gown and went to the window. The moon shimmered on the expanse of lawn and a crystal reflecting pool in the gardens beyond and played a staccato of light and velvet shade with the line of lime trees that led to a small orangery. Someone's cat, a spotted furry little creature, prowled the night, stopping from time to time to fling himself into the air at a night-flying bug.

She smiled to herself. It looked so inviting, the still June night. And who would know if the mistress chose to take a solitary stroll under the moon? The east pavilion housed few servants; no one would see or hear her. There was a small side door that led to the outside. She lit a candle and moved quietly through her bedroom to her boudoir—like a private sitting room—beyond. When she reached the corridor, she was startled to hear a loud noise.

Surely it was a human cry! And coming from Noël's room across the passageway. *Dieu!* she thought. He was having another nightmare. She hurried to his rooms, peering about the antechamber to see if Fouche had decided to spend the night; seeing no one, she went into Noël's bedroom.

He lay writhing on his bed, the sheets thrown back in a tumble. He was naked except for his underbreeches, and his bandaged and sling-braced arm. His chest and side wounds had healed sufficiently to be left unbound; only the bumpy and angry red scars still remained. His bare skin glistened with sweat. He moaned and cried and rocked his head from side to side, then shouted something unintelligible. His wrenching movements were so violent that Charmiane feared he'd throw his weight onto his own injured arm.

She set down her candle, leaped forward and pressed him onto his back again, all the while murmuring soothing sounds.

"What?" His eyes flew open and he sat bolt upright, glancing frantically about the dim room. "What? What?" He gasped and panted, as though he'd been running wildly for hours, and he shook all over.

"Hush, Noël. Hush! It's all right."

"What?" It took him a long minute to return to himself, for the gasps and cries to subside. Then he stared at her, groaned and closed his eyes. He rubbed his hand across his face in a slow gesture—so forlorn and despairing that it broke her heart.

"What is it, Noël?"

"Just a dream," he mumbled. "Don't concern yourself."

"Tell me about it."

He opened his eyes and frowned. "It's just a dream, I tell you. Go back to bed."

"Tell me," she insisted. And then, "Is it always the same?"

He stared in stubborn silence, then slumped back against the pillows and sighed. "Yes. Only it isn't a dream. Would to God it were."

"Then what is it that terrifies you so?"

He made a sound like a wounded animal, all pain and uncomprehending suffering. "Not terror. Horror. The horror of it. I'm always back in Russia." He looked at her, stricken. "Do you know how cold it was? They told us that after we crossed the Berezina it sometimes dropped to thirty-five below. And that's where I am, when I dream. Climbing over mounds of dead and frozen corpses to get close enough to a fire to keep warm. Only they're not all dead. And they cry, and they moan, and they lift their arms for succor. And I can do nothing." He sighed again and waved a dismissing hand at her. "Go to bed. It will pass. It always does."

She felt it was a deliberate evasion, as though he were afraid even to talk about it. "And then what happens?" she persisted.

"Charmiane...damn it..."

She groped for his hand and squeezed it encouragingly. "Please."

He began again, the words low and halting, as though they were being dragged out of him. "Everyone is hungry and cold. Desperate for warmth. For food. One of the men...God, it's impossible to tell he's a man. We all look like bundles of rags. Beards. Skin blackened from the cold, as if it were burned. And red watery eyes. Hardly human. This thing...this pile of rags and filth is hacking at a dying horse for food. And we crowd around, ready to kill each other for a piece. The man . . . in his haste, and shaking, cuts off two of his own fingers." He choked back a sob. "And we watch with envy as he sucks at his own blood, his fingers shoved in his mouth. Like a hungry baby at the breast. Sucking."

"Oh God, Noël."

"There's more." He blinked back his tears. "Someone set a peasant's cottage on fire for more warmth. Do you know how mad you can get when you're cold and starving?" He pulled his hand free of hers and clapped it over his eyes. "No more," he groaned. "For the love of God, no more."

"Tell it all," she said firmly. "Once and for all, tell it all."

"One of the men . . . began to cackle like an idiot. He threw himself into the fire and laughed all the while his body . . ." His face twisted in agony and he began to sob. "I can't. I can't."

She sat on the edge of the bed and put her arm around his shoulder. "You must."

He took a tortured breath and went on. "Even before his charred corpse had stopped smoking, a poor desperate wretch staggered to him. Reached out. Oh God, have we come to this? He tore off a piece of blackened flesh and . . . and put it in his mouth. There was a man beside me. He began to weep and pray. I knew he meant to feed off the corpse and was suffering in moral agony. I still had a piece of horse meat I'd been chewing on. I begged the man to remember his humanity. I offered him the horse meat. He took it, weeping his gratitude. The tears froze on his face, I remember. And then, before he could eat the meat, he fell at my feet, dead."

"Oh, Noël. Alas!"

His sobs were becoming uncontrollable, shaking his shoulders in a storm of grief. "They crowded around. Picked the burned corpse clean. Down to the bones! Oh, the horror. I was no better. I pried my horse meat from the dead man's fingers. Broke his bones to do it. I think I would have . . . killed any man who stopped me. Lord Jesus!" he implored. "Is this why you died? So men could sink so low?"

Charmiane's own tears burned her eyes. She gathered Noël's trembling form in her arms and cradled his head against her bosom. His body was racked with sobs, as though the telling of the dream had opened the floodgates of his torment and grief. She could do nothing but hold him, and murmur softly, and pray that God would bring him peace at last.

The moon was low in the sky before she was able to calm him enough to persuade him to sleep again. Sleep, she thought. It was a wonder he dared go to sleep at all, knowing the horror that awaited him in his dreams.

It was a changed man who came out to the terrace to join her for morning *café au lait* the next day. Quieter, with a serenity that hadn't been there before. The bright gaiety was gone, and she scarcely missed it. She had thought it a mask; it warmed her heart that, after last night, he no longer felt the need to wear it with her. Perhaps the role had been forced on him. Adam was the "serious," the sober, responsible brother. Noël had had to carve out his own identity and had chosen a mask as different from his brother as possible: the carefree, always laughing scapegrace. But perhaps the part of him that she had seen last night—the dear vulnerability that she saw sometimes when his guard was down— was as much a part of him as his charm and his smiles.

Still, some of his restraint this morning was clearly due to embarrassment. She had seen him stripped of his defenses, and he wasn't comfortable with that. Not yet. He drank his coffee, and commented on the mists that still hovered over the pond, and strolled up and down on the terrace, admiring the fit of his brother's boots. Distant remarks. Small talk. Even the presence of the flirtatious Suzanne didn't seem to tempt him or shake his reserve.

"Thank you." He nodded impersonally as the maid poured him another cup and bent low to show him her *décolletage* at the same time. He turned his head away to pick up a spoon and stir his coffee. Suzanne flounced off, her pride injured. Charmiane smothered a laugh. Noël looked at her. "*Le diable!* What am I to do? Call her back and pinch her?"

She giggled. "If you don't, I'll begin to think you've taken a turn for the worse."

He started to laugh, then looked her in the eye. His blue gaze was direct, as though he'd suddenly decided that his deliberate distance was false pride under the circumstances. He put his hand over hers. "Thank you," he said softly. "For last night."

"Noël, my dear," she said—and he *was* dear to her—"the heart can't hold such pain. Sooner or later it must overflow."

He looked out at the sunny day as though he didn't see it. His voice, when he spoke, was low and muffled. "I have drowned in horrors for too long. Till they rise up and choke me. And still I live and breathe."

He was too close to the edge. She pulled him back. "And play chess badly. And pinch the maids when you shouldn't."

His eyes, warm with gratitude, flew to her face. He laughed his relief. "And pinch the maids."

"What else can you do?"

He smiled. "I should like to hold you in my arms."

"Hmph! Now I know you're getting better. You sound more and more like the Noël of old."

"And growing older by the minute, without the comfort of your kisses." He grinned as she blushed, and finished his coffee. In a moment he was serious again. "You're a warm and comforting woman, Charmiane. A man can consider himself lucky if..." He shrugged. "Ah, well. And whom do you weep with?"

"My pillow has shared an ocean of tears."

"And whom do you weep for?"

She gulped back the sudden rush of tears. "Armand." But even as she said his name, she knew it wasn't entirely true. Armand was almost a stranger when she thought about it. Until she and Sophie had returned to Paris, Armand had been a man she scarcely knew: he had appeared in Switzerland perhaps half a dozen times through the years. When he died, she had wept as much for the idea of "brother" lost as for the corporeal brother.

No. When Armand had died by Adam's cruel hand, her tears and grief had gone far beyond her brother. She had wept for her sweet dream of love—born, like a budding spring flower, in a moonlit garden, nurtured by tears of loneliness and yearning, nourished by sweet words scratched on paper in the glow of a midnight candle. And killed by the reality of the cold, heartless man she'd truly married.

"You're thinking of Adam." Noël stared at her, his eyes dark with sadness.

She tried to laugh. "Don't be silly. How do you know?"

"There's a look in your eyes that you get only when you think of Brother Adam. Or speak of him. Savage and terrible. Filled with hatred. What did he do to earn all that?"

"He tore out my heart," she whispered.

"Charmiane..." He reached across the table and stroked the side of her cheek with gentle fingers. "Poor Charmiane." His touch made her shiver, and his eyes seemed to probe her very soul.

It was too much to bear, the tenderness in eyes that were so like Adam's, yet so wondrously different. It would be very easy to love Noël. And she mustn't. All she had was her honor. She mustn't lose that. She jerked her head away from his hand and stood up quickly, praying to keep her voice from trembling. The sound of it was unnaturally high and forced even to her own ears. "Forgive me, brother-in-law. I must find Prosper. I have so many errands for him today. We'll have lunch in the rose arbor, I think. They're in bloom, and quite lovely. I'll see you then?" Without waiting for a reply, she escaped his disturbing nearness. And her own weakness.

In the next few days, she found her salvation in the use of Prosper as a shield whenever Noël was with her. At her command, Prosper waited at her elbow during meals, lest she want a shawl, a handkerchief, a fan. She discovered that she needed him to carry things as she strolled in the gardens, moved about the château during the day. And when they chose the horses for her cabriolet, Prosper sat with them and nodded his approval. Anything to keep the boy near her, to keep his intruding presence between her and Noël.

And Noël knew it. She saw it in his eyes when he looked at her; in the angry toss of his head when he'd go to help her down a staircase and Prosper would be there first, his little hand held out to his mistress. Noël spoke less and less, lapsing into unhappy silence at their growing estrangement. But what could she do? She was fighting for her honor, clinging to her last shred of common sense. What could she do but keep him at bay? She struggled against blossoming desire; but she wanted him so much her body ached at night when she went to bed.

And she no longer had the safety of thinking that his wooing was only lighthearted sport. He wanted her, as well. She couldn't deny it to herself. He was impatient now with the maids, brushing them aside when they gathered about him, all giggles and coy smiles. I desire you, his eyes seemed to say, as he looked at Charmiane. Only you.

His impatience extended to his body. Despite Bazaine's protests, he had stopped wearing his sling. Often Charmiane would see him from a window, pacing back and forth on the terrace, swinging his arms, flexing his muscles, as though he couldn't wait to be whole again.

There must be something she could do, she thought, to recapture the carefree innocence of their first few weeks together, before his unburdening tears and her tender comfort had created an intimate bond between them that was killing them both.

She smiled brightly across the table at him one afternoon as they were finishing lunch. He leaned back in his chair, pulled a cheroot from his pocket and scowled as Prosper scurried forward to light it for him. Charmiane forced a laugh. "You're beginning to resemble Adam more and more," she teased.

He exhaled, then managed a wry smile. "Is that the supreme insult?"

"No. Only to say that I've...missed my jolly companion. Shall we have a game of chess this afternoon?"

"With Prosper making the moves for you, so that our hands won't accidentally touch on the board?" When she flinched at his sharp words, he softened his tone. "I think I'll see if the grooms can find me a gentle horse. I'd like to ride."

"No. I'm sure it's too soon. The bones in your arm mayn't have knit well enough yet. It's foolish. I have an idea," she said quickly, as his frown deepened. "It's a lovely day. Why don't we take the cabriolet and ride into the hills? You can take the reins, so you don't feel idle."

"Will Prosper be with us?" he growled.

"Well, I thought it would be nice to bring some refreshments. We'll need Prosper to help."

"Of course." He stubbed out his cheroot with an angry gesture and left the table.

But by the time they started out in the cabriolet, he seemed to have recovered some of his old good humor. He complimented her on her costume—she had put on a pale pink muslin gown and a large, peaked straw bonnet—and even allowed Prosper to squeeze in between them on the narrow seat.

It was a bright June day. The sky was clear and blue, though low on the horizon a few clouds had begun to gather. And when they passed the half dozen tenant farms and climbed the hills that surrounded Adam's estate, the wind blew fresh and brisk. It tugged at Charmiane's skirts as she alighted from the carriage and fluttered the tails of Noël's coat. Why did she have to notice how handsome he looked in Adam's clothes: the buff riding breeches clinging to his muscled legs, the polished boots, the broad-shouldered blue coat that matched his eyes? Fouche had tied his cravat in neat folds; despite the expensive clothing, he was a handsome gentleman, not a foolish dandy. His tan had begun to deepen again, and his blond hair to take on the streaked glow of summer. Her heart thumped at the sight of him stepping so purposefully from the carriage.

Before she could stop him, he'd reached for her hand. "Come," he said. "Let's picnic at the top of the hill. Prosper, bring the hamper." He pulled her along and they raced up the hill together. The wind was stronger here, but the sun was warm. Almost as warm as his hand in hers. She felt so happy that she almost forgot that such happiness as Noël could bring her was forbidden. Reluctantly she pulled her hand away and directed Prosper to arrange their picnic. Fresh strawberries dipped in sugar, glasses of chilled *kirschwasser*, sweet cakes studded with raisins and nuts. Sprawled on the grass, they ate in near silence, with Prosper's adoring eyes fixed on Charmiane, and watched a shepherd on a distant hill gather in his flock. At last they rose to go. The clouds were coming closer now, and the sun would soon be covered.

Noël pointed to a nearby stand of birches. "While Prosper is packing up, let's stroll under the trees. I can use the exercise."

Charmiane hesitated. But after all, the trees were nearby and in plain view of Prosper. "Of course," she said.

They walked together, though she evaded his hand this time. The wind was quite strong now; she put one hand on the brim of her bonnet to keep it from turning inside out with a sudden puff. Noël stopped and turned to her. In a swift gesture, he untied the ribbons that held her hat. Charmiane cried out as a gust lifted the hat from her head and sent it spinning and tossing down the hill, carried on the strong breeze.

"My hat! Why did you . . . ? Prosper!" As the boy dashed off after her hat, she turned to follow.

"No!" Noël's strong arm circled her waist and he pulled her toward him. "Not this time," he growled. "You'll do without your protection for a few minutes." He tightened his hold; his hard body pressed against the length of hers, sending tremors through her that left her weak.

"Name of God, Noël," she choked, "what do you want of me?"

"Tell me in words what I read in your eyes. Tell me you want to be kissed."

"No, no. Have a little pity." She began to weep. "Noël. Please."

His eyes held her in their spell. "Kiss me first," he said, "and then tell me no." His head bent to hers and she trembled, knowing herself powerless to resist. And lost if he should kiss her.

Just then, Prosper tugged at her skirt. She started, and wrenched herself from Noël's embrace. Prosper held out her bonnet. She snatched it from him, whirled about and raced down the hill to the waiting cabriolet. By the time Noël joined her, his face twisted in an angry scowl, she had managed to calm herself. And on the silent ride home, as the sky grew as dark as Noël's visage, she framed the words she would have to say, to make him understand once and for all that she was Adam's wife, however much it pained them both.

"May I speak to you alone?" she asked as they entered the château.

"Without Prosper?" His voice was sharp.

She ignored the sarcasm. "Please come into Adam's library."

She hated the room. It was where Armand had died. But it seemed the wisest place to speak, Adam's library. A masculine room, filled with reminders—for her and for Noël—that she wasn't free. That she belonged to his brother. She closed the door and smiled thinly at him. "Noël, you must understand that what happened on the hill . . . mustn't happen again."

"Are we to ignore our passions?"

She managed a nervous laugh. "What passions? A brief flirtation? A passing infatuation? Really, Noël, it's nothing more. And if you can't understand that, I'll . . . I'll have to send you away."

He searched her face. He must have read it, the determination she felt. He turned away for a moment. When he looked again at her, she saw Noël's mask. His mouth twisted in his familiar lighthearted smile. "Have you no pity for a wounded soldier? Not even one kiss?"

She shook her head. It was too painful to laugh.

His eyes were pleading, dark with desire, though he still smiled. She felt herself weakening. "Not even one?" he asked. "Even the warrior Paris could dream of fair Helen. But what shall I . . . ?"

She gasped, her eyes widening with shock, and sank into a chair. "Oh, my God, can it be possible?" It was too awful to contemplate.

"What is it? What's the matter?"

"You said . . . fair Helen. Just like . . ." Oh, God. She could see his blush even through his tan. Her heart sank.

He waved an impatient hand. "It's just a phrase," he muttered. "Anyone can say it."

"No. I was *his* fair Helen. I was . . ." She stared at him, her eyes imploring the truth. "And now *you* say the words. Noël, for the love of God. *Did you write Adam's letters?*"

He groaned and covered his eyes. "This gets too complicated."

"Did you?" she cried.

He nodded. "Yes."

Dear heaven, she thought, let me die. "And signed Adam's name to them?"

"Charmiane, please, I . . ." He sighed in resignation. "Yes. I signed his name."

"Oh, God," she choked. "Did Adam know?"

"Yes, of course." He moved forward to grasp her hand, but she shook him off.

"Oh, you villains! Both of you! How could you? To play such a careless game with my heart?"

"Charmiane, listen to me. I swear to you that Adam loves you."

"*Adam* loves me? Don't you understand? I fell in love with the man who wrote those letters!"

"No," he growled. "You fell in love with the man in the Tuileries Gardens."

Her brain whirled with the perfidy of their deception. She was beginning to doubt everything, doubt her sanity. "Was it Adam in the garden? Or was it you?"

He ran his hand through his hair in a gesture of desperation. "It was Adam in the garden, Adam you married, Adam who loves you."

"No. That was a night of madness. An unreal dream. And Adam was a stranger, pretending for a few hours to be something he's not. I've seen the real Adam. A heartless monster. God forgive me, I pray for his death to release me."

His voice was ragged. "Charmiane. Don't. He loves you."

She looked at him with tear-filled eyes. "And I loved the man who wrote those letters. The man I thought I was marrying. Damn you, you let me marry *him*, knowing it was you who'd won me. That it was you who . . . Was it a joke? That special bond of twins you talked of? Was it a game between you?"

He groaned. "No. Never."

"When you were here, before the wedding. You said he owed you money for a favor. Was that the favor? To use your . . . charm to win him a bride? Did it amuse you, to court me in the letters while you did your brother a service?"

He swore softly. "I helped him buy some horses, that's all. In God's name, Charmiane . . ." He strode to her, pulled her from the chair, tried to gather her in his arms. "I meant every word in those letters."

That only made it more terrible to endure. "Then how could you let me marry him?" With a cry of grief, she tore herself from his embrace and ran from the room, nearly colliding with Bazaine in her haste to escape. She raced up the stairs to her rooms and flung herself across her bed, pouring out her despair and heartbreak into her pillows.

Chapter Fifteen

He threw himself disconsolately into a chair as Bazaine bustled into the room. Those damned letters, he thought. He would have kissed her in another moment, and she would have been his. Swearing her love and hearing his answering vows. And nothing else would have mattered.

Bazaine cleared his throat. "You look tired, *monsieur*. Will you rest before dinner?"

He grunted and stared at a row of books on a high shelf.

Bazaine put a stack of papers on the desk, opened up the ink pot and dipped in a quill. He looked toward the door through which Charmiane had just fled, then proffered the pen. "It's none of my business, but how long does *monsieur le comte* intend to keep up this masquerade? Your promotion to general of brigades will come through soon. How much longer can you take a sick leave without reporting to the Emperor?" Again Bazaine held out the pen. "Monsieur de Moncalvo?"

He waved him away. "I'll sign them later."

"For God's sake, *monsieur*. Tell her."

He sighed. "Tell her what? That I'm the monster she married? That drunken madman who staggered in here last winter and killed her brother, and then . . ." He rubbed his hand across his eyes, then looked at Bazaine and laughed—a dry, sardonic bark. "I rather thought you enjoyed the game, you old devil. I've swallowed more insolence from you in the past month than I allowed in all your ten years of service."

Bazaine smirked. "A humbling experience, I trust, *monsieur*."

He frowned. "Was I proud? Was I arrogant?"

"A little heavy-handed, perhaps. But you were young."

"'How are the mighty fallen.' Noël used to say I never learned to be anything but a soldier.''

"And are you learning now?" Bazaine's voice was deep with sympathy.

"Perhaps more than I want to. I wish I had Noël's easiness."

Bazaine smiled. "I think you've done rather well. Though I don't think your brother is usually quite so free with his hands. Your pinches and pats were all the talk in the servants' wing."

He laughed bitterly. "Charming Noël. And now my wife suffers because she thinks she's in love with charming Noël. Who wrote her love letters on his brother Adam's behalf. I'm my own rival. Absurd, isn't it?"

Absurd, he thought. And impossible. He was beginning to wonder who he really was. Not Noël, though a part of him had enjoyed the relinquishing of command this past month or so. But surely not the madman who had returned from the horrors of Russia with his soul shriveled and haunted and his nights racked with awful dreams. His drinking had begun at his garrison on the Elbe. All those weeks of watching the remnants of the Grand Army drag across the frontier more dead than alive, and having to patch them up and put them into new uniforms and assign them to another regiment, to another opportunity to die for a cause he himself no longer believed in. But when he drank, he could go to sleep without fear; the stupor from too much cognac kept the nightmares away.

And then he'd come to Bonneval. When he pictured those weeks now, in his mind, it was through a haze of alcohol and pain and rage. He had stormed about and barked orders and lashed out in a drunken fury. And she had been the nearest target.

His memory of her in those weeks was of a white-faced, trembling little mouse, deferring to his tyrannies with a humility that had only angered him the more. He had felt trapped in a spiraling whirlpool that seemed to engulf them both: he raged, she cringed, and his frustrated response was more rage. As for Noël . . . The servants had been eager to repay his wrathful outbursts by telling him of Noël's visit. In malicious detail. And that only made him more cruel to her. He told himself it was stupid to be jealous of his brother. She was marrying *him*, wasn't she? But it had been impossible to forget that she'd kissed Noël with warmth.

And then, of course, he'd killed her brother. He scarcely remembered that night, he'd drunk so much. Afraid to claim the bride who so clearly disliked him, who shrank from his kisses,

Even now he couldn't remember all the details, he'd been so drunk. He *thought* it was an accident, her brother's death. But maybe a part of him—the soldier still fighting a war—had meant to kill. He didn't know anymore. It all seemed so unreal in retrospect.

And then, that last night. He had wanted her so much. Wanted her comfort. Wanted to leave her with a child, so he could die in peace. But the hatred in her eyes had burned his soul, ripped out what was left of his humanity, until all he could do was brutalize her. Strike her, cut her hair, frighten her into obedience. He would have been ashamed to treat a *whore* so badly. And that was worse, even, than killing her brother. He closed his eyes and groaned aloud.

"You shouldn't have let her think you were Noël," said Bazaine.

He opened his eyes. "What would you have done? I needed a tunic. Mine was torn and bloodied. I took one from a dead man. It wasn't even from Noël's regiment. But she thought it was."

"And you let her think so."

How could he explain it, even to Bazaine? He had come home, thinking he would die anyway. With his shattered arm, the pike slash to his breast, the festering bullet wounds. The surgeons hadn't held out much hope unless the arm was amputated. So he'd come home to die. Come home to face her hatred once more, and beg her forgiveness if she'd let him. And—wonder of wonders. She'd mistaken him for Noël. And the look in her eyes, which had curdled his heart with its implacable hatred, had become soft and caring. Who could blame him for wanting to die with that tender gaze bent to him? He was a beggar, warming himself at an unaccustomed fire. Her smile revived his soul. Couldn't he be forgiven if he was reluctant to tell the truth, to abandon that warmth and see the loathing return to her eyes? Bazaine could tell her everything after he was dead.

Good old Bazaine. He'd recognized him at once, of course. But he'd kept the secret, watched over him in the first few days so he wouldn't reveal the truth in his delirious ravings. And after that, as he'd recovered despite the surgeons' predictions, it had seemed too late to tell her of his mistake.

Besides, he'd enjoyed playing Noël's role. Burdened by too many responsibilities through the years, he'd always envied Noël's lightheartedness. When Charmiane had called him by his brother's name, he'd felt an odd sense of release: To pretend to be Noël was to *be* Noël. To cast off Adam's burdens and cares for a little while. He'd found himself able to laugh more, to flirt with Charmiane, to behave like a schoolboy again. To call her beautiful lady, as she said Noël had done, and see her eyes light up. *He'd* never been much good at thinking up compliments. At least not until he had to try to think like Noël.

What was it his old tutor had often said? You call a man an ass ninety-nine times, and the hundredth time he brays. It had been so with Charmiane. She'd seen him as a monster, called him a monster; he'd responded by behaving like a monster most of the time, even when he tried to control his drunken rages. But now she looked at him and saw Noël, and he was delighted to find a playful, gentle side to himself again.

It had been frightening, of course, to give up the cognac. Every night had brought fresh terror, knowing his dreams would return. Horror piled upon horror. The frozen corpses of Moscow danced with the rotting carcasses of Germany to the music of screams and moans. And he danced among them, more dead than alive. It had taken all his willpower to resist the pull of the liquor, its blessed forgetfulness. But he couldn't afford to drink heavily now. Drink would bring back Adam the monster. Or at the least—if the passage of time had begun to blunt his rages— drink might allow him to slip, reveal himself to her. And that was the last thing he wanted then.

"I think you ought to sign these papers now," said Bazaine. "So I can send them off." He waited while Adam crossed to the desk and signed the papers, then tucked them into a portfolio. "Fouche tells me you're sleeping better," he said.

"Yes."

"I'm concerned about Fouche. I think he's begun to suspect. *Monsieur le comte* had one or two nightmares in the spring, if you recall. For all his drinking."

"Then tell Fouche the truth, and swear him to secrecy. And yes. I'm sleeping better." It had been her doing, of course. The easing of his torment. It still surprised him, thinking back, how close he'd come to complete insanity. The nightmares, the feelings of panic, the cold sweats and trembling. After all the years of soldiering, he'd assumed he was hardened enough to be unaffected. Perhaps Noël, who could laugh more, was luckier than he.

It was only the shock of thinking he was going to die at Lützen that had stopped his slide into madness. A slide that had started even before the Tuileries, when he'd begun to dream of dying. He probably would have ended up in the madhouse at Charenton if it hadn't been for Charmiane. First with the letters. He'd never been able to talk of his fears in all his years of soldiering. Not even with an agreeable *fille d'amour*, who'd have been happy to listen sympathetically for a few extra francs. But Charmiane . . . He'd known it at once, in the Tuileries. That this was a woman who could comfort his bleeding heart. And he'd poured out his soul in the letters and drawn strength from her replies. And survived the Russian campaign.

And she was still his good angel, pulling him back from the edge of despair and madness. Since the night she'd forced him to tell his dreams, comforted his unashamed tears, he'd begun to sleep better, as though his silence had been a festering sore, needing lancing and release to heal. Sometimes now, when he awoke in the morning, he was aware of the song of birds, the smell of summer, the everyday sweetness of life that he'd forgotten. She'd done that for him, with her tender care and concern.

But she was so much more that he'd never suspected. He'd loved her at once in the Tuileries. But he'd thought her fragile and young. Dependent on others. And after he'd returned from Russia, he'd seen only her cringing fear, her servile deference. But why not? She'd deferred to that domineering husband of hers and thought it her duty. And then *he'd* come home, like the company commander, still giving orders, and robbed her again of her independence.

It had been a revelation to find so much more in her. A lively spirit. A strength and a competence that perhaps she herself was unaware of. He liked being "Noël," stepping back, allowing her independence, encouraging it. He thought he'd married a child bride; he was beginning to discover a woman, if he gave her the chance. He was learning so much about her, and about himself, as well. He had never known what really pleased a woman beyond the minimal wooing to get her into bed; he'd never taken the time. But every time she told "Noël" what she hated about Adam, and every time "Noël" had the courage to do and say things that Adam would have been too constrained to do or say, he learned a little more.

He sighed and covered his eyes with his hand. But it was becoming too complicated. Charmiane was falling in love with him, that was evident. Only it was Noël she thought she loved. Her confusion and despair had been all too clear, even before his slip of the tongue had made her think that Noël had written the letters. But if he told her the truth now, she'd hate him all the more. To her grief at Armand's death, her horror of the night he'd treated her callously for his pleasure and abuse, would be added disgust at his betrayal.

No. He wasn't willing yet to lose the sweetness his days had become. He was comfortable, carefree in Noël's skin—at least for the time being. He wasn't ready to give that up. Perhaps when her love had deepened a little more, it would be easier to tell her. She could forgive a man she loved. She could scarcely forgive a man she still thought she hated.

"I had another note from Monsieur Noël," said Bazaine.

He lifted his head. "Yes?"

"He bought another horse for you in Strasbourg and sent it off to the *hôtel* in Paris. I've forwarded him the purchase price and his commission, as usual."

"How is he?"

"Back with his regiment in Germany and awaiting orders. He's piqued at his promotion to lieutenant. He wonders if I can't use some of my old connections to get him demoted. He doesn't want to ask you."

Adam smiled crookedly. "Carefree, irresponsible Noël. Laughing his way through life. I saw him go down at Lützen. I thought he was dead. And to get up without a single scratch...? The gods seem to smile upon Noël." He laughed in bitterness. "And Adam's wife upon Noël's impostor."

Bazaine frowned. "*Monsieur le comte*, do you want *me* to tell her?"

"Good Lord, no! I think I want a chance to court my wife first."

"And what happens when she finds out, as she must, sooner or later?"

"Maybe by that time..." He lapsed into silence. Maybe he would have won her love, and her trust, by then.

"And Monsieur de Moncalvo, her husband? Where is he, Monsieur 'Noël'?"

"Let her think, for the time being, that he's safe in Germany." He shrugged. "Or missing. What the deuce does it matter to her where the hated Adam is?"

"I still think you ought to tell her. Only a fool would play such a mad game." At Adam's warning scowl, he stepped back and bowed in deference. "As you wish, *monsieur le comte*."

Adam stared at his retreating back. It was right, what he was doing. And damn Bazaine and his old-womanish concerns. He'd wear the mask of Noël for a little longer. And then he'd tell her. He promised it to himself.

* * *

A jagged bolt of lightning flashed down from the sky and separated into branches, like a giant hand reaching to touch the earth. Standing at the window, Charmiane shivered. It was like the hand of God, coming to touch her with its curse. She loved Noël. But until she knew if Adam lived or died, it was forbidden love. And she'd never felt more wretched, more miserable, in her life.

She should have guessed that Noël had written the letters. All these weeks, every time he spoke or looked at her in silent communion, she might have known that he was the man who had touched her soul with his words. And she couldn't hate him for what he'd done. Knowing him, his generosity, she imagined that he'd thought it was simply a kindness for his brother. Hadn't he called Adam tongue-tied around women that fateful night of the ball? And if he knew that she'd already succumbed to Adam in the gardens, what harm in strengthening his brother's position with a few love letters? He probably wrote the first few as a romantic exercise, and then was caught up in the emotion, until he forgot he was writing for his brother and wrote them for himself. From the depths of his own heart and soul. How could he have guessed the mischief they would cause? She remembered how he'd visited before the wedding and asked if she liked Adam's letters. Perhaps he'd begun to have an inkling, even then, of the strength of her feelings for the author of the letters. Perhaps he'd wanted to see her, to touch her heart, one last time— before losing her to Adam. Oh, if only he'd spoken up then!

She pulled her dressing gown more tightly around her body. It was chilly at the window. The storm had howled for hours, a cold and fierce onslaught, rare for June. Afraid to face Noël, she'd had her dinner brought in on a tray, then sent it back again, untouched. She'd prayed for sleep, but it wouldn't come. And now the wail of the midnight wind echoed her own voice: What to do? What to do?

For both their sakes, she must send him away. She couldn't bear his nearness, knowing how much she loved him. And his desire for her, if satisfied, would brand him with the mark of Cain. It was one thing to steal a brother's mistress. But not his wife.

She jumped as a large crash reverberated through the château. It sounded like the voice of doom. She trembled, then shook off the fanciful thought. After a few moments she heard voices, shouts in the passageway beyond her rooms, running footsteps. She snatched up her candle and hurried from her suite, making for a knot of people who seemed to be crowding into a small drawing room in the middle of the pavilion. She saw Bazaine, and Noël beside him. "What is it?" she asked.

Bazaine turned and gave a little bow. "One of the trees in the park fell against the side of the château."

She peered over his shoulder into the room. "Is the damage serious?"

"No, *madame*. The window, of course, is smashed. And a desk that sat before it. Perhaps a few stones in the lintel. But nothing that can't be repaired. I'll see to it in the morning."

"Very good." She waited for a few minutes in case she was needed as the activity died down and Bazaine shooed the servants back to bed. She was aware of Noël's eyes on her; more aware that his dressing gown, thrown on in haste, scarcely concealed his bare chest. She had meant to escape him, but by the time she was ready to leave, Bazaine and the few remaining servants were moving off in the opposite direction, toward the stairs, and she was left to return to her rooms alone.

Noël took the candlestick from her hand. "Let me escort you."

"No, I . . ." Was there no evading him?

"I *am* going in your direction," he said gently. "My rooms are there."

She nodded silently and they moved down the passageway together. She had never been more conscious of his imposing height, the easy grace with which he moved, the subtle scent of cologne about him. And when they reached her door, and she turned to take her candle, and her fingers brushed his, she trembled at the warmth of his hand. She moved into her boudoir and set the candle on a small table, then turned.

He stood at the door, watching her, making no move to go. Even in the dim light she could see the yearning in his eyes, the hunger that parted his lips—those beautiful lips that she ached to kiss. The blond streaks in his hair glinted in the candle's glow and echoed in the golden tufts that thatched the muscles of his chest.

A despairing moan rose in her throat. "It isn't fair," she whispered.

"Life never is," he said angrily. "Don't you know that yet?" The sharpness in his voice was like a slap, and she began to weep. At once he closed the door behind him, strode into the room and pulled her into his arms. "Oh, my love," he said. "Let's take what we can. Seize the moment." His voice was a husky seductive murmur. "Charmiane, I love you."

"Do you? Do you really?" It was too wondrous to be true.

"Always and forever." He kissed her softly, a kiss of such sweet tenderness, his lips caressing hers, that she trembled and clung to him. She was loved, and his mouth told her so, his hands—stroking her gently through her dressing gown—told her so. He kissed her again and again, tasting her mouth, gliding his lips across her cheek to rub against the downy softness of her neck and ear. With the hesitation of a young lover fearful of being refused, he slipped his hand into the opening of her dressing gown and caressed her breasts through her nightdress. She burned with impatience, desire a hot flame within her. He seemed content only to explore with soft lips and gentle hands; indeed, when he released her mouth to step back, untie her dressing gown and slide her nightdress off her shoulders to the floor, his face was filled with wonder and delight. As though tonight were the first time he'd ever made love, and she was his precious beloved and the focus of his rapture. Her heart exulted in his love; yet it was strangely humbling as well, to know she mattered so very much to him.

"I love you too, my dearest," she said. God forgive me, she thought. She untied his dressing gown and ran her fingers across the hardness of his bare chest, feeling the buds of his breasts stiffen at her touch. She had touched his body as his nurse, and her hands had ached to caress, not minister. Now she gloried in the feel of him, the ridged muscles of his chest and sides, the downy golden hairs that felt like velvet, even the smooth warmth of his healing wounds. "Noël, my love," she whispered. "Take me to bed."

He shrugged out of his dressing gown and let it fall. His lower body strained at his underbreeches; he removed them with shaking fingers, then reached for Charmiane's hand. "Come to bed, then, my love." He pulled her toward her bedroom, taking the candle on his way. "I want to watch you," he said, "while I make love to you." He led her to the bed, urged her down and lay beside her.

His movements were slow and unhurried. His mouth took hers again and again, his tongue stroking the inner edge of her lips till she moaned and clung to him, burning with desire. He kissed her breasts, her flat belly; and when, in her impatience to have him within her, she let her knees fall wide, he dropped his head lower and planted kisses on the quivering, intimate warmth of her. She groaned and shivered at the thrill of his mouth.

He made love to her with a kind of awe, stopping to smile tenderly, to let his eyes drink in her eager body spread before him.

It was so different from Adam's hungry haste, Henri's air of boredom. Noël seemed almost reluctant to bring their loving to climax, as though he were sorry to have it end.

At last, goaded by her impatient moans and gasps and unable to contain himself any longer, he entered her. A slow, gliding thrust that made her cry out in pleasure. Again and again, hard and slow, until she thought she'd go mad with the exquisiteness of the sensation. It was only at the very end that his control was exhausted: with a choked cry, he quivered violently and then was still. After a moment, he lifted his head and smiled down at her; by the light of the candle she could see tears in his eyes. "My love," he whispered. "I never knew it could be so sweet."

She reached up and stroked his cheek. "I don't think I've ever known pleasure until now. Henri . . ." She shuddered.

"And Adam?" His voice held a sudden sharp edge.

She remembered the humiliation and pain of Adam's last night. "Never!" she cried.

He moved off her and sat up in bed, his back to her. "But I thought that . . . in the Tuileries Gardens . . ."

The whore Adam had picked up in the Tuileries, she thought bitterly. That's all she'd been to him. It shamed her now to think how her body had responded to his in the garden. "Never," she said again. "His very touch sickened me. I hate him!"

He put his head in his hands. "So you say. Is there no forgiving him? Ever? Nothing he can do to make amends?"

"Let him give me back my brother. My honor. My self-respect. I hate him so much, I can never forgive all he's done. If it should happen that he's dead in Germany, I wouldn't forgive him even then. And when they planted his marker in the churchyard, I'd go every day and spit on it."

He groaned into his hands. "You hate him so much." He lifted his head and looked at her, his eyes soft and pleading. "But if he were to beg your forgiveness . . ."

"No. There's no forgiveness in my heart this side of the grave."

"But to have nothing save your hatred . . . ? Forever?"

Her mouth twisted in bitterness. "I wonder if he knows—or cares."

"Yes," he choked, "I think he does. God knows he does. Charmiane—" he turned around and clasped her hand in his tight grip "—I can't defend him. His behavior was indefensible. But every man has a breaking point. Where he crosses the line to madness."

She shook her head. "No! I can't accept that."

His features hardened into anger. "You have to be young to be so self-righteous," he growled. "If you can't forgive Adam, at least don't speak ill of him again."

"Why not?" What did it matter?

He leaned forward, his eyes burning with intensity. "Because *I'm*..." he began in a rush, then stopped, seemed about to speak and finally shrugged. A gesture of resignation. "Because I'm his flesh," he said at last. "And I feel the pain."

She heard it as a rebuke, and it stung. She had a right to hate Adam, didn't she? She frowned. "If he's so precious to you," she said defensively, "how is it you're able to betray him with his own wife?"

He stared and then began to laugh. A bitter laugh, a high-pitched laugh of grief and despair. Like a madman confronting his image in a twisted mirror.

She trembled in fear and bewilderment. Somehow she'd blundered where she had no right to be. The bond of twinship was a mystery beyond her understanding. Let it be between them alone. She held out her hand to him. "Noël," she said softly. "Don't. I'm sorry."

He pulled her into his arms and pressed her close to his breast. "God help us both," he groaned. The misery in his voice was echoed in the moan of the wind outside.

They slept in each other's arms as the storm abated. But when Charmiane awoke, just before dawn, she stirred him awake, eyes wide with sudden panic. "Quickly!" she said. "Go, before the servants come." He seemed reluctant, eager to make love again. But at last her uneasiness at being discovered persuaded him. He kissed her, grumbled a little, retrieved his nightclothes and was gone.

She felt giddy with happiness as she sat across from him at the breakfast table in the morning. It was all she could do to keep her face from betraying her, with the servants hovering nearby. And Noël was no help—grinning like an idiot, silently mouthing "I love you," so she blushed scarlet.

"Really, Noël," she whispered when she thought the maids couldn't hear, "behave yourself. If someone should see or hear..."

The grin widened. "They'll think your brother-in-law, the rake, is more wicked than usual this morning." His eyes twinkled. "And determined to make love to you today, before the sun is high in the sky." He cleared his throat and managed to look serious as Suzanne came near to refill his cup. "I *am* determined, sister-in-law. Will you make the arrangements?"

"Y-yes, of course," she stammered. What was she to say now, with the girl listening so intently? "If you . . ." She thought quickly. "If you think you're ready to ride, Noël, I'll have the grooms arrange a gentle horse. But I insist on riding with you. I don't intend to see my weeks of nursing go for nothing."

He contrived to look unhappy about that. "I'll feel like a child with a nursemaid," he muttered, "but if you must . . ."

They rode out together, laughing like children who'd played a trick on a watchful schoolmaster. They galloped past fields golden with early hay, and scented vineyards, and meadows dotted with bright red poppies. At last they found a patch of lush green grass, dappled with sunlight and nestled amid a stand of trees, far from farms and fields and the intrusion of the world. They slid from their horses and kissed—the impassioned kiss of lovers who had chafed at the need for restraint.

Noël threw himself down in the thick grass and pulled Charmiane beside him. "Lord, I've missed riding," he said. "I've missed kissing you."

She took off her riding hat and laughed. "You kissed me only a few hours ago. You haven't ridden in weeks."

"I think I've missed the kisses more," he said, and leaned over to cover her lips with his burning mouth. As tender as he had been last night, he was an impatient lover this morning. He tugged at the buttons of her jacket, opened it wide, reached for her breast to knead it with strong fingers. She gasped and writhed under his loving assault, her body hot and eager for him. And when he pushed up her riding skirt and searched and found her vulnerable core, she arched her back in an agony of joy, roused to a peak of feeling, of sensation, she hadn't thought possible. With a quick gesture he released his manhood from the confinement of his riding breeches and plunged into her.

They rocked together in a savage, pounding union, crying aloud in their ecstasy until the meadow and trees faded, the sunlight faded, the bright day vanished. There was only the glory of their passion, the incandescent brightness of their love. At last—and all too soon—they climaxed in a wrenching, mutual spasm that left them spent and glowing with satisfaction.

Charmiane sighed and made a halfhearted attempt to straighten her clothes, her tousled hair. Noël had rolled over to rebutton his breeches, and now he leaned on one elbow and stared down at her. "I think I could look at you forever." He reached out, plucked a pink clover from the grass and stroked it across her lips. The blossom was fragrant and cool, soothing her burning mouth, still tingling from his impassioned kisses. "I haven't felt so free, so deeply in love, for a long time," he said. "I hadn't thought I could ever feel so young again." His eyes were clear and direct, as though he were allowing her to see into his very soul.

She smiled tenderly. How could she ever have thought that Noël was light and frivolous and nothing more? "You're very serious when you want to be," she said. "It surprises me sometimes."

He scowled. "Do you mind if I'm not smiling Noël all the time?"

"Oh, my love. Smiling or frowning, lighthearted or serious— I love you." She trembled as he bent to kiss her again. I shouldn't be so happy, she thought. It was wicked. But she loved him, and not all her misgivings could change that.

But of course they did. The warm days of June advanced: it was summer now. They rode out and made love under the trees, or waited until the château stilled at night to slip stealthily into each other's beds. And the more Charmiane's happiness grew, the more her conscience nagged at her. It was wrong, what they were doing. And she lived in fear that the servants would discover their relationship. God help them both if Adam should ever learn of it! He was capable of killing his own brother, heaven knew.

And she had begun to be troubled by something that was casting a shadow on their love. Noël seemed completely free of the guilt that gnawed at her. Somehow it lessened him in her eyes, that he could be so indifferent to their betrayal of Adam. It only made the burden heavier for her to bear.

He grew more lighthearted and reckless as the days went on. He would reach across the table to lace his fingers through hers when they dined; or help her into the saddle with hands that lingered too long about her waist; or sit beside her at the piano as she played, blowing gently in her ear. And finally there came an evening when he stopped to pull her into Adam's library for a kiss. And Bazaine was there.

Charmiane hastily pushed Noël away. "If you'll set up the chessboard, Noël, I'll join you in the drawing room in a moment. I want to speak to Bazaine first."

She found it impossible to look at Bazaine. She played with Armand's ring on her finger and cleared her throat. "I...should like you to forget what you've just seen. It was a harmless kiss.

A very...sisterly kiss. It isn't necessary for Monsieur de Moncalvo to learn of it. *N'est-ce pas?*"

He gave a little bow. "Of course, *madame*." His expression was serious, but his mouth seemed to twitch.

It made her uneasy and cast a pall over her evening with Noël. By the time he came to her bedroom, she was quiet and withdrawn. He seemed aware of her mood: when they climbed into bed he simply cradled her in his arms and stroked her hair. "The world is far away when I'm with you," he murmured. "How do you do it?"

She choked on a sob and pulled away from his embrace. "I wish I could do it for myself."

"Charmiane, *ma chère*, what is it?"

She dabbed at her eyes. "I look at you and I see his face. Adam's face. I was miserable with Henri. But I never betrayed him. I try to tell myself that...perhaps Adam is dead, and I'm free. Free to love you and to push aside the remorse I feel."

"Charmiane..."

"But I'm only deceiving myself."

He rose from the bed, wrapped his dressing gown around himself and went to stand at the window. "Do you want me to go?" he said at last.

She was filled with agony. "How long will it be before all the servants are gossiping about us? Carrying stories to Adam?"

He turned from the window, frowning. "Do you care enough for Adam to regret your..."

"Betrayal?" she said bitterly. "Infidelity?"

His voice was urgent. "*Do* you? Does a part of you hold him still in your heart, despite what he's done?"

"No! If he were dead, I'd rejoice in a moment. But I've betrayed my own honor. Broken vows I swore to."

"But if he were dead, and you were free to be mine?"

"My conscience would torment me still."

"And if he lives. Could you come away with me and live without the Church's blessing?"

She turned her head away. He must know the answer to that. "Please, Noël. Must you pursue this?"

He was dogged in his insistence. "If he lives, what will you do?"

She sighed. "Somehow I'll reconcile myself to being his wife, God save me."

"And love?"

She choked. "I'll never stop loving you."

"Even if I should prove as . . . flawed as he?"

"No. Never."

He seemed to make a decision. He strode to the bed, sat beside her, took her by the shoulders. "What if . . . what if Adam should return? Beg your forgiveness, treat you with the honor he should have shown from the first. Show you the gentler side of his nature. Could you . . . learn to love him?" She shook her head vehemently. He rubbed his hand across his mouth. "Well, then, could you learn to live with him?"

"Yes. If he were to do all that."

He nodded in satisfaction. "And then, perhaps someday, love would follow."

"Noël!" she cried. "Why should you want me to love him?"

He smiled tenderly. "Because of that nagging conscience of yours. You can never love Noël fully, openly. Joyously. For all the world to see. Maybe if you give Adam a chance, you can find that love with him."

Her heart was in splinters. "And you'd be happy?"

"Nothing would please me more than to have you fall in love with Adam."

"Oh, God," she sobbed. "How can you be so noble, so self-sacrificing, when your heart must be breaking as mine is?"

"My sweet Charmiane, I'm not noble." His voice cracked. "The only thing I am is cowardly. Promise me you'll give Adam a chance."

She clung to him, weeping. "Yes."

"I'll speak to Bazaine tomorrow about leaving. I won't write to you. Let it end cleanly."

He made love to her then with a quiet sweetness. It was a tender affirmation. A last celebration of their love. And a sad farewell.

"You have everything you need, *monsieur*?"

Adam slipped his arms into the coat that Fouche held out for him and nodded at Bazaine. "I can't take very much. Not without seeming to steal from 'Brother Adam.' But I'll stay a week in my *hôtel* in Paris and have my tailor make me some new uniforms."

"Oh, *monsieur le comte*," said Fouche, "I wish you'd let me come with you."

Adam clapped him on the back. "You can best serve me by keeping my secret. Now off with you, and see that I've packed enough shirts."

Bazaine handed Adam a small packet. "Your promotion, General Bouchard. Your orders. Bank notes and a letter of credit. What will you do?"

Adam tucked the packet inside his waistcoat. "I'm to report to Marshal Berthier in Dresden on the fifteenth of July. If the armistice holds..." His smile of optimism was a lie, and Bazaine knew it. After the French victories at Lützen and Bautzen—won at a terrible price in men and horses—a temporary truce had been declared. Discussions were taking place even now between the Emperor and the Austrian ambassador Metternich. In exchange for a general declaration of peace, France was to give up Lorraine and some of her occupied territories; otherwise, Austria would join the war on the side of Russia and Prussia.

Adam had received private letters from some of the men surrounding the Emperor. Everyone, including Berthier, had begged Napoleon to accept the terms. But the Emperor was adamant, still insisting—as he had throughout his career—on one decisive victory before agreeing to peace. But a victory with what? Adam thought bitterly. An army of children?

And in the meantime, the armistice was madness for France. A tactical blunder that the young General Bonaparte wouldn't have committed. He should either fight that decisive battle now or settle for peace. This delay was only giving Austria the chance to arm herself. And now the rumors were that the English commander Wellington had routed Joseph Bonaparte—Napoleon's brother and the King of Spain—and would soon look to the soil of France for conquest.

Bazaine cut into his reverie. "When do you expect to return?"

"It could be months. God only knows."

"And Madame de Moncalvo?"

"She'll await my return with trepidation, I'm sure." He sighed. "The young have a fearful code of honor, Bazaine. Terrible in its rigor. Do you remember when you were that young? And felt no need to compromise with life?" He thought again of Charmiane, with her implacable hatred for Adam, her consuming guilt for loving Noël. His own feelings weren't nearly so ordered and neat. In a strange way it pleased him, her guilt. In an age of loose women who cuckolded their husbands with shameless impunity, it was rare to find a faithful heart, a dutiful soul. He even felt a twinge of guilt himself for his relentless seduction as "Noël." But she had repaid him, all unknowing, by insulting Adam's sexual prowess in the Tuileries Gardens. He wasn't sure whether it bruised his manhood or amused him in a sardonic way: that her unwavering hatred should make her reinterpret that night.

"You should tell her before you go."

"No, Bazaine. The pain of her brother's death is still too fresh. It's only been four months. She still weeps too much over him. Let the wounds heal. And then a kinder Adam will return. One who doesn't frighten her."

"I still think you ought to tell her now."

"You're probably right. But I can't." He saw the rebellion in Bazaine's single glittering eye. "I want your oath that you won't tell her unless I die."

"Begging your pardon, *monsieur*, but you're a coward."

He scowled, his hands curling into fists. Then he relaxed, sighed, even managed a rueful smile. "Yes, I know, you old devil. Your oath."

He said goodbye to Charmiane on the terrace, watched by the servants and a sad-eyed Prosper, who had become his loyal shadow. It was a strained parting, with formal kisses and handshakes. But what else could he do? Another private farewell would have been too painful for Charmiane. "Be of good cheer, my dearest," he said softly, seeing the tears well in her eyes. "If I survive this war, I promise you happiness. And if I die, remember our love, and forget the rest."

Chapter Sixteen

"I don't understand you, Bertrand. No matter how much I bring you, you say it isn't enough. I'll soon exhaust my allowance, and then what am I to tell Bazaine?" Charmiane paced the sitting room of the little cottage and shivered. "I wish you'd put another log on the fire. It's cold."

Bertrand de Domfort threw a piece of wood into the fire and kicked it angrily. "Are you losing the heart for it, after all this time?" He pointed to a doorway and the darkened room beyond. "You've asked more than once why the presses are silent when you've visited. Why do you think? While I buy wood for the fire, Georges looks in vain for ink we can afford. For cheap paper. And you live like a queen."

"What about some of the other émigrés? Can't you sell another subscription to *La Voix*?"

"Not before Christmas. And not with France's economy in ruins, thanks to the Tyrant." He laughed bitterly. "Not everyone is married to a man who stole a fortune in diamonds. And now you complain?"

"Alas, don't reproach me! It's only that it's very difficult . . ."

"Bah!" He tossed himself into a chair. "Will you tell that to your poor murdered brother? To Gaston, flogged and branded and exiled to Guiana?" He looked at her with his sad eyes, dark with accusation, then pointed to an old battered trumpet hanging from the mantel. "Or will you tell it to poor Jean-Pierre in Heaven?"

She bit her lip. "I wish you wouldn't keep that. It haunts me every time I come here."

He softened. "I'm sorry. How cruel I am to you. And in your condition." He rose from his chair and put his arm around her,

guiding her carefully to the sofa. He looked at the soft round-
ness of her swollen belly. "Forget the past. Remember only that
we do what we do for the future. For your unborn child. To claim
his rightful heritage, his titles of Chevrillon and Viollet."

She sighed, feeling shamed by his rebuke. "I'll see what I can
do about more money. In the meantime, I'll finish writing the
Flaming Sword's next polemic. If I can't deliver it myself before
Christmas, I'll send it to you by way of Sophie's letter." She
smiled as Prosper came into the room. "Did you find something
to eat?" He nodded, went to the window and pointed out to the
gray December afternoon. "Yes, of course," she said. "We
should go."

Wrapped in a warm cloak with a fur-lined hood, she allowed
Prosper to help her into the cabriolet, hop in beside her and pick
up the reins. She shivered. Lord, but it was cold. She wasn't sure
how long she could continue to make these trips, not in her condition. She turned around and waved at Domfort, standing
mournfully at his door, then settled herself for the ride back to
Bonneval.

It was a nice cottage that Bertrand had bought with the pro-
ceeds from her diamond-and-emerald earrings. Snug, private,
with room for the printing press. On an isolated road just outside Pontoise, about the same distance from Bonneval as was
Paris. It had become quite easy for her—during the long summer and fall, as her belly grew with Noël's child—to lie and tell
Bazaine she was visiting Sophie in Paris, and then to turn her cabriolet toward the west instead of south. And when the weather
was nice and she and Prosper started out early enough, she could
visit with Sophie *and* Bertrand and still be back at Bonneval before dark. And no one the wiser.

Though she had maintained her suite in the Paris *hôtel*, and
stayed there occasionally, she didn't really like to be in the capital very much now. The war situation had gone from bad to worse
all summer long. Napoleon had refused the Austrian offer of
peace, and the Emperor Francis had declared war on France.
There had been the successful battle of Dresden at the end of
August—Napoleon's last triumph. But in October, the combined forces of France's enemies had crushed the Grand Army at
Leipzig, and Napoleon's subjugated territories of Holland and
Northern Italy and the Confederation of the Rhine had declared
their independence.

Napoleon had led the remnants of his army back to France in
November, hacking their way through the German town of

Hanau to do it. France was exhausted. Yet only last week the Emperor had appeared before a joint session of the Legislative Body, the Senate and the Council of State, asking the country for fresh sacrifices and calling for a new army of three hundred thousand men. The rumormongers in Sophie's salon had it that he'd be fortunate to find fifty thousand. He had lost two armies—nearly a million men—in fifteen months. Who was willing to serve now?

Paris was an odd combination of gaiety and gloom—like a troupe of clowns at a funeral. The Emperor had ordered public entertainments and dancing in the streets. And the *Marseillaise*, banned for so many years, was being played again to stir up patriotic fervor. Yet the Tuileries, it was said, seemed like a palace where someone had died.

Bazaine, with his old army ties, had learned that Metternich had offered peace again in November. France would return to her natural frontiers of the Rhine, the Alps, the Pyrenees. But Napoleon had hesitated, and the offer had been withdrawn. Now Paris was in a ferment, protesting the further conscription of men, the taxes, the interminable war. There were still cheers in the streets when the Emperor passed by, but some said that the crowds had been hired. And on the fringes could often be heard other cries: *"Vive Louis XVIII!"* and "Down with the Tyrant!" The dream of the émigrés, the restoration of the Monarchy, seemed closer than ever.

And she, through *La Voix* and its calls to the Royalists, was helping it come to pass—though not without some uneasiness. She glanced at Prosper, sitting contentedly beside her, tugging on the reins. "What will happen to us, Prosper, if the Emperor falls?" He looked at her. She wasn't at all sure he understood her much of the time; indeed, the reading and writing lessons had long since been abandoned as hopeless. But she liked to talk to him, to see his smiles when she smiled, his frowns when she seemed troubled. "Shall I still be the Comtesse de Moncalvo? Marquise de Viollet? Or simply Madame Bouchard?" She giggled. "Ah, but *which* Bouchard, Prosper? That's the question."

His eyes darted to her face with an expression of alarm. She patted his hand in reassurance. "I like the one, but not the other. The same as you do. But I yet have a husband." She assumed that Adam was still alive. A brigadier general now, Bazaine said. He'd been assigned as a staff officer to Marshal Berthier and hadn't seen fighting all summer or fall. The last they'd heard, he was still on the German frontier.

"Perhaps I'll force my husband to divorce me, so I can marry Monsieur Noël. You'd like that, wouldn't you?" She laughed ruefully. "But I wonder if Noël would." Noël was alive too, according to Bazaine. Promoted to lieutenant. He'd fought at Dresden and Leipzig and had emerged safely from the hell of battle. She'd wept for joy when Bazaine had told her. And then, Napoleon's army, retreating from Germany, had been struck with an epidemic of typhus. Thousands had died. But Noël, with his usual charm, had found an Alsatian peasant girl to take him out of the filth and corruption of the army hospital and nurse him in her own cottage. In exchange for what? she thought with a twinge of jealousy. Why had Bazaine told her *that*?

Little fool! She had no hold on his heart. They'd parted forever. And if he chose to forget her in the arms of another woman, why should it matter to her? He could scarcely know that he'd left her with more than a memory.

The baby stirred within her and she jumped in surprise. Prosper looked at her, his eyes questioning. She chuckled. "Yes. He kicked again. Would you liked to feel him?" At his eager nod, she guided his hand to her belly and watched in delight as his face lit up in a radiant smile. Before she could stop him, he bent and planted a kiss on the rounded swell of her belly, then turned away, his downy cheeks flaming red. She gulped back the sudden rush of tears. "I'll let you hold him, Prosper," she said tenderly. "Whenever you want."

Noël's child. She wasn't sure what to tell Adam, if he should return unexpectedly. By her calculations, the baby was due early in March. But, of course, had it been Adam's, it would have been conceived that terrible night in April, before he left for Germany, and she would have been in her ninth month, as everyone at Bonneval thought. Not her seventh. Perhaps if Adam stayed away until after the birth, she might be able to deceive him: tell him the baby was late, small, slow in developing. Confide in Bazaine and have him change the date of birth on the records—for the sake of the twins' amity.

Lies heaped upon lies. She tried to ignore the gnawing of her conscience—and the pain in her heart. She'd sent Noël away. The wisest course. What else was she to do? Divorce Adam and marry his brother? Even if he'd allow it, which was doubtful, where was her assurance that Noël would marry her anyway? He was wild, reckless, free. For a brief moment she'd seen a deeper, dearer side to him. But thinking of it now, with the clear-eyed perspective of time, she wasn't sure that he was the sort of man to be tied to a wife, even for the sake of the child. It was better to stay married to Adam. To make her peace with him eventually, if she could, though her stomach churned at the thought. But it was best for the child. And was it so wicked, after all? The child would carry the Bouchard name, the Bouchard blood.

Her heart sank at the sight of the coach standing before Bonneval, and the several horses with military saddles in tow. Adam was home. A groom helped her from the cabriolet and led her carriage to the stables. Prosper ran ahead to open the door for her, but it was clear from the look on his face that he would have preferred to bolt, to avoid the master.

Adam stood at the great staircase in the vestibule, speaking to a young officer. He had exchanged his bright green Dragoons' uniform for a dark blue one with gold embroidery, epaulets and aiguillettes; his *chapeau bras*—the large bicorne hat that he carried under one arm—was edged with gold braid. He looked more imposing than ever. Charmiane assumed all this splendor was because of his promotion to senior staff officer, but it didn't help to quell the sudden rush of fear that the sight of him had produced.

He turned, his eyes sweeping her and coming to rest on her belly. His face lit up and he smiled—a smile of such warmth and joy that her heart caught. For a moment, he looked just like Noël. But, of course, he was Adam. And terrible. She conquered her fear and bobbed her head in a formal salute. "You might have told me, husband, that you were returning," she said coldly.

The smile died on his face. *"Madame."* He bowed and clicked his heels. "I've been posted to Paris to serve Marshal Moncey. But I thought to enjoy the holidays and the New Year here, if that doesn't inconvenience you too much." He indicated the officer beside him. "Permit me to introduce Lieutenant Aulard, my adjutant. He'll be staying at Bonneval for a day or two. Will that disrupt your schedule?"

"Not at all." In truth, she was grateful for Aulard's presence. A civilizing influence on Adam, perhaps. She held out her hand. "Lieutenant. We'll dine at six, if that's agreeable to you." She turned. "Prosper?"

The boy scurried forward, anxious eyes on Adam. Adam scowled, which only made Prosper quake the more. "Tell the boy to get out of here," Adam growled. "I'm tired of being looked at like an ogre."

"Prosper," she said smoothly, "go and tell Antoinette I want my green velvet gown for this evening."

Adam raised a questioning eyebrow. "Antoinette? I thought Bazaine had given you Yvonne for a maid."

She shrugged. "I sent her packing months ago. Insolent little snip."

For some reason, that seemed to please him; he turned to Aulard with a smile. "I have an independent wife, you see, Lieutenant. What else have you done while I was away, *madame*?"

"I'm sure you know," she said sourly. "I'm sure your spy, Bazaine, has written to you." It was too much to hope that Bazaine wouldn't have told him about Noël. "Surely he's told you everything."

"Not everything." He stared at her belly and smiled again. "I believe he did mention a cabriolet and team. And something about hiring a decorator for your suite."

She gulped. It had been wildly extravagant of her. But after Noël had gone, her rooms in the east pavilion had seemed too sad, too cramped. With her condition, Adam would scarcely demand his conjugal rights; it seemed safe to move back to the large suite across the hall from his. But after a week she had found the dark green color and the decor too heavy and oppressive; it had taken months, and a small fortune, to make the changes to her liking. She took a deep breath. "It . . . didn't suit my taste, what Bazaine had done. He gave me a free purse. I'm sure you'll be pleased," she added quickly.

He shrugged good-naturedly. "No matter. So long as you're pleased."

It seemed wise to escape while he was still smiling at her. Lord knows what he'd ask about next! "Until six, gentlemen," she said, and flew up the stairs with as much grace as her bulk allowed.

Dinner was a difficult affair. Lieutenant Aulard laughed and joked, pleased at the unexpected comfort of his surroundings after so many months in the garrison. He seemed oblivious to the tension in the air, Charmiane's barely disguised hostility toward her husband. Adam was making a conscious effort to be sociable, introducing topics of conversation whenever the talk lagged. But since his good humor was clearly tied in with his pleasure at Charmiane's condition—would he be so pleased if he knew it was Noël's child? she wondered bitterly—she found it difficult to shake her sense of guilt and responded with curt answers or not at all. Besides, Adam's kindnesses appeared forced to her, not at all like the Adam she remembered, the cruel, drunken Adam she knew him to be. She began to wonder if Noël hadn't spoken to him, encouraged him to show the "gentler side of his nature," as Noël had put it.

He cleared his throat. "You look charming in green, *madame*. But why didn't you wear your diamond-and-emerald earrings?"

She hesitated for only a moment, the lie long since prepared. "Alas, I've misplaced them." She smiled at Aulard. "More goose, Lieutenant?"

"Misplaced?" growled Adam.

She took her courage in hand and stared him full in the face. "I wasn't myself the night you gave them to me. I might have inadvertently thrown them away. Do *you* remember anything about that night?" She batted her eyelashes innocently and watched him squirm. At least he had a shred of conscience, the brute!

"I'll have to replace them," he managed at last, his voice strained.

She smiled again at Aulard and put her hand to her diamond necklace. "Am I not the most fortunate of wives, *monsieur*? My husband gives me jewels with madcap generosity. I feel as wicked as a grand courtesan of the *Ancien Régime*, being courted for my favors." God knew that was all she meant to him!

She joined Aulard in amused laughter but managed to steal a glance at Adam. To her surprise, he sat stone-faced. Not a scowl wrinkled his brow. Indeed, the only sign of his heightened emotion was the working of his jaw, the muscles hard against his cheeks. She began to realize that whatever her provocation he didn't intend to say anything, to rage, to terrify her. Perhaps it was Aulard's presence or perhaps he intended to make amends for his past behavior; but the awareness of his forbearance gave her a sense of power that made her reckless. The more he tried to be kind and restrained, the more she laughed with bright gaiety and threw sly insults at him, disguised as wit. Aulard, all unaware, shared her jokes and complimented General Bouchard on his wife's cleverness.

Seeming defeated at last, Adam lapsed into his customary silence for the rest of the meal. But when they'd retired to the music room for coffee, he tried again. "Perhaps you'd like to come to Paris for a few weeks, *madame*. I understand the opera is exceptional this season."

She shook her head. "I find Paris depressing at the moment. All those—" she almost said parvenus, then decided it was a little strong, with Aulard there "—those newly appointed aristocrats fearing for their positions should Bonaparte fall." She knew, from the look in his eye, that he'd heard the contempt behind her words.

Instead of challenging her, he chose to take another tack. "Paris," he mused. "Yes. It was my understanding that you only meant your cabriolet for local trips to the villages. Now Bazaine tells me you go to Paris unescorted."

"With Prosper," she said quickly.

"A child."

"I only go to see Sophie. I'm careful to avoid the low quarters, as you requested." Ordered, she thought, remembering his rage that day. With Aulard's presence as her shield, she decided to confront him openly. "Do you object?" she asked with some belligerence.

He cleared his throat. "I only question the wisdom of it, in your condition."

"My condition? *Fi donc!* I won't be brought to bed for mo— weeks and weeks yet." She turned away to hide the spots of color that had sprung to her cheeks. She'd nearly said "months." And he would have known the truth. Her own uneasy conscience made her snap at him. "Perhaps you'd like to provide me with a military escort," she said sarcastically, and then held her breath.

His eyes flashed at her tone, but he merely bent his head and took a sip of coffee. "Pray God it never comes to that," he said quietly.

"Then I'll continue to go alone, if you don't mind," she ventured, and was relieved to see his nod of agreement. She felt like a victorious soldier planting her flag on the field of battle, her enemy vanquished.

But when she would have retired for bed, he held on to her arm, bid Aulard a pointed good-night and scowled down at her until the other officer had left the room. Then his expression softened. A man trying to be reasonable. He sighed and released her arm. "Does it make you happy, all this venom?"

His resemblance to Noël, when he stopped frowning, only increased her bitterness and regret. "Does it make *you* happy to know you're a murderer, a lustful defiler, a tyrant?"

He stared at her, then sighed again and turned away. "God," he muttered, "it's a losing battle."

"Does that mean I'm dismissed, General Bouchard?"

"Damn your stubborn will!" He swung to her and pulled her savagely into his arms.

She trembled at the look in his eyes, so dark with uncertainty that she wasn't sure if he'd hit her or kiss her. Their glances locked for a long moment, and then he pushed her roughly away. She needed no more encouragement to flee his side. She hurried to her rooms, ignoring the trembling that refused to be stilled; a trembling that had more than fear about it. That felt like desire.

God help her, for a wild moment she'd *wanted* him to kiss her.

He was silent, withdrawn and moody for the next few days, particularly after Christmas, when Aulard returned to Paris. Charmiane was filled with dread, awaiting what she knew was an inevitable outburst. Antoinette had reported that some of the other servants had told Adam of Noël's recuperation and extended stay at Bonneval. "What was *monsieur le comte*'s disposition, when he was told?" she asked, fearing to hear the answer.

"Not . . . good, *madame*. Especially when it was suggested to him that you were very . . . friendly to Monsieur Noël."

"Dieu!" she gasped. "Wicked gossip. What a cruel thing to tell him."

"Indeed it was, *madame*." If Antoinette had her suspicions, her face didn't betray her.

Charmiane turned away, knowing her own face was an open book. "What did *monsieur le comte* respond to such a wicked insinuation?" She tried to sound offhand.

"He was very angry and defended *madame*'s honor."

"Oh, dear." It only compounded her guilt. She almost wished he *would* confront her directly. His rage would be easier than this silence over Noël.

The weather turned colder as the New Year approached. Prosper came down with a cold and was sent to bed. Charmiane sat in her boudoir day after day before the comfort of a warm fire and tried to finish the article for *La Voix* that had been promised for weeks. But how could she concentrate with Adam home? With his masterful presence in every room? She hadn't realized how free she'd felt all those months he was away. Now, despite the changes in his demeanor since the spring—the kindnesses, even a surprising gentleness—she found herself deferring to him again. Awaiting, as she had with Henri, the inevitable moment when his patience was exhausted and he would turn on her in a fury. For surely his pose of goodwill couldn't last. Hadn't she already seen the true Adam?

"May I come in this morning?"

Charmiane looked up from her desk, startled. Adam stood in the doorway of her boudoir, smiling. "Of course," she stammered, and rose from her desk, closing her leather writing case on the Flaming Sword's inflammatory words.

"I haven't seen how you've redone your suite," he said. "May I?" He stepped into the room without waiting for a reply and took a turn around her boudoir.

She'd had it redone in a soft blue. Blue silk draperies edged in gold braid covered most of the walls as well as the windows; the ceiling was swagged and draped with shirred panels of the same material, like an exotic tent in some romantic, faraway kingdom. A velvet sofa with mounded pillows was tucked into a mirrored niche at one end of the room, and the furniture—cabinets, desks, chairs—was of finely inlaid and gilded wood. Sevres porcelain flower bowls, candelabras and figurines added delicacy to the room, and a pale cream carpet, sprigged with blue forget-me-nots, covered the floor. The bedroom beyond and the small bathroom, with its tub and other personal amenities, were done in the same blue silks and velvets, relieved in the bed hangings and at the windows by white satin embroidered all over with gold fleurs-de-lis.

"Very handsome," said Adam as they returned to her boudoir. "I compliment you on your taste. However—" he smiled crookedly "—as to your judgment in the matter of the fleur-de-lis..."

"The symbol of *my* France," she said. "Did you think you'd married a Republican, not a Royalist?"

He sighed. "I'd hoped I'd married a realist." He crossed to her desk. "Are you sending New Year's greetings to your aunt? Ask her if she needs more money."

She hesitated, thrown into a panic. "My aunt? Oh, yes. Yes, of course. I shall indeed." She laughed uneasily.

He frowned. "What is it?" He reached out to her writing case.

"No!" she cried, feeling the blood drain from her cheeks.

"What? Am I being maligned to good dear Aunt Sophie?" His voice was heavy with mockery. Before she could stop him, he had opened the case. She held her breath. He stared at the writing, his hands curling into fists as he read. Then he swung to her, brandishing the paper under her nose. *"Did you write this?"*

"Y-yes," she whispered in terror.

"The Flaming Sword. They speak of his vitriol in Paris. And that damned subversive sheet *La Voix*. That's you? *You're* the Flaming Sword?"

"And Armand." The thought of her poor brother made her strong. "Before you killed him," she added with venom in her voice.

"Morbleu!" he swore. "Are you mad?" He held the paper before him and read aloud. His hand shook with rage. " 'This despot, this dictator, who forces the children in Holy Church to honor him as God Himself...' You wrote this? 'Rise up, you faithful. Follow the Flaming Sword and welcome the Tyrant's enemies as the saviors of France! *Vive le Roi!*' " He threw down the paper and stared at her. "My God, Charmiane. I don't believe this!"

"Why shouldn't I do it? The sooner your kind falls, the happier day it will be for France!"

"Happier day? Do you know what it was like in the old days? Beyond the romantic notions of the *Ancien Régime* that your fool family poured into you? A corrupt society in so many ways. And it was more than twenty years ago! Even if we could turn back time, that's not a society that France should welcome!"

"It's not welcome by you, God knows! I can hear your self-interest in every word you speak. *You* have everything to lose if the Monarch returns. Well, I say let the proper aristocrats take their places again."

"My God, all those idiots of the Faubourg Saint-Germain have filled your head with nonsense! May I remind you, Madame de Moncalvo, that *you're* now the new aristocracy?" His voice rumbled in fury.

"Bah!" she said, and swirled away from him.

He made an effort to calm himself. "Tell me why," he said.

Her eyes filled with tears. She fingered her brother's ring. "For Armand and his lost love. For all the other unfortunates who suffered unfairly. Perhaps it's a kind of redemption that the living owe the dead."

He rubbed his hand across his mouth. "I forget how young and innocent you can be. How long has this been going on? Since Armand died?"

"No. Since you went away in April."

He laughed sharply. "I see. It wasn't the killing of your brother that outraged you. It was the violation of your person by your lustful husband. Is that how women think?" He held up his hand to still her sputter of protest. "Who's involved in this with you? That white-haired jackal who called himself your brother's friend?"

3

"Bertrand de Domfort has been a loyal friend! And ally." She hesitated, then shrugged. Let it all be told. "And collaborator. Yes."

He shook his head in disgust. "The unescorted trips in the cabriolet. Of course. To meet with your fellow collaborators. In Paris?"

"No. Bertrand has a country house."

"What about money? From what I know, your Domfort hasn't a livre. He's been singularly unsuccessful at finding favor with the right people. Did you give him money?" At her silence, he grabbed her by the wrist, his hand a tight clamp. "Damn it, Charmiane, I'm losing my patience with you! Did you give him money?"

"Yes!" she burst out. "And the emerald earrings, as well! Now let me go. You're hurting me." Her lip curled in malice. "Unless you enjoy playing the bully and ordering me about."

He winced at that, released her and ran his fingers through his hair—a gesture of exasperation. "Don't you understand yet? What you did was stupid and dangerous. It's one thing to talk treason in your Aunt Sophie's salon. It's quite another to write and publish sedition against the Emperor!"

"Are you concerned that the scandal would ruin your career?"

"My God, you little fool," he growled. "The Emperor has spies everywhere, noticing the shipments of ink, the sales of printing presses. He's particularly sensitive to propaganda. You could be found out and shot for what you've done! And still you reduce this to some petty argument between you and me?"

It made her blood boil, the way he spoke to her as though she were a child! He had only his own interests at heart, the selfish brute. She knew it clearly. While *she* was fighting for a noble cause, picking up the torch that Armand and others had dropped along the way. "You can't begin to understand," she said scornfully.

"I can't and I won't," he said with finality. "Since you seem incapable of responding to reason, I intend to give you orders."

"Like one of your adjutants?" she sneered.

"No. Like the stubborn child you insist on being. You may thank the gods for your condition, *madame*. Otherwise I'm not sure that my treatment of you might not include the punishments due a child! Now. You are forbidden contact with that rascal Domfort except in the social setting of your aunt's salon. He is not to have another sou. You are to forget the Flaming

Sword, cease your writing and destroy whatever papers or records you may hold."

"Am I to be confined to my rooms? Or to Bonneval?" The words were meant to be bold, but her voice was shaking.

"You have complete freedom," he said, "but only if you behave yourself. Do you understand?" Without waiting for an answer, he turned on his heel and stalked out.

"Oh!" She had never felt more angry, more helpless, in all her life. She picked up a porcelain statue and flung it across the room, feeling satisfaction as it splintered against the wall. A child, indeed! Petty argument, he had said. As if Armand's death, her violation, were unimportant! You have a duty to yourself, Noël had told her. Well, he was right.

She rang for her maid. "Antoinette, go and have my cabriolet made ready. And then come back and help me dress."

"But Prosper . . . his cold . . ."

"I'm going out without him. He's not well enough for it on such a cold day. Don't worry. I'm quite capable of handling the team myself." As soon as Antoinette had left the room, she hurried to the chest that held her jewels, pulled out her diamond necklace and brought it to her dressing table. With a scissor and a small knife and a great deal of straining, she managed to pry loose one of the large stones. *La Voix* might not speak again with *her* voice, but it would live and triumph.

Bertrand de Domfort was just sitting down to a late luncheon when she arrived at his cottage, shivering against a day that had turned bleak and raw. He was surprised and delighted to see her; more delighted still to see the huge diamond she held out to him. "Charmiane, my sweet adored! Flower of all that's good and generous. I bless you. Armand in Heaven blesses you."

"I wish I could do more. As it is, I'll have to lie and tell Adam that one stone fell out of the necklace." She joined him for lunch, wondering when to tell him that this was the last time she could help *La Voix*. To tell him that she hadn't the courage to defy Adam by continuing her writing. Bertrand hadn't asked for her new article, though it was weeks since she'd given him anything to print. As they finished the meal, she rose. Perhaps she'd see which of her tracts was on the press; it might make it easier to open the difficult conversation that way. She pushed open the door to the printing room and gasped. "*Mon Dieu!* But where's the press?"

He hesitated. "I sold it," he said at last. "It was getting too dangerous. Besides, if the Tyrant falls, there's more important work to be done than printing. I told that to Georges months ago.''

"Months ago?'' She remembered the silent presses all these weeks. "When did you stop printing?''

"October.''

She stared at him, bewildered. "But you needed money, you said. I've given you money every week since then.''

"I've been using it to reestablish my position as a Domfort. When the Monarch returns to the throne, I want a place of influence in society. It will be easier to claim the Domfort title if I have property.''

"But . . . I've brought you a fortune!''

He smiled. She remembered, suddenly, that she hadn't liked him very much when they'd first met. She saw coldness in the smile in spite of his sad eyes. "I thank you for your help,'' he said. "You've enabled me to buy a *hôtel*. It's being furnished even now.''

She sputtered with outrage. "But you used me! It was greed, not patriotism, that fired you!''

He shrugged. "Perhaps a little of both. But you knew I was ambitious. Why shouldn't I do what's best for me? *La Voix* has done its part. Supplied me with funds, connections to the Faubourg Saint-Germain.''

She sank into a chair, overwhelmed by his words. By her dark thoughts. "You wanted to marry me. Was I part of your ambition? Henri's claim? Was that why you pursued it on my behalf?''

His eyes glittered with a naked desire that frightened her. "I always wanted you. But your late husband's holdings would have been welcome.''

"And when I married with Adam?''

"I kept hoping the war would make you a rich widow.''

"Curse you.'' She stood up and held out her hand, fingers shaking. "Give me back my diamond.''

He laughed softly. "I think not. Not unless you want your husband to know what you've been doing all these months.''

She drew herself up. "You're wasting your breath, villain. He knows.''

"Ah, but does the world know? Shall I noise it about Paris that General Bouchard's wife is a traitor?''

She reached for her cloak and her bonnet. "I'll take my chances. You have nothing to connect the Flaming Sword to me.''

He leaped for her and wrenched her away from the door. "Sit down!" He flung her onto a chair and glowered over her. "I want the rest of that necklace."

"Don't be absurd," she sneered.

He laughed, an ugly sound. "I think your husband will give it to me, to get his wife back safely. A soldier. A man of honor. Men of honor are so easily duped."

She felt a chill as the reality struck her. "*Mon Dieu!* You'll kill me, won't you? As soon as you get the necklace." When he nodded, she sank back against the chair, her hand over her eyes. "Was I so very blind? From the first. You used me. And Armand too, I'm sure."

"Your brother was a weakling," he said contemptuously. "Do you know how wearying it became? To give him his mercury and animate his corrupt body and keep his recklessness from destroying all our work?"

She stared at him in horror. "But you were his friend!"

"Until he stopped being useful. And by that time I'd met you."

"My God," she whispered, "you have no conscience. No soul. What do you want?"

His eyes were the cruelest she'd ever seen. "To take my place as a Domfort," he said. "As they denied me, damn every one of them. But the name will be mine. The title will be mine. As it was meant to be, if there were a God in Heaven!"

"The name?" she asked, bewildered. "But you *are* a Domfort." Hadn't she heard the story often enough from Armand? The family waiting to go to the guillotine? Bertrand alone emerging from the prison alive, his hair turned white from the terror of his days?

"A Domfort on the wrong side of the blanket," he said bitterly. "The bastard son. Raised on the estate with Bertrand the wastrel heir and the others. But never quite the equal of the legitimate children. Only equal when the family was denounced and thrown into the Conciergerie."

"They went to the guillotine, all of them. But not you."

"We were all condemned. I watched them go, one by one. And exulted. I befriended one of the jailers. I knew where my father had hidden some jewels. In exchange, the jailer conveniently 'lost' my condemnation papers. I was released after the fall of Robespierre. My hair was white by then. And the first person I met called me Bertrand and said how I'd changed. We'd always resembled each other, Bertrand and I. So I went abroad as Bertrand. Applied for papers as Bertrand. And when I petitioned the

Emperor for my return to France, it was as Bertrand. And no one—not even those who knew my dear half brother and me—has ever questioned it. Nor ever shall. Money is a powerful disguise. With your necklace to open doors and give me my father's title of *baron* no one will ever doubt who I am.''

"You monster!'' She leaped from her chair and hit out wildly at him. He deflected her blow and wrestled her back into the chair, managing at length to pin her arms behind the back of the chair and fasten them securely with a cord.

He reached for his overcoat and shrugged into it, holding the diamond like a priceless treasure. He smiled, the narrow-eyed smile of a snake. "I'm off to Paris, my dear. To sell your diamond. And arrange for a dupe to act as a go-between in your ransom so your husband can't connect it to me.''

She leaned forward and spat at him, filled with helpless rage and frustration. "And then you'll kill me, you coward?'' she sneered.

"Not right away,'' he said softly. "I promised myself the day I met you that I'd have you someday. I'm a very patient man. I've waited twenty years to claim my name. And two to taste your body.'' He clapped his hat on his head. "I'll be back late tonight. Think of me until then.''

Chapter Seventeen

"Will you dine soon, *monsieur le comte*?"

Adam roused himself from his reverie and looked at the footman. "Yes. And send *madame*'s maid Antoinette to me now."
He crossed to the library window. It looked as if it would storm tonight. He hoped it wouldn't make traveling impossible tomorrow. He was eager to be in Paris to learn what he could of *La Voix* and to see if there was any danger of it being connected to Charmiane. The little fool! Even now he trembled at the risk she'd taken, the mortal danger to herself, to his child.

His child. Conceived in hatred, he guessed, the night he'd used her so savagely. No wonder she'd told no one for months, not until her condition began to show. Not even "Noël," though she must have known by then. And Bazaine had kept the news from him in his letters so as not to worry him, he said. But they both knew that an unhappy, unwanted pregnancy carried its own special risks.

And now he'd added to her unhappiness, done what he swore to himself he'd never do again. He'd bullied her, frightened her, even threatened to beat her. God! He was no better than her first husband.

But damn it! She was partly to blame. When he'd been "Noël," she'd stood her ground as an equal. Why was it, as a wife, she seemed to think that servility or childish rebellion was her proper role? The odd thing was, he could understand her idealism, even if it was dangerous and misguided. It was her manner that had finally made him lose his temper. That and her unwavering hatred, no matter what he did.

He groaned aloud. He almost wished the real Noël was here to give him advice. He'd been a soldier from the age of seventeen.

What the deuce did he know of women and love besides the few giggling girls in the Brittany of his youth, a legion of nameless whores from every nation and the forward garrison wives who seduced a lonely soldier into their beds for their own amusement? Scarcely love, any of it. And now, because of his own clumsiness, he seemed even further than ever from being able to tell Charmiane the truth.

"You wanted to see me, *monsieur*?" Antoinette stood in the doorway.

"Yes. *Madame la comtesse...*" Lord, this was awkward! "Does she seem...of an agreeable disposition this evening?" Perhaps over dinner he could behave with more kindliness and reason.

"Oh, *monsieur*, she's gone. I thought you knew."

"What?"

"Before noon it was. Off in her cabriolet, without even Prosper for company."

"Damnation!" he burst out. Gone to Domfort? Her aunt? He pounded his fist in his palm. And after his warning! "That stubborn little... Where does she go in her cabriolet?"

Antoinette cringed at his anger. "I don't know, *monsieur*. Paris, I always thought. But, *monsieur*..." She hesitated in fear, then went on. "I think you should know that *madame* left her diamond necklace out. And one of the stones is missing. I'm sure it wasn't missing when I put it away. I'm most certain, *monsieur*!"

He cursed again. She'd taken a diamond. That meant Domfort for sure. And who knew the way to his cottage besides Charmiane?

Prosper! He raced to the servants' wing to find the boy. He found Prosper in his room, huddled in front of the fire, coughing and still showing the effects of his cold. At sight of Adam, the boy seemed to shrink into himself, his eyes wide with terror. Adam cursed his own short temper, but there was no time to win the boy over. Only a direct approach now would do.

"Listen to me, boy," he said, as calmly as possible. "I know you have no love for me. But as you love your mistress, and as you love my brother, Noël..." He nearly snorted aloud at the absurdity of this: to have to make friends with a child who'd been his friend, all unknowing, for weeks last summer. "I beg you to help me. Your mistress has taken her carriage."

Prosper's eyes widened at that. "Yes," said Adam. "She's gone. To visit Monsieur de Domfort, I think. She shouldn't be out alone in her condition, so close to term. You *do* understand that?'' The boy nodded vigorously. "Good. Unhappily, I don't know where Domfort lives. If you do, can you show me on a map?'' Prosper looked stricken. Adam groaned. "You can't read. I forgot. Well, you'll just have to ride with me and show the way as we go. Get dressed warmly and meet me at the stables.''

It was already turning dark when Prosper joined him. Damn, he thought. They'd have a devil of a time finding their way now! But Prosper grinned and held up a piece of paper. It had a crudely drawn picture scrawled on it. It seemed to be a bridge. *"Pont,"* said Adam, scowling. *"Pont?* Does it sound like *pont*?'' At Prosper's nod, he racked his brain. He knew some of the villages near Bonneval but not all. "Pontoise! Of course. Is Domfort's cottage near Pontoise?'' At Prosper's excited nod, he smiled broadly and hoisted the boy into his saddle. "Come along, boy,'' he said. "We're going to have a ride you'll never forget!''

Despite his wish to remain calm, he spent the ride picturing Charmiane with that snake Domfort, laughing happily at her cleverness. Short of throttling her, he didn't know how he was going to make her understand the seriousness of her actions, the folly of her treason.

Domfort's cottage was dark when they reached it, holding a lantern before them to show the way. Oh, God, thought Adam. If she's not here, where could she be? Then Prosper, who'd slid from the saddle and run to Domfort's stable, threw wide the door and showed him Charmiane's cabriolet and team. Numb with dread, Adam burst into the cottage. It was as cold inside as out. No fire burned on the hearth, no candle lit the gloom. Charmiane, her face drawn, sagged in a chair to which she'd been cruelly tied. While Prosper built up the fire, Adam loosened her bonds, wrapped her in a blanket from Domfort's bed and held her in his arms.

The words of reproach died on his lips. "Charmiane,'' he murmured. "Thank God. Thank God.''

Charmiane pulled the blanket more tightly around her. It was cold, the wind was gusting fitfully, and they'd only been on the road for half an hour. She wasn't sure how much more she could endure. Her body ached, a dull pain that had begun in the small of her back. And between the night and the dark road, it would be another two hours at least before they reached Bonneval.

She glanced over Prosper's head to Adam, sitting stonily in the cabriolet, the reins in his fists. His face, by the light of the lantern, was hard and unreadable. She'd been surprised at his tenderness, the way he'd held her tightly, his warmth giving her strength. And more surprised when he'd confined his scoldings to a muttered "Completely unnecessary, if you'd had a little more sense in your head." She'd murmured an apology, but when she'd haltingly told him of Domfort's betrayal, his vile past and the theft of the diamond, Adam had merely shrugged. "Let him have the diamond," he'd said. "And his unearned title. If he's that desperate, I can only pity him. Besides, if we denounce him, he'll implicate you."

That had surprised her, his generosity. "You mean you won't kill him?"

He'd laughed sardonically. "Why? To make another martyr for you to grieve over?"

That had made her think of Armand and Domfort's strange words. Now she took her courage in hand and broke the heavy silence. "Why does a person take mercury?"

"For the pox. Syphilis. You do know what that is?"

"Yes." She was glad he couldn't see her blush for Armand's shame. "And mercury cures it?"

"There's no real cure. But it helps. Unless you take too much."

"And then what?"

"The cure becomes worse than the disease. I've seen men suffer for years because of mercury poisoning. Tremors and headaches. Rages and tears. Men cry like babies over nothing, shake for hours, talk with longing about suicide. All reason seems to vanish, and memory sometimes. A kind of madness takes hold. A dangerous cure, needless to say."

That started her to thinking, recalling Armand in those last months before his death. Could it have been possible? He'd certainly wept a lot. And his tremors had broken her heart. And Domfort had said he was reckless. But mad? It was too sad, too terrible to contemplate.

The cabriolet gave a sudden sickening lurch and tipped to one side. Adam reined in the team, leaped from the seat and pulled the lantern from its hook. He cursed softly. "The wheel is broken, damn it. I suppose we can leave it here and take the horses. You and Prosper will ride my saddled horse; I'll manage a carriage horse without a saddle."

She hesitated. She hated to be a bother after all the trouble she'd put him to tonight. Still . . .

"I can't," she ventured. "I'm shivering now. And I have a pain . . ." She wrapped her arms around her belly.

"It must be your time," he said calmly.

"It can't be! It's too soon. I . . ." Oh God, what could she say? If she were truly in labor, it *was* too soon. She was only six and a half months gone, and the baby would never survive. But she couldn't tell him that. It would have to be her own private agony.

Adam was already marching down the road, the lantern held high. After a few minutes, he returned. "I've found a woodcutter's cottage. The man has agreed to take Prosper and my horse and go to Bonneval. They'll come back with the large coach so you can finish the journey in comfort. In the meantime, we'll stay warm and snug in the man's cottage."

Her body was beginning to shake uncontrollably. Perhaps she was in labor after all. "What if they don't return in time?"

He reached up and lifted her down, cradling her in his strong arms. "That's why I'm staying with you. I've been an accoucheur many a time. Camp followers always seem to give birth after a battle, and there are never enough surgeons, never mind midwives." He carried her into the cottage and set her on the woodcutter's small cot. While he gave the man final instructions and a sack of coins for his trouble and put the carriage horses in the barn, Charmiane tried to reassure a wide-eyed Prosper.

"Go home and go to bed," she said gently. "I'll see you tomorrow."

When they'd gone, Adam took off his greatcoat and hat and, despite Charmiane's feeble protests, helped her undress down to her chemise. He bundled her into the bed, built up the fire and came and sat beside her. "How do you feel?"

She grimaced as a sharp pain tore through her. "Maybe it's only something I ate."

"And maybe not. Tell me when the next one comes." When she made a face again, squeezing her eyes against the wrenching spasm, he put his hand on her belly. "No," he said, "it's not something you ate. You can feel it—the way the muscles tighten into a mound."

His hand was warm and comforting on her belly—she yearned to blurt out the truth about Noël, to share her fear that the baby was dangerously premature. "Adam . . ." she whispered.

He patted her hand. "Don't be afraid. They should get to Bonneval by midnight. The carriage will arrive in plenty of time.

You'll be snug in your own bed long before this Bouchard makes his entrance into the world.''

The pains grew in intensity, catching her with such sharpness that she held her breath. Adam soothed her, mopped her damp brow, stroked the strands of hair back from her forehead. Meantime, the wind increased, howling mournfully around the stones of the cottage and rapping at the windows with impatient fingers. By midnight the snow had begun; by dawn, with the storm still raging, they both knew the coach wouldn't arrive in time, if at all.

Charmiane was exhausted. It was impossible to sleep with the pains coming so quickly; impossible to focus on anything but the wrenching agony of her swollen body. Adam smiled his encouragement and rubbed the ache at the small of her back, but there was little more to do except wait. Charmiane passed her tongue across her dry lips. ''Talk to me,'' she whispered. ''To help the time pass.''

He dampened her lips with a wet cloth. ''What shall we talk of?''

''How—'' she cringed as pain tightened her belly, held her in its fierce grip, then subsided ''—how did Armand die?''

He rubbed tiredly at his eyes. ''I wish I could tell you,'' he said. ''But it's a blur. I was very drunk that night.''

She still felt anger at his violation. ''And other nights, as well.'' A cruel thrust. Seeing the pain in his eyes, she almost regretted her words.

''Am I never to be forgiven for that night?'' he asked. He stared at her and then laughed, a sad, humorless laugh. ''No. I'm not. Your face, as usual, speaks to me with rapier clarity.'' He sighed. ''But you asked about your brother. I'll tell you what I remember. He came to pick a quarrel with me. His stupid pride. He'd decided that my giving a stipend to your aunt represented an insult to the Chevrillons.''

''That doesn't sound like Armand. He would have been glad for Sophie!'' She said the words, but she wasn't sure they were so. Armand *had* been irrational those last weeks, nursing his resentments against the upstarts who had robbed him of his life, his love, his station.

''I've wondered if Domfort had something to do with Armand's state of mind. He certainly urged on your brother. I remember I tried to reason with Armand. I begged him to embrace me as a brother. Because of you. I think I started toward him.'' He blinked his eyes as though he were trying to clear his memory. "And then we were fighting. I know I didn't want it. I kept backing away, crashing into things, trying to avoid him. He was screaming curses at me, I remember. And Domfort...I couldn't tell if he was glad or sorry it had come to this."

She burned again with remorse, thinking of how she'd so misjudged Domfort, been so blind to his hungry ambition. "Perhaps both," she said bitterly. "What did he have to lose? He was able to use Armand's death to keep me guilt-ridden, bleed me for money. And if Armand had killed you, I would have been the rich widow, ripe for Domfort's wooing. Oh, God," she choked, "was there ever a more willing dupe than I?"

"Don't, Charmiane. Don't." He sat on the edge of the cot and gathered her in his arms. "We learn from life. That's all the teacher we have." He held her while she wept. Held her and comforted her until a violent spasm wrenched her out of his arms and she writhed on the bed, fighting the urge to scream aloud. When she subsided against the pillows, gasping in relief, he smoothed back her hair and managed a bleak smile.

"Armand," he said. "I don't remember killing him. I wish to God I could. It torments me not to remember. I think it was an accident. I think I was trying to avoid his lunge, but I can't remember! God help me, I was too drunk to remember."

"*Do* you think it was an accident?" She had never considered it, never given him the opportunity to explain, seeing him as a black villain from the first.

"I don't know," he said, anguished. "I know I didn't want to kill him. But I drew my sword. I fought with him." He groaned. "It was an unfair contest. He behaved like a madman. I should have had the sense to walk away. Then maybe he'd be alive today."

"And maybe he *was* a madman," she moaned, struggling against fresh tears. Dear Armand. Dear heart. "Domfort told me this morning that he'd been taking mercury." She hesitated, then reached up and stroked the side of Adam's cheek. Whatever else he was, he had deserved more of her understanding than she'd given him. "Adam," she said, "I'm sorry. I...Dear Mother of God!" She cried out as her water gave way in a great rush.

"It will be soon now." Adam threw off his coat and rolled back his shirt cuffs. He had found several clean sheets in the woodcutter's chest; now he tucked them under Charmiane's hips. The pains were coming fast now, with an urgency that left her gasping. Her legs quivered as she dropped them wide. She pushed and strained, feeling the baby exploding from her womb. She felt a surge, a fierce stretching of her membranes, and Adam let out an excited shout. "Yes! Push once more!" Then he cursed softly.

She raised herself on her elbows to see that his face—wreathed in expectant smiles but a moment before—was now drained of color, his jaw slack. She sank back against the pillows. She didn't want to see. "It's dead, isn't it?" she whispered.

He took a towel and wrapped something in it. Something small and gray that barely filled the palm of his hand; and when he spoke, it was with the distant, commanding voice of General Bouchard. "There's nothing to be done. I'll bury it when the snow stops. It's important for you to pass the afterbirth." He kneaded her belly, working the placenta loose. Then he wrapped her in towels to stanch the blood, covered her, ordered her to sleep. She was too exhausted to feel anything. Not pain. Not grief. Not even remorse, knowing that he would mourn a child that wasn't even his.

She awoke to pain. Her womb, having done its work, was now cramping and tightening in the process of returning to normal. She sat up in bed. It was cold. The door to the cottage had blown open, and Adam didn't seem to be about. She staggered out of bed, tottered to the door and stared out at the morning.

The snow had stopped, but the sky was still gray. Adam was there, on a hill a small distance from the cottage. He was in his shirtsleeves, a shovel in his hands. Before him was a cleared patch, well trampled, the snow mixed with dirt. As she watched, he shoveled more snow onto the bare patch and tamped it down. Then, like a great shattering explosion, he let out a roar, lifted the shovel and smashed it against the trunk of a tree. Again and again, with savage blows, while his howls reverberated against the bleak hillside.

Charmiane began to tremble, feeling his pain and rage. He knows, she thought. *He knows.* Now she remembered that during the last frightening moments, the final, painful rush of the baby, she'd cried out Noël's name. And Adam was no fool. He could tell from the size of the baby that he couldn't possibly have sired it.

It was terrifying to watch his rage, to be reminded of the cruel bridegroom he'd been in the spring. But she felt anguish, as well, for this man. And terrible pangs of guilt, sharper than any labor pain she'd endured all night. "Oh, Noël," she whispered, "what mischief have we done in the name of love?"

Adam turned and saw her at the door. His face was terrible in its grief. It tore at her heart. Whatever he'd done, he hadn't deserved an unfaithful wife. Charmiane quivered violently, her head buzzing, and sank to the floor, senseless.

"Your papers, *madame*." The young soldier stamped his feet in the trampled snow around the city gate and waited while Charmiane fished in her reticule for her papers. His frozen breath hung in the still air.

"Ciel," she said, handing over the documents. "Since when do we have armed guards at the gates of Paris?"

"For more than three weeks now, *madame*. The war, you know."

She frowned. Everyone knew that France's enemies had crossed the Rhine at the end of December and were now on French soil. But Napoleon had left Paris to do battle only a week ago, on the twenty-fifth of January, taking a fresh army with him and leaving behind his reassurances. "Is Paris in danger?" she asked.

The soldier puffed out his chest. He seemed very young, his chin soft and unwhiskered. "Not while the Guard is here, *madame*! Your papers are in order." He handed them back, saluted her and motioned to her coachman to pass through the gate of La Villette.

She leaned back in the coach and closed her eyes. It would be nice to see Sophie again. And married! The invitation had caught her by surprise. Sophie's first "At Home" as the Duchesse d'Auvergne. She'd met Charles d'Auvergne at Sophie's salons a few times—a wealthy former aristocrat who'd wormed his way into the Emperor's favor, been appointed to a good government position and had his title reinstated. But she'd had no idea that he and Sophie . . .

She sighed and opened her eyes. Sophie's letters had been singularly unsympathetic since she'd lost the baby. Filled with veiled suggestions that if she should be fortunate enough to lose her husband as well in this campaign, she might come to her senses and find a proper Royalist for her third husband.

She sighed again. In some ways, she felt as though she'd already lost her second husband. Whether it was the pressure of the war that kept him constantly dashing off to Paris or her own burning guilt at her betrayal, they seemed always at odds. He was cool, distant, preoccupied; she needed brightness and gaiety to keep her grief at bay.

She'd taken to entertaining at Bonneval, glittering little suppers for the local gentry. Afternoon card parties and *soirées musicales*. She found the people as tedious and unpolished as she had at her wedding supper. But they supplied companionship, and it kept her from thinking of the fragile bundle that Adam had buried in the snow barely a month ago. She moved among her guests like a mechanical toy; her laughter was brittle, and her smiles were as false as the corkscrew curls the women pinned on to appear fashionable and young.

It had infuriated Adam, all her frivolous amusements. He had come to Bonneval unexpectedly more than once in the past month to find her surrounded by her guests. He had scowled and stomped off to his rooms. And once, to her horror and shame, seeing her flirting with a young *baron* who smiled and kissed her hand, he had taken the man and thrown him bodily from the house. She tried to persuade herself that his somber and angry mood was only because of the gravity of the war, his military burdens. But she knew in her heart that she was the object of his anger. A faithless wife who had carried his brother's child.

The carriage stopped. Darnaud opened the door. "We're here, *madame*. Rue de Varenne. I'll pick you up at four this afternoon. Will you stay in Paris overnight?"

She thought for a minute. She didn't know where Adam was. Sometimes he spent the night at the various barracks in and around the city, but sometimes he stayed at their *hôtel*. "No. I'll return to Bonneval tonight." Coward, she thought.

Sophie's new house on the rue de Varenne was superb. The furniture was expensive and elegant, and every room was filled with paintings, antique statues and choice porcelain. Sophie greeted her warmly; but Jeanine, coming into the drawing room to hand her mistress a cashmere shawl, lifted her nose in the air and passed Charmiane by, as if to say, My mistress is rich now, too! Charmiane congratulated Sophie on her marriage and allowed d'Auvergne to kiss her on the cheeks. She moved among the formerly titled guests who longed to regain their stations and noticed—almost for the first time—the bored flick of a hand taking snuff, the autocratic snapping of fingers to a laggard footman, the indolence and the arrogance of the old aristocracy. *Mon Dieu,* she thought. They're no better than the parvenus at Bonneval desperately trying to be the New Society. And perhaps a good deal worse. The parvenus, at least, had earned their airs and titles.

And when the talk turned to politics, she felt a stirring of real anger. She had endangered her life as the Flaming Sword to defend these people? They had done nothing to support the Monarch during the Revolution except flee with their riches; now, smelling Napoleon's defeat, they sat back and gloated and let men like Adam die for them.

"Monsieur de Talleyrand says it's the beginning of the end," said Sophie complacently.

A fat *marquis* with a quizzing glass held it up to his eye and examined a passing young servant girl. "Yes," he said. "The Bourbon supporters are beginning to rise in the provinces. I've even heard—" he lowered his voice "—that Talleyrand has been in contact with our exiled Monarch in England."

"*Vive Louis XVIII,*" murmured another man. "Now all we have to do is wait for the allied forces to liberate us. Ah, *monsieur le baron.* Come and join us."

Charmiane looked up. Domfort had come into the room. So it was *monsieur le baron* now. And her diamond had done it. She could tell by the smug look on his face that he no longer feared her denunciation. *Dieu!* Surely he didn't mean to greet her as though nothing had happened between them, the villain!

He did. He moved at once to her, a bland smile on his face. "Charmiane. My dear. I'd hoped you'd accept Sophie's invitation. You're looking superb, as always. I heard about your unfortunate loss. Please allow me to express my deepest regrets."

She stared at him. This was the man who would have killed her. Whose mistreatment of her had likely caused her premature delivery. "You bastard," she muttered. "You damned hypocrite. My husband is more generous than I. I wish I had the savagery in my heart to kill you, as you deserve."

He shrugged. "You had best look to yourself. When the Tyrant falls, where will you be? Married to an upstart when you might have had me and Henri's legitimate title."

Sophie, standing nearby, clicked her tongue. She had clearly heard only the last of Domfort's words. "I don't know why you didn't pursue Henri's claim, Charmiane. To let Troche's family have it! I still remember him. Fawning little toady of a servant. And his daughter was no better than a whore."

"What of his daughter?" Charmiane remembered that Adam had said Troche's family deserved Henri's money. Especially Troche's daughter.

Sophie laughed. "Oh, my dear. I remember Eugène speaking of it. In the old days, before the Revolution. He played cards with

Henri sometimes. Poor Henri had to send the girl away finally. She'd disgraced her father and had a child out of wedlock. A poor twisted deformed thing that had to be put into an asylum. She claimed afterward that it was Henri's child and bothered him for money. What could he do but send her away?''

"But that's monstrous!" cried Charmiane.

Sophie looked astonished. "My dear! He was very generous. But for his warm feelings for Troche, he would have had the girl horsewhipped and imprisoned for such slander. It was his privilege, as an aristocrat."

She didn't know how she endured the rest of the afternoon. Adam had been right. Right to give Henri's money to the Troche family; right in his understanding of the moral bankruptcy of the *Ancien Régime.* She'd seen only what she'd been taught: the beauty of privilege. But someone had had to pay the price. The Troches of this world. The Adams and Noëls, whose blood and energy had allowed these selfish parasites to endure.

She sat in her carriage, her head in her hands. Did she have a single ideal left? Sophie was a shallow, self-interested old woman, Domfort a betraying snake. Even poor weak Armand had been less than she'd imagined him through her romantic haze. His bitterness, his illness, had twisted his reason and common sense long ago.

Only God was just, punishing her for her adultery by taking away her child.

And Adam. Had she misjudged him? There was so much of him that was good, that was kind and understanding. The more she learned of him, the less certain she was of his wickedness. Armand's death. The family Troche. She had been quick to judgment, deaf to the possibility that he might be in the right. She began to weep. What did it matter now? It was too late. She'd betrayed him, and he'd never forgive her. And even if he did, what was she to do about Noël? God help her, she still loved him, still dreamed about their sweet summer idyll, still thought of his moving letters and the passionate man to whom she'd given her eager body. How could she start afresh with Adam now? How could she forget the love she'd found with Noël?

She rapped on the roof of the coach. Darnaud opened the little door above her and looked in. "Have we passed the gate of La Villette yet, Darnaud?"

"No, *madame.* We're just in Montmartre."

"Find me a church nearby," she said. "I should like to pray."

* * *

Adam knelt before the altar, crossed himself, then took a seat in an empty pew. The church was deserted, which suited him in his cheerless mood. He wanted to be alone with God and his thoughts. He had put aside his uniform today, tired of being clutched at by terrified old women who wanted to know if the enemy would dare to attack Paris itself. But in civilian clothes, as he'd discovered this afternoon, he was as easily prey to those who demanded to know why an able-bodied Frenchman wasn't in uniform.

He leaned back in the pew, overcome with weariness. The work never seemed to end—the meetings, the messages, the inspections, the juggling of limited troops and supplies. The only blessing was that the last of his nightmares had gone; he was too tired even to dream these days. It was their birthday next week, his and Noël's, and he hadn't even had the time or energy to write a letter to his twin. Thirty-six, on the eleventh of February. "Here's to you, brother," he whispered. "God keep you safe."

Lord knew where Noël was now. They'd dined together in Paris, when Noël was on his last leave. A quiet dinner. A final farewell, perhaps. They'd talked about their childhood. And then Noël had marched off with the Emperor's forces to meet the enemy. A motley army, with maimed and crippled veterans, forest rangers and customs officials added to the remains of the old Grand Army and the untested young conscripts. But perhaps Noël was luckier than he. At least he'd be fighting under the command of experienced veteran officers and the Emperor, who was still the most formidable tactician in Europe. Even with his back to the wall.

But *he* had been reassigned to the National Guard to fortify and defend Paris and its environs should it come to that. Under the command of the Emperor's brother, the deposed King Joseph of Spain. A lazy, ineffectual, unmilitary man. He'd been unable to hold out against Wellington in Spain; how the deuce could he be counted on to protect Paris? Well, at least Adam's immediate superior was Marshal Moncey, a career officer and a thoroughly competent soldier. If only they had the troops! What they had was a handful of boys—raw recruits who'd been issued a shako, an overcoat and a musket or fowling piece they didn't know how to use. Every day now in Paris, batches of conscripts were being shot as deserters.

And the Emperor was at the breaking point. He had given his farewell to the officers of the National Guard in the snowy courtyard of the Tuileries. Adam, in attendance, had been appalled at the scene. Gone were the appeals to glory, the noble sentiments, the national pride. They had been harangued by a little man, a frenzied, desperate man, his face distorted with rage, who seemed more concerned with his own fate than with the country he was dragging down with him after too many years of war. A man who could order the National Guard to turn Paris into a fortress, to defend it to the last man and be buried in the ruins if necessary.

And there was no one left to advise him. Force him to accept the coalition's peace offer, no matter how personally degrading. For the good of France. But through the years the Republican had become the Dictator; the liberator of France had become mad with power and his own glory, gradually replacing honest advisers with flunkies who agreed with everything he said.

Adam sighed. He'd long since stopped fighting for the Emperor, for France, for a cause. Now he went to war because he was a soldier, and it was his duty. But Lord, he was tired.

Too tired even to mourn the loss of his child. "Noël's" child, he knew now, conceived in their great love, not in anger and lustful rage. He wondered if Charmiane thought he suspected "Noël" of fathering the child. Not that it mattered. *She* didn't seem to be suffering with the loss. Her indifference had infuriated him. He had never seen her more bright and happy, in a frenzy of merrymaking and shallow coquetry, as though the world weren't crumbling around them.

He groaned aloud and covered his eyes with his hand, fighting against his tears. He needed her so much. Needed the simplicity of their love, without the complication of his lies and duplicity. But there was no time. No time for explanations, no time to win her as Adam, no time to sire another child before the twilight fell. No time for anything.

He buried his head in his arms, his body shaking with sobs.

"Noël?" A soft voice behind him. "Noël, is it you?"

He turned. Charmiane stood in the church doorway, her hand to her breast, eyes filling with joyous tears.

He hesitated. He yearned to call out the truth. No! It's Adam, and I love you. But he hadn't the courage. This might be the last time he'd see her. Love her.

"Yes, my dearest love," he said, "it's Noël," and went to her.

Chapter Eighteen

They kissed in the vestibule of the church—a mad, wild kiss filled with hunger and desire and great joy. Charmiane smiled up at him and dabbed at a tear that lingered on his lash. "Noël, my love."

He kept his arms around her, as though he never wanted to let her go. "Where can we be together for a while?"

It was too cold to be outside. Too dangerous to go to Adam's *hôtel*. But she'd seen a small tavern just down the street from the church. She went out to her carriage, told Darnaud and the coachman to wait for her at the *hôtel*. She didn't know how long she'd be. Then she and Noël walked hand in hand to the tavern and found a quiet table in a corner. The wine they ordered sat untouched; they drank in the sight of each other like thirsty souls drinking their last.

"Charmiane," he murmured. "I thought I'd never see it again. That look of love in your eyes."

She groped for his hand and brought it to her lips. "So much has happened. I lost the child I was carrying."

His voice was a strained growl in his throat. "I know."

"Oh, Noël, it was yours!"

He gulped and stared up at the beamed ceiling of the inn. "I know."

"How I've longed for you, my love. Longed for someone to share my grief. To hold me and cherish me."

"I'm here." He leaned across the table and kissed her. "Put aside your grief. Smile for me, just for a little while, and tell me you love me."

"No matter what's to come. Yes, I love you," she whispered.

He stared at her for a moment, all hungry longing, then turned and called out. "Innkeeper! Have you a room?"

She put her hand on his arm. "Noël, please. I can't." How could she betray her marriage vows again? No. It was more than that. It was Adam. How could she betray Adam, who was deserving of her loyalty, if nothing else, after his tender concern that night in the woodcutter's cottage?

"Oh God, Charmiane," he groaned. His eyes were filled with dark despair, a deep, elemental need she couldn't ignore. Who knew if they'd ever meet again?

She nodded her consent and allowed him to lead her upstairs to a little room under the eaves. They undressed quickly, shyly, not looking at each other, like lovers meeting for the first time. But when he made love to her, it was with a passionate burst of frenzy, and he cried out in release as though the sound had lain within him, imprisoned by his own restraints, yearning to break free. After a moment, he rolled over and stared up at the ceiling.

"You're my savior," he said. "As always. Whenever I think I can't go on, you're there with your love and your sweetness, giving me heart and hope for the future." He closed his eyes and passed his hand across his mouth. "I should like to tell you something, I think."

She sat up and looked at him, the beautiful embodiment of all her dreams of love. His face was strong, despite its fatigue, and the power of his hard-muscled body made her heart beat faster. She lifted a languid finger and traced the line of scars on his chest, then followed a path across his ridged stomach to a tuft of blond hair just above his navel. He twitched and opened his eyes, surprise mixed with a sudden gleam of desire.

"We've had too much gloom," she said. "What's happened to my carefree, laughing Noël? Do you remember last summer how we made love, filled with joy and happiness? It was always summer then. Make love to me now, Noël. As we did then."

"Charmiane, we must speak seriously."

"Later. For now, make me feel young and free again. And beloved."

He took her mouth in a lingering kiss, and when he took her body it was with an unhurried delight, as though tomorrow would never come. She gloried in the feel of him within her, in the knowledge that she was adored. And when he fell into an exhausted sleep, he held her close, cradling her in the bend of his arm. She sighed in contentment, never wanting to leave his warm, sweet embrace.

* * *

It was night. The little tavern room had grown quite dark. She heard the shout of a carouser outside the window, the rumbling clatter of carriages and horses. *Dieu!* What was she doing? Had she lost her senses? Darnaud still waited for her at the town house! And what if Adam was there tonight and not at a garrison? Her heart froze in dread. She'd never be able to keep the guilt from her face if he should ask where she'd been.

She extricated herself from Noël's arms and dressed quickly by the dim light of the lamp in the street below. She couldn't stay until morning. She dared not stay to hear what Noël wanted to say to her. He'd only ask her to leave Adam, she was sure. And that was something she wasn't ready to contemplate.

"*Adieu,* my love," she whispered to his sleeping form. She hurried downstairs, tipped the innkeeper to hail her a passing carriage and sped off toward the rue Saint-Honoré. If she was lucky, Adam wouldn't be there. She'd avoid Darnaud's questioning looks, lie to Bazaine when they reached Bonneval late tonight and try to live with her conscience.

God help her. She couldn't keep away from Noël's arms, from his bed, when he needed her. But she realized now that a part of her *did* care for Adam, in spite of everything.

"Ah, Prosper, won't it be nice to see spring again? In less than a week!" Charmiane smiled up at the blue sky. The March sun was warm on her face, and the sharp breeze that whipped at the ribbons of her bonnet—while still cool—bore the scents of loam and early flowers and green buds. The weather in February, and even into March, had been dreadful—the coldest winter in years. For three weeks the temperature had hovered at eighteen degrees below the freezing point. Charmiane, weakened by her pregnancy and stillbirth and further worn by the giddy round of dinners and entertainments, had been felled by a cold that had kept her bedridden for a fortnight.

But now the sun was shining and her health was restored. A happy circumstance. She should be happy. But Noël was off to war again, according to Bazaine. And Adam was waiting for her in Paris.

She could only guess at his mood from the note she'd received. Not a note, really. More like a command. An order. From his adjutant, Lieutenant Aulard. Madame de Moncalvo was to come to Paris at once. General Bouchard wished to have a seri-

ous talk with her on a matter of grave importance. She was to
come in the carriage, with Darnaud and the coachman.

Prosper glanced up at her and offered the reins of the team. She
shook her head. "No," she said, "not now. Perhaps I'll drive the
cabriolet for a while after we pass Montmorency." She was beginning to regret disobeying Adam in the matter of the large
coach. It had seemed such an unimportant thing, which carriage
to take, when she'd started out. The sun was shining, they'd be
in Paris in just a few hours, and she'd been confined to Bonneval for so long she yearned for fresh air. Surely he would understand. But as they'd traveled, she'd begun to realize why he must
want to see her. The "serious talk" could only involve her infidelity with Noël. Perhaps Adam even knew of their tryst in
Montmartre at the beginning of February. If Bazaine knew Noël
was off to war again, perhaps it meant the brothers had met in
Paris before Noël left for the front. Noël had blurted something;
Adam was furious and had decided to speak openly and confront his wife at last. Seen in that light, her defiance in taking the
cabriolet was an act of folly. Already she could feel a tight knot
growing in her stomach in anticipation of one of Adam's angry
outbursts.

She was surprised as they neared the outskirts of Paris to find
the road crowded with large traveling coaches and small carriages, heavy with baggage and filled with women and children.
They seemed well-to-do and traveled at a leisurely pace. Charmiane breathed a sigh of relief. It was clearly not a panicky ex-
odus from the capital, merely a precaution, as the wealthy citizens
of Paris sent their loved ones to the safety of country homes. Still,
it was a sign that the war was coming close.

There was a long delay at the gate of La Villette. The carriages
were shunted aside to allow the passage of wounded French soldiers into the city. They lay in hay-filled farm wagons, their heads
and arms and faces bandaged, or sat slumped astride a plodding
horse, a leg encased in rags, an empty sleeve flapping. Their uniforms were torn and dirty, caked with mud and dried blood. One
soldier rode along completely enveloped in a large cape, his whole
head and face covered by a single tied-on linen square, with only
a slit for his mouth; a young boy walked in front of him, holding the horse's reins, guiding the sightless rider along the road.
Charmiane found herself studying every soldier, dreading to see
one beloved face in that sorry procession.

She was taken aback to see the dark side of war firsthand.
Adam's letters—Noël's, that is—had touched her, but there was

still distance. Up till now—except for Noël's terrible wounds last summer and the occasional one-legged veteran on the streets of Paris—the war had been, for her, merely reports from Bazaine and the gossip of the locals around Bonneval.

All during February and the beginning of March, Napoleon had won victory after victory against a far larger enemy, leading his little band of soldiers in lightning strikes against the combined forces of Russia, Austria and Prussia. In five days alone he had won four victories: Champaubert, Montmirail, Château-Thierry, Vauchamps. He had sent back to Paris eight thousand prisoners to be paraded through the streets to the accompaniment of triumphal cannon shot from the Invalides. In a stirring public ceremony, the Empress Marie-Louise, now Regent in her husband's absence, had exhibited ten enemy flags taken at Montmirail and Vauchamps and had been showered with shouts of pride and an outpouring of loyal affection by the citizens of Paris.

That was glory. This dirty, bedraggled group of soldiers didn't seem to be a part of the same war. And now it was being said that despite the Emperor's stunning victories, the Coalition had hardened their terms for peace. France was now to return to the borders she had held in 1792, before the Revolution. When he heard that, Napoleon had roared like a trapped lion.

They were allowed at last to pass through the gate. Someone had scrawled on it *A Bas le Tyran!* and a grizzled workman was busy with mop and pail, scrubbing off the treasonous words. They made their way to the town house and clattered into the inner courtyard.

Madame Fleuve, the housekeeper, greeted Charmiane warmly. "Good day, *madame la comtesse*. We haven't seen you in many weeks. Do you have baggage? Shall I put your suite in order?"

"No. Not just yet. I don't know if I'm staying." She handed a maid her redingote and bonnet. Upon being informed that Adam was waiting to see her as soon as she came in, she tapped nervously on his library door and entered at his brusque command.

He sat at his desk, writing. The table before him was strewn with papers, and at his elbow were the remains of lunch, barely touched. The top of his uniform tunic was unbuttoned, and he needed a shave. He looked vulnerable, not frightening. He glanced up, smiled and rose from his desk, holding out his hand to lead her into the room. "Charmiane. Come and sit beside me." He guided her to a sofa and sat next to her. His hand was warm in hers, his eyes gentler than she'd ever remembered them. "I'm

sorry to bring you here, at a time like this. But I can't leave Paris.
And there are . . . difficulties between us that should be resolved.
Before it's too late."

She stirred uneasily. It was clear that he intended to be understanding of her betrayal. And that only made it worse. Whatever he had done to her, she had paid him back in kind. The
letters? She could almost forgive him now, as she'd forgiven Noël.
He'd wanted a wife and children amid the uncertainties of war.
He'd made that clear enough at the Tuileries. Who was to blame
if—in his desperation—he'd used Noël's letters to woo her? Who
was to blame if they'd misjudged each other? If they'd been ill-
matched from the first? It wasn't Adam's fault that she'd fallen
in love with his brother. "Too late?" she asked. "Are things as
hopeless as that?"

"We've been ordered by the Emperor to fortify the city. God
knows King Joseph will botch the job. There are no entrench-
ments, no barricades. And half the National Guard are only
armed with pikes." He looked at her and managed a bleak smile.
"That's not your concern. But yes, we could all be annihilated if
the enemy attacks. That's why I want to clear the air between us."

She stood up and moved restlessly around the room, twisting
her hands together. She didn't want this interview. She didn't
want to see the hurt in his eyes when she spoke of Noël. And
know that she was the cause of it. Oh God, he'd never wanted to
speak about Noël, about the baby's father, before. Why now?
"The air is cleared," she said with finality, praying to put a quick
end to this. "You've explained about Armand's death. I understand. I...I forgive it. You. As for that night...many a soul has
done worse under the influence of drink."

"That's not why I sent for you," he said gently. "Though I
thank you for your forgiveness."

"You didn't 'send' for me," she said, more sharply than she'd
intended. "You ordered me."

He frowned. "I didn't have time to write to you myself."

"A matter of such life-and-death concern and you didn't have
time?"

He was on his feet. "Damn it, Charmiane . . ."

"Excuse me, General Bouchard." Aulard stood at the door. He
bowed to Charmiane—*"Madame"* —then turned again to
Adam. "The courier is waiting, sir. If you don't sign those letters now, they won't get to Marshal Marmont tonight."

Adam sighed and turned to his desk. "Yes, of course."

"It would be very simple, sir, wouldn't it? If the Emperor accepted the peace terms, as you've all been urging him to do."

Adam laughed bitterly. "They're not peace terms anymore, Aulard. Now the allied forces will accept only unconditional surrender. But God knows even that would be welcome."

Aulard shook his head. "Marshal Marmont has been heard to whisper that the Emperor is incapable of envisaging defeat."

Adam sighed again. "I suppose that's true. And we shall all go down because of his folly." He handed Aulard the signed letters. "Is there anything more?"

"Only a question for *madame la comtesse*. The stable-boy wanted to know whether to unhitch your team, *madame*. Your little pageboy has been having difficulty conveying your wishes."

"No. I thought perhaps to do a bit of shopping this afternoon in the Palais Royal. A spring bonnet, perhaps."

Aulard bowed again and backed out of the room. "I'll tell the groom."

Adam raised a quizzical eyebrow. "Shopping?"

She blushed. It did seem frivolous of her, and perhaps insulting as well, since he'd sent for her on a matter of some importance to himself. "I'm sorry," she stammered. "I didn't think."

He shrugged. "No matter. I'm more concerned that Aulard spoke of Prosper and your team. Does that mean you took the cabriolet?"

"Why not? It's a lovely day."

"I specifically asked you to take the carriage," he said, his voice mildly reproving. "The roads are dangerous. War creates its own lawlessness."

He was right, of course. She'd been foolish. And deliberately rebellious. She could see that now. And his gentle tolerance only rankled her the more. "I'll do as I wish," she said sourly, "unless you choose to order me about again, General Bouchard."

He clenched his teeth and made a hissing sound. "Why do you *do* that? You throw out words like challenging gauntlets! Are we always to be adversaries? I don't think we've ever had a conversation as husband and wife where you haven't attacked me with harsh words. You said you forgive me for Armand. What good is your forgiveness if I can never expect a gentle word from you?"

Now she saw it in his eyes. The pain. It was so, what he said. She'd protected herself from him by attacking first, with cruel words. Until this minute, it hadn't occurred to her that he could be hurt as much by her words as by her unfaithfulness. It only added to her guilt. The sooner this interview was through, the happier she'd be.

"Why did you send for me?" she asked, her unease making her sound cold and impatient. "If you're so concerned with my safety, say what you must and quickly. So I can get back to Bonneval while it's still light."

He swore under his breath. "You're determined to make it impossible, aren't you."

He stared at her, his eyes burning like blue flame, then reached for her and pulled her savagely into his arms. His mouth ground down on hers with passionate intensity, demanding her surrender, draining her of all will. She could scarcely stand; only his arms, tight on her shoulders, kept her from collapsing in a quivering heap. He had kissed her like that in the Tuileries, and she'd forgotten until now. Forgotten that this man had the power to fill her with desire. To make her tremble with longing.

She broke from his embrace, her eyes filling with tears. "Adam . . ."

A discreet knock at the door. It was Aulard. "I'm sorry, General. The major is waiting for orders. In the drawing room."

Adam took a deep breath, squared his shoulders, buttoned his tunic. "Wait for me, *madame*," he said. "We'll settle this once and for all."

She was glad he was gone, if only for a few minutes. It would give her time to collect her chaotic thoughts. Calm her racing heart. Was it possible to love both brothers? Noël for his gentleness, Adam for his strength? But that was wicked! Maybe she didn't love Noël. Maybe she'd been drawn to him because she'd misunderstood Adam at first. Misjudged him. Treated him unkindly, then reaped what she'd sown. And Noël had come along—so different, so unfrightening. But of course she'd never deliberately tried to challenge Noël, to antagonize him. Which was more than could be said about her behavior toward his brother. She could see that now. "Oh, God," she whispered. "Which one do I love?"

She paced the small room, tormented by her thoughts. She pulled a book down from a shelf, riffled the pages, stared at them with sightless eyes. She picked up Adam's pen, scratched a few circles onto a blank paper, then put it down next to a disordered pile of letters. And stared, feeling the blood drain from her cheeks. One of the letters was signed, simply, "Noël." She lifted it, hands shaking. She didn't recognize the handwriting.

Dear Brother Adam,

I told you I should never have taken that promotion. It's sheer madness, leading those charges. How the devil did you manage to do it for all those years? My luck finally gave out, and I swear I have my silver epaulets to thank for it.

Paris must be a holiday for you, compared to what Champagne has been. The weather has been impossible, with more d---ed forced marches than I care to remember. Up until a week or so ago, the roads were covered with mud and slush, and we slept in the open beneath a freezing sky. A very inhospitable province this, in winter. A barren land, scoured by cold winds, without adequate shelter. And the foraging leaves something to be desired. I've decided I'm not as young as I was when we went to Moscow.

We were successful at the battle of Craonne on the ninth of March. The Emperor still knows how to maneuver. They gave me some sort of d---ed medal; I'd gladly trade it for a decent omelet right now. Laon, on the next day, wasn't as successful, for either France or myself. We were forty thousand against Blücher's hundred thousand. With Marshal Marmont in command. A good man, but he's not the Corsican, G-d knows. But, what the h---. We're f---ed anyway. I plan to sit out the rest of the war, such as may be left to fight, patching myself together in Brittany.

Laon is still held by the enemy. A skeleton force. Some of us managed to slip out after the battle, mangled bodies and all. No sense in spending time in a Prussian prison. Though the German women, I hear, are agreeable f---s. Didn't our Emperor brag as much after his wedding night?

I'm in the old church in Saint-Gobain, west of Laon, if you should want to get a letter to me. This letter is being written by a sweet, innocent young Sister who blushes every time I dictate an obscene word. And so I'm using as many as I can, d--- it, because she's so charming when she blushes. I'm not sure, however, that she's writing them down. You must let me know in your letter. Though Sister will have to read it for me, since I can't focus my eyes very well yet. And I'm not sure I can trust her, the little minx.

Now that I've coaxed another blush out of her—I want to add in all sincerity, Adam, that I pray this letter finds you safe and well. I thought of you on our birthday last month and wished we could celebrate together, as we did in the old

days. I would have written to you, but I was slaying drag-
ons, and Prussians, that day.

God keep you, brother.

Noël

Charmiane stood trembling, her hand to her mouth to stifle her
cry of dismay. Noël. Wounded. God knew how seriously. And
needing her. But Adam wanted her, too. And in his way, he
seemed to love her. What was she to do?

She took only a moment to decide. She pulled a sheet of paper toward her, dipped the quill and began to write.

Dear Adam,
Forgive me. I can't live with you as your wife until I know
my own heart. Let me go away. If I return, it will be because I've searched my soul and my conscience. Because I
want to be yours. Until then, take care of yourself.

Charmiane

Perhaps if she went to Noël and saw him again, she could resolve her doubts at last.

She rang for her redingote and bonnet and hurried out to the
courtyard. Prosper was already there, feeding apples to her pair
of grays. "Come, Prosper." His eyes were wide and questioning. She laughed softly, feeling an odd sense of release after all
her months of conflict and confusion. "Yes—" she laughed
again "—we're going shopping. For answers."

"Fifty centîmes for this bowl of soup?" Charmiane stirred the
thin broth and stared indignantly at the proprietor of the inn.

"Be lucky you have it, lady. You won't get soup like this in
Saint-Gobain. Not nowhere near as good. Not with everybody
hiding what they got, in case the Cossacks come through. My
sister butchered her cow last week and salted up the meat. Then
buried the barrels under her cellar. It's better than having some
damned German soldier help himself to the whole cow."

She looked in disgust at the bowl, then at Prosper, who
shrugged stoically. "I don't mind the thin soup if your meat is
hidden or stolen. I mind the fifty centîmes!"

"Take it or leave it, lady. This is wartime. I charge what the
market will bear."

She nodded in resignation and handed the man a sou for the
two bowls of soup. They had been on the road for three days now

and, God willing, would reach Saint-Gobain tomorrow morning. The journey had taken far longer than it should have. Her teeth rattled from the jounce of the cabriolet over pitted roads where—in the past two months—gun caissons and marching men and horses had churned the mud and snow into deep ruts that made traveling almost impossible. They had seen no soldiers about, but the occasional looted village they passed made it clear that foraging, marauding armies had come this way. Charmiane hoped it was only enemy troops who stole from the peasants, but she knew in her heart it wasn't so. Hadn't Noël told her, in one of his letters, that the Emperor expected his troops to live off the land? And devil take the unfortunates who lay in the path of those rapacious armies.

She was glad at least for the accident of her planned shopping trip in Paris. She seldom traveled with much money, but that day she'd had a great deal in her reticule. Ordinarily she and Prosper would not have been able to make this journey, even if they'd stayed in the worst flea-infested inns along the way. She wished she'd had the sense to take a change of linen from her rooms in the *hôtel* before dashing off on this mad trip, but it couldn't be helped. Perhaps in Saint-Gobain she'd locate a draper's shop.

It wasn't difficult to find the old church in Saint-Gobain. It dominated the little town, its ancient spires reaching to the heavens in silent homage. She was met at the door of the church by a solemn-faced nun in a wide starched headdress that bounced when she walked, in frivolous counterpoint to her serious demeanor. "I'm sorry, *madame*. If you've come to pray, you'll have to use the little chapel. We've turned the nave into a hospital."

Charmiane hesitated. "No," she said. "I've come to see...my husband's brother. We've learned he's here."

"And who might that be, *madame*?"

"*Brigadier*...No. He's a lieutenant now. Lieutenant Noël Bouchard." She felt as guilty as a child stealing tarts and wondered if it showed on her face.

The nun laughed softly. "That one. He's a devil, your brother-in-law. Always making Sister Agnes blush. And threatening to kiss Sister Claire when she goes to change his dressings."

She bit her lip in dismay. "Was he badly wounded?"

The nun smiled gently. "*Madame*, they all were. Or they would have gone back to Paris in the ambulances right after the battle. But your brother-in-law..." She said the word in an odd way, as though she suspected there was more to the relationship than that. Charmiane's face probably gave her away, as usual. "Your brother-in-law seems to be making a splendid recovery. The doctor thinks he'll recover his sight fully when the injury to his head heals. As for his leg . . .''

She felt the tears burn her eyes. "His leg, too?" she whispered.

"He was very fortunate that he was found in time. He might have bled to death. Saber cuts are quite destructive. Fortunately, none of the slashes damaged a vital sinew, and the surgeons decided to save the leg. He will limp, though. Permanently, if it's God's will. We can only hope, *madame*."

"Let me see him." She prayed she wouldn't weep in front of him. But she knew the sight of him would break her heart. And to limp forever? Never to dance the waltz with such gaiety, as he had in the Tuileries so long ago?

She followed where the Sister pointed, making her way through the rows of bodies stretched out on the stone of the church and cushioned only by mounds of straw. Hundreds of wounded men, it seemed. It was clear that the nuns had done all they could with what they had, but many of the bandages were no more than filthy tatters, and the smell of infection was strong in the air. She passed a young soldier writhing in pain, twisting and turning so the light sheet that had covered him slipped away and showed a soiled stump where one leg had been.

And then she was on her knees, staring down at Noël on his straw bed. He had one arm thrown across his eyes. His head was completely wrapped in a thick bandage, like a large turban; and, by the lumpy outline of the sheet, she could tell that his leg was similarly bound. He moaned and stirred, and his dear mouth twisted in pain. In spite of herself, she gasped to see him, her heart wrenching within her breast.

He lowered his arm, looked up at her and even managed a crooked grin. "What?" he said. "Shall I have a beautiful woman to cry over me?"

She stared in shock and disbelief. The eyes were the same. The nose, the mouth. The voice. And yet. And yet. She was looking at a stranger. "Dear God," she whispered. "But you're not Noël!"

Chapter Nineteen

He blinked and squinted at her. "Am I dreaming? Or are you truly the lovely creature who married Brother Adam?"

She couldn't stop shaking. "You're not Noël." Hadn't she loved Noël, laughed with him, carried his child? "You can't be Noël! Who are you?"

He laughed, then groaned and held his head. "The same man I was nine days ago, though a little the worse for wear. Thanks to a damned Prussian shell and a Russian saber. Such as I am, beautiful lady, I'm Noël Bouchard, and none other."

"But I nursed you after Lützen. You were . . . different. Have you changed so much? Is it my memory?"

"I wasn't wounded at Lützen. But Adam . . ." He chuckled softly. "*Mon Dieu.* Has Brother Adam revived our old game?"

Her head was spinning. "But in Paris . . . February . . ." she stammered.

"I left Paris at the end of January. I'm afraid, my dear Charmiane, that—though it pains me to say so—we've only met three times. My loss, I must confess, but there it is."

"Three times? That's . . . that's absurd!"

"First, at the ball, where you were the most beautiful creature around. Then those few days I spent at Bonneval before you married Adam. And you kissed me." He grinned. "A particularly pleasant memory. And now, here. Like a lovely angel of mercy come to rescue me. If you've had any other dealings with 'Noël,' I can only assume that Brother Adam has been playing games with you."

"What do you mean, games?"

"We did it all the time when we were children. To my benefit, more often than not. He was much better at his lessons than I. He took many an examination in my stead."

"I don't understand. Do you mean that Adam was...pretending to be you? Last summer after Lützen? No. No. It must have been you. The wounds...Your chest. Your arm."

"See for yourself," he said, tugging at the open neckline of his shirt. She stared in disbelief. The skin was smooth and unbroken. "I told you," he went on. "I didn't get so much as a scratch at Lützen. But Adam nearly died, Bazaine wrote me. Where did you nurse him?"

"Bonneval." She choked back her tears, feeling the sharp sting of Adam's betrayal. "He said that he was Noël."

"I wouldn't have thought my sober brother could be so playful. And with his own wife? I hope, for my reputation, 'Noël' didn't behave badly."

Had Adam been playing a game? "How could he have done it?"

"I told you. When we were boys together, we deliberately learned and used each other's mannerisms. It was great sport for both of us. I could frown and lose my temper when I wanted to." He laughed ruefully. "No one expected *Adam* to be jolly when he didn't want to be. And Adam always took on the burdens of the world. It was a relief for him, sometimes, not to have to be the responsible twin. Of course the game was only effective on someone who didn't know us well enough to see the differences. Don't you remember, at the ball, how easily you were confused?"

"But why should he play at being you?"

His eyes were warm with sympathy. "Perhaps he thought it was what you wanted. Only you can answer the why of it, beautiful lady."

It couldn't all have been Adam. It couldn't have! "But you wrote the letters, didn't you? From Russia."

He looked surprised. "Not a line. Why should I? Adam's quite capable of speaking for himself. I'm sorry," he added as she covered her face with her hand. "Has Adam behaved like a complete scoundrel?"

What could she tell him? In a moment's revelation she had lost two lovers: her dear Noël and an Adam she was just beginning to trust and respect. What was left except the memory of a man who had deceived her? Not once, but a multitude of times. "Why?" she cried aloud, lifting her tearstained face to Noël.

"Only you can answer that."

She couldn't think clearly now. Not while her heart was still so filled with pain. She looked down at Noël. For the first time she was aware of how haggard he looked, of the way his skin was stretched taut across sunken cheeks. She glanced around the church. The stone floor, even with a layer of straw, had to be a hard bed, and still damp and cold from winter. *"Ciel,"* she said, dabbing at her tears. "You can't stay here. Let me take you home."

"Alas. The good Sisters said I shouldn't travel while my head still hurts or I would have been out of here like a cannon shot as soon as Sister Claire's back was turned. If you truly want to be an angel of mercy, Charmiane, my sweet, you'll bring me something to eat. They seem to have depleted their stores of everything except turnips. And while the good Sisters may have God's ear, God clearly doesn't have a *chef de cuisine* to advise his flock!"

Charmiane smiled in spite of herself. It wasn't just the subtle differences in their looks. There was a reckless gaiety, a devil-may-care easiness about the real Noël that the sham Noël had lacked. No wonder she'd thought last summer that his flirtations seemed obvious and occasionally forced. Adam playing at Noël. She liked this Noël at once, grinning at her through his pain. She'd loved that "Noël," so gentle and vulnerable beneath the good humor. But of course he didn't exist. He was merely a creature of Adam's fashioning, created for...what? To seduce the wife who had denied him her bed? She sighed and turned her mind to the business at hand. "You can't travel. But can you be moved? Perhaps I can find a comfortable inn where you can rest and regain your strength."

"If you promise to feed me, beautiful lady, I'll follow you anywhere." He smiled, his eyes twinkling. "If you throw in a kiss for dessert, I'll be your slave for life."

In the end, the Sisters agreed that he could be moved on a stretcher laid across a wagon. At least for a short distance. They carried him out with care, his knapsack filled with his few belongings perched on his chest. He wasn't to sit up until his vision cleared and his head ceased its throbbing. The enemy shrapnel, though luckily failing to penetrate his skull, had produced a severe concussion.

Charmiane found a reasonably clean inn outside Saint-Gobain, on a country road that seemed to have been overlooked by the scavenging armies. The beds weren't too lumpy, and the food, while simple country fare, was plentiful and nourishing. Under Charmiane's care, Noël's strength grew every day. He flirted with her, charming her with his irreverent humor. Flat on his back, he managed to play card games with a Prosper who—after his initial shock—was delighted to find this Noël even more of a jolly companion than the other "Noël" had been.

After three or four days, his headaches stopped. Charmiane, coming into his room to change the dressings on his leg, found him sitting up in bed. "Fit as a fiddle," he crowed. "I'll be dancing in a week." And surely his recovery was nothing short of a blessing. Charmiane had already replaced the large enveloping bandage on his head with a wide band; now his hair fell carelessly over band and forehead, so he looked less like a wounded soldier than a mischievous little boy who'd taken a tumble.

She tucked in the edge of the bandage on his leg and patted his knee. "The swelling has almost gone away. I'll have to see if Prosper can find you a pair of crutches, now that you can be upright."

He studied her face. "You're a tender nurse. Does Adam know where you are?"

She looked away. "No."

"Write him a letter and tell him," he said gently.

"No."

"It hasn't been a good marriage, has it? Adam never wanted to talk about you the few times we met. And Bazaine wrote that there was some unfortunate business about your brother."

"Adam . . . killed him in a duel."

He whistled. "No wonder he wanted to be Noël for you, not Adam. Do you hate him so much?"

"No. I don't know." She wrung her hands.

He laughed softly. "Your face betrays you, beautiful lady. And the weeping I've heard from your room at night. I think you love him."

She felt choked by her anguish. "How can I love him? I don't even know who he is."

"Who he's always been. A good man. Not as winning as his brother, Lord knows, but—" he shrugged good-naturedly "—who is?"

"Tell me about him."

"Perhaps you know more about him than you realize. We're very different. You've learned that, I think. I always found it amusing that we should have chosen the branches of cavalry that most suited our natures. The Dragoons are heavy, serious. They lead the 'shock action,' as the Emperor always said. The first wave of charges. But I'm a Chasseur. Light cavalry, like the Lancers and Hussars. We're the gadflies **of** the army. Pursuing a retreating army, raiding. All lightning strikes."

She laughed, remembering the different troops she'd seen from time to time in Paris. "And all swagger and bravado."

He grinned. "Yes, I suppose so. It goes with the uniform."

"Are you jealous of each other, you and Adam?"

"In some ways, yes. We're so different. He's everything that I'm not. Including married, more's the pity. His gain. My loss." He put his hand over hers, a surprisingly friendly gesture, with no suggestion of anything more. "But I think there's more amity than hostility." He chuckled. "And I suppose, when it came to women, he was more jealous than I. Because of my exceeding charm."

Her mouth twitched in a smile. "Of course."

"I'm not jealous of his successful army career," he said more seriously, "but I am in awe. To be a soldier for so many years and with such distinction . . . it's not the life for me, the devil knows. I don't know how Adam's borne it all these years. I should have gone mad. For a while, though, I even began to wonder about him."

"What do you mean?"

"I never saw him like he was in the spring of 'twelve. He was always serious. But there'd been laughter in him before. But that year . . ." He shook his head. "Every time our paths crossed, all the way to Moscow and back, he seemed to be stretched to the breaking point. The worse conditions became, the angrier he got. Filled with black rages."

She stared, mouth agape, remembering Adam's return from Moscow. "Until I thought I'd married a madman," she whispered.

"Maybe you did. The madness of war can unbalance even the strongest soldier. But he seemed more like his old self when we met in Paris this January. Quiet, of course. It's his way. But solid, not restive. Whatever his demons were, he seemed to have quieted them."

"Mon Dieu." She was seeing a picture emerge: a very human man, with human weaknesses, who hid behind his letters, his brother's mask. And only then feeling free enough to reveal his heart and his fears. But a good man. A tender and caring man. Hadn't he proved it in the woodcutter's cottage, if she'd had the sense to realize it? All her certainties of a raving, ferocious

monster were melting away like winter snows. "How did he get so rich?"

He laughed. "Poor Adam. It always bothered him. It was when he was still a young soldier. Only nineteen, if I remember it right. It was the only time he ever disobeyed an order. Emigrés were still being detained and arrested at the borders in those days. But there was an old man, a *marquis*, I think. His name was on the list of the proscribed. Not only didn't Adam arrest him, but he left his post to see the man safely into Italy. The *marquis* was old and sick; he died on the trip, bestowing his carriage on Adam as his last wish."

She gasped. "The diamonds!"

"Yes. A fortune hidden under the seats. Adam didn't use it for years. He put advertisements in the papers, looking for the old man's relations. No one ever came forward. But dear Brother Adam, with his Catholic conscience, has always felt a certain amount of guilt for enjoying the old man's largesse."

"Conscience is a rigorous taskmaster." How often had she obeyed Sophie, Henri, even Adam, out of a sense of guilt?

He chuckled. "I wouldn't know. I try to avoid mine as much as I can."

"I'm surprised Adam never shared his wealth with you."

"Quite frankly, I didn't want it. All that burden and responsibility. I buy horses for him sometimes. My eye for horseflesh is better than his. And he pays me a commission. And perhaps someday if I decide to buy a horse farm or a fishing boat or—" he shrugged "—whatever catches my fancy, I'll come to him for a loan. I'm simply not as ambitious as he is."

Somehow she didn't quite believe that. He was proud, as proud as Adam in his way. Determined to earn what he had, to deserve it. The only difference was that he hid his pride behind laughter. Adam scowled and defied the world to find a chink in his armor. No wonder they could play at being each other: despite what Noël seemed to think, they were opposite sides of the same coin. She smiled tenderly. "I like you, Noël."

"But you don't love me. You love Adam."

She still felt such confusion. Adam's masquerade, for whatever reason, had been dishonest. And there had been so many opportunities for him to make it right, to explain everything. To ease the guilt he knew she felt over her "infidelity." She couldn't forgive him for his silence. Not yet. "I don't know if I love him," she said.

"At least write to him. Tell him that you're with me. That I love you madly, but I'm willing to give you up."

"Do you?" she asked, taken aback.

"I could have, you know. Once on a time. But though I might steal Adam's women, I wouldn't steal his wife. I'm not so wicked as that! There *is* someone, however. Lying in that church, with my head pounding like an enemy cannon, I kept thinking of her."

"The Alsatian girl? The one who cared for you when you had typhus?"

"The devil! Did Bazaine tell you all my secrets? She was very sweet and very helpful. And very silly. I think we both tired of each other at the same time. No. The woman I remember wanted to come all the way to Russia with me. And I wouldn't let her. It probably saved her life. But she wasn't in a forgiving mood when I came back."

"In Strasbourg, *n'est-ce pas?* I remember your speaking of it when you came to Bonneval last year."

"Yes. We spent the week quarreling violently. Among other things. And then she ran off with my friend Hautecoeur. A Hussar, and very dashing."

"Is she still with this Hautecoeur?"

"No. I heard he was killed at Leipzig. I wonder..." He stared up at the ceiling; his eyes were dreamy and faraway. "I wonder where Martine is. Maybe she went home in these difficult times. I think, when I can get around on crutches, I'll go and look for her."

"Do you love her?"

He seemed taken aback by the direct question. He frowned for a moment, then laughed. "More than I've ever loved any woman, I suppose. But I'm suddenly full of envy for Brother Adam's domesticity." He rubbed his chin in thought. "I might even marry the little vixen. I still have my last pay. Enough to buy a wedding dress. Yes. I'll go find her. Her village is near here. La Ferté-Milon. They might know something."

She clicked her tongue. "The very idea! You're scarcely fit to travel alone. We'll go in my cabriolet. But if your Martine isn't there..."

He held up a silencing hand. "Peace. I'll go back with you to Bonneval to recuperate. Will that make you happy?"

They set off for la Ferté-Milon the next day. Charmiane penned a simple note to Adam. Nothing could be resolved until they were face-to-face. She was visiting a friend in la Ferté-Milon; she promised she'd be in Paris before the first of April. She mentioned nothing of Noël, preferring to deal with Adam's masquerade in person. She still had lingering doubts about her feelings: she signed the letter merely "Yours," not "With love."

They reached Martine's little town as evening was falling and found rooms in a tiny inn. Noël, hobbling around after dinner on his new crutches, was impatient to wait for morning to search out his Martine. "Martine Rollin," he said to the innkeeper. "Do you know her? Her family?"

"Martine? Don't know a Martine. There's Rollins, though. Two sisters. They keep to theirselves. Weave baskets, down by the river." He slapped at Noël's dark green tunic and smiled broadly. "Chasseur, are you, young fellow? Had a cousin was. Died at Vitebsk. Jean Prunières. Heard of him?"

Noël shook his head impatiently. "No. Tell me about the sisters."

"Odd ones. Not friendly. Not so pretty, neither."

"No other Rollins?"

The innkeeper tapped his forehead with a grimy finger. "Daughter. Came home. Left again, with a man. Pretty enough to be a lift-skirts, but the man married her all the same. I wouldn't have."

Noël frowned. "What did she look like?"

The innkeeper winked and held up his hands as though he were clutching a woman's breasts. "Like that. Begging your pardon, *madame*." He shrugged at Charmiane. "Hair like gold, too."

Noël turned away, but not before Charmiane caught a flash of disappointment in his eyes. "Married, you say?" he asked.

"Married, bedded and gone."

"Noël." Charmiane put a sympathetic hand on his arm.

He maneuvered his crutches and himself to a bench near the fire. "Go to bed, beautiful lady. I'll sit up and have a pint or two." His mouth twisted in a wry smile that didn't quite hide the pain. "Don't look so sad. It wasn't meant to be." He jerked his chin in Prosper's direction. "Leave the imp with me for an hour or so. I'll teach him to cheat at cards, as the Emperor does."

"Good night then," she said. On an impulse, she darted forward and kissed him on the cheek.

"Don't do that again," he said softly, "or I might not let you sleep alone."

She was surprised, when she came down for breakfast in the morning, to find him already up and out in the courtyard of the inn. He was seated at a trestle table, gazing rapturously across at a lovely young woman with dark, luminous eyes. Nearby in the courtyard waited a sturdy carriage and team. The coachman nodded to the young woman. She stood up, smiled at Charmiane, still standing in the doorway, and bent and kissed Noël on both cheeks. His hand went around her neck, pulling her face down to his. He stared deeply into her eyes, then kissed her again, a solid kiss, firmly on the mouth. Her cheeks turned a bright pink and she hurried to her coach. In a moment, and with a great clatter of hooves, the carriage had departed through the courtyard gate.

Hands on hips, Charmiane accosted Noël. "*Who* was that?"

He grinned and scratched at his forehead beneath the strip of bandage. "A very...accommodating young widow. She came in last night after you'd gone to bed. On her way to Coutances. Charming Brittany accent. I haven't heard it for a long time. Certainly not expressing such tender sentiments."

She looked at his bandaged leg. "You didn't spend the night with her!" she chided. "Not in your condition."

He laughed. "I was wounded. But I'm not dead!"

Shaking her head at him, Charmiane sat and breakfasted, then went inside to settle their account with the innkeeper. Noël clumped in on his crutches to announce that Prosper and the cabriolet were waiting in the courtyard.

"Be you Bouchard?" Two women stood in the doorway of the inn, carrying a basket between them. They might have been young, they might have been old; it was difficult to tell. Their graying hair—dirty white threads scattered among faded yellow strands—was greasy and unkempt. Their bodies sagged, thin breasts hanging over aprons set high, in imitation of the current fashion. If they had ever been pretty, their looks had withered like the first bloom of youth. "Be you Bouchard?" The woman who had spoken smiled, a toothless grin.

Noël stared at them. "Who wants to know?"

The other woman pointed to the innkeeper. "Him said there was a blond Chasseur here. We thought it might be Bouchard, come looking for her. Martine. Talked about him often enough. The little *putain*." She shook her head. "Bad blood. Bad blood. She should have ended up like her old man, with her head in a basket." She turned about and spat on the floor.

Noël scowled. "You're her mother. Where's Martine?"

"Only decent thing the whore ever done. Marry that lowlife when he asked her." She held out the basket. "He didn't want this, though. Here. If you're Bouchard, it's yours."

Noël hobbled forward and looked into the basket. His face turned white. "Damn," he whispered.

The women put down the basket. "Be you Bouchard? Yea or nay?" At Noël's wordless grunt, the women smiled at each other, muttered "good riddance," turned about and left the inn.

"Noël, what is it?" Charmiane crossed the room and looked down into the basket. She gasped, her eyes widening in astonishment. Lying in the basket was a baby. Its eyes were a deep, intense blue and the sparse hair on its head a lovely golden color. A pretty child, despite its dirty clothes and a rash on its face from neglect. It appeared to be four or five months old, as near as Charmiane could tell. "I'm sure there's a mistake, Noël."

"No." He breathed a heavy sigh. "I've already been counting the months in my head. That week in Strasbourg. It fits. And Hautecoeur was as dark as a Gypsy."

She smiled, a tentative smile. "Well then, I suppose we'll have to take it with us. They didn't even say if it was a boy or a girl." She knelt and unwrapped the baby's diaper. She looked up at Noël, still teetering above the basket. "You have a son," she said softly.

"Oh, God," he muttered. "What the devil do I know about children?" He balanced on his good leg and reached down to touch the baby. His crutches slipped and he went crashing to the floor, landing heavily on his shoulder.

"Noël!" cried Charmiane, abandoning the baby to put her arms around his waist and help him right himself.

He let out a roar. "Leave me alone! I'm not a complete cripple!" While she watched, agonized, he painfully retrieved his fallen crutches and hauled himself to his feet. His brow was damp with perspiration from the effort, and his face showed the strain. "I'll see to the carriage," he growled, and limped to the door.

The child had begun to cry. Charmiane sent the innkeeper's maid to buy a nursing bottle if she could, a spare vest and a few diapers. It would have to do until they arrived at Bonneval. At last the baby was fed and changed. Charmiane carried the basket out to the courtyard.

Noël was on horseback. One of Charmiane's grays had been saddled and loaded with his knapsack and his crutches. Prosper, at Noël's direction, was rehitching the other horse to the cabriolet. *"Mon Dieu,"* cried Charmiane, "where are you going?"

He laughed in his old carefree way. "Off to catch up with my widow from Brittany. I could do worse than recuperate with the smell of the sea. I've paid the innkeeper for the saddle, so don't let him charge you."

"But what will you do?"

"Continue on my irresponsible way, Adam would say. The child is better off with you. If Adam wants to adopt him . . ."

"How will you live?"

"I have a little money in a bank in Brittany. I'll rejoin the army when my leg is better. If there's still a France to fight for. Or maybe I'll leave the country. I've already beaten the odds by staying alive this long through the madness."

"Noël, don't go." Her heart was breaking as she saw through his bravado to the wounded soul beneath.

"You'll be safe," he said. "God knows the war may be over by now. But if not, the Coalition will be moving on Paris. Find the road we were on yesterday, then go northwest from there and get to Bonneval as fast as you can. I think you'll avoid any fighting that may be going on around Paris."

"But Adam's in Paris."

"It doesn't matter," he said sharply. "Go to Bonneval and stay there until you're sure of what's happening. Do you understand?"

She began to weep. "Please don't leave, Noël. Don't leave your child."

He grinned and saluted her. "Tell Adam I owe him for this horse." He wheeled about and started out of the courtyard. At the gate he stopped and twisted back in his saddle. "Goodbye, beautiful lady," he said. His voice cracked. "Name my son Martin-Victor." Then he was gone.

Near tears, she settled into the cabriolet with Prosper, placing the basket with its precious contents at their feet. She felt lost. Lonely and alone. Not even Prosper, gazing at her with adoring eyes, could fill the empty part of her heart. Noël was gone. God only knew if they'd meet again. And Adam . . .

Adam. She stared at Prosper, astonished at the thought that had just struck her. "Adam wrote the letters," she said slowly. "*Adam.* Long before his masquerade. Those dear, heartbreaking letters." Prosper smiled, bemused. It didn't matter. She felt as though a great burden had been lifted from her. How blind of her not to have realized it until now! Those letters, filled with love and aching need, had come from Adam. The intimacy, the tenderness and vulnerability had been Adam. Not a frightening god but a man who looked to her to restore his spirit. It was the letters and the man who'd written them that she'd fallen in love with all that time ago. The real Adam. A little bit like the playful "Noël," filled with laughter, that he'd pretended to be; a little like the strong, commanding Adam who'd intimidated her because of her own youth, her miserable life with Henri. And all the times he'd made love to her: the hungry haste in the garden, the sweet exuberant couplings at Bonneval, their last desperate, needy encounter in Paris. It had all been Adam. She remembered what Noël had said. She *did* know Adam. She'd simply never put the pieces together until now.

She smiled at Prosper, her eyes shining with joyous tears. "I love him. Do you realize that, Prosper? I *love* him." Prosper still didn't seem to understand what she was talking about. But if his mistress was happy, so was he. He grinned and clicked to the horse, and they started on their way.

It was at a crossroads, less than half an hour later, that the idea occurred to her. She loved Adam, and Adam was in Paris. How foolish, then, to go to Bonneval when her love waited for her in Paris! The signpost at the crossroads said Meaux. She was unfamiliar with much of France, but she remembered that the public coach bringing her and Aunt Sophie from Switzerland in January of 1812 had passed through Meaux on its way to the capital. It meant going south and not northwest, as Noël had admonished her. But how far out of the way could it be? And if there was any sign of trouble at Meaux, she and Prosper could still turn toward Bonneval and avoid Paris. She pointed to the road. "That way, Prosper."

She began to regret her decision the farther south they went. The sight of burned and sacked towns became commonplace. From what she could learn, the armies had come through a month or so ago, yet she saw sad-faced peasants who still poked among the ruins, searching for what few possessions might have been overlooked.

Whole towns seemed abandoned. Failing to find an open tavern, they bought their dinner—bread and cheese, a pail of milk—from a farmer; nightfall found them near a dilapidated hut. Charmiane had no idea how close they might be to Meaux, and the cloudy sky promised to be dark and moonless. "We'll stay here for the night," she said. The hut was bare, but they managed to collect a pile of leaves and pine branches for beds before it became too dark to see. Huddled together under Charmiane's redingote, with the baby in its basket nearby, they fell asleep to the sound of cold rain on the roof.

The sun was shining in the morning. Charmiane felt heartened at the sight: she hadn't cared to think that she'd made an unwise decision. And they'd come too far to retrace their route, even if she could find the way again. There was no breakfast for her or Prosper, but she'd saved a bit of yesterday's milk for the baby. While she fed the child, she ordered a reluctant Prosper to go outside and hitch up the horse. She laughed at the boy's expression of longing. "As soon as we're home, Prosper, you can feed the baby and hold him and play with him to your heart's content. I promise." She watched him go, his eyes shining in expectation.

After a moment, a strange sound came to her through the open door of the hut. A raspy, coughing sound such as a man might make in his throat before spitting. She put down the baby and ran outside. She saw a huge monster of a man, bearded and in an unfamiliar uniform. His long coat was wrapped by a wide sash with two pistols protruding from it. He had his hand on the bridle of the horse. Prosper had leaped onto the man's back, his child's arms around the massive neck, his pretty little face screwed up in a scowl. Guttural sounds, provoked by his outrage, issued from his throat.

"Take your hands off my horse!" cried Charmiane, rushing forward to pound at the man's arms.

"Nyet!" the soldier said, and swore at her in a strange language. He brushed at her impatiently, as though she were a gnat buzzing around him. Grunting in anger, he reached behind him, caught hold of Prosper and scraped him off his back. With one bearlike paw, he held the boy aloft for a minute; then he dashed the little body against a tree. There was a sickening crack.

"Bastard! Villain!" Charmiane leaped for the soldier again. He turned, raised his arm and gave her a swipe to the side of her head that sent her sprawling to the ground.

He laughed, a sneering, ugly laugh, then leaped to the horse's bare back, kicked it savagely with his spurs and raced off down the road.

Still dazed from his blow, Charmiane crawled to Prosper. He lay twisted on the ground, his head bent at a grotesque angle. He seemed calm and at peace, but the light had already gone from his eyes. As gently as she could, she gathered him into her embrace, smoothing back the soft straw of his hair. His mouth moved, lips twisting and pressing together. With a burst of strength, he forced out a single word—a halting, whispering, wheezing sound, but recognizable as a word. *"M-ma-man,"* he breathed. A smile as sweet as an angel's spread across his face, then he closed his eyes.

He died in her arms, his head resting on her lap. She sat for a long time, still stroking his forehead while her hot tears dampened his bright pageboy's livery. She remembered the joy he'd taken in it, his happiness at serving her. He'd served her too well, at the end. What did a horse matter against his life? Prosper, she'd named him. So he might grow and thrive. *"Ah, Dieu,"* she sobbed.

The crying of Martin-Victor roused her at last. There was nothing she could do for Prosper. Martin-Victor was the future. And Adam. And the child she was now almost sure she carried. Conceived during that desperate night of love in the little tavern of Montmartre. She must think of them now.

With a broken tree branch, she scraped out a shallow grave in the soft, rain-dampened earth, then lined it with pine boughs. She tore the silk lining from her redingote and wrapped Prosper's frail body in it, placing him gently in his last bed. She covered it with dirt, knelt and said a prayer for his young soul. Then she put on her coat and bonnet and picked up the basket. The sight of the cabriolet, which she'd have to abandon, reminded her of the dangers that might lie ahead. If a Russian deserter was scavenging this far into France, what else could she encounter? She opened up her reticule and removed the large number of coins within. Wrapping them in a handkerchief, she tucked them into the baby's diaper. A less than dainty hiding place but probably the safest, under the circumstances.

She decided to continue in the direction of Meaux. Surely there she could hire a carriage to take her to Paris. March was nearly over. The roads would be dry and thawed after the winter but not yet impassable from spring rains. Besides, if she came to a main thoroughfare, it would be metaled with broken stones and cinders, and the carriage could fly all the faster.

In only a day or two, she reckoned, she'd be in Paris. And Adam's arms.

Chapter Twenty

It was more than a week before she saw Paris again. And by then she had learned so much of war firsthand that she wondered how Adam could have endured for all those years. She had come across whole villages of starving people: what the French troops hadn't requisitioned, the advancing enemy hordes had demanded as reparations. She had passed abandoned and broken wagons and cannon, all the brave accoutrements of war—now useless. She'd seen women, still dazed weeks later from the horror of repeated rapes. And corpses left rotting in the spring sun while the living foraged for food to keep themselves alive.

She was grateful she had her money in gold. Though it cost her a great deal, she could almost always find a shopkeeper or a tavern owner who had a little food hidden away and was willing to part with it for gold. There had been no carriages obtainable at Meaux, but a helpful cobbler had suggested she go down to the Marne River on the chance that there might be a boat. The Marne, she knew, ran into the Seine, and thence to Paris. She had hoped at Meaux to write letters to Adam and Bazaine, asking for rescue. But the war had put an end to mail delivery; without information, no one wanted to venture into a region that might be overrun with troops.

She found a boat on the Marne, a leaky little barge with a canvas lean-to at one end. The boatman was an evil-looking man with rotted teeth, and when he grinned at her it made her flesh crawl. But he was going downriver and would take her—for an exorbitant fee. "Consider yourself lucky," he said. "Not every man wants to go all the way to Paris in times like these."

She sat well away from him in the boat, guarding herself and the baby, not sure from his leer whether it was her person or her money that interested him. She found out soon enough. After a few hours they reached the juncture of the Marne and a smaller river. The baby had begun to cry; lifting him in her arms, Charmiane went ashore to find food. By the time she returned, the boat was gone from the shore, carrying with it her redingote and bonnet and the baby's basket. She could see it in the distance, on the little tributary, moving rapidly away from the direction of Paris. He'd never intended to convey her to the city—only to take her money.

She walked then, following the path of the Marne. She found a linen shop and bought several cheap fringed scarves—the traditional costume of the French working woman—to use as diapers for the baby and to cover her head and shoulders. She felt safer, anonymous, in such garb. She ate what she could buy or find, slept under hedges and in ditches or curled up in ruined and abandoned gun caissons for a night's protection. The rains drenched her and the baby; the early spring winds chilled her. Her traveling shoes wore thin, her feet ached. Once or twice she was able to find another boat—merchants moving their goods out of the reach of marauding hordes or toward a ruined town to take advantage of needy customers with inflated prices. She was cold, hungry, uncomfortable, her energy sapped. It didn't matter. Each ride, each league she walked, brought her closer to Paris. And Adam.

She arrived at last at Nogent-sur-Marne. A helpful goodwife allowed her to wash and dry the baby's diapers and spend the night on the floor of her barn. In the morning, Charmiane asked about boats to Paris.

"You don't want a boat, lady. The river curves away from Paris from here on. It will take you out of your way." The woman pointed down the road. "If you walk, you'll reach the Bois de Vincennes. If you walk apace, you can reach Paris before noon."

She was already exhausted and footsore from her journey, from the weight of the baby in her arms. So it was well into the afternoon before she limped up to the Vincennes gate.

Two things at the gate caught her eye at once: a cart loaded with amputated limbs being trundled out of the city for disposal in some distant field. And a handful of enemy soldiers guarding the gate. Her heart sank. Only as she neared them did she feel a measure of relief. They spoke German. It was a small thing, but after the horror of the Russian soldier and Prosper's death, she was grateful at least to be able to communicate with these soldiers, enemy or no.

She shifted the weight of the baby to her other hip and approached one of the soldiers, a young man with a kind face. "Is the war over?" she asked in German.

He looked at her torn and filthy gown, her tattered shoes, her unkempt hair straggling out from beneath her kerchief, and nodded in sympathy. "Your Emperor abdicated yesterday. It's over."

She gulped. "And who rules France now?"

He slapped at his chest. "We do. Until the generals can decide what to do."

She sighed and rubbed a tired hand across her face. The days had faded into a blur for her, a time of weariness and pain and concentrating on survival. "What day is it today?" she asked.

"Thursday. The seventh of April." He frowned. "Sunday is Easter, and I won't be home in Berlin to celebrate."

"I'm sorry," she said. "Was there much fighting in Paris?"

"Only in Montmartre. Your Marshal Moncey and his troops defended for a day and then surrendered. A bloody fight."

"Moncey?" she whispered, feeling her blood run to ice. Adam was under Moncey's command. For the first time the possibility struck her. He might be *dead*. All this time, through the exhaustion and pain of the past week and a half, she had kept the vision of Adam before her. The thought of him had sustained her. Now she remembered that Noël hadn't wanted her to go to Paris. She'd thought it was only because of the fighting. Now she realized that he'd wanted to spare her this: the horror of wondering if Adam lived.

She reached for the papers that she'd kept tucked in her bosom. "My *hôtel* is in Paris," she said. "Grande rue de Verte. Am I permitted to enter the city?"

He looked at her papers, nodded and passed her along. She made her way slowly through the eastern part of the city toward the rue Saint-Honoré. The tricolor flag of France no longer floated above the public buildings; now, everywhere she looked, she saw the white flag of the Bourbons. In anticipation of the King's return? she wondered. But what did it matter who ruled France, if Adam was dead?

Except for an occasional building that seemed to have been damaged during the final bombardment, the city went on as though it were a normal spring day. Citizens strolled about, sat at café terraces ordering lemonade or ice cream, tipped their hats to the foreign soldiers who congregated at every corner and ogled the women. It wasn't difficult to see who the Royalists were—

those malcontents from the Faubourg Saint-Germain who had waited more than twenty years for this day. They sported flamboyant white cockades on their hats, trailed white scarves from the lanterns of their coaches, fluttered white banners from the balconies of their *hôtels*.

Paris was occupied by Austrians and Prussians, Russians and Bashkirs, and the Tuileries Palace was guarded by troops from the farthest corners of Europe and Asia. Charmiane passed the sentry boxes on the Place de la Concorde, manned now by Cossacks and Russians, and skirted the Champs-Elysées. The vast field was filled with enemy troops in a bewildering array of uniforms. They had set up their tents and straw huts among the trees and now sat and slept and laughed in little groups. Several German musicians were playing, watched by a group of laughing French citizens. A Russian Cossack, stripped to the waist, was trimming his red beard in front of a broken mirror. The smell of cooking meat came from dozens of camp fires, while dogs raced through the park, barking and begging scraps. It was a chilling sight to see the glorious city occupied. Degraded by the presence of the enemy in its midst. Even the staunchest Royalist must feel a pang of dismay at France's humbling.

Charmiane turned north at the Grande rue de Verte. Despite the baby's weight, she found herself running as she neared Adam's *hôtel*. She tugged furiously at the bell and waited, peering through the iron gate, her heart in her mouth. At last Madame Fleuve, the housekeeper, emerged and crossed the cobbled courtyard to the front gate.

The older woman gasped. "Madame de Moncalvo! Thank God you're safe and well! We . . ."

She waved an impatient hand at the woman. "Does my husband live?" she demanded.

"Of course, *madame*."

Charmiane sobbed and sank to her knees, clutching Noël's child to her breast. "He lives," she whispered. "Adam."

Madame Fleuve put a comforting hand on her shoulder. "*Madame*, where have you been?" she said gently. "Whose infant is that?"

Charmiane lifted the child to the housekeeper. "Take him and see that he's bathed and fed. He's Monsieur Noël's child."

"Of course. *Monsieur*'s brother. He spent many a visit here. He's well?" Madame Fleuve cradled the child in arms that seemed comfortable with an infant.

"Yes, he's well." Charmiane nodded and pulled herself slowly to her feet, wiping at her tears. "Is *monsieur le comte* here now?"

"No, *madame*. He's at a meeting. With that...German." She sneered the word, then shrugged apologetically. "They've quartered a Prussian officer with us. *Monsieur* says I should treat him with honor, but . . ." She shivered. "In a French household. The very idea! We expect General Bouchard in several hours. He'll be quite pleased to see you, *madame*. He's been frantic with worry."

"But he knew I was safe. Didn't he get my letter about la Ferté-Milon?"

"*Madame*, we've been at war. The only letter *monsieur* received, as far as I know, was the note you left him the day you went away. Three weeks ago. I don't know what it said, but he was beside himself. He stared into a mirror for a very long time, as though he weren't even seeing his own reflection. And then...oh, *madame*, it was terrible! He smashed the mirror with his fist."

She began to weep again. "Oh, Adam." Had he tired of being his own rival?

"*Madame*, you look exhausted. Come inside where we can tend you properly." She bustled Charmiane inside. In a moment they were surrounded by a host of servants, maids and footmen, all overjoyed to see the mistress and eager to be of service. Madame Fleuve directed them all like an army officer. A maid was dispatched to Mademoiselle Minette, linen draper, on the rue de Miromesnil, to bring back infants' diapers and vests, nightgowns and nightcaps. And someone was to find a healthy wet nurse. Nothing was too good for Monsieur Noël's child.

Charmiane was hurried to her suite and deposited in a hot tub. She was bathed and fed at the same time; all the while Madame Fleuve told her what had been happening in Paris.

The enemy had attacked the city on the thirtieth of March. The Emperor, far to the south, had not arrived in time to direct the action. Marshal Moncey and his forces had defended the capital in a fierce battle at the Clichy gate. But after a full day of bloody fighting, and seeing the cause lost, Marshal Marmont, at King Joseph's direction, had capitulated. Napoleon, hearing the news as he neared the city, had turned about and led his men to Fontainebleau. Marmont and Moncey, allowed to leave the city after the battle, had marched the remnants of the gallant defenders of Paris to join the Emperor.

On the following day, Tsar Alexander of Russia and the King of Prussia had led their victorious armies down the Champs-

Elysées. For the first time in hundreds of years, Paris had seen an occupying army. Madame Fleuve sniffed. "At least the Emperor of Austria had the decency to stay away, having driven his own daughter from the throne of France! God knows where the Empress is today. And Bonaparte's son, the little King of Rome."

"But what's to become of France now?"

"Hmph! The Senate lost no time in declaring the Emperor deposed and rallying to the enemy. A bunch of secret Royalists, only interested in keeping their powers. I always thought so. Only yesterday they invited Louis to return from England to take the throne. In the meantime, Monsieur de Talleyrand, who certainly knows which side of the fence to jump to, has been appointed the head of the provisional government. It's all a lot of nonsense, and I haven't been able to buy a decent cut of mutton for weeks now!"

"Did Adam stay at Fontainebleau for a while, then?"

"Oh, no. I think the Emperor wanted the army to keep on fighting. But the Marshals stormed into his private chambers at Fontainebleau, they say, and announced that they refused to fight another battle. What could the Emperor do but agree to abdicate? The officers—and General Bouchard, of course—came back to Paris after that. We've been very fortunate. The Tsar has personally pledged to guard the city against pillage."

Charmiane gulped, remembering Prosper. "It was a pity the Tsar didn't have the same concern *before* he reached Paris."

"*Madame*, you look very tired. Why don't you go to bed?"

"No. I want to be dressed and waiting when my husband returns." She dabbed at her tears, her heart filled with love and longing. "I want to be very beautiful for him, I think."

In the end, despite Madame Fleuve's protests, she was dressed in a deep gold gown, her hair curled and perfumed, her nails buffed. She agreed to sleep in a chair until Adam returned, cautioning Madame Fleuve to wake her the moment he came in.

It was dark when the housekeeper came to her, carrying a candelabra. She tapped her on the shoulder. "Madame Bouchard, the General came in an hour ago with several officers and senators. They've been in conference in the library."

She sat up and rubbed her eyes. "*Fi donc!* Why didn't you wake me?"

"*Madame*, it was impossible to inform *monsieur* of your arrival. Not with the gentlemen around. But now they've begun to call for their hats, and *monsieur* will soon be alone in his library." She smiled and patted Charmiane's hand. "I thought you might like to announce your presence to *monsieur* yourself."

"Yes." She hurried down the stairs to Adam's library and softly opened the door. He stood at the window, his hands behind his back, and stared out at the night. Charmiane's heart caught. This was Adam, who loved her. Who had always loved her. From the discouraged set of his shoulders, she could imagine the bleak look on his face. If he'd never received her letter from Saint-Gobain, he must be sick with worry.

Suddenly he stiffened and his chin shot up as though he were sniffing the air. He was roaring before he even turned around. "The deuce! Who dares to wear my wife's perfume?"

She stared, seeing on his face, in his eyes, the fear that drove his anger. Could he have been afraid all those times he'd raged? Afraid and—as Noël seemed to think—a little bit mad? "It's my perfume," she said gently. "Why shouldn't I wear it?"

His face had gone white. He closed his eyes for a moment, then he clenched his fists to still the trembling that had begun in his hands. "Well, *madame*," he growled, "have you decided to come home at last?"

Her whole being brimmed with happiness and love. He loved her and he needed her. And the dear man couldn't unbend even for a minute. Somehow it made him all the dearer to her, his fragile heart. She smiled indulgently. "You look tired. And thin. Have you been eating enough?" She couldn't stop smiling, drinking in the sight of him. Her dear love.

He muttered under his breath. "This interview amuses you? Your aunt has been prostrate with cóncern. There hasn't been a day when she hasn't plagued me with inquiries. With tearful messages. And you dare to stand there grinning?" His voice rose in outrage. "Where the deuce did you go without telling me?"

"You needn't roar like a lion," she said complacently. "I did write to you. It's not my fault if the postal service was less than competent in these trying times."

"You think it's a joke? You had no right to leave in the first place! Your duty was at your husband's side!"

"*Mon Dieu.* How fiercely you frown and shout at me. Noël smiles so much more often."

That slowed him down for a moment. "Will you mock me?" he sputtered. "Will you throw my brother in my teeth?"

"I can't help it if I like Noël more than I like you."

He appeared stunned. And speechless at last.

"I love Noël," she whispered.

He turned away, head bowed, and covered his eyes with his hand.

She put her hand on his arm. "Be Noël for me."

"What?" He turned. His blue eyes were guarded and bright with a sudden, terrible fear.

"You're the Noël I love. Be Noël for me."

"Damn it, what are you talking about?" he muttered.

She tried to put her arms around him. "Oh, you dear, foolish man."

His chin was set in a stubborn line. "I'm Adam. I've always been Adam."

"Are you so determined to resist me? If I must, I'll tear open your shirt to find Noël's scars."

He wavered, then groaned in resignation. "When did you know?"

"I left your brother in la Ferté-Milon a week and a half ago. I saw his letter on your desk, that day you sent for me. I went to find my heart in Saint-Gobain and found a stranger instead. And then I knew."

His eyes were filled with pain and anguish. "Oh God, how you must hate me."

"That's why you did it, isn't it? Because I hated you for Armand."

"And for that shameful night. I kept seeing the look of horror on your face. The terror. But my madness and despair had driven me on. And every time I saw you cringe in my presence it made me all the angrier, until I became the reflection of myself in your eyes. When I came home from Lützen, I thought I was going to die. All I wanted was your forgiveness."

"Oh, Adam."

"It wasn't deliberate at first, my deception. I swear that to you. The error was yours. You saw the tunic I'd borrowed and thought I was Noël. And I saw eyes that filled with warmth—and trust. Eyes that didn't burn with hatred for a monster. An assassin. It was all too easy for me, at first. I was tired of being hated and feared. My body was in pain. My soul couldn't endure more. And then, later . . . I suppose it was the coward's way, to let you go on thinking I was Noël."

Her cheeks were wet with grateful tears. "Oh, my dearest Adam. I love you. I must have been blind not to know, not to understand. The man in the Tuileries. The letters. The Adam who held my hand while I labored, and comforted me. Always you. Always my love."

His eyes held the shadow of hope. "Can you love me? Can you forgive me?" At her eager smile, he crushed her in his arms, taking her pliant mouth in a burning kiss. She clung to him, feeling welcomed, adored. Home at last. He lifted his head and looked at her, his eyes troubled and filled with regret. "I can't be Noël for you. The easy, free-spirited Noël you loved last summer. I'm sorry."

"Oh, my dearest. You're not Noël, true enough. But you never were. You forget I've been with Noël. And for all his laughter and all his bonhomie, he guards his heart as charily as you do yours."

"But . . ."

"Don't you understand? You were Adam, not Noël, last summer. Adam, with all his constraints put aside. Thinking you played Noël's part you could be yourself. The dear man I love, who hides so often behind the soldier's mask."

He cleared his throat, a habit she'd come to realize he used to cover his deepest emotions. "How is my brother Noël?"

"He's very like you in some ways. He's fine. He was wounded at Laon. You remember he told it in his letter. But he's whole and should be well soon enough." The thought of Noël reminded her of something she had to deal with. Something that tore at her conscience. "Adam, forgive me."

"Forgive *you*? For what?"

"I was an unfaithful wife. Or thought I was."

He shook his head. "No. That was unfair of me, Charmiane. I was doing everything in my power to seduce you. I needed you so much."

"If it will make you feel better, my conscience gnawed at me all the time."

"Yours was no sharper than mine, knowing I'd deceived you."

"Tell me about Paterne," she said, filled with a sudden remembrance.

He frowned. "Paterne?"

"The groom at Bonneval. The one you . . . beat so savagely."

He ran his hands through his hair. "I was drunk, to begin with."

"The nightmares? The ones that 'Noël' spoke of? They made you drink?"

"Yes. I think I was as close to madness as I ever came, in those months. I recognized Paterne. He was a runaway from service. I saw him on the Russian campaign, before we'd even reached Vilna. The men were dying of thirst and dysentery and fever. Paterne, like thousands of others, only waited for his compan-

ions to die before stripping them of their uniforms and equipment. I saw him on the march, tearing a ring from an officer's
hand. But the officer wasn't quite dead yet. And when Paterne
couldn't get the ring off, he pulled out a knife and lopped off the
finger, as well. I remember how the officer screamed with his
dying breath. When we made camp, I sent for Paterne, meaning
to put him under arrest. But I learned that he'd deserted that day.
I guess, when I saw him at Bonneval, it was the final horror that
sent me over the edge."

"Oh, Adam. If you'd only told me what was in your heart
from the beginning. Only your letters..."

He laughed, a sharp, bleak sound. "When I met you at the
ball, I was sick of life. Almost praying that the next campaign,
the next battle, would end it for me. You were warmth. You were
love. You brought me back from the abyss for a little while. When
I killed Armand, I knew from the look on your face that I'd killed
myself, as well. Then you thought I was Noël. To tell you otherwise would have been to give up my life once more. I wasn't brave
enough for that."

She knew instinctively that this was a confession, an open-
ness, that he'd never allowed himself before. She put her arms
about his neck and smiled tenderly. "What does bravery have to
do with it? You were human, clinging to life and love. Can I reproach you for that? Should you reproach yourself?"

His arms tightened around her, warm and comforting. "I
wanted to tell you so often. I planned to tell you, at last, the day
you left." His voice cracked with emotion. "But you made it very
difficult for me."

She burned with remorse. "I was blind. It's strange. I forgave
'Noël' everything. But...Adam? Maybe it was because of Henri.
I suppose I was afraid of another marriage like that. I fought you
at every turn, even when it wasn't necessary. And then, after Armand, after that night...*Dieu*. I was so self-righteous and un-
forgiving, so quick to judgment. So..."

He kissed her softly on the lips. "So young, so innocent and
trusting." He looked deeply into her eyes and sighed. "And now,
no more, I think."

"Oh, Adam, it's not simple, is it. Life. How could I ever have
thought it so? The questions, the answers. So simple." She
sobbed and clung to him. "Adam, the horrors I've seen! And
little Prosper... He's dead."

"Oh, God. I'm sorry for Prosper. For your suffering. Sorry I
deceived you. Sorry you had to grow up this way."

"What will happen now?"

"To France? I don't know. Years ago, when I was young and filled with hope and enthusiasm, I saw nothing but a glorious future. Liberty, equality, fraternity. It sounded so wonderful. It began so bravely. And now, what's left? Petty hagglers and opportunists. The losers look to see if they can save what they have, and who needs to be flattered and cajoled. The winners squabble over the spoils and connive for positions in the new government. The Royalist sympathizers have been agitating in the newspapers for the restoration of the Bourbons. That black hypocrite Domfort has distributed a new issue of *La Voix* every day this week. If the King comes back to power, he intends to be remembered as a loyal supporter."

"And if the King does return?"

"We can only hope he'll preserve some of the democratic changes that came with the Revolution. And if not..." He shrugged.

"We make compromises with life, don't we?" She felt very old and very wise. Armand hadn't been able to compromise; he'd been consumed with bitterness long before the poison of mercury had destroyed his body and his mind. And Henri, lost and useless without his title and his money, had found solace in tormenting her.

"Nothing's inevitable but change," he said.

"And us. What will happen to us?"

"There's talk that the Emperor's officers will be discharged at half pay, which might create hardships for some. Though I've been kept on for the time being. To effect an orderly transition from the occupying troops to the National Guard, once the King returns to power. I don't know if I'll be allowed to keep my title. But we'll not want for money. I had Bazaine bury my diamonds weeks ago. I own the *hôtel* and the château outright, and Bazaine has invested well for me through the years."

She began to laugh. "And of course you're in a very fortunate position, having had the foresight to marry a *true* aristocrat."

He smiled broadly, then hugged her tight. "Oh God, how I need your youth and optimism." His voice shook with emotion.

"Adam." She stared at him in wonder. Each minute was a revelation. "You're afraid sometimes," she said.

"Does that surprise you?"

"It would have, a year ago."

"Dear Lord, but I love you," he murmured. His eyes were filled with warmth and gratitude, like a man who's come upon a wondrous treasure. "I don't know what will happen in France. I can only pray for an end to wars and Terrors and tyrants. But I know I can't face the future without you."

"The past is gone," she said. "As you tried to tell me so often. We can never return to Sophie's world. It's too late. I can see that now. And all we have is each other. Our faith in a better future for France."

He laughed. He sounded almost young. Carefree. Her "Noël." "I feel as though I've been given a reprieve on life. I want to fill our house with children."

She giggled and danced away from him. "You may regret your wish."

"How so?"

"Noël has a baby boy. There was a girl, a Martine Rollin."

"I remember her. He spoke of her before the Russian campaign."

"We seem to have...acquired the child. Noël wants us to adopt him. And then...it may be too early to tell, but I think I'm pregnant again."

"Charmiane!" His eyes sparkled with joyous tears. "Oh, my beloved." He lifted her in his strong arms and swung her around the room.

"Excuse me, sir. General." Lieutenant Aulard stood at the door. "General von Carlstadt wishes to discuss the details of tomorrow's meeting with Talleyrand before dinner tonight." He smiled, seeming aware for the first time that his commanding officer stood—quite unmilitarily—with a woman in his arms. Aulard bowed and clicked his heels together. "Good evening, Madame Bouchard. Welcome home." He raised a questioning eyebrow to Adam. "General, what shall I tell von Carlstadt?"

Adam cleared his throat. "Aulard, have you ever been in love?"

A self-satisfied grin. "Many times, sir!"

"Good. Then you appreciate the value of delaying tactics. A little diversionary maneuver on your part, for an hour or two, would be most helpful."

"But, sir..."

Still holding Charmiane, Adam strode to the open door. "General Bouchard has a more pressing engagement. Do I make myself clear?"

Aulard smiled uneasily at the sudden sharpness in his commander's voice. "Of course, sir."

"Good." Adam swept up the stairs with Charmiane in his arms, marched purposefully to her suite and tossed her onto her bed. He laughed—carefree and joyous—and threw himself down beside her. He kissed her resoundingly on the mouth, then kissed her again, his lips covering every inch of her face. "I think," he murmured, seeing her tremble with longing, "Aulard will have to delay through dinner, as well. I don't intend to be disturbed by anyone or anything."

She wriggled happily beneath his caressing hand. "Not even if there's rioting in the streets, General?"

"France will have to survive without me—without us—for a few hours."

"Dear, dear Adam," she whispered as he rolled over and imprisoned her body with his. He was warm. He was comforting, his lips on hers. His breast and hips. His . . . She grunted and pulled her mouth away. "Your buttons hurt, General Bouchard," she said with a gentle laugh.

"Forgive me. An unnecessary intrusion." He stood up and pulled her to her feet. He tried not to smile. "But then your gown, too, is an intrusion—for what I have in mind." He paused, his hands on the buttons of his tunic, until Charmiane had removed her spencer jacket, her necklace and earrings. Only then did he take off his tunic and set to work on his waistcoat and cravat.

Charmiane had undressed to the last two items of clothing—her petticoat and chemise—when she realized that he had become quite still. She glanced over her shoulder in his direction. He was seated on a carved armless chair, clad only in his flowing white shirt, the rest of his clothing in a discarded heap at his feet. His hair shone like spun gold in the light of the candles, and a gentle smile played on his lips. But it was his odd stillness that tantalized her. "What is it, Adam?"

His eyes were half-closed and heavy with passion. His sensuous lips parted slightly; she heard the soft whistle of his breath. "You're so beautiful," he said, "I just wanted to watch you."

She blushed and smiled, a little shy, a little proud of her lover's admiration. Self-consciously, yet glorying in the willing body she offered him, she finished undressing. His warm glance was as thrilling as his caresses.

"Come here," he growled. Then, as though he'd realized it was too much like a command, he held out a supplicating hand. "Please."

She moved across the room to stand before him. Still seated, he reached up, pulled the combs from her hair and spread the fragrant tresses. She bent to kiss him, covering them both in a curtain of dark curls. His arms encircled her, strong hands playing up and down her back so she shivered in delight and anticipation. Hungry for him, for the feel of his naked flesh against hers, she tugged at his shirt, and together they pulled it over his head.

She looked down at his potent body. He was poised and hard and waiting for her; she hesitated for a moment, then straddled the chair and lowered herself onto him. He gasped in pleased surprise, leaned back and closed his eyes. His hands tightened about her waist, moving her body up and down on his; a gentle rhythm that thrilled and excited her.

It was fitting, she thought suddenly, that they should be making love in just this way. In all the times that they'd made love— even when he was pretending to be Noël—he had always been above her. Dominating. Conquering. Now, for the first time, they were equal. Face-to-face, arms around each other, giving and receiving love in equal measure.

She rode him with a passionate need. His hips rose to meet hers in an ever-increasing frenzy until they climaxed in a sweet chaos of burning kisses and moans and tumbled curls.

She sighed in contentment and nestled her head in the curve of his neck. He was still within her, and she never wanted to be parted from him. He seemed to feel the same need. "Hold me," he murmured, clutching her more firmly to him and standing up. With his arms around her, her legs entwined about his torso, he carried her to the bed and lowered her gently, so they were still joined.

He smoothed the damp hair from her forehead, kissed her tenderly and smiled, his blue eyes soft and hazy with love. "Beautiful Charmiane. My beloved. I want to make love to you every minute of every day that we're together. To keep you imprisoned in my arms. In my bed."

She giggled. "Such extravagant sentiments. You sound like my lover 'Noël,' from last summer."

"Do you know how often I wanted to shout it aloud, every time we met in secret last summer? 'This is *my* woman. I have a right to her!' "

"You had a right to my heart. Always." She reached up to caress the scar on his chest. "Noël's" scar. It still seemed a little unreal. That it had always been Adam.

He smiled. "You were a tender nurse."

"Hmph! You were a wicked patient. Always flirting. Completely unruly."

There was a sparkle in his eyes that warmed her heart. But he kept his expression serious. "That wasn't me," he said defensively. "That was Noël!"

"Oh! It must be nice to have a twin to hide behind!" She might have said more, but he stopped her with a burning kiss that filled her with renewed desire.

He lifted his head at last and grinned down at her. "Now," he said, "who am I? Adam or Noël?"

She gazed into eyes that held love and joy and laughter. The laughter that had always been in him—only needing her, *her* to bring it out. "Oh, my dearest," she answered, her heart swelling with wonder and gratitude for the beautiful man who bent above her. "You're Love."

* * * * *

Author's Postscript

Napoleon unsuccessfully attempted suicide by poison on the night of April 12, 1814. On April 20 he bade farewell to his Old Guard in the courtyard of Fontainebleau, and embarked for his exile on the Isle of Elba on April 28.

Louis XVIII entered Paris on May 3, 1814, after an absence of twenty-three years. His reign inaugurated the White Terror—bitter and savage retaliatory measures against the former Revolutionists, particularly in the provinces.

The old aristocrats regained their titles, but not their lands; only those confiscated holdings that still remained the property of the government were returned to them. Napoleon's aristocrats were allowed to keep their legitimately purchased holdings as well as their titles, although they were at first snubbed by the returning émigrés.

The soldiers of the Grand Army saw their pensions cut by half, while the returning aristocrats—with little experience or training—were given high military positions as senior officers over them. However, those officers who had distinguished themselves under the Empire were eventually accepted by the King and incorporated into a new, merged society.

Harlequin Historicals®

History is now twice as exciting, twice as romantic!

Harlequin is proud to announce that, by popular demand, Harlequin Historicals will be increasing from two to four titles per month, starting in February 1991.

Even if you've never read a historical romance before, you will love the great stories you've come to expect from favorite authors like Patricia Potter, Lucy Elliot, Ruth Langan and Heather Graham Pozzessere.

Enter the world of Harlequin Historicals and share the adventures of cowboys and captains, pirates and princes.

Available wherever
Harlequin books are sold.

H·A·R·L·E·Q·U·I·N
American Romance®

RELIVE THE MEMORIES. . . .

From New York's immigrant experience to San Francisco's great quake of 1906. From the muddy trenches of World War I's western front to the speakeasies of the Roaring Twenties, to the lost fortunes and indomitable spirit of the Thirties . . . A CENTURY OF AMERICAN ROMANCE takes you on a nostalgic journey through the twentieth century.

Glimpse the lives and loves of American men and women from the turn of the century to the dawn of the year 2000. Revel in the romance of a time gone by. And sneak a peek at romance in an exciting future.

Watch for all the A CENTURY OF AMERICAN ROMANCE titles coming to you one per month in Harlequin American Romance.

Don't miss a day of A CENTURY OF AMERICAN ROMANCE.

The women . . . the men . . . the passions . . . the memories . . .

Harlequin romances are now available in stores at these convenient times each month.

Harlequin Presents
Harlequin American Romance
Harlequin Historical
Harlequin Intrigue

These series will be in stores on the 4th of every month.

Harlequin Romance
Harlequin Temptation
Harlequin Superromance
Harlequin Regency Romance

New titles for these series will be in stores on the 16th of every month.

We hope this new schedule is convenient for you. With only two trips each month to your local bookseller, you will always be sure not to miss any of your favorite authors!

Happy reading!

Please note there may be slight variations in on-sale dates in your area due to differences in shipping and handling.

HDATES